WILL HOUSE

OLD SCHOOL SECRETS

HENRY BROOKS

This edition published by PiquantFiction in 2016
PiquantFiction is an imprint of Piquant.
Piquant
PO Box 83, Carlisle, CA3 9GR, UK

ISBNs:
978-1-909281-46-2 OD
978-1-909281-47-9 MOBI
978-1-909281-48-6 Epub

British Library Cataloguing in Publication Data
A catalogue record for this book is available from the British Library
ISBN 978-1-909281-46-2

This is a work of fiction. All characters, organizations, and events portrayed in this novel are either products of the author's imagination or are used fictitiously.

Cover design by Abigail Vyner-Brooks
Typesetting by ProjectLuz.com

CONTENTS

ACKNOWLEDGEMENTS

Birthing any book is a laborious process and one that cannot happen without various literary obstetricians at each stage! Like good gynaecologists Pieter and Elria from Piquant have been monitoring the foetal growth since 2009. They chose a very able editorial midwife in the novelist Leanne Hardy, for which I am very grateful. I also wish to thank people like the author Andrew Sibley who, amongst others, gave their time to check the scientific and historical detail. And also my wife Ruth who gave many hours to the final editing process during a four week vacation on Lake Constance. There are also a number of young people: Connor, Abigail, Miriam, Matthew, Laura (to mention the few I can remember), who read early drafts and made comments; you are the book's honorary aunts and uncles. This book was a late term baby and it came after a long labour, but I hope that it will prove to be a great blessing and strength to young people around the world. Remember: *Nihil Auctoritas!*

Henry Brooks,
Lake Constance, Germany
30th Aug 2015

Dedicated to my nephews and nieces:

David, Daniel, Hannah, Freddie, James, Digby, Hannah, Esther, Mary, Lettice, Margot, Cecily, Blaise, Hugo and Florence.

(Something to read when you are older – in fact, much older!)

PROLOGUE

Pupil in Tragic Suicide at Top Public School.

It has been revealed by local police that a pupil from St Columba's School, five miles south of the Cumbrian coastal town of Whitehaven, was admitted to Westmorland General Hospital earlier today after a suspected suicide. The boy, who cannot be named for legal reasons, was said to be suffering from severe wounds to the abdominal regions, and pronounced dead on arrival. A police spokesman told reporters that it was too soon to speculate on the cause of death but they were certainly not ruling out foul play at this time.

The school, which is one of the oldest and most prestigious schools in Europe, attracts the sons of the wealthy elites from across the world. And they are no strangers to controversy either, due to the closed – some say secretive – nature of the monastic order on which the school is founded. The brothers of St Columba, some of whom are teachers at the school, claim a monastic heritage dating back to the times of the Celts. It is claimed that they did not ally themselves with the Catholic Church at the Synod of Whitby for which they are still held with suspicion even today by established denominations. One monk approached by this paper, but who did not wish to be named, said, 'We are careful that the indulgence and self-sufficiency of our Latin brethren does not pollute our simple lifestyle and earth-bound spirituality.'

Although the school office have refused to comment to this newspaper, they have posted a statement on their website to say that the parents of the boy had been contacted and that the school were assisting the relevant authorities with their enquiries into this 'tragic accident'. An emergency number was also given for concerned parents, but as yet there is no more information forthcoming.

Times and Star, *22ⁿᵈ July 1996*

....

St Columba's School
Whitehaven
Cumbria

28ᵗʰ July 1996

Dear Mr and Mrs Percival,

Further to our conversation by telephone at the weekend, it is with the greatest pain that I write to you following today's inquest to offer once again our most sincere condolences. James was an outstanding student, bright, earnest and a great favourite with the teachers. He will be sadly missed by us all.

As I am sure you know, we have worked hard with the police and the coroner to ascertain all the facts, and it has appeared that James had been taken up with certain ideas during the weeks just prior to his death. It may have been these ideas, the coroner thinks, combined with nervous exhaustion over exam pressures, and lack of sleep that contributed to the decline in his mental health. The psychiatrist said that James' paranoia about secret societies and persons coming 'after him', is very typical for someone experiencing severe levels of mania in a manic depressive episode.

Some of these issues, particularly the sleeplessness, were being treated by our nurse, but the decline was so rapid that I am afraid there was not enough we could do. Although the coroner was careful to praise the school at all points, I confess I still blame myself that we could not do more. Though it may be of little comfort to you in your time of grief, you can be assured that we will work tirelessly to ensure that such a thing will never happen again at St Columba's.

Yours sincerely,
George Hanover
Headmaster

1

SCHOOL WITH
A PAST

10, 9, 8, 7, 6, 5, 4, 3 … 2 … 1! Happy New Year, everyone!'
Loweswater village hall exploded with the sound of cheering and party poppers. Will moved through the crowd of family and friends, shaking hands and giving hugs where necessary, but still finding it hard to hide his disappointment. Back outside in the crystal winter night, he dug two chilled hands into his pockets and gazed out over Crummock Water, deep into the mountains. The air crackled with distant fireworks and the shrill laughter of a hundred-plus local revellers.

Soft leather scuffed the gravel behind him. 'There you are! What on earth are you doing out here alone?'

'Nothing – just thinking, that's all.' His shoulders slumped further and his eyes moved toward the ground.

Hannah slipped her arms around Will's waist and, shivering, pulled herself close. Peering over his shoulder she whispered, 'Have you got the Millennium Bug?'

'No.'

'Umm, not still sulking about next week?'

'No – well, perhaps a bit …' Will gazed up at the stars and sighed. 'Look, I can't shelve how I feel, even on Millennium night. I wish I could, but I just can't, that's all.'

'D'you want to talk about it?'

'What, again? No, it won't change anything. I'm off to Hogwarts and we're not going to see each other for months at a time.'

Hannah laughed and pulled Will around to face her. 'Hogwarts? You said St Columba's was nice?'

'Well, yeah, nice and old and by the sea, but can you see me fitting in with all those toffs? Will Houston from the Liverpool Comprehensive – they're gonna love me there.'

'Oh, come on. Stop being melodramatic! There'll be lots of nice lads there, you'll get the extra help you need for your dyslexia, and there'll be no pretty girls to distract you!' She squeezed him. 'And it's only fifteen miles away, so you'll get to come home every now and again … perhaps more than Prince Von Coburg!'

'Oh, Hannah, you should've seen the place! His dad had a helipad built at the school so the pampered prince could be airlifted at the end of each term! I thought the guy showing me round was ribbing me!'

'Now, there you are, laughing again! Good. Listen, I'll get our coats and you can take me for a walk to the lake and say two thousand nice things about me – how about it?'

'Okay, okay, you win – but no more tickling, or you'll not get one, never mind two thousand!'

They spent an hour walking round the lake, watching the fireworks reflect on distant shores, and they prayed together at her suggestion. As Will got to number twenty-three on his list of nice things, he began to feel it hadn't been such a bad Millennium party after all. He pondered this while letting the water run onto his trainers. *I mean, here I am finally living in the place I love best and walking arm-in-arm with the girl of my dreams.* His life *had* seemed mapped to perfection – until, that is, his parents had got cash-rich from the Liverpool house sale and started talking to that weird Russian professor who lived nearby. Conrad Inchikov had just landed a job teaching Philosophy at the prestigious private school called St Columba's, where the facilities were top-notch, especially the one-to-one extra dyslexia tuition Will so desperately needed, particularly starting his 'A' levels.

The snows came one night later, so Hannah and Will made the most of their final week of freedom outside in the winter wonderland. On Thursday they cross-country skied the south Buttermere ridge on a sparkling, cloudless day with views right across the Irish Sea to the Isle of Man. On Friday they spent the morning sledging on the side of Melbreak, and then had an afternoon reading together by the vicarage fire with a pot of tea whilst Hannah's family were out. Saturday saw the snows melting, and Hannah took Will out riding, though she still laughed and compared his stubborn stiff and unbending technique to that of her father. After lunch they took an afternoon trek along the shores of Loweswater and up over the fells, cantering back through the old cobbled farm courtyards as the evening drew in. Sunday was church as usual; and after lunch in Granny's kitchen Hannah chatted with Will's mum, who was re-checking his suitcase ready for him to leave, while Will flicked through his CDs and tried not to be irritated by how much the others were enjoying themselves.

He said goodbye at teatime, an ill wind in the yard spoiling the work he had done on his hair. He waved back and touched the window, tracking Hannah's face as the car pulled away. Loweswater writhed dark and turbid as the car sped past and made the steep climb out of the valley to the coastal plain. They passed the graveyard, the war memorial at Lamplugh. *I wonder how it feels leaving for war.* The butterflies in his gut, the clammy head and hands. A moment later another pothole jogged his head back against the headrest, putting an end to the catalogue of injustices that were sending him away from the valley for three months at a time.

His dad did most of the talking as usual. 'You will remember to get your assignments in on time … to brush your hair … and your teeth, and for heaven's sake don't slouch … and look at the teachers when they are speaking to you.'

Will blotted it out, tugging at the stiff neck of his Grandfather's Harris tweed sports jacket, which the old man had been more than keen to pass on to him. 'Never wears out, this stuff, really good quality … seems a shame.' It would now be his everyday jacket at the new school where, as far as he could see, the clocks had stopped in the 1930s. As the car passed some kids at a bus-stop in Frizington, Will shrunk down slightly into his seat and half covered his face, placing his leather padded elbow on the side of the car door.

The half-hour journey seemed interminable in some ways, yet it was still over too soon for him. The dark clouds billowed and tossed, casting grey gloom across the bleak landscape. The car descended towards the rugged coast from where the fifteenth-century priory tower loomed into view. Soon the weather-worn red sandstone buildings that formed the school complex emerged, nestled in a valley among the cliffs, with the driving sea just a hundred metres from the entrance. At the back of the school buildings he watched groups of boys kicking balls on rugby and cricket fields – all friends, all happy to be back no doubt. As the car rounded the last bend, a shudder ran down Will's spine. The jagged remains of the Druids' stone circle came into view against the skyline one kilometre down the coast. A storm was rolling in as their car pulled through the stone gates. Will gazed up at the stylized dragons perched on top of the pillars. Hogwarts, all right!

Just inside the gate, a rowan tree bent in the wind over a stone porter's lodge. A burly man in his late sixties and dressed in overalls came out of the lodge, and Will's dad stopped to ask for directions. Will's sweaty palms finally fumbled the car window open, and the man touched his cap. 'Storm's brewing tonight, all right!'

'Hi, could you tell us where St Alban's House is?'

The generous ruddy face squinted. 'Now then, you must be one of these two new sixth-formers we've got coming, eh?'

Will smiled. 'Yeah, that's right, how'd you guess?'

The man looked pleased and rubbed his square chin. 'Well, old Arthur don't forget a face, know 'em all, young Master – Master …?'

'Oh, Will – Will Houston.'

'Right, Master Houston. I'm pleased to meet you, lad, and if there's aught I can do for you while you're here, you just come see me and I'll sort you out. You'll find Alban's house down the end on the right.'

'Thanks a lot. I'll see you later.' As the window juddered back up, Will let out a pent up breath.

They drove at the required five miles per hour past the priory as the monks shuffled out into the cold winter's evening. The first splatterings of rain were coming on and all the monks who headed for the cloistered quadrangle had their hoods up.

'They look creepy,' Will said.

'Stop it,' his dad said. 'They do a good work here. Anyway, I thought you were all for religion after last summer.'

'Yeah, I am – just don't get where all the Darth Vader gear comes into it.'

Will's dad pulled up outside the medieval ramparts of St Alban's and switched the engine off. 'Look, Will, you're not going to be a smart alec here and get into trouble? This is a good school; you're going to get the best help.'

'Yeah, so everyone keeps telling me – for my disability.'

'Oh c'mon, stop being so touchy. Anyway, it's not just that. These people send more lads up to Oxford and Cambridge than any other public school, and their science facilities and reputation are second to none.'

'Yeah, I know, the next generation of politicians, generals and scientists. I've read the spiel.'

'Will, listen to me. You can go in there with a chip on your shoulder but it's only you who's going to miss out. Come on, Will! This is a chance I could never have dreamed of when I was growing up! You could get such a head start here if you buckle down … and you will give it your best, won't you?'

Will sighed and rubbed his forehead. 'Yeah, sorry, 'course I will. C'mon, let's get this stuff out the car.'

They mounted the steps and were met by the duty prefect. He was lean and stiff, with immaculate sandy hair and an acne-pitted face pinched like a shrew. He addressed Will's dad: 'Good evening, Mr Houston, welcome to St Alban's house. Name's Sidmouth, duty prefect tonight. I'll see you both in.'

As Will marvelled at how anyone his age could speak like Prince Charles, he noticed Sidmouth glancing disdainfully at their Mondeo parked among the Range Rovers and Audis. He greeted Sidmouth, 'Hi, I'm Will. How're you doing?'

'Very well, thank you. Welcome to the school.' Sidmouth turned abruptly to some younger boys inside the entrance. 'Pierson and Smithers, stop gawking and get these bags.'

'Yes, Sidmouth,' they said, relieving Will and his dad of the bags they were carrying.

'Right. If you'll follow me, please.'

They were led into an oak-panelled hall and up the stairs to a long corridor. 'Right, Houston. You're down here at the very far end. You're sharing with another new sixth-former who's coming later in the week. The room's a decent size, bit draughty, but the views are good if you go in for that sort of thing.'

'Oh, Will won't mind the draught,' said Will's dad, 'but tell me now about this other lad Will's going to be with – is he local?'

'No, from London – he's Sir Alan Rawkins' son – you know, the famous biologist. Anyway, he's left Eton and is on his way here.'

'Wonder why,' Will's dad mused.

Sidmouth turned down the corners of his grey lips and shrugged. 'Probably wants a decent education.' Will raised an amused eyebrow at his dad, who smiled back.

As they reached the end of the corridor, the boys dropped the bags beside the door. Sidmouth walked into the room first and turned on the light.

The room had two metal beds with tough-looking mattresses, two old desks and two sets of drawers. The walls were pitted with pinholes and Blu-Tack® marks, and the central light gave off an unwelcoming and dingy yellow glow. Will made a face. His dad nudged him. 'I'm sure "our kid" will make it look a bit more homely with some pictures and his Everton lamp, eh.'

Sidmouth managed a begrudged smile at Mr Houston's Scouse comments. 'No doubt. Well, you must excuse me, I have things to attend to. Just send Smithers and Pierson away when you've finished with them. This is the senior gallery – it's not for juniors unless they're fagging for you.'

'Oh, okay.'

'I'll be back in half an hour or so, when you've had a chance to unpack.'

Pierson and Smithers did a fine job of emptying the car, even bringing in things they were not supposed to. They seemed highly amused by the Everton Football Club lamp and handled it with whispers as if they had never seen one like it before. By the time Will parted company with them and had said goodbye to his dad, the room looked only moderately less sparse, but, Will thought, it's a good start at least. Sidmouth was back as promised and looked around the room without emotion. 'Right? Good. Interesting lamp-shade! It'll be prayers in a minute, Houston, so anything you want to ask now?'

'Well, yeah, why's everyone so interested in the lamp-shade?'

'I dare say they've never seen one before.'

'I don't get it.'

'You'll find that gentlemen play rugby, and, if you want my advice, if you don't want to be known as a pleb, you'll get rid of that lamp-shade before anyone else sees it!'

Will's hackles were well and truly up, but he remembered what he had promised his dad, so simply said, 'Thanks for the advice.'

'That's all right – no one else will tell you. Anything else?'

'Are you the, like, head boy in Alban's?'

'Me? No, that's Dundas. He'll be with the others having his sherry with Father Bede before prayers.'

'Others?'

'Brummell and Wordsmith, the senior house prefects. You'll meet them soon enough. Now, is there anything else?'

'Yeah, food, if there is some. I'm starving!'

'8 a.m., breakfast. Anyway, come on, there's the bell for prayers.'

A bell echoed around the walls and Will followed Sidmouth downstairs to where evening prayers were to be endured. Boys poured out of every corridor, converging on the stairs like rats. They entered a panelled common room, where a set of folding doors at one end had been pulled back to reveal a small alcove with an altar. There was excited chatter as everyone took their seats, older boys on chairs, others on benches and radiators, and those who looked the youngest on the floor. Sidmouth stayed by the door and Will, noticing how everyone stared, did his best to look cool. He wandered over to one of the radiators and a junior boy stood up to let him have the seat.

'No, no, that's okay, I'll sit down with my back against it. It's gotta be better than having your back against a freezing window.'

Will squatted down on the floor just as he heard Sidmouth's voice: 'Elliot, you snivelling amoeba, get your butt off that radiator when a sixth-former needs it or I'll have you running to the Druids' circle three times before breakfast!' The room hushed straight down to a few whispers.

Poor Elliot stammered, 'But Sidmouth, I just, just …'

'Its okay,' intervened Will. 'He did offer, but I'm okay here, really.'

'Nonsense, no sixth-former sits on the floor. Elliot, shift!'

'I said no,' insisted Will. 'Thanks, but I'm fine where I am.'

Sidmouth's face was rapidly changing colour and he looked as though he would have spoken again were it not for the sound of doors opening and the house master, Father Bede, and three older boys entering. Will assumed these were the prefects. Among the hushed whispers from the younger boys he heard the almost hallowed names of Dundas, Wordsmith and Brummell. Any remaining whispers soon subsided and the unseated boys quickly found seats. Father Bede was a tall though slightly stooping man with unkempt white hair, circular spectacles and small eyes hidden beneath a furrowed brow. Will's granddad had known this man from his war years, though he'd said very little about him – a bit strange as Will thought about it. The monk walked with a limp and his robes followed the jarring motion of his gait like curtains catching on a stiff runner. He walked to the front without acknowledging anyone in particular. Will eyed the other three. One was immaculately turned out, with collar-length hair combed back in place and a dark-blue sports jacket with a tan waistcoat; the others only wore jumpers under their jackets. Will also noted this first boy's tanned leather ankle-boots. The second boy was quite scruffy by comparison, and the third was a tall, ginger-haired guy who spoke to Sidmouth: 'All present?'

'Yes, Dundas, all in.'

'Good man, take your seat.' Dundas took his seat as well and, from the back, surveyed with evident satisfaction the sixty-two boys in front of him. Will cast a glance around the room in wonder. *Blimey, these guys really take themselves seriously, as if they're really mini adults and this is a real world.* A moment later the dark thought dawned on him; *this is my real world from now on too.*

This place was to be – near enough – his school, home, family, everything combined for the next two years, and at this moment he didn't think he would last out two days.

All this and more Will was taking in as his mind wandered during the prayer time. Father Bede rattled off a series of readings and Celtic prayers from a book in his monotonous voice. When he had finished, he started to leave. The boys stood. 'Um,' Bede muttered, 'Welcome back,' and left the room. The boys waited and the house head came to the front. There was no sound except the noise of creaking wooden furniture joints.

'Right, gentlemen! Welcome back. Trust you all made the best of your Christmas break.' Some younger boys nodded in adulation, muttering his name 'Dundas' as an affirmation. 'As you know, it's the house matches this term and we want to put a strong team together to thrash the daylights out of those lazy cretins in St Oswald's! We'll do practices this week and see what you're made of. A few reminders: No walking on the grass outside Father Bede's study, and anyone found with muddy rugger boots in the common room will have me to deal with, understood?'

'Yes, Dundas,' they murmured again, some with humour, most with fear.

'Good. Don't forget to make yourself acquainted with Master Houston over there, our new senior, and don't forget to be ready for chapel at 8.25 sharp tomorrow morning. Sidmouth, you'll see everyone is ready. Okay, dormitories to bed, and no talking after lights out or I'll send Brummell round with his cricket bat!' There were shy giggles as the younger boys filed out and some of the older ones started pulling their chairs up to the television in one corner.

Dundas approached Will as he got up. 'All right, Houston? Get settled in?' He held out his hand.

'Yeah, yeah. Everything's fine, thanks.' Will took the tight grip.

'Good. Sidmouth make sure you had everything you needed?'

'Yeah, everything.'

'Good man, good man. Are you a rugby player?'

'Um, could be – don't know, not really tried before. We were a footy school where I came from.'

'I see. Well, you mustn't let that hold you back. You look sturdy enough, and if you can face 'em down without blinking, you could be our man. We'll see next week.' Dundas walked off and two other lads Will's age came over to introduce themselves.

'Hi, I'm Thornton. This is Clarkson. We're on your corridor and probably have some of the same classes.'

'Yeah, okay – how you doing, guys?' Will's shoulders relaxed as these two seemed more friendly in manner and eager to talk. Together they went back up to the corridor, or 'gallery' as they called it, where Thornton and Clarkson shared a room.

'Wow, you guys sure know how to decorate!' Will exclaimed as he entered their room. Every inch of wall space was covered with tie-dyed drapes, even the ceiling. There were also many posters, some of James Dean, a few of girls and others of rock bands.

Clarkson took an easy chair. 'Nah, everyone does it like this; there's no magic, but I'm glad you like it.' Clarkson was stocky and dark-haired; Thornton was very fair in complexion and also very thin.

'I just imagine it's like some Turkish bazaar or something – it's really cool.'

'Hey, want some tea or something?' Thornton was filling a kettle in the sink.

'Sure. Tea's fine, thanks.'

'Yeah, and none of that fancy stuff – get him some of my Yorkshire tea,' Clarkson said. It appeared that he was a rarity at the school in that he prided himself on not being quite as posh as everyone ought to be. They enjoyed their strong Yorkshire tea and gossiped about the people in the house.

'You certainly made an impression on Siff – I mean, Sidmouth,' Clarkson said. 'Thought he would explode when you wouldn't budge before prayers!'

'Yeah, why'd you do that?' Thornton asked.

Will shrugged. 'Just didn't fancy a cold back against that window. And I don't like bullies. What is it with you lot, getting kids to run around for you all the time?'

Clarkson laughed. 'Listen, the fagging system is as old as this place, which is pretty old, right, so unless you want a heap of trouble, you just go with it.'

'Trouble?'

'Yeah, amigo, trouble! Not from me – I couldn't give a toss if they all want to be little Hitlers and have their power fling, but the guardians of the system – you know, the prefects – will give you merry hell if you mess with their hierarchy.'

'So how does it work?'

Thornton got up to refill the pot. 'What – fagging? Oh, well, basically, when you become a senior, like us, you get to choose a kid from the lower years to be your fag, a sort of servant. Not for everything – they'll do your shoes, your boots, make you drinks, carry your books sometimes, clean your room. But don't listen to Clarkson. It's not all bad for them – they get privileges, get to come up on the gallery, talk to other seniors, which they'd never get to do otherwise. And anyway, it was a lot harder when we came. The seniors were pretty violent back then. By comparison, we're soft touches. Anyway, we've done our bit and it's time to reap the benefits, so don't listen to Clarkson's drivel. He's just complaining 'cos his fag can't make tea strong enough.'

'Hah, very funny, Thornton! At least mine knows how to use a kettle! No, Houston, I hate the whole thing. If I had my way, I'd move to St Oswald's house. They've got a lot more sense and their head of house, Fox, has got some seriously forward-thinking ideas. They're all radicals over at Oswald's.'

'Oh yeah, when he's not drunk,' Thornton said with a snigger, 'or smoking the old wacky-baccy with Brummel and the Dragoons.'

'Brummell's the guy at the back of prayers – the cool one, right?'

'Oh yeah, Mr Cool,' Clarkson said, breaking into a whisper. 'He's right in with the Dragoons, only one in Alban's to get in, and he's not got the money or connections like the others, but the Prince likes him, so he got in.'

'Dragoons?'

Thornton said, 'Yeah, we've had 'em since the 1780s. They were a set modelled on the Prince of Wales' Light Dragoons.'

'Eh?'

'Oh, some mock regiment so George III's son could play soldiers with his mates. It wasn't for real fighting,' Clarkson said. 'Just dressing up and stuff – bit like our lot!'

'They're basically the "in-gang" if you're loaded or seriously connected, which Clarkson isn't!'

'And I'm glad I'm not if that's what megabucks do for you. No, I've got better things to do with my time and money than waste them on designer clothes and booze.'

'But this Fox guy you like, he's a Dragoon, is he?' Will asked.

'Fox? No, he just hangs out with them sometimes, as they can get their hands on booze, sometimes even girls!'

Will raised an eyebrow. 'Women, here? There can't be a town for miles.'

'Oh, you'd be surprised what the Dragoons can pull,' Clarkson said. 'I heard that last year they got a load of girls from a school in Carlisle down here by train.'

'Oh, come on, it's just hearsay! Anyway, Houston was asking about fagging,' Thornton said.

Will scratched his chin. 'Yeah, the whole thing sounds weird to me, but you say I've got to choose one or I'll be in trouble. Anyone you suggest?'

'There are a couple left in Alban's, but they're pretty useless,' Thornton said.

They talked though the options and none sounded promising. Though Will liked the idea of being served like that, he knew it did not spring from the best of motives and he couldn't imagine Hannah or his parents approving. They left the subject without conclusion and Will chewed it over. *Maybe I could slip through the net unnoticed?*

Will had a hard time keeping warm that night and he slept badly because of the draughts and the unexpected sense of isolation that seemed to gnaw at his inner being like a slow toothache. When he did eventually sleep, the noise of the sea winds blasting the leaded panes of his room set his mind to dreaming that he was out there in the Irish Sea, a lost, lonely soul amidst the vast rising walls of cold water, clinging only to the oars of his little boat.

Next morning, after a scant breakfast of cereal and toast, Will walked with Thornton and Clarkson to the priory for chapel. The wind had dropped, though the skies were still ominous with inky black clouds. As they went through the huge sandstone portico on the eastern entrance Clarkson remarked, 'Abandon hope all ye who enter!' They laughed, but as they stepped inside the chapel Will felt a wave of dampness and cold envelop him like a shroud. The smell of incense and mould were so thick you could almost taste them.

'Think this is creepy?' said Thornton. 'Man, you wanna see the crypt! They say its foundations are Roman and before that it was a place where the Celtic Druids worshipped.' He pointed to a small arched doorway in a dark recess on the opposite wall. Will gave an involuntary shudder.

'What do you mean "worshipped"?' Clarkson whispered as they got into their row and knelt on the hard wooden kneelers. 'They still do – that's what my brother told me. On dark nights with full moons, they meet down there or at the Druids' circle and drink the blood of sacrificed chickens.' He broke off into a giggle. 'Woooo!'

'Clarkson, don't be a wally! Don't take any notice, Houston, he's such a sucker for any conspiracy,' Thornton said. 'No, all I was going to say, before I was interrupted, was that there are some very old sarcophagi – you know, stone coffins – down there and it's supposed to be haunted.'

'Yeah, haunted by Druids! Listen, my brother says that half the monks and the teachers are really Druids! They keep alive ancient rites in this valley, and it's all been going on for over a thousand years.'

'Give us a break! How does your brother know? I suppose he saw them!'

'No, actually it was another teacher who told him.'

'Yeah, I bet ...'

At that moment all whisperings were overtaken as the plain chant echoed from the cloisters adjoining the priory and the black-hooded monks entered in procession amidst the swirling incense. It all seemed so very ancient, so timeless, so mesmerizing, a way of life unchanged for hundreds of years. *It's as if these mournful chants occupy another realm entirely, one without mobile phones, televisions or even a twenty-first century.* These hooded men, this haunted music, this way of life pre-dated the Normans and even the Saxons; they were living markers that spanned the ages of English history, even church history. *How strange to be sitting here!* Will felt his breathing slow, his shoulders relax, his thoughts float inarticulately about his mind.

After the readings and prayers a grave, grey-faced monk called Abbot Malthus addressed the boys. He carried a gnarled wooden crook and walked down to the rows to talk about the new term, his voice slow and deliberate. His face was sallow and drawn, his head balding with great tufts of white hair. He was tall and his torso gnarled, like the ancient oaks that grew in those parts. He spoke about the new season that was upon the school. 'The earth is waking from her slumbers. We, too, should be waking from the winter of our Yuletide pleasures to rise to the challenges of a new term.'

He paused and looked around at the boys when he had finished his address. Will felt the heat of the abbot's gaze upon him for an uncomfortable second. The abbot strode away with his monks in procession and one of the lay teaching staff stepped to the front.

This man was plump, dressed in a smart pinstriped suit and had a large head with wavy grey hair. 'It's Mr George, the Head,' Thornton whispered. Mr George also spoke about the new term, repeating much that had already been said. He spoke at length of the school's reputation: 'Gentlemen, let our school motto, *Lux et veritas, virtus et proficere* – Light and Truth, Virtue and Progress – serve as a guide as we come to our work, that we may honour those many great scholars who have become the great public men of our day. Particularly in the realms of science, our dedicated staff are expecting outstanding achievements this term as many of you gear up for your final exams this summer. They also look forward to receiving the son of our nation's most eminent biologist, Sir Alan Rawkins, into the school. As you see, our reputation for excellence in science is spreading far and wide, and you all have much to be proud of as you go forward this term to pursue the light of knowledge.'

Will took very little in, apart from the mention of his new roommate. He drifted with tiredness, but also with questions about all that Clarkson had said about the Druids. Could it be true? Was it likely? Thornton nudged him and he came to. 'Hey, wake up! Let's go. You've got work to do.' And so he had.

2

THE SECRET CODE

It was a difficult first week at St Columba's as there was so much that was new. Will was too busy to be bogged down by it. Just finding your way to the classrooms was a task in itself and would have been near impossible but for Clarkson's and Thornton's help. The school had been successively enlarged over the centuries, and each group of buildings had a connecting stone passageway, giving the place a disorientating, warren-like feel. On many occasions Will would give up and get any passing junior boy to show him the way. At the centre of this musty web was the Great Hall, with towering, gothic windows, an impressive fan-vaulted ceiling and oak-panelled lower walls. On his first Monday Will stood for a full minute on the stone steps at one end to take it all in.

'Wow, that's massive!' he said to Thornton.

'Yeah! The ceiling dates to the Tudor era, the window mullions even earlier. That little door in the side is the library entrance. We can take a look after English Language, but we'll have to get going now or we'll be late.'

'So, what's this Mr Conlon like?'

'Oh, old Colon? It's what we all call him. He's stiff as a board but can spot bad grammar at fifty paces!'

And indeed he could. The erect and dictatorial Mr Conlon gave no quarter to idleness in the execution of the 'Queen of Languages'. He moved and walked as if he were wrapped in barbed wire under his grey suit. He did not take too kindly to Will's written work. 'Your entry form says you suffer from mild dyslexia,' he said, removing his glasses and forcing a smile that almost shattered his pinched face. 'Of course, I am no expert on these modern literary diseases, but I will not stand for slovenliness in my class when it comes to punctuation or grammar. Let us hope the extra help the school is so generously lavishing on you will improve your offerings to my table.'

After the class Thornton was reassuring. 'Don't mind him – he's like that with everyone! Anyway, look, we've got English Lit after lunch with Toupee Taff, and there'll be some fun to be had as the wind is up!'

'The wind's up? What on earth do you mean?'

'Oh, you'll see! A rare treat to compensate for Colon's class.'

Thornton and Will were back at their house for lunch, with the ever-present junior boys waiting on tables. Father Bede came to the top table flanked by his senior house prefects. They all stood behind their chairs and said the Latin grace.

> 'Benedic, Domine, nos et dona tua,
> quae de largitate tua sumus sumpturi,
> et concede, ut illis salubriter nutriti
> tibi debitum obsequium praestare valeamus,
> per Christum Dominum nostrum. Amen.'

After they had sat down Will asked Clarkson, 'So what does all that mean? I meant to ask you this morning.'

Clarkson was already helping himself to a bread roll. 'What, the grace? Oh, I dunno – something about getting nutrition so we can better serve Christ. How was chemistry?'

'Awful! I've never got the hang of all those symbols and stuff.'

'And Fizzy – what d'you think of him?'

'Who, Mr Fortesque? I can hardly understand him – he dithers and waffles on as if we weren't even there. And all that wild white hair. He looks like Einstein!'

'Yeah, he's an oddball all right. Pass the butter, please. Did you notice his missing finger?'

'No!'

'Oh well, he hides it well. They say that he was dithering one day as to where to put a test tube with some chemicals in. He couldn't decide which holder to use, and the thing just exploded and messed up his hand!'

'Oh, man, that's rough!' Will said, tasting his beef soup.

'Oh, you'll get used to the food, Houston, don't worry.'

'No, not the soup. The hand! Mind you,' Will said as he swallowed, 'the soup's pretty rank too!'

They laughed and did the best they could to finish before games. Will hadn't thought that his football boots would stand out quite as much as they did as he lined up with all the other boys of his house for the match's trials that afternoon. They were looking for a junior and senior team, and Dundas and Brummell patrolled the ranks of hopefuls, or, in the case of boys like Thornton and Clarkson, the unhopefuls! For them, games, particularly those involving getting wet and muddy, like rugby, were something to be avoided if possible; an attitude that at St Columba's was, according to Clarkson, viewed as 'cowardice bordering on treasonous insubordination'.

'Dundas and Brummell look tense,' Will said, when the two had reached the other end of the line out of earshot.

'We did rubbish last year against Oswald's in the semi-finals,' said Thornton, his spindly legs shivering.

'Did Oswald's win?'

'What, Fox's lot? No way, they hardly practised!'

'But they beat us?'

'Yeah, there's the disgrace of it! Dundas won't let it happen again.'

'Which house won, then?'

'Aiden's. Their head prefect, Pitt, is the head boy too. They've been unbeatable since I've been here.'

'Where's that other house prefect, the scruffy one?'

'What, Liam Wordsmith? You wouldn't find him here – he'll have his head in a book somewhere … Oh, look out, here comes Dundas again!' Will braced up as they passed, and felt his toes curl as Dundas cast a glance at his footy boots.

They did running exercises and ball passing for twenty minutes before trying some formations for the scrums. Dundas dealt with the senior team, Brummell with the juniors. Dundas seemed pleased with Will and put him as a centre in the line because of his speed and agility. Will was pleased, as he had never been singled out at his old school in sports, though his previous summer at the farm and all his adventures in the valley had made him broader and more daring.

At one point a hairy eighteen-year-old called Grenville powered down on him full speed with the ball. The ground shuddered at his approach, turf and mud ascending in clods right and left. For a moment it was all Will could do not to dive for cover. Grenville passed to his left, thighs like tree trunks. Will flung himself sideways toward them, linking his arms around Grenville's waist, then letting them slip down and tighten around the muddy legs of the goliath runner. The giant came down with a sudden thud, ploughing like a meteor into the wet turf for several yards. Will held on for dear life as if behind a derailed carriage, with Grenville's boot studs digging into his stomach. Both lads lay winded for several seconds, Grenville worst. Will eventually sprang to, extending a hand to lift the other.

Dundas yelled, 'Nice ballsy tackle, Houston. Just what the house needs! Now get back in the game!'

Later, Will did some impressive kicking, almost equalling the height and length of Brummell's legendary 'magic boot'. Thornton and Clarkson looked impressed; they all did.

On the way back to the house Dundas jogged past Will. 'Nice one, Houston. You're on the team, but get rid of those stupid things on your feet or you'll make our house the laughing stock of the school!'

The boys all showered together and when Will finally got the nerve to hang his towel on the peg, a junior boy who was not wholly through puberty said, 'Don't worry, Houston – it was worse at the junior school! There we had to swim starkers and then run round the sports pitch afterwards to dry off!' Will nodded and found a free shower in the corner where he tried to imagine what his mates in Liverpool would think if they could see him now.

After the shower ordeal Will followed others down for tea and toast, which more than made up for the humiliation. This was not dinner, which was served after the afternoon lesson; more an interim filler after games which gave the older boys yet another opportunity to lord it over the first-years. Will was ravenous, and the six-slot toaster had to be worked overtime by poor little Elliot to keep the shouting boys from throwing spoons and knives at him. A first-year called Gordon congratulated Will for his tackling and kicking. Will shrugged. 'The ball was there and they said "Kick it", so I did. Didn't know I'd be any good at it.'

'Well, I wish I could be good at it. The juniors could really use a good kicker, and I'm rubbish at everything else, apart from study.'

'Hey, listen, I tell you what: you rescue Elliot off that toaster and I'll teach you what I know sometime, okay?' The boy grinned and went off to help his beleaguered friend.

Later on that afternoon, Thornton delayed Will outside Toupee Taff's English classroom. 'Now look, give me a minute to get in and open the window, then come in slowly, okay?'

'Well, okay, but hurry! I don't want to be late.'

After a minute of reading the name plate on the door, Will knocked at the classroom door of Mr Blake, the English Literature tutor. 'Yes, yes,' called out Mr Blake. 'Come in, dear boy. It is the hour, upon my word; 'tis the hour.'

Will opened the door softly and saw a rotund man in his late sixties sitting at the desk. He had a mouth crammed with an assortment of jumbled teeth placed at random in his generous chops. He wore a beige suit and his hair was spuriously combed forward and across his otherwise bald head. A draught rushed past Will that lifted the bulk of Mr Blake's hair arrangement from his head. This delicate piece of hair sculpture was so well formed with Brylcreem that it lifted up as one, so that it looked as if his whole head were an egg with the crown lifting up and waving in jest.

For a moment Will simply stood there and marvelled at the sight of the hair hovering at a sixty-degree angle, before he heard the muffled sniggers and saw Thornton by the window in fits of giggles. Will knew he would explode into laughter at any moment so said, 'Sorry, wrong class', retreated and shut the door.

After a few minutes' drying his eyes another boy approached the door. 'Oh, wind's up,' the boy said with a twinkle. He knocked and they both went in. Mr Blake's hair saluted them at a full eighty degrees before falling to its repose on his shiny head. 'All right, all right, silence, you imbeciles, and open your Preludes, and see if Romantic poets can't rescue you from the excesses of your modern scientific education,' said Mr Blake in an obvious attempt to hide his embarrassment.

The last lesson of that day was biology. Clarkson bumped into a lost Will in the Great Hall. 'Hi, Houston. Didn't Thornton give you directions to the science labs?'

'Yeah, but I spent a few minutes trying to find Mr Gibb's class and just ended up here again.'

'Never mind. I've got science with old Gibbon too – the labs are just up here.' The two made their way up the steps and along further, deeper corridors. The natural light faded for the last lesson of the day, the neon ceiling light replacing it with its harsh, bluish glare. Of all the sciences, Will had always been able to get along with biology; he loved animals and insects, and it seemed so much less theoretical and more 'see-able' than physics or chemistry. As he entered the room, Will caught sight of the gowned form of his biology teacher. *Can see why they call him Gibbon, those long arms and squat, primate-like form!* He observed the ruddy, bulbous face with large, brown, hairy moles on his neck and cheeks, and straightway imagined the man might be some fantastical root vegetable yet to be discovered in the upper Amazon.

'Come on, come on,' Mr Gibbs snapped. 'Haven't got all day.'

Will followed Clarkson into the damp where it seemed that everything had that musty smell that got into your clothes, and where the mildew and moss were clearly visible on the stone window mullions.

They were two minutes late, and only three desks remained, one of which Clarkson took. Will went for one of the remaining two desks in the back-left corner under a window, but as he did so he felt all eyes on him and heard a few whispers.

Will had never seen anything like these desks before. Not here the metal-and-chipboard efforts, for these were almost like sleighs with metal runners. They were ancient-looking wooden affairs with inkwells and huge, deep desktops whose lids lifted to reveal a storage drawer.

Will chose the farther of the two remaining desks and heard more muffled whispers as he sat down. A boy behind him whispered, 'He's got the cursed desk – ooooh!'

'Silence at the back, you insignificant amalgam of cells and protoplasm!' shouted Mr Gibbs. He smiled under his beard towards Will and pushed some half-rimmed spectacles back up his stubby nose.

Clarkson put up his hand. 'Please, sir, I thought we were the next generation of great leaders and scientists.' A chuckle spread around the room.

Mr Gibbs walked to the front of his desk and grabbed a jar. 'Thank you, Mr Clarkson, for reminding us all of our potential greatness. What you may be for a few years after you escape my clutches remains to be seen. Maybe you'll be the next Crick or Watson, or Rawkins.' He smiled again at Will but then his face returned to a dead-pan expression. 'Or maybe you'll be a secondary-school science teacher – who knows? But there is one thing I do know,' he continued, now raising the sealed glass container and shaking something brown around in the clear liquid. 'You're all food for the worms, boys, no matter how great your intentions! A hundred years from now you'll be pushing up daisies … with me.' Will squinted to see the jar. 'It's my knee-cap, Mr Rawkins. Welcome to the class.'

'Oh no, sir, I'm Houston. Will Houston.'

'Oh, I see, the local lad – ah, my mistake. Right, gentlemen, we are here to uphold at least two elements of the school's motto. You will have to decide on light and virtue for yourselves, but it's my job to give you truth and thereby progress. One of the great men of my time, when I was in research at Oxford in 1977, was a Frenchman called Pierre Teilhard de Chardin. Regarding the truth of all truths he said these immortal words: that evolution "is a general postulate to which all theories, all hypotheses, all systems must henceforth bow and which they must satisfy to be thinkable and true. Evolution is the light which illuminates all facts, a trajectory that all lines of thought must follow – this is what evolution is." Yes, gentlemen, all systems of truth must henceforth bow to this light that illuminates all facts.'

Mr Gibbs' Hush Puppy shoes let out a high-pitched squeak as he paced the worn parquet floor. He scanned the faces and with a frown glanced at Will's desk as he continued, 'The sooner we are acquainted with the facts, the sooner we can get used to our place in this world. A blade of rice has twice as many genes than you, so in this world you're nothing special, especially not you, Clarkson! You cannot fight against facts like evolution; you cannot break nature's laws, though some have tried and found themselves broken by them. Now get your biology texts from those desks of yours.'

Will opened his desk lid. Cobwebs and dust covered the various textbooks, so much so that Will did not notice the carved lettering on the underside of the lid until he put his books back in the desk after the class. They were carved with a knife or perhaps a compass, and Will read them softly to himself as he sometimes did to help him get the meaning:

> Gibbon's Brave New World:
> No God, no life after death,
> No absolute right and wrong,
> No ultimate meaning for my life;
> Just a meat computer with no free will.
> Percival 1996
> The truth lies in here
> 12.0195. P.LXVI.

'What's that you've got, Will?' asked Clarkson, who had come over to Will's desk. Will showed him the desk lid. 'Oh, Percival, poor git,' said Clarkson. 'They say his mind had gone before he checked out.'

'What d'you mean – who was this Percival, and why's this desk not been used for so long?'

'Sorry, mate, I should have warned you not to sit there. I wasn't thinking.' Clarkson pushed the lid down. 'Come on. Let's get to prep.'

'Yeah, but who was he?' Will felt the hairs on his neck tingle.

'Not so loud. We'll talk outside.'

Mr Gibbs spoke up from his desk, where he was waiting for the boys to leave. 'Percival was an obsessive, idealistic fool, and you'd do well to take a warning from him.'

'What did he do, sir?'

'Tried to break the laws of science, but they broke him. Now, on your bikes, both of you.'

Outside in the corridor Will was still in the dark. 'Well, come on, what happened?'

Clarkson was cagey. 'Look, I don't know all the details, it was back in '96, just before I got here, but it was in my brother's time; basically the guy went off his head and killed himself at the Druids' circle.'

'What! Killed himself? How? And what's old Gibbon mean, talking about breaking science's laws?'

'Hey, I don't know anything else. I could call my brother if you want, but I know it was a massive scandal back then and everyone has to wear black ties each summer on the day it happened.'

Will felt the goose bumps appear on his arm, and an involuntary shiver run through his limbs. 'Clarkson, do call your brother after prep. I want to know.'

Will was still struggling through an English essay when he heard a knock at his door. It was Clarkson.

'Okay, here's the spin, right. Apparently Percival was a junior and a bit of a weirdo, a bit religious too, and he got hung up on some idea about evolution – but not just that: also the Druids and an ancient prophecy about the Millennium.'

'Conspiracy is right up your street, isn't it?' Will chucked his pen down and stretched out, still feeling stiff from the rugby.

'Well, exactly! My brother got most of this stuff straight from Percival, but even he stopped giving him credence after a while as the stories got more and more dangerous.'

'Hang on. Dangerous? What d'you mean, this ancient prophecy?'

Clarkson looked back down the corridor and shut the door fully. 'My brother never told the police, but Percival claimed that an ancient curse had been found in one of the tombs in the crypt when they were doing some excavation in the '70s. Percival said that a scroll, written on a vellum parchment, possibly of human skin, said that if some sort of Druidic rite was performed on the Millennial solstice, then the earth would be at peace for another thousand years and not descend into chaos and burn up and stuff.'

'Come off it,' Will said. 'Sounds like some naff Indiana Jones movie – I mean, where's this scroll now?'

'Ah, it mysteriously disappeared in the '80s.'

'So how did Percival know what it said?'

'I dunno – he told my brother that he'd read a transcription of its runes in a book in the school library.'

'Blimey! I wouldn't mind getting my hand on that book, would you?' Will said with one of his dangerous looks.

'Forget it; the library is massive and anyway, my brother said he looked in every book he could think of.'

'And?'

'Nothing, so he figured Percy had just gone gaga. He was being bullied a lot and it just got to him, I guess.'

'Yeah, yeah, but remember what old Gibbon said about "science's laws" – there was more to it than that, I bet.'

'Well, maybe, but we'll never know now.'

'You didn't say how he died.'

'Oh, that's the worst bit. He dragged a knife across his stomach and was found by his best friend the next morning in a pool of blood and guts in the centre of the stone circle.'

'Urgh! Poor guy – and the friend! How come he was the first one there?'

'I don't know, Poirot! The poor git was a first-year, probably sent on a morning run. Anyway, enough of this. It's dinner time – come on.'

Will found it very hard to get the images out of his mind as he sat silently with his shepherd's pie. Even more spooky was that he had found himself the first one in nearly four years to sit at the 'cursed desk'. Was this providence? He shook his head and took a mouthful. Probably just coincidence.

Will saw through the week without any other major events until he was back in the biology lab on Friday. He and Clarkson were in first that day, but even so Will deliberately chose Percival's desk, as if somehow drawn to it. Mr Gibbs noticed it and looked up from his desk. 'Wouldn't you be more comfortable somewhere else?'

'No, I'm comfy here, thanks.'

'Not superstitious are you, sir?' asked Clarkson.

'You will find, Mr Clarkson, that I am a great many things, but religious and superstitious are not among them. How could I be any use to you if I dished out truth with one hand and mumbo-jumbo with the other?'

By this time Will was getting his books out. As he lifted the desk lid he examined the inscribed text again.

> Gibbon's Brave New World:
> No God, no life after death,
> No absolute right and wrong,
> No ultimate meaning for my life;
> Just a meat computer with no free will.
> Percival 1996
> The truth lies in here
> 12.0195. P.LXVI.

What did the 'The truth lies in here' mean? Did it refer to the preceding lines of text? Was Percival saying that he thought the above lines were true: that there really was no hope in a world without God? Or was he perhaps saying, a bit more subtly, that the biology teacher's creed was in fact a lie, that *Gibbon's* truth *lies* here? It was very perplexing. And then there was the nine-digit code; what did that mean? Perhaps it was a date, but what of the extra digits?

The last two lines seemed to have been inscribed at another time and with far less precision, perhaps in a hurry. Did 'The truth lies in here' refer to the nine-digit code – *yes, it must!* But what was that code? Perhaps it was a library code. The code of the missing book? A wave of cold adrenalin rushed through his body, leaving his arms momentarily limp. He propped the lid open with his head and worked through the implications. Quick as a flash Will leaned over towards Clarkson: 'Pssst, give me that library book of yours.'

Clarkson got up and walked over to him. 'What's this? You interested in socialism?'

Will took the copy of *The Rights of Man* and looked at the spine. 'Blast it! Only six digits.'

'What d'you mean, six digits?'

Will showed him the desk-lid inscription.

'Wooh, unless …' Clarkson whispered.

'Unless what?'

'Clarkson,' Gibb's voice thundered down the classroom, 'stop whispering sweet nothings to Houston behind that desk lid and get back to your seat.'

'What?' Will repeated to Clarkson with desperation.

'Well, I'm not any good with Roman numerals but the last three digits could be the page number, only in disguised form!' Clarkson got up and crossed back to his seat. Will hid behind his desk lid for a moment longer. Perhaps Clarkson was right, but if so, why would Percival go to such trouble to hide the book's identity? Who or what was he afraid of?

3

A Second Adam to the Fight

All right, you lot, let's get started. Open your *Brandon's Standard Biology* textbooks at page 32, please.' Mr Gibbs crossed to a large poster showing a man with some test tubes. Will recognized the man from other textbooks, as he had unusually chunky glasses. With his one-metre wooden ruler, Mr Gibbs pointed at the poster. 'Stanley Miller in 1953. Why do we remember him, please? Anyone? Yes, Keats.'

'He simulated the earth's original atmosphere in those test tubes and made amino acids by adding electrical charges.'

'Good. And that is important because …?'

'Because he showed that the building blocks of life could easily be made with the right atmosphere and a bit of lightning, sir.'

'Good. Keats, take your seat. Amino acids make proteins, proteins make cells, cells make organisms and organisms evolve by random mutations and natural selection into other life forms – like Mr Clarkson, for example.'

While the boys tittered, Will was reading the notes someone had scrawled in the margins of his textbook. He lifted the lid of his desk to check – yes, the writing matched Percival's style. He had underlined the section on Stanley Miller's experiment and written in the margin: 'Seriously doubted by 1970, totally disproved by

1995.' Will was about to start on the rest of the detailed scrawl when Gibbs moved onto his next poster.

'You will observe that in the next section in Brandon's introduction to evolution, he outlines Darwin's tree of life from his masterpiece, *The Origin of Species* – without doubt the most important book ever to have been written.' Will at once recognized the image on the poster from his old school science lab. He had always found it somehow reassuring that every organism was in some way connected. He glanced down to see if Percival had made any note; he had: 'Everyone knows that the Cambrian Explosion turned Darwin's tree into an orchard.' Will thumbed his chin wondering what on earth Percival meant by that. Gibbs continued his parade.

'And then we have Haeckel's embryos, clear and convincing proofs to those sceptical Victorians that in our earliest developmental stages we still retain many vestiges of our aquatic ancestral past.' Will looked up to see the poster of Haeckel's sketches, another one he knew well. They showed comparative images of the embryos of a fish, a salamander, a hog, a calf, a rabbit and, of course, a human. There were enlargements of the human tail and the gill slits in the cheeks. He glanced down and saw Percival's scribble. He had crossed out 'embryos' and put 'forgeries' in its place, with plenty of dates and details in the margin.

Will had no time to read them as Gibbs moved on. 'Now, someone else please give the name of this creature.' Gibbs pointed to a reptile-like bird on a fourth poster.

Will volunteered the answer in front of him: 'Archaeo – arghh, Archaeo – something, sir.'

'*Archaeopteryx*, Houston. Glad you were paying attention; thought I might have lost you in your textbooks.' Mr Gibbs turned and processed rhythmically back towards the whiteboard, waving his ruler gently as he spoke. 'Now, tell us why this fossil is so important.'

Fig.6 Tree of Life

The tree of life is a metaphor describing the relationship of all life on Earth in an evolutionary context. Charles Darwin talked about envisioning evolution as a "tangled bank" in On the Origin of Species (1859); however, the book's sole illustration is of a

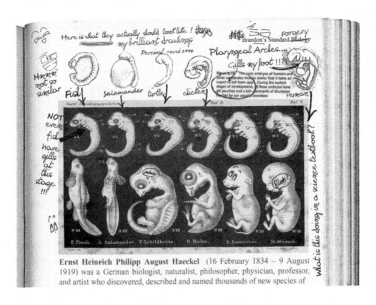

Ernst Heinrich Philipp August Haeckel (16 February 1834 – 9 August 1919) was a German biologist, naturalist, philosopher, physician, professor, and artist who discovered, described and named thousands of new species of

35

Will unwittingly started to read what Percival had written: 'Hailed as the great transitional fossil that showed the colossal leap between reptiles and birds, but now regarded, even by some eminent evolutionary scientists, to be an extinct form of bird and nothing more.'

It took Gibbs a moment to stop waving his ruler and turn around. 'What did you say?'

'Well, just what it says here in the –'

'I should have known it when I saw you – another of these gullible creationists who want to rid the world of science and go back to the Dark Ages! Well, I've got news for you, sonny: the black robes have been replaced with white coats. The clerics and the mumbo-jumbo are still around, but the world's moved on and we're not going back!'

'Well, sir, I don't know if I am a creationistic person actually – I've never really thought that much about it. I just –'

'– Just thought you'd have a scoff at established scientific history and have your little say? Well, what about this, then?' Gibbs held aloft a copy of *National Geographic* magazine with a picture of a dinosaur bird on the front cover. 'Archaeoraptor, dug up in China last year – proof that reptiles were the ancestors of modern birds. What does Mr Houston have to say about that?'

Will glanced down at his textbook, his cheeks beginning to flush. Of course, Percival's notes were written three years before 1999 and said nothing of this fossil link. 'Come, come, now, is our eminent school palaeontologist silent on the most significant find in its field for a century?' The other boys were now laughing openly, and Will could feel his cheeks getting hotter and hotter. 'But we need your wisdom to guide us in case the most respected palaeontologists are wrong! Please don't deprive us!'

There was a crushing silence as Gibbs stood, holding the magazine aloft with one hand and with his other hand on his hips. Just when Will could bear it no longer, there came a sharp voice from near the door: 'It's a fake!' Will peered with an audible sigh of relief down the aisle. And there, leaning in the doorway, was a dark, curly-haired boy dressed in a black jacket, black jeans and black cowboy boots with what looked like spurs on (though, in fact, there were only the buckles and under-chains without an actual spur). His open white shirt was not tucked in. He was wearing a bohemian bead necklace with another similar beaded bracelet on his wrist.

Gibbs wheeled round. 'What did you say?'

'Archaeoraptor's a fake – they're pumping the blasted things out of Liaoning Province in China! They know that we want the fossil link, so they make it – it's big business.'

'Who says?'

'Read up, man! The *Geographic*'s apologized for being so thick – everyone knows.'

'Well, suppose it is – and I'm not saying you're right – but what about *Tiktaalik*, dug up in Canada last year, eh? Half-fish, half-amphibian, with modified fins for walking. Suppose Canada's faking them too, eh? These are proofs of evolution, boy – wake up!'

'You'll find that Tiktaalik's fins weren't attached to the main skeleton, so anything more than swimming would have been difficult.' The class laughed.

'Yes, but it's an intermediate –'

'Or just an extinct weird lobe-finned fish like the coelacanth – though not as weird, say, as a platypus! Anyway, you can argue it both ways. Like you could with Archaeopteryx: it had avian lungs, feathers and brain case; I hate to give anything to the creation loonies but there's nothing to say it ain't an extinct bird and not a link at all.'

'Rubbish! Of course they're both links! Every scientist worth his salt says so.'

'Yeah, maybe – but, like I say, maybe Archaeopteryx is another extinct species, or maybe the creationists are right and the

which is not extinct

similarities between birds and dinosaurs are the result of a common designer. All I want to know is, why are there only one or two supposedly transitional fossils to showcase, when so much money's been given to these guys for a hundred and fifty years to get their act together? I mean, they find one interesting fossil to debate every ten years; then they jump up and down and get themselves into *Nature* magazine, but they never talk about the Cambrian Explosion and how all these different creatures just appear in the rocks out of the blue.'

'All right, we've had enough of you, boy! Now, what are you doing in my class – and where's your tie?'

The boy slunk into the lab. 'Well sir, it's like this: I just got here! I haven't had a chance to find a fag to unpack my stuff, and, anyway, I didn't want to miss my favourite lesson.'

'Oh, then you must be young Rawkins!' Mr Gibbs changed his tune immediately and went to shake his hand. 'I'm a great fan … er, follower of your father's work! Please take this seat over here.'

Rawkins dragged his heels as he made his way to Mr Gibbs and took his hand. 'My father's a jerk, sir.'

'I beg your pardon!' Gibbs recoiled and took back his hand at the blasphemy. 'Your father is one of the country's most –'

'My father,' Rawkins said, slumping into his chair, 'is an undistinguished zoologist and a third-rate philosopher who writes controversial books popularizing other people's work, which makes lots of money for his publisher and gets him on chat shows.'

'But … but his scientific wor –'

'He's an embarrassment in academia. He's never persisted in any field of inquiry and he knows how to talk for England, and that's all.'

Gibbs appeared briefly stunned, but then he said, 'Well, I'm sure when you are older you will appreciate him more than you do now. You'll find your textbook in the desk; we're on page 33 now. Right, where were we? Ah yes, the progress of Darwin's dangerous idea; Miller's experiment, the tree of life, Haeckel's embryos, the fossil record, and now, of course, Java Man and the famous picture.'

Gibbs strode back down the classroom and pointed with his ruler to the poster of the walking apes turning into men that Will knew so well. 'Perhaps Clarkson would like to read to you about the most famous fossil associated with human origins for the benefit of Mr Houston and the rest of us.'

Clarkson stood up and read, 'These fossil remains, dug from a riverbank in Indonesia by Dutch scientist Eugène Dubois in 1891 and 1892, have come to represent the missing link between modern man and our earlier, smaller-brained ancestors.'

'Yes; hence we have been able to establish what you see in the poster here. Right, thank you, Clarkson: you may sit down, if that is all right with your friend Houston in the corner.' Gibbs glared at Will as if in challenge.

Will was already riled by Gibbs' bullying and slightly emboldened by his new roommate, so he stared Gibbs out for a moment before saying, 'Well, actually, no.'

'Oh, so you would like to have a go at the established fossil record now, would you?'

'I don't know, but someone's written in my book that all that Dubois found was a skullcap, three teeth and a thigh-bone. It says, "Even evolutionist scientists admit that the skullcap was from a head that would have held a modern human brain and that Java Man throws no light whatever on our past. DNA studies suggest that both Homo erectus and Neanderthals interbred with modern humans. If that's true then they're all the same species."'

'Well, Houston, don't you think it strange that the textbook writers and your teacher haven't been made aware of this new data?'

'Strange and blasted embarrassing, I'd say.' Rawkins threw his book down onto his desk, put his hands behind his head and stretched out.

'Meaning?' Gibbs was clearly losing it, though Rawkins seemed totally oblivious.

'Meaning, the guy at the back's right and the numpties who write textbooks and the people who teach kids should do their job properly and know what they're frigging talking about.'

'Your father wrote the foreword to this book. Did you know that?'

'What I know is that my dad loves to see his name in print and probably never read any of the rubbish in it.'

'Mr Rawkins!' Gibbs bellowed. 'I think you've said quite enough.'

'Oh, well, you did ask.'

'You're just a sour little rich kid, bitter about your father's achievements and eager to debunk everything he's working for.'

Rawkins' hands fell to the desk and he looked away to one side and then back at Gibbs with a slow nod.

'Yeah, yeah, that's probably true – but that still doesn't rescue all your icons from the truth.' He pointed casually to the row of posters.

'Oh, I see. You'd like to explain it all away for us, to join Houston and the debunkers of knowledge in the name of what, pray? These girly ornaments you're wearing – perhaps you're a Romantic, like old Blake down the corridor, or maybe you've "looked inside yourself" or outside at nature and seen mystical deities rather than "nature red in tooth and claw", eh?'

Rawkins put his elbows on the desk and then slowly and deliberately put his head in his hands. 'No, I'm not here to join your monastery.'

Seeing the forlorn, deflated Rawkins, Gibbs pressed his advantage. 'Oh, well, so you're a seeker after truth and virtue?'

'Perhaps; maybe – but without the virtue, though it all hardly matters now.'

'Oh well, the class is open to you.' Gibbs swept his hand. 'Please, take my desk and teach us, seeing that our fathers have fallen so short!'

Rawkins remained in his pensive state for a moment as if not even hearing or caring what Gibbs had said. To Will this was the strangest part of the whole dramatic event, but in a moment Rawkins was back on his feet. 'Okay, let's start with Brandon's iconic images.' He walked to the front and sat on Gibbs' desk. Gibbs stayed near the back of the class, a growing look of dismay apparent in his toad-like eyes. Rawkins' eyes were moist, as though with tears. 'Right, where should we start with these babies?'

Will spoke. 'Yeah, tell us about what Stanley Miller proved about the building blocks of life.'

'Miller proved squat! By the '70s most scientists acknowledged that his predictions about the original conditions of the earth's atmosphere were way off!'

Mr Gibbs seized his chance. 'But wait a minute: Brandon does indeed give details of this later in the textbook – where is it? … here, page 237. Ah, yes, he says, "Further experiments carried out according to the more recent predictions of the original atmosphere still produced organic molecules when electricity was applied." There, I think we've all heard enough from Mr Rawkins junior, who hasn't managed to fill his father's shoes quite.'

Rawkins did not budge from the front. 'Thank you at the back, but you'll find that the two organic chemicals that were created – rarely mentioned by the textbook writers – were, in fact, formaldehyde and cyanide, so no go there.'

Keats said, 'But why won't they do to build life?'

'They fry proteins, and you need at least two hundred and fifty proteins to build anything. Even the fumes fry the blasted things. So no proteins, no organism.'

Clarkson leaned forward and raised his hand. 'All right, Mr Rawkins.'

'Please, call me Raucous!'

'Okay, Mr Raucous. What about the tree of life?'

'I don't want to take away from what Darwin gave us, but his tree of life fails dismally to explain the fossil record; he knew that more than anyone. So many life forms seemed to just appear out of nowhere without an ancestor, but he just figured, "Well, hey, we've only been digging up fossils for fifty years; let's give it a bit longer and the lads will come up with missing links to fill in my blanks."'

'Yeah, so where are we now with them?' asked Clarkson, starting to sit forward on his seat, as were one or two others.

'Well, obviously we've had about a hundred and fifty years to get more fossils, and they just turn that tree on its head; rather than finding lots of little organisms gradually evolving into the larger, more complex ones, you actually get a biological "big bang" in the Cambrian period, where lots of stuff with radically different, complex body plans just appears from nowhere.'

'Hey, come on. What d'you mean "a bang"? How sudden are we talking about?'

Will could see Gibbs' trembling hand thumbing through the textbook as Rawkins went up to the huge rectangular whiteboard. 'Now, I'm pretty rubbish on geology, coming from such a distinguished line of biologists an' all, but it would be something like – oh, and by the way, some geologists, particularly religious ones, reject the long ages in the geological column, saying that the whole lot was laid down in one or more catastrophic flood events. But be that as it may, let us suppose it does exist …' He drew a huge rectangle on the board and marked it off like a rugby field. 'Okay, so this is your first XV's match pitch, halfway line, etc. Now imagine this is all of human history, and you start walking from the touchline at this end. You look down and you see a single-celled organism. "Interesting," you think, so you keep on going, and going. You pass the 22-metre line, then the halfway line: nothing, just single-celled organisms. You keep going, and now you've walked almost to the other touchline before you see a sponge and a few worms. You take one more step, and then, bang! Within one footprint's length. From out of nowhere, you've got all these new, complex body plans – you know, fish, trilobites and stuff. No gradual progression as predicted. Just, bang! All there.'

Gibbs heckled. 'But that's the point, you imbecile! Darwin was right; the fossil record is still incomplete. You can't make an argument for your religious propaganda from "non-evidence". And anyway –'

'Excuse me, sir,' Clarkson interrupted, his hand raised slightly with incredulity. 'But isn't a hundred and fifty years long enough? I mean, what on earth is this stuff doing in a school textbook?'

'Thank you for your astute observation, Mr Clarkson, but it is most probable that the missing ancestors were soft-bodied and therefore did not survive fossilization – though that may have escaped our new teacher.'

Rawkins didn't even blink. 'Your answer, Mr Clarkson, is that perhaps they'll stumble across some new sedimentary layer in the Congo; yes, a hundred and fifty years is long enough for most people; and as to the "soft-cell" argument, sir, there are plenty of soft-bodied creatures preserved as fossils that survived from within and before the Cambrian period, so it's not a good place to start a credible argument.'

Clarkson was about to speak again when Gibbs stepped in. 'No, boy, we've had enough of you, and your girlfriend in the corner, for one class. Let's move on, shall we? Rawkins, take your seat.'

It was obvious to everyone that Gibbs was looking for a way out, but Keats now raised his hand and Gibbs said, 'Ah, Keats, sense at last! What is it, boy?' Will turned to observe the lean, sensitive boy in the far corner whom he had already noted as something of a teacher's pet.

Keats' hands shook with rage as they clenched the textbook in one hand and his glasses in the other. His eyes were bloodshot and filled with tears as he stood up. 'No, sorry, sir, this won't do – it won't do at all! What the ... what on earth have we been doing all these years if –'

'Now calm down, Keats; there's no need to get so het up. There are plenty of intermediate fossils.'

'Where, for heaven's sake, where? And if they are so blasted compelling, why have we got this ... this ... this rubbish in our textbooks! My dad's busting his guts to keep me at this school, to get me this education and –'

'Now can you see?' Gibbs shouted at Will and then at Rawkins. 'Can you see what you've done? Are you happy now, destroying this boy's foundation with all your wild theories based on who knows what? Can't come up with any proper answers, can you? Just ridicule everyone else's work. You're pathetic, both of you! And what have you got, eh? NOTHING. That's what you've got. NOTHING!'

Echoes of his fury resounded down the corridor. 'Look who's talking!' Will thought when Mr Hill, the physics teacher, popped his head round the door. 'Everything all right, Charles?'

'Yes, yes, blast it, everything's under control, thank you.'

Mr Hill shrugged, smiled and left. Rawkins slouched back to his desk, but Keats spoke again. He wiped his eyes and seemed more collected. 'And what about Haeckel's drawings?'

'Never mind that now, Keats. We can look at that later.' Gibbs walked back to the front of the class. Keats looked at Rawkins.

'Don't look at me, Keats,' Rawkins said. 'Get a life! I mean, haven't they got the Internet in Cumbria? Google it! Everyone knows they're fakes.'

'They are not fakes! Sit down, Rawkins,' Gibbs bellowed.

'How long,' Keats said, 'I mean, how long have people known that?'

Rawkins slumped into his chair. 'Er, hello, since the 1870s.'

'The 1870s! Then what are they doing in this book – I mean, how faked?'

'Rawkins, shut up and don't answer that,' Gibbs said. 'Keats, face the front – and the rest of you, too. Now listen: Haeckel may have been a bit zealous –'

'That's one word for it!'

'I said "shut up", Rawkins … a bit zealous in the execution of his drawings, but the basic theory still stands and the work has value.'

Keats turned back to Rawkins. 'Is that true?'

'Keats, face the front or you'll be in trouble. We don't care what Rawkins has got to say.'

'But I do, sir!' said Will, who always dug in his heels with bullies.

'So do I!' Keats said as the class muttered similar sentiments.

Clarkson seemed to nail it. 'Yeah, come on, sir. Talk about tails that wagged the dog! I mean, how many times are you prepared to say that the basic theory is sound when each pillar turns out to be a pile of –'

'RIGHT, FINE! Have it your own way! I'm not paid to teach a bunch of undisciplined, disrespectful know-it-alls. Have your blasted answers. I'm going to see the headmaster. It's not the first time we've had smart alecs, and we know how to deal with them!' Mr Gibbs threw his ruler at the whiteboard and stormed out the room, leaving the class in stunned silence.

Rawkins fiddled with his bracelet. 'Blimey! Are all the teachers here so uptight?' There was general laughter from everyone except Keats, who shook his head and said, 'This isn't funny.'

'Come on, Keats. You'll not get into trouble,' said Clarkson.

'That's not what I meant. I mean, don't you care? Can't you see what this means?' Then, after an awkward silence, 'How much were they faked, then?'

'Well, he used the classes of animal that looked like they proved his point rather than other classes that didn't. Then he only used the most similar; so, for amphibians, he used the salamander rather than a frog, because a frog looks so different.'

'Yeah, but that's not totally faking it, is it?'

'No, it's loading the dice. But then he also chose the mid-point stage of development, where the embryos look most similar, rather than the earlier stages, which tell a different story.'

'Yeah, okay,' said Clarkson. 'He's stacking the deck but –'

'And then he went and faked the drawings to make the evidence fit.'

'How?'

'Oh, he used the same woodcuts to draw out the embryos of different classes just because he was so sure of his theory; then he distorted his drawings to exaggerate the features he wanted in order to make the link between humans and fish.'

'And the gills?'

'The pharyngeal arches – that's what you call them if you want to be a clever Dick, like me – the pharyngeal arches develop into the neck, throat, face, ear and various glands like the thymus, thyroid and parathyroid. They've got nothing to do with gills. I mean, not even fish have gills at that stage of development!'

'Right. That's it!' said Keats. 'I've absolutely flipping well had it with this rubbish!' He gripped the offending pages and ripped them from his textbook. 'I'm not going to sit here and take it any more. Just wasting time and my dad's money.'

Rawkins smiled and the class, egged on by Clarkson, started doing the same thing. Will got up. 'Woa, woa, wait up you guys – that's no solution.'

Keats was incredulous. 'What? Don't you care we've been sold this crock all these years?'

'Yeah, sure I do, but those books aren't yours, and you're just giving ammunition to old Gibbon.'

'Stuff the fascists,' Clarkson said, as he stood on his seat and shouted with theatrical zeal. 'Rip the lies out and maybe they'll get new books for the next generation! Come on, lads, up the revolution!'

Will shook his head but he could do little to stop the mob fever that ensued as the students tore pages from their books and flung them into the air. Will put his book back into the desk and started for the door as the bell rang for prep. Rawkins was already out in front of him, and Will caught him up.

'Hey, I'm Will Houston.'

'Adam Rawkins. Nice lesson!'

'Yeah! Thanks for rescuing me. Gibbs has really had me on the ropes! Man, I was starting to pray –'

Adam turned and raised a hand. 'Look, I don't care if you're some sort of religious fruitcake but I'm not, okay, so don't crowd me.'

'But why d'you take on Gibbs, then?'

'Because he's pig-thick, and because he's a bully like my old man, and …' He hesitated. 'It was something to do.'

'Something to do!' Will said, gesturing back down the corridor. 'You've started a flipping revolution down there! Something to do?'

'Hey, don't look at me! I just answered a few questions. You're the one who started it.' He smiled so that Will could see his canine teeth, and then it began to sink in.

Will's mouth hung open for a moment. 'But … but all along you still believe Darwin?'

'Yeah, why not? Better theory than any of the alternatives. Sure, they need to sort their stuff out. I mean, just 'cos a car has a wobbly hub-cap, doesn't mean the wheel is crooked. You creationist wackos have your own list of red herrings. Or haven't you heard of the Paluxy footprints, the shrinking sun, the decaying speed of light and the Guadeloupe skeleton?'

'No, I dunno much about any of it.'

'Well, bully for you: keep it that way. If the grown-ups can't pull stuff together, I wouldn't waste your time trying to figure it out too closely.'

'And the alternatives?'

'Hey, dude, if God's a viable option for you, good for you! Have a nice life!'

'And he's not viable for you?'

'Yeah, well, that's complicated, so, like I say, don't crowd me.'

They had reached the Great Hall by this point, and Adam walked away as if without a care in the world. It was only then that Will realized that he hadn't told him that they were room-mates. But he had just seen the library door and remembered the code scratched into his desk lid. He had written it on the back of his hand. The small library door beckoned, and he descended the great steps and made his way to the alcove where it was located. As the oak door closed behind him, Will found himself in another world: not at all small, as the door suggested, but a room almost as large as the Great Hall itself. In fact, it had the same high-vaulted ceilings and tall Gothic windows on the far wall. A huge study area at the far end held tables, like so many small altars under the Great West Window. The rest of the space was given to wooden bays with books and secluded study areas. Each bay was garnished with heavy oak sculpture: leaves, fruit and other ornaments crowned with one-armed angels. Higher alcoves between the windows held plaster statues of saints in the stonework above.

If the first two digits indicated the bay, the book should be there – bay twelve. *0195*. Will found 0194 and 0196, but an empty space gaped between them. With his fingers he drummed the shelf for a moment. What about the library computers? He did not yet have a password so he went to the librarian. The small, grey, humourless Brother Brendan evidently liked boys to practise patience. Tap, tap, tap the librarian went at his computer, but no eye contact. Will marvelled at the man's legendary cone-like head.

No wonder Clarkson called him 'Truncheon'. He did eventually look up but then only sighed as Will explained that he was new and hadn't yet been given a password. Brother Brendan spoke slowly without taking his eyes from his computer. 'I see. Give me the number, then.'

'No, that's the problem: they've not given me one yet.'

Brother Brendan sighed again. 'The book number or name!'

'Oh, right, that. I have the book number.'

'Yes, yes, when you're ready.'

Will read out the number and Brendan typed it in. 'Ah yes, it says it's in the back room.' He turned, and, raising his voice as much as was permissible in the library, called out, 'Reece, bring me 12.0195, please.' He carried on typing until a nervous voice came from a room behind his desk. 'Could I please have a word with you, Brendan?'

'Yes, what is it?'

A young man with a sallow, greasy face appeared at the doorway. 'A private matter, Brother.'

Brendan sighed and went into the back room and shut the door. After five minutes, Brother Brendan reappeared, looking flustered. 'You are sure you have the right number?'

'Oh yes, pretty sure. Did you find it?'

'Write your name and house down here, please.'

He pushed a notepad towards Will and Will obliged. 'Have you got it then?' Will asked.

'No, no, but we'll let you know if we find it.'

Will lingered for a moment, disbelief showing on his face. But Brother Brendan sighed one last time and said, 'I have work to do, thank you.'

No sooner was Will outside the library than he realised he'd left his books behind. He slipped back inside.

'Has he gone?' Brother Brendan whispered. The librarian picked up the phone. It must have rung for a few seconds before someone answered. Will stood perfectly still, clutching his books to his chest. 'Yes ... it's me,' he heard Brendan say. 'I thought you should know that a new Alban's boy called Houston has been snooping around, looking for a certain book: 12.01 ... yes, that one ... No, of course I've no idea how ... Yes, yes, you'll look into it ... Good. Goodbye.'

4

MIDNIGHT EXCURSION

Will used half the prep time to clear his head in Monks' Wood on a bank behind the school. What an afternoon it had been! He looked down from the wood onto the priory and out to the sea. Another storm was coming.

He returned to his room, expecting to find Adam there, but he wasn't. The room was a total mess, with Adam's clothes strewn everywhere. Will was cursing that he had managed to get such a disagreeable roommate when he noticed that even his own things had been emptied out all over the place. 'What the …!'

'Hey, what have you done with my stuff?' Adam stood in the doorway. 'Oh, it's you again! What are you doing here?'

'I'm your roommate; welcome home.'

'What's happened to my stuff?' Adam said, picking up his leather jacket.

'And mine too – someone's been through my drawers and books!'

'Thieving swine! Better not have touched my baccy!'

'No, somehow I don't think that's what they were after,' Will said. He picked up his books and sat on the bed while Adam ranted on. Will began to bite his lip. Had this something to do with him being in the library asking for a certain dangerous book? But that was only an hour ago. Adam was all for getting Dundas, but before he could go, an out-of-breath Elliot rushed in. 'Well, what is it?' Adam snapped.

'Bede and Dundas want to see you both in his study!'

Adam got up. 'Good, about time this sort of thing was taken seriously.'

Dundas stood by the fire while Father Bede sat at an untidy desk tying a fishing fly. The boys filed in and acknowledged Dundas, who looked very grave. Father Bede strained his eyes to the lamp to make an awkward loop and did not look up.

'Well, sir,' Adam said, 'I suppose you've heard how someone's been in our room …'

Father Bede spoke as if he had not heard. 'The last time I had a third-year in this study was about two years ago. I don't like being disturbed by school affairs, but a most alarming situation was brought to my attention this afternoon. The headmaster tells me that there was a riot in Gibbs' biology class today, led by you two. He says that school property was vandalized.'

Will swallowed hard. 'Well, sir, I think there was a slight mis –'

'Tush, I don't care for Gibbs; can't see why the school can't limit the staff to old boys. And I care very little for business outside Alban's walls.' His voice rose. 'But what I am bothered about is when I am charged with the trouble of telephoning both your parents. Dundas, on the other hand, is concerned that your ungentlemanly outbreak today has jeopardized the house reputation … and therefore I will leave you in his hands. That is all.'

The boys looked at each other, not quite sure what he meant. Dundas put his sherry glass down and barked, 'Right, you two, the prefects are waiting upstairs.'

As they moved towards the door, Father Bede said, 'Houston, a word please, in private – thank you, Dundas.' The other two left and the door was shut. Will observed the fly being tied on the desk and the fisherman's knife attached to the fishing bag that hung nearby. Will's own grandfather used a similar slender, curved knife to gut fish.

'Did your grandfather say that he knew me?'

'Yes, sir.'

'He ties a mean fly, your grandfather. He's a good man.'

'Yes, sir.'

'I am going to tell you this because I am a friend of your family, Houston.' He focused his grey-blue eyes on Will for the briefest second. 'This is an old school; it will be here long after you've gone. I wouldn't meddle in things you cannot change, all right? Stay away from things that don't concern you. Got it?'

'What, biology? But –'

'Yes, that too,' he said, cutting the tying thread with his knife, pointing it at Will and then pointing towards the door. 'Now run along and don't keep the prefects waiting.'

'Yes, sir.'

Will found himself quite out of breath and unusually weak at the knees when he left the study and started on his way up to the senior gallery to find the prefects. He met Clarkson in the hall. 'Hey, how did you get on with Bedo? You look awful.'

'They're going to call my parents,' Will said.

'Bummer, man! Anyway, better than getting suspended or being handed over to the prefects!'

'That's where I'm off to, actually.'

'Oh, right, sorry.'

'Why, what can they do?'

'Damn sight more than the teachers, buddy. I'd get going, if I were you.'

'Right, thanks.' Will started the stairs, his steps heavy. 'By the way, how's the revolution?'

Clarkson's face lit up. 'Quality, dude, spreading like wildfire! Whole school's talking about it. You can die happy!'

'Very funny.'

As Will entered the senior gallery, a sulky but defiant Adam was coming out of the prefects' study. As they passed each other, he made an obscene hand gesture in the general direction of the prefects' room.

Will tapped softly on the door and heard Sidmouth's voice a second later: 'Enter.' The prefects' study had leather armchairs and was oak-panelled, as was everything at St Columba's as far as Will had seen. Brummell had his feet up by the log fire, Wordsmith was sat in a corner and Sidmouth stood behind Will by the door. Dundas stood by the window with another tall boy whose face Will could not see. This boy looked out the window for the duration of Houston's interview.

'Right, Houston.' Dundas' fingers and thumbs rubbed constantly against each other, his breathing sharp. 'What the dickens has been going on?'

'Gibbs asked a question, I read a comment from my textbook that someone had written in the margin, and the guy just blew up and –'

'Oh, come on, Houston! Who wrote it, you or Rawkins?'

'No, some guy called Percival.'

'P – Percival!' Dundas exclaimed, his face draining of colour. He turned towards the boy in the window with a wide-eyed stare. The tall boy glanced back at Dundas, then raised a hand to his chin. 'Who got the class to rip pages out of the books?'

'Look, it wasn't me. Actually, I tried to stop them, but they were so cheesed off at the bull they were being fed, they reacted like it was a revolution or something.'

'Ah well,' Wordsmith mused, 'what did the poet say? "Bliss was it in that dawn to be alive, / But to be young was very heaven!"'

'Yes, all right. All right! Thank you, Liam.' Dundas said.

'If I were you –,' Sidmouth began.

'Shut up, Sidmouth, I'm not asking you.' Dundas looked again at the tall boy in the window and then said, 'Right, Houston, here's the deal: the next time you do anything to shame this house or in any way bring your prefects into disrepute, you will appear before the Senate. Tomorrow, you will run five times to the Druids' circle before breakfast with your clever roommate. Then you will write an apology to Mr Gibbs, which you will give to me, and I will go and kiss his you-know-what for all of us and see if I can smooth this thing over. And Houston –' For a moment Dundas looked almost paternal.

'Yes?'

'It is our A-level year, we don't need any extra stuff to deal with, right?'

'Yes, Dundas.'

'Good, now get out of here before Sidmouth persuades me to do something worse!'

Will was back on the stairs a minute later as the supper bell rang. At dinner and prayers, he spent almost all the time in silence, thinking about what had been said and what on earth he would write to Gibbs. Afterwards he went straight to his room. Adam lay on his bed reading a book called *The Donor*, while young Elliot folded his clothes for him and organized them into the drawers.

'So you got out alive,' Adam sneered, without looking up.

'Yeah, just! I see you've got domestic help.'

'Elliot was all that was left, and I can see why! Can't fold a shirt to save his life and says he's never pressed trousers before – think of it! Boy needs a good kicking.'

'I'm a quick learner, Rawkins,' Elliot said as he shut the drawers. 'I'll learn.'

'You'll have to, won't you? Now lose that suitcase and don't forget I'll need to be able to see my face in those brogues for Sunday.'

'Yes, Rawkins.'

With Elliot scuttling down the corridor with the shoes, Adam looked at his watch. 'Right,' he said.

'What? Gonna write that letter to Gibbs?'

Adam snorted. 'I need a drink. Should make last orders if I go now.'

'You're going to the pub after what just happened?'

'Yes! And what are you going to do, spend your whole life living inside a Dundas-shaped box? Think they'll make you a prefect if you play by the house rules and drink sherry with Bedo in his study? Life's too short, dude, way too short.' Adam opened the window by the basin and climbed out onto the rusty drainpipe. His boots snagged half-way down and Will whispered, 'Are you okay?'

Adam scowled. 'No, I'm not; this pipe-work is a blasted disgrace; someone could really hurt himself.' He looked up and grinned. 'Remind me to mention it to Dundas tomorrow!'

Clarkson, Thornton and Elliot came round to find out what had gone on with the prefects, and they talked for half an hour about everything else that had happened that day. It turned out that the 'Senate' was a special gathering of the senior prefects of each house, and their range of punishments was severe. Thornton reeled off in great detail how, even after the legal ban on corporal punishment, the Senate often used the 'board of education on the seat of learning' on serious offenders.

'What,' exclaimed Will, 'and no one tells anyone's parents?'

'Their parents would laugh at them,' Clarkson said. 'They'd have got the birch on their bare backsides, and that draws blood; the board just leaves bruises.'

'And boys stand for it? What about the police?'

'Sure they do; you leave this place with the reputation as a grass or a traitor to the house, that sort of thing follows you through life,' Thornton said with earnestness.

Clarkson sniped, 'And you can kiss goodbye to cushy little jobs in the city or at the foreign office that people like Thornton have been bred for.'

'Get lost! There's nothing wrong with getting on in life, accepting your place and responsibility,' Thornton said. 'Can't all be radicals, can we?'

They carried on talking about the school system for another ten minutes. Will was enthralled by the whole thing: part-disgusted by the elitism, part-excited by the opportunities it might open up for him in later life. He had a picture of himself in ten years' time as Her Majesty's Ambassador to some Caribbean island where they drank ice-cold Lilt, where he could have Pimm's parties by the embassy pool and spend his days scuba-diving.

Elliot and Thornton left, and Will spent a while telling Clarkson about what had happened at the library and how his room had been ransacked within the hour. Clarkson was furious, and the more he went on about it, the angrier Will got too.

'Do they lock the library?' Will asked.

'No, 'course not; no one would dare to burgle it.' Clarkson paused. 'Wait, Will, you're not suggesting –'

'Too right! That book's there, and there's a reason why they're hiding it. Are you coming?'

'Tonight? You mean, tonight?'

'Yeah, when else?'

'With the Night Boggy knocking around?'

'The Night what?'

'Night Boggy – you know, night watchman: doesn't miss a trick.'

'Who on earth's he?'

'No one knows, and no one crosses him, either.'

'Well, look, they're gonna shift that book, I reckon, so, if we're going to get it at all, then the sooner the better. Come on, man. Life's too short! Are you with me?'

Clarkson grinned. 'Of course, mate! Up the revolution!'

They both shimmied down the drainpipe and kept to the shadows along the cloisters and passageways leading to the Great Hall.

At each critical juncture Will scouted the next section with his keen eyes and ears before going further. They slipped through the creaky south doors to the Great Hall. They had moved with such stealth that the noise of those Elizabethan iron hinges sent a shudder through their bones. The moonlight came full through the tall east windows, and the boys sank quickly into the shadows by the lockers as they moved towards the library. At the door, Will put his hand on the handle, but something made him pause. He listened. What was that noise inside? The faint rustle of garments, and … footsteps. Someone was coming to the door!

He grabbed Clarkson, covering his mouth and pointing to the niche nearby. They were barely in the shadow of that alcove, and indeed scarcely hidden by it, when the library door opened and a hooded monk came out. His robes, scented with incense and nicotine, brushed Will's body as he silently passed. Neither boy breathed or moved. They waited for another minute in sheer fright, trying to listen for further sounds above their thumping hearts. Clarkson tried the door a second time. It opened, and they entered. Will tried the handle of the back-room door, but it was locked.

'Look, blast it! It's locked, Will. Let's just get back to the house before we're busted. This place gives me the creeps,' Clarkson whispered, looking up at the statues in the alcoves.

'No, I want to get in that room. Help me find the key, will you?'

They searched Brother Brendan's desk and Will found a key hidden behind some files. He tried it in the lock. It fitted and they were in. It was not a big room. There was no window, so they shut the door and turned on the light. There were piles of books around the room.

'Right, come on. Let's look through these books: you do that shelf; I'll do the trolley,' Will said. After two minutes the boys knew that they were on to a loser; there was nothing. 'Are you sure there's no other hiding place?' Will asked.

'No, that's it. Now come on, let's get out of here.'

As they moved towards the door, there was a noise outside. Will killed the lights. The faint creak they heard was the main library door opening. Clarkson grabbed Will's arm. A powerful torch beam showed through the cracks of the door but moved away again as the boys crouched breathless in the dark. The footsteps went the length of the library and then back again. The torchlight shone through to them one last time before the library door opened and shut. *Phew, that was too close!* Will thought. He put his hand on the floor to push himself up and felt a small piece of paper. He turned on the light to examine it.

'I don't believe it!' he whispered.

'What is it?' Clarkson said.

'I'll tell you later! Come on, let's go.'

They locked up and moved into the Great Hall once again. The beams of the torch were refracted in the glass window at the end which they had used to get in. 'Night Boggy! Don't fancy that way. Any suggestions?'

'Yeah, follow me,' Clarkson said. They headed up the steps and right to the science labs. Will kept looking behind. There was no torchlight now. Through the labyrinth they crept until they rounded a corner and heard the most deafening hammering sound.

'What on earth is that?' Will said.

'Don't know, but we can't go back. Let's take a look.'

'Okay, but don't expose yourself.'

'Hey Houston, leave the jokes to me!'

They crept around the corner to the part of the corridor outside the science teachers' studies. The Roll of Honour boards were fixed high on the wall either side of the mighty oak doors into the lecture theatre. A young boy stood before them, nailing a piece of paper to the doors. Beyond the boy, at the next turn of the corridor, torchlight could be seen getting brighter. Night Boggy! The boy looked to his left, where he must have seen the light and then darted down the corridor toward Will. He ran straight into Will at the corner, and for a moment Will just stared at the lad's rabbit-like eyes. Eventually the boy said, 'Evening', gave the hammer to Will, then added, 'Toodle-oo', racing off back towards the Great Hall.

Will and Clarkson lost no time either as the light got brighter. Will stuffed the hammer into his belt and grabbed Clarkson, and they both belted off at top speed, not stopping until they were well clear of the Great Hall and within sight of the drainpipe.

It was then that they saw a body lying on the ground. 'Who is it?' asked Clarkson.

'Rawkins! Come on, he's drunk. Probably fell off the drainpipe!' They helped him to his feet. 'Come on, Rawkins, let's get you inside.'

'Disgrace that drainpipe! I'm gonna file a complaint to Bede now! C'mon, you two.'

Will grabbed him. 'No, climb it again, slowly. Honestly, Rawkins, why d'you get so drunk?'

'To forget,' he said out loud.

'Sshhh!'

But Rawkins spoke louder. 'To forget the brevity and meaningness … meaninglessnessness of this miserable life, I will "not go gently into that good night".'

'Yeah, all right, save it for inside, before Sidmouth or the Boggy gets us!'

They got him up the drainpipe and into bed, and when they were alone, Adam sobbed, 'To forget, blasted stupid – forget that I must be nothing for ever. You know it was the Mayans who gave us zero?'

'Uh, no – how nice of them.'

'They gave us zero, everyone gives you zero, what a farce, what a stinking, pointless farce, a fointless parce. But I'll not go gently into that good night! I'll rage, Houston, "rage against the dying of the light". Urgh – think I'm gonna be sick.'

He was, and Will was handy with the bin and a towel. Will noticed that Adam had carved '8000' into the wall near his pillow.

The noise brought Clarkson in again. 'Keep it down! It sounds like an elephant's giving birth!'

When Adam eventually finished voiding the contents of his stomach on the bedroom floor, they cleaned him up and gave him some water. After that he crashed out and said nothing else.

As Clarkson left he said to Will, 'Oh yeah – what was that piece of paper?'

Will took it out of his pocket, unfolded it and held it up under the light. 'This, my friend, is conclusive evidence that we were just minutes too late.'

'What's it say?'

'It's a library book insert for *Ancient Archaeological Sites and Rituals of Celtic Druidry in West Cumbria* by Mr J. Hanover!'

'And the number?'

'Matches exactly, of course!'

'The sly devils! So we're scuppered.'

'Oh no we're not! You get on to your brother and find out who the teacher was that told him about the Druids' cult. I'll see whether I can get a copy of this book elsewhere. We'll soon see why page 66 has to be kept such a secret.'

'Houston, this is a bit – well, you know, spooky, real, and stuff. Don't you think we'd better take this to Dundas now?'

'Hey, let's just find out what the book says, okay?'

Clarkson went back to his room. Will flicked the switch on his desk lamp and went to close the curtains. It was then he noticed a shadow peeling away from the undergrowth, and moving silently but surely toward the priory.

5

A Run-in with the Bullies

The alarm clock sounded all too soon the next morning, and it took Will more than a little energy to encourage his roommate in their pre-breakfast 'penance'.

The boys scrambled into their games kit and headed up the coastal path against a sharp autumn wind that chaffed their ears and knees. Adam seemed to fancy that he'd be able to blag it about doing the run five times. Sidmouth would supposedly be watching from the house, but he wouldn't be able to see through the thick mists now rolling off the sea.

They walked the first section as Adam had a hangover. Will did not ask him what he had meant by some of his comments the night before. Adam had not bothered to ask why Will had been out so late at night either.

Within ten minutes they had taken the fork to the right along the cliff path leading to the promontory where the circle was situated. The sea crashed on the rocks below out of sight. Will pinched his rugby shirt tightly as they drew nearer. The mists eventually gave way and grey forms appeared, taller and taller, darker and darker – perhaps fifteen of them between ten to twenty feet in height. Adam turned back before they had passed even the first monolith. 'Come on, no one's giving us a medal for going any further. Let's get back.'

They went back down the narrow path, walking faster than before, Will all the while looking over his shoulder. As they neared a low wall, Adam hunkered down out of the wind, 'Listen, Houston, my head is splitting, mate; need some shut eye. You be a hero if you want. Just give me a nudge on your last lap okay?'

Will went on alone four more times, back up the path and along the craggy ledge. Each time the circle seemed a different shape, each time more jarring, more jagged, more threatening as the mists whirled by. On the last circuit he saw a lone man in the centre of the circle. At first Will thought that his eyes were playing a trick on him but, sure enough, a man, maybe six feet tall, with broad, slumped shoulders stood in the circle, facing away from Will. Will wanted to go back but his feet became rigid, as if rooted to the ancient earth. Something was odd about this man. The man began to fold his arms, then pinch his eyes with his right hand. He was muttering.

Will's knees trembled slightly but nevertheless he moved closer to the circle and passed the stones. The figure stood motionless, the winds driving the mists around him. Strange beast-like shapes patrolled the outer perimeter of the circle obscured in the haze of stone and mist. Perhaps the size of small horses, they moved with purpose. Will screwed up his eyes. It was like a bad dream, and everything seemed to be happening too quickly. A great rush of adrenalin made his heart race. He heard the beasts' breathing, as if someone or something was coming after him; but then the creatures disappeared off side and he wheeled round again. They were not there. Only Will and the man in the centre were left. What were these creatures? Will's heart thumped like a hammer on his ribs. And who is this?

Just then, the man looked round, straight at Will. He was old, maybe sixty or more, unshaven, and had a distant, mad look in his eyes, the sort of look that doesn't see you, that looks past you. Will opened his mouth to say hello but nothing came out. A low, deep-throated growl sounded behind Will. The soft tread of feet came closer and closer to his back.

The man raised his hand. 'Don't move a muscle, boy.'

Is he kidding? Will thought, *I couldn't move right now even if I wanted to.*

The man spoke again, this time with a gruff voice of command that echoed off the rocks. 'Grendel, Beowulf, come!' Two huge furry shapes passed either side of Will – Irish wolf-hounds standing higher than his waist. Will gingerly drew his hands up to his chest, barely daring to look. 'What are you doing here?' the man asked.

'I – I was on a run.'

'Oh.' The man looked at the ground for a moment and then strode away from Will out of the circle into the mist. The dogs waited, looked back at Will and then disappeared too. He leaned against a stone to catch his breath. After a minute he half ran, half stumbled, back along the path to the safety of the school gates. There was no sign of Adam by the wall, but he met the gardener with his wheelbarrow. Arthur was talking to a thin woman in a blue overcoat with long grey hair, when his eyes met Will's.

'Well, I'll bid you farewell Matron, and a good morning to you – Master Houston, isn't it?' The school matron turned, and peered down her long nose at Will before leading her bike away. Arthur took off his cap and put out his calloused hand, which Will grasped and shook. 'Look like you've had a fright, lad.'

'Well, I've just been for a run.'

'Oh, ay, in trouble already, are we?'

Will breathed out and looked down, remembering his father's last warning.

'Here, lad, come in and I'll get you a cuppa, eh?' Arthur propped his wheelbarrow by the gate-post and led Will into the shed behind the wall. 'Fill that kettle up and grab a seat while I fettle these here tree straps.'

Arthur's manner reminded Will of his great-uncle who was a shepherd back in the valley; uncomplicated and settled. All the tools were arranged in their places along the wall, and the workbench that ran beneath the windows was lined with jam-jars of nails and screws. Arthur washed his hands and rubbed some Nivea cream onto his eczema. Will observed the redness and cracking around the old man's fingers. 'Used to get that too,' he said. 'Not nice.'

'Ay, I've only got it quite recent, like, but I won't complain – there's plenty worse off than me.' Arthur smiled and went to the bench. 'Doctor says to wash my hands less. I says, "Doctor, have you seen how mucky my hands get!" They're a queer bunch, them doctors, live in t' different world.'

As Will stumbled to make two mugs of tea, he tried to tell Arthur what had happened in the science class and explain his predicament. Arthur listened, saying every now and again, 'I see' or 'Oh, ay', though he did not stop fixing his tree ties. Will put his tea down.

'So you see, now there's all this fuss, and the prefects have me down as a trouble-maker, and Father Bede has called my parents. And then there's all this stuff about whether God made us, or evolution did, or both – and I'm caught in the middle.' Will sighed. 'Oh, your tea's there, by the way.'

'Oh, I know it is, lad, but I always like to finish a job once I've started it. Right, there, done! Now let's have that tea.' He looked into the mug, 'Ooh, lad, fetch us another tea-bag! Looks like it needs a bit of colour.'

They sat down in two battered armchairs, and Arthur stirred his tea-bag round in the mug. After a long pause he said, 'Now you see, lad, I have a very simple faith. You know, I work out here with nature and I see God in all that's around me, an' that's special, really special, and not something I take for granted. Oh, I know there are folks with their degrees and such, want to make themselves names by proving this, that and t'other, but this spot's a miracle, this is, all of it, and sometimes you've got to fight for it, lad.'

'Are you on your own?' Will asked.

'In a way, yes. Cancer got the wife. That's her there.' He pointed to a photo of a plump, jolly woman standing outside the cottage. Will recognised it as the gatehouse cottage just outside this work shed.

'And is this your son?' Will said, pointing to a young soldier sitting on a tank.

'Ay, that's our Chris. His tank took a shell in the Gulf War. Abbot let us bury him at the priory.' Arthur touched the photo with tenderness.

'I'm so sorry,' Will said.

'Ay, lad, them were bitter times, but my faith pulled me through in a fashion.'

'But you must have questioned it all?'

'Ay, I did – but we hope for something better. We have to, don't we?'

'Totally,' Will agreed.

''Cos there can't be nowt worse than living in a world where there's no hope of aught better, and that's the truth.'

They finished their tea, and Will took his mug to the sink. 'Ay, lad, you leave them and get yourself back.' Arthur went to the sink to wash his hands yet again and Will returned to the house to shower up, a great deal encouraged by the old man.

After breakfast Will went to the school shop via the lecture theatre in the science department. He was hoping to have a look at the theatre door to see what the young boy had put there the night before. But when he got there he found a crowd and spent five minutes just getting within viewing distance. Seeing Clarkson at the front he shouted to him to find out what was going on. Clarkson came back brandishing his mobile phone and fighting as much for breath as to get clear of the crowd. 'Oh, boy, this is big. This is massive!'

'What is?'

'It's a challenge to the science department about evolution. It's got to be something to do with our class yesterday.'

'Oh, no! What does it say?'

'Well, let me see. I got a fairly decent picture. Right. Here it is. "We want to know how a school that has banned God from its science department can explain the following:

'"'The First Cause of the universe in the light of recent cosmological advances

'"'Anthropic principle: e.g. how the laws of the universe have been fine-tuned to accommodate life

'"'The origin of life

'"'Irreducible complexity in molecular machines

'"'The Cambrian Explosion

'"'Human consciousness

'"'Signed, The Invisible College … *Nihil auctoritas*" – or something?'

'Who on earth are "The Invisible College"?'

'I don't know – another secret school club, perhaps.'

'Maybe. By the way, have you called your brother yet about that teacher who told him about the Druids?'

'Not yet, but I will tonight.'

'Well, mention this invisible whatsit to him when you do.'

'Yeah, okay. Are you coming down to watch the first XV play after lunch?'

'Yeah, sure. Who are they playing?'

'Sedbergh. We'll whip 'em!'

The boys parted, and Will wandered down to the shop, thinking about the poster. As the science teachers were away until Monday, the challenge was read by every boy in the school over the weekend, and the effect was nothing short of sensational.

Following the rugby that afternoon, Dundas collared Will on the way across to the house to ask if he was responsible for the poster. When Will shook his head, Dundas appeared relieved. 'Good. Glad to hear it. Look, just put this business behind you, Houston. I didn't want to say anything last night with the others there, but I think you have a really good future here if you keep you head down. You're fast, and that's no mean right foot you've got. We could use a good man for the house matches.'

'Thanks. The match today was amazing. Your tries, and Brummel's drop goals really won it for the school.'

Will had not been slow to notice the near god-like status in which the first XV players were held by the rest of the school; how they had erupted with cheers and songs at every bit of good play during the game, and how they lauded and greeted the players, not least Brummel and Dundas, as they left the pitch.

'Yeah, there was some good play today. But remember, you just keep out of trouble, right?' Dundas jogged away.

Clarkson came to Will's room later that night. 'Good. You're alone. Listen, I've just got off the phone to my brother.'

'What did he say?'

'The teacher who told Chris about the Druids was Mr John, the headmaster's younger brother, and you'll never guess what: he was the one who started the Invisible College!'

'So what is this college, then?'

'Well, he didn't know 'cos he never went, but Percival did, and my brother said that Mr John lost his job when Percival died.'

'Woo, that sounds like a cover-up to me. And you don't know what he was teaching them?'

'No idea. Chris said he was an archaeologist by training, but he taught history at the school.'

'Yeah, whatever – but what about at these secret meetings? He was probably filling their heads with spooky stuff about the Druids. I don't like it. The whole thing stinks.'

There was a pause before Clarkson asked, 'What about the book – did you find out anything about it?'

'No, couldn't get on the computer.'

'It was free a minute ago. Let's have a look now.'

They found the house computer station free in the common room and so logged on, going straight to the Amazon web site. The book was listed as unavailable, but there was a link for Mr J. Hanover's name, which Will clicked on. He found two other archaeology books by a Mr John Hanover, and then he began to get a strange, queasy feeling in his stomach. He copied the author's name and pasted it into Google to search under images. As the images loaded, Will's hands recoiled from the mouse and keyboard.

'Hey, what's the matter?'

'I've seen him.'

'Where? My bro says he went abroad after he lost his job and hasn't been seen since. I mean, are you sure?'

'I'm sure, all right! Hair's a bit longer but, yeah, I saw him this morning at the Druids' circle! Frightened me half to death! Not surprised he went abroad! There's more to Percival's death than anyone's saying.'

'Look at the name and the eyes; its gotta be the head's brother.' Both boys sat motionless for a moment, and then Clarkson concluded, 'Well, I don't know we should get too involved if this guy's back in the country.'

'You suit yourself, but it seems to me that Percival's blood could be screaming out from the ground, and we've been given some clues by providence or whatever and shouldn't be too chicken to follow them.'

'Oh great – now God wants us to solve the mystery suicide!' Clarkson cast up his hands. 'A mandate from heaven to get our hides kicked!'

'All right, don't be melodramatic – but I'm not letting it drop.'

'Whatever. You're starting to sound as paranoid as Percival was!'

'And how do you know that?' Will's cheeks flushed hotly.

'Because of what my brother told me. He said he was intense, critical, bitter and stuff.'

'Yeah, well, I'm not those things, but neither is this just going to go away.'

The next day was Will's first Sunday. Dressed in dark suits, the entire school assembled in the priory for Sunday worship at 10 a.m. It was the only time the whole school was together, and it was expected that either the abbot or the headmaster might say something about the recent disturbances in the science department. Will, Adam, Thornton and Clarkson were forced into the front row by the ushers, trying to look as innocent as they could when the hooded monks filed in to take their pews in the choir. Abbot Malthus came last of all, and after some hymns, he strode to the lectern, barely three metres from where Will sat.

'This morning, I find myself like Our Lord's brother, Jude, who wished to write to his friends about their common salvation but instead had to defend the faith against secret men who had crept in unawares and disturbed the community of faith. I have received word that there are, among our honest number, deceitful fundamentalists. Fanatics who have been creeping about in the night, and carrying out their work of deceiving and troubling you all.'

Malthus scanned left and right, though Will felt his eyes rest mainly on himself. In those pregnant seconds Will tried to loosen his collar to let the heat from his chest.

'So that you are troubled no longer, dearly beloved flock, I will say this once and for all: there is no argument, and there never has been any argument, between true science and the Christian faith.' Malthus let his crook rise then fall on the stone floor, sending out a hollow bang that echoed off the pillars with his words. 'That's right! The orthodox view of the Christian church can quite easily accommodate Mr Darwin; there is no issue. From Philo of Alexandria to Augustine of Hippo, the church has always encouraged an allegorical view of the opening chapters of the Bible. They are there to reveal deeper truths about our fallibility and the infinite nature of our Creator, not to comment on science. But these literalist fanatics ...' His eyes narrowed, then widened on Will, who could now see the veins in the whites of the old man's eyes. '... falsely force science and religion to oppose each other, causing thousands to lose their faith. These dreamers think they can undermine two hundred years of geology and two thousand years of traditional Christian teaching with their unorthodox brand of religious intolerance and bigotry. Their God is small and restricted, confined to the six days their little minds can comprehend. This God will not do for me, and I do not recognize him as the God and Father of Our Lord Jesus Christ, gloriously present in all forms of creation. *Can you?'*

As those last words reverberated, and died away, the abbot finished as tenderly as he had started. 'So, my dear children, fret not yourselves because of the wicked; our enemy, the devil, will always masquerade as an apostle of light – call it Intelligent Design, Creationism, or any other "ism" or schism – but neither be unvigilant in your uprooting of such who destroy the faith of others, for they are a cancer in the community of faith.'

He looked with one last fleeting and terrible glance at the front row, then raised his arms in benediction. 'The one who rips up his science book one week will rip up his hymn-book the next. I know you all to be sensible, so think on what I say, and repent or confess if you have need. Our Saviour is merciful, *even to the undeserving*. The Lord bless you.'

As they filed toward the door, Thornton echoed all their thoughts. 'Well, I don't know about you two, but I feel as guilty as hell, and I haven't even done anything wrong.'

'Man, thought I was going to faint,' Will replied, but he now also felt a glimmer of hope. Perhaps there was no dilemma after all. He had only been reading the Bible in the last six months, and he certainly found bits complicated; perhaps that was all it was. As the boys filed into the corridors, Will found himself singled out by a very red-faced headmaster.

'Houston, isn't it?' Mr George ruffled out the black gown that he wore over his suit.

'Yes, sir.' Will let his friends sidle off while he stepped out of the shallows to where Mr George stood by the crypt door.

'Yes, I thought I recognized you from the interview.' He feigned a smile, straightened his cuffs and tidied his cufflinks. 'See here, I heard about the incident last week. I ... er ... hope you were listening this morning?'

'Yes, sir, I was.'

'Our abbot is a very scholarly man; he knows what he's talking about.'

'So you think it's okay to be a Christian and believe in evolution?'

'Yes, of course! Haven't you been listening at all? There is no conflict. Now see here, Houston, I have a Masters in biology, and the fact that God used something as elegant as evolution to create us only strengthens my faith.'

'But in our class –'

'In your biology classroom it is important that you study only what can be observed. Evolution can be observed; the miracle of special creation cannot be observed. That is why you have an RI classroom; that way, it all makes sense, everything in its proper place.'

'But Mr Gibbs said –'

'Mr Gibbs is an ultra-Darwinist, a materialist, if you like, but he's a good man. No, he doesn't share our faith, but his tough approach is good conditioning for the lads going out into the world of science, I know.'

Will wanted to believe him, but it sounded so bleak, so harsh. 'But Percival's notes said that there were … well …'

'My dear fellow, we can't poke fun at apparent gaps in Darwin's theory and say "Hah, there you are; there's proof of God" – it's absurd, unscientific. Supposing the scientists fill that gap? What would that do to your version of God then? Listen, evolution works, it helps us with medicine, antibiotic resistance, agriculture and pest resistance, in industry, aeronautic design, software and computer-chip design – and I could go on.'

Will shuffled his feet. 'Didn't know that, sir.'

'No, but that's why you're here: to open your mind to the future, to the possibilities. And as for anything you read written by Percival, I wouldn't be led by him one jot. Just ask any of the senior boys; they knew him. He was poisonous and bitter, not a team-player. I was at school with his father, poor fellow, and they were alike that way: literalists, small-minded evangelicals – a family thing, no doubt. There was just no talking to either of them. If they had had their way, we would have joined the RI and biology classrooms together! They would've taken us back to the Dark Ages before science, back to astrology and all that mystic nonsense!'

'I see, sir.'

'Good, good! Well, anyway, Dundas gives me to understand that it's all sorted out now, so we need not mention it again. But I just wanted to be clear about the vandalism.'

'To the books? No, it wasn't me –'

'No, not that. I refer to the lecture-theatre door –'

'– and the Invisible College?'

His eyes narrowed. 'Listen, there is *no* Invisible College. I've seen to that.'

'You've been to see Mr John about it?'

'Well, I –' but then he stopped, his eyes widening. 'What do you know about my brother?'

'Nothing, really, but I had to do this run yesterday, and I saw him at the Druids' circle.'

The headmaster took hold of Will's arm tightly. 'Now listen very carefully: I don't know what he's told you, but I warn you to keep well away from him. He already has plenty to answer for; it nearly cost us everything here –' Mr George stopped abruptly, and released his arm. 'See here, Houston. I've spent my life building this school's science department to international acclaim, and I do mean "international". Mr Gibbs took my place when my father stood down as head and I stepped up. It's been a long, hard slog to get us where we are now, and my brother, *my brother …*' He looked to one side in disgust. 'Just keep away from him, now he's back from heaven knows where, or it will be worse for you, got it?'

'Yes, sir.'

'Well, on your way, then.'

Will went along the connecting corridors to the Great Hall to find his friends. He had his hands in his pockets and let his elbows bang into the pillars as he stewed in his thoughts. *Why do they always assume the worst? That I'm always up to something? What's wrong with these people? Why are they so uptight?*

At the far end of the Great Hall he heard muffled cries for help. Boys jeered and ran towards the far-left corridor. He went to investigate and found Thornton among the twenty or so boys crowded outside a doorway. The cries for help came from inside a classroom.

'What's going on?' asked Will, when he finally managed to get to where Thornton was standing.

'Oh, nothing unusual: hook-wedgy.'

'Hook-what?' Will peered over the head of the boy in front and saw three boys lifting a junior up towards some coat-pegs and hooking his underpants onto them. The boy's face could not be seen because the three bullies had pulled his coat-tails over his head, but he cried out again, 'Please don't, I won't do it again.'

Will felt his blood rising, and started clenching and unclenching his fists. 'Oh, what's the matter with you people?'

'Hey, don't get involved! They're top seniors, and the kid must deserve it for something.'

'Like what? Didn't press their trousers neat enough?' And though Thornton tried to stop him, Will pushed the other boys aside, walked past the whiteboard and shouted above the laughing. 'All right, that's enough!'

There was an almost instant silence as the smaller of the three, who wasn't holding the junior up, turned to him and said, 'Oh yeah, and who are you to be giving me orders?'

'Someone who's not going to stand by and let three cowards pick on a small boy.'

'Very noble, I'm sure, but you quite mistake the matter.' His voice was nasal, aristocratic with a slight Germanic accent. 'We're here to punish an offender against our traditions, and you are interrupting us, sir!'

'And what great tradition has he broken to be publicly humiliated like this?'

'That's our house business and not yours! Now get lost before I thrash you.' He picked up a riding crop from the desk and pointed it at Will.

Will said very softly, 'I'm not going.'

'Oh, I think you will, sir.' The other boy moved closer.

Will shook his head. 'You let him down and then I'll go.'

The boy laughed and nodded to the other two. 'As you wish, then.'

They let the junior boy go. He dropped onto the hook and hung there by his underpants. There was a sound of ripping. The boy cried out in pain and Will winced. He stepped forward to get him down, only to be met by the riding crop.

The bully rested it just under Will's chin. 'I've done my bit, so now you go.' He jabbed Will's chest, and Will slowly raised his arms, as if in surrender.

Will's nostrils flared. 'You're standing in my way.'

The bully prodded the crop at Will's chin. 'The door is behind you!'

There followed a deathly silence, concluded by Will announcing, 'Let me help you find it …' Without warning and at lightning speed, he took hold of the riding-crop hand with his inverted left hand. Will twisted his left hand back round, locking the other boy's arm straight, then used his right hand to force the boy's head onto the desk with such speed that it nearly knocked him unconscious. 'It's that way!' And with a shove he sent him flying towards the shocked faces at the door. The boy sprawled on the floor winded and stunned.

Will, now in possession of the crop and thoroughly revved up, pointed it at the other two boys. 'You want some too? It's all for free today.'

They had no time to answer as a voice came bellowing down the corridor, 'What in heaven's name is going on down here?'

The boys scarpered, including the bullies, who picked up their friend and helped him out of the room. Seconds later a tall boy strode in. Will recognized his curly blonde hair and tweed jacket at once: it was the mysterious boy from the prefects' study.

'What the …?' he shouted to Will, who was the only one left, struggling desperately to lift the screaming boy. But Will was in no mood for more accusations. 'Shut up and help me get him off that hook.' The boy cried bitterly with pain but they managed to get him down and reveal his tearful face.

The tall boy's face softened immediately. 'Ben!' The younger boy sobbed uncontrollably, while he stuffed the straggling remains of his underpants back into his trousers. Pitt swore. 'Who did this to you, Ben?'

The boy shook his head. 'You know the house code. I can't tell you – they'd make my life even more miserable.'

'It was Coburg, wasn't it? I saw Clarendon and Tarleton helping him down the corridor.' Will's face dropped at the name. Coburg was the famous prince he'd only heard about until now. 'Did they do it to get at me?'

'No. I slept in and forgot to get him up and ready for chapel.'

'Oh, for heaven's sake! You just play into his hands! Why don't you – I mean, how many times do I have to tell you –'

'I didn't ask to be his fag!'

'I know, I know,' the older boy said more tenderly, putting his hand upon the younger boy's shoulder. 'I wish it could have been different, little brother, believe me.'

Through the tears the younger boy forced a mischievous smile. 'Anyway, just as well he didn't find me peeing on his toothbrush!'

There was a pause while they looked at each other before the elder smiled and spoke. 'Idiot,' he said, but then his face turned more serious. 'Coburg was clutching his head. Did you hurt him back?'

'No, *he did*,' the boy said, looking over at Will. 'Thanks.'

'Oh, and what did you do?' the older boy asked Will.

Will shrugged. 'Showed him the door.'

'I'm afraid you may have brought a great deal of trouble on yourself, meddling in another house's affairs. I'll do what I can for you, but they may want your blood. I suggest you see your prefects as soon as you can, Houston.'

'You know my name?'

'I do indeed, and I thank you for your sympathy for my idiotic brother, however misguided –'

'Misguided! I just don't get you people – you'd sit back and let –'

'Don't talk back to me! How dare you? No one ever died of a wedgy. My brother knew the rules; sleeping in was his mistake and one he'll never make again.'

'I'm sure he won't.'

'Good, then we are agreed; the system works. And you might do better yourself to obey what your house prefects instructed you the other night, if you want to last out the term.'

He shook his head and took the riding crop from the desk. 'Right, I'm off. Better take this back to the Black Prince before he accuses St Alban's of giving refuge to thieves of Crown property. Ben, I'll talk to you later, and, like I've said, Houston, I'll do what I can for you.' He ruffled his brother's hair and left the room.

Ben beamed at Will. 'So you're the guy everyone's talking about, the one who stood up to the Gibbon about evolution!'

'No, that would be my insane roommate who doesn't even believe in God! I just asked the question.'

'Must have been some question!'

'Well, perhaps it was – or maybe the abbot was right.'

'Malthus! His view of orthodox Christianity is as gnarled and twisted as that old crook he carries. I wouldn't give a Refresher chew sweet for his take on church history.'

'Really? And what makes you such an expert?'

'Me? Oh, my brother used to tell me things before ... well, never mind that, but he got me interested, anyway, and then I read up about stuff ... It *is* important – you know?'

'Yeah, I figured that out. Everyone's so uptight, including your brother. What is he, anyway? Like a prefect or something?'

'Willie? No, he's the head boy, though, of course, you must call him the "honourable Pitt esquire" if you don't want to get into trouble ... or just plain "sir".'

'Right, I'll remember it.' And then under his breath Will muttered, 'One thing everyone loves here; names and titles!'

'Oooh, and you're just the reformer!'

'Hardly!'

'Oh yeah, and what do you intend to do about the evolution debate?'

'Look, as far as I'm concerned, it's not my fight – just a huge thing that I can hardly get my head round for myself. I'm here to pass my exams and keep my parents happy, and I seem to have got into more school trouble in one week at this place than in all my other schools put together … so subject closed.' Will started for the door.

'Strange – I thought you'd be the one to take Perciv –' Ben stopped.

'What did you say?'

'Nah, nothing – just thinking.'

"You were going to say Percival weren't you? Now what do you know about him?'

'Nothing.' Young Ben Pitt raised his hands feebly. 'Anyway, thanks for the help.'

'It's okay – just don't lie in next time.' Will left and wandered back to his house for lunch, wondering why the boy's face seemed familiar.

He only twigged it as he passed the drainpipe by his window. Of course, he knew it! The wedgy kid was the boy with the hammer!

6

THE BULLIES' REVENGE

Where d'you learn to fight like that?' Thornton had gathered a crowd around Will as he went up the house steps.

'Taught by an old soldier. Thanks for sticking around to help.'

Thornton looked down. 'Pitt would have had our guts. Anyway I told you not to mess with the Dragoons.'

'You didn't say who they were.'

'You didn't give me the chance, Jackie Chan. Anyway, doesn't matter now. You're dead meat, mate. Prince Von Coburg will have your guts.'

The lunch bell rang, and after a good roast, Will was summoned to the boot room by Brummell. Will was anxious, but it was obvious that Brummell had heard nothing about what had been happening.

'Right, Houston. Dundas and I think you have some promise and he wants me to give you a little extra tuition this afternoon; see that golden foot of yours.' He handed Will an old pair of boots with heavy, square-ended toes. 'Did me when I was your age. Put 'em on and meet me outside in ten minutes.'

They spent an hour doing various types of kicking, but Will was frustrated with the boots and couldn't match Brummell for power or accuracy. Brummell was confident and very encouraging. 'I know it's hard with the square toes, but it's best.'

'You speak like you had footy boots too.'

'I dare say Dundas has forgotten, but I did once.'

'You did? But you're a Dragoon!'

Brummell scratched at the designer stubble on his chin, and looked back toward the school buildings. 'Wasn't born a Dragoon like some, but I soon sorted out my clothes and accent – yes, and my boots!'

'Yeah, but you got in – I mean, you're one of them.'

'I live in Chelsea, I keep them in touch with what's in. I'm useful – that's all, okay? Anyway, come on, let's work on your breathing and pacing.'

Will didn't talk with Brummell again that afternoon, but he felt that they had some common ground, and it gave him hope that he would fit into this strange new world after all.

The next morning, Monday, Will had double maths first thing, which he intensely disliked. The teacher, Ms Sykes, was an Oxford Ph.D. graduate and, as Clarkson warned Will, 'as fearsome as they come – militant feminist is Dykes, absolutely hates men, so I'd keep your head down if I were you.' It was good advice, and Will was for once able to watch other boys being emasculated in class rather than himself. He fared better in art with Ms Woolfe, whom the boys called 'Shaggy Sheila' on account of her slight facial hair. Will found her very encouraging about his life drawing but was quite shocked when he went into her back room to fetch her glasses and found a pile of books on the New Age and Eastern Mysticism. He was even more surprised to find out later that she had originally been Mr Conlon's wife and that, after sixteen years of childless marriage, she had divorced him, and moved in with Ms Sykes.

He had English Lit before lunch, and Mr Blake cornered him after the class as the others left. They spoke for some time about his essay on Kubla Khan, though Will felt Mr Blake had something more on his mind. It was only as Will was preparing to leave and placing the essay in his folder that Blake said with surprising feeling, 'Dear boy, I see the profound doubts in your work and your eyes. You are not the first.' Will was not sure what he meant.

'My doubts?'

'Yes, dear boy, doubts. You are like Tennyson, barely holding on to faith now the Enlightenment has come to explain everything away, but, as I say, we have all been there. I too, at one time.'

'And what did you do, sir?'

'I came to teach at this school,' he said, using his hand to comb his hair across his head. 'I am a Romantic, my lad, not like George Eliot or Arnold – they shrank under the pressure and abandoned their faith altogether. No, I see things quite differently. Let them mock on, Voltaire and Rousseau; they "cast their sand into the wind, and the wind blows it back again". I fear not; I know what I know.'

'And do you believe the Bible, sir?'

Blake looked steadily at Will, grinning suddenly with his garbled teeth. 'Dear boy, I was just saying I understood those who struggle with the barbarities and complacencies of the scientific age. I am here if you need a friendly ear.' Will thanked him and left.

After lunch and games, Will was even more surprised, for he had quite forgotten that he was due to be sitting in a classroom facing his grandparents' friend, the eccentric Professor Conrad Inchikov. The professor had obtained a part-time post to teach philosophy, and as the old man stood at the front, writing on the board, Will wondered how the erratic character he had come to know the summer before would have a chance of controlling a class full of riotous boys.

Inchikov acknowledged Will with a stern nod.

'Read, please!' He pointed to the whiteboard.

The boys fumbled and giggled. 'What, do they not teach you Latin? Very well, "I think, therefore I am." My name is Inchikov – you may call me "professor". Your school has employed me to give you one lesson a month so that you may be able to think and therefore be. Do not look so worried, William, there will be no exam or qualification – they do not think it important enough for that.' At this point Will was actually thinking about the group of boys he'd seen staring at him in the Great Hall as he passed.

'No.' Inchikov looked across the grassy quadrangle towards the science department. 'Perhaps that would take too much time away from the real business of moving the world on by science.' He looked back at them. 'However it is, you have me and I have you, and together we may look at the world and see the history of ideas.'

At that moment, Adam came in late and sat with Will.

'Sorry, sir. Got lost in the warren.'

'Then you are no different from most men, but this is why we are here.'

'To talk about ideas?' Adam said. 'Thought it was facts that changed things.'

'Wrong, foolish boy! Who told you such nonsense? Ideas are what make men, make the world, drive history! Each of you is a fish, and your bowl is your preconceptions, your unquestioned paradigm. You don't know they are there – they surround you so completely, but by them you see the world. By them, what you call "facts" are seen and given value. Give me an idea and I'll show you the world.'

'Whatever,' Adam said, and pushed his pencil box across the table.

Will, wanting to save the professor from the same slaughtering that Gibbs had got, said, 'What about Darwin's idea? I was told it helps us with medicines and computers and farming and stuff.' Adam looked interested.

'Perhaps – I wouldn't know; but remember it also gave us – to a certain extent – Marx, Stalin and Hitler.'

'Oh come on!' Adam said.

Inchikov flashed his grey eyes. 'You think this is fancy on my part? Well, I am Russian; I am the fulfilment of Plato's dream: every child an orphan raised in a bureau, and these scars –' he pulled up his sleeves and thrust them at Adam's face, his wrists dark red with hideous, deep wounds '– are the Gulag's reminder that ideas are more important than guns. This is not academic, boy. What I tell you here are things I know, things I have seen.'

The whole class was silent as the shaking man rolled down his sleeves. He stared at them for further moments, the ghosts in his eyes chilling them all. Eventually the old man looked to the window, taking an audible breath.

It was Will who broke the deafening silence, 'Professor – the scars?'

'I have plenty more, but they are not visible.' He turned back to the class. 'What you need to know is what scars you have.' Inchikov paused and observed their faces. 'Inside, in your mind, who has given you lenses to see the world, I wonder?'

'Were the Commies evil men?' Will asked.

'You cannot use terms like "good" and "evil" to describe them; they were not men in that sense, not as we would see it, for they had remade men into something else. No, you could not say *evil*; such words would mean nothing to them.'

'But you *are* implying that there is something evil about Darwin's idea, aren't you?' Adam said, almost under his breath.

'I never said so. Ideas are ideas; why men give them credence and how they use them is not something my profession allows me to judge. I am a philosopher. I will show you the other goldfish bowls; you decide which one will be yours.'

'Sir, you said you would tell us about Darwin's idea.'

'Ah yes, that ancient promise to free us from Olympia! Well, some ideas have a life of their own, some fade, some … some are ancient and won't go away until they find full expression, their full force. Evolution is such a one as this.'

'Do you mean that it was older than Darwin?' Will said.

'Darwin? My boy, what do they teach you in this place? There is nothing new about evolution. Greek philosophers gave us forms of organic evolution as far back as the sixth century BC. Anaximander claimed that life evolved from the sea and only later moved onto land, and Empedocles wrote of our non-supernatural origins, and even suggested a form of natural selection. Years later Aristotle would compile his four influential biology books, not on Galápagos but the isle of Lesbos. He too was obsessed with finding out the relationships of living things. He gave us a "scala naturae", a hierarchical classification system called a "Ladder of Life" or "Chain of Being", placing organisms according to complexity of structure and function, some higher, some lower.'

Will whispered to Adam, 'Did you know that?'

He whispered back, 'No, I did not; shut up.' Adam then spoke straight to the front. 'So we got it all a long time ago from the Greeks?'

'That's not what I said; some ideas pop up in many places and philosophies at once, seeking to rise, to find hearers. We could visit the Taoist Chinese thinkers such as Zhuangzi, who lived around the fourth century BC. He speculated that species evolve in response to differing environments. Humans, nature and the heavens are in an existing state of constant transformation known as the Tao. Then we could meet the Roman Titus Lucretius Carus in 50 BC and get him to read us his poem "*De Rerum Natura*", "On the Nature of Things", and you would hear how the cosmos, the earth, living things and human society appeared through purely naturalistic mechanisms without any supernatural involvement. It would be an Italian best-seller fifteen hundred years later.'

'Then what?' Will asked, looking round and realising that the professor had never needed rescuing at all.

'Then the idea slept after its exertions. Like the ring of power in Tolkien's tale, it was hidden for a time. The Greeks went, the Romans went, the great library of Alexandria was burned. But I fancy the idea slept for a reason: she slept while that other daughter of Athena, Stoicism, was at work in Christendom, preparing the ground for her great rise.'

'Sorry, sir, you're losing me,' Will said.

'The Greeks, I mean, Houston, the Greeks; their division between the sacred and the secular, the evil flesh and the pure spirit: it lived on, passed to Rome, and then entered the Western civilization. It's part of your goldfish bowl, even now.'

'Wouldn't have anything to do with Augustine, would it, sir?' Will asked, remembering what Ben had said about Abbot Malthus' sermon about Philo of Alexandria and people like him.

'Yes – and others. Why?'

'Well, you said they divided stuff up. I mean, would they divide, say, the science and the RI classroom?'

The professor looked at Will for a while with utter astonishment before he spoke softly. 'Oh, yes, it is quite the Greek way of seeing things.' And then, after another pause: 'There is hope; perhaps you shall learn to think as a man after all.'

'So what happens – Darwin finds the idea again two thousand years later, right?' Adam said.

'No, the idea was found by another unlikely Gollum, in the Great Library at Alexandria; the Internet of its day, the epicentre of the world's knowledge database. It was finally lost when the Muslims seized it. Many Greek texts of philosophy and mathematics were preserved and taught at Islamic universities by eastern Christian scholars, and many other ideas were kept alive by Muslims like Al-Khazini, Al-Jahiz, Miskawayh and Al-Haytham, who carried on writing about organic evolution. Hundreds of years later, when the West was on more peaceful terms with the Islamic world, the Greek manuscripts were released to the West. Evolution wanted us to find her doctrine again, and she knew her time would be soon.'

'Well, I bet it shook 'em up, sir,' Adam said.

The professor walked to the window and looked across to the science labs. 'What?'

'Greek science, sir – made an impact.'

'Yes, of course, the rediscovery of Greek works filled a huge intellectual vacuum in Europe. A vacuum that was left, by the way, by a partitioned, Greek-thinking church which looked down on "natural philosophy", as they called it, as something connected with the unholy, secular realm. Of course, this would push many restless intellects directly into Greek philosophy when they came to study the natural world, seeing everything through Aristotle's goldfish bowl; a missed opportunity, some say.'

'But didn't the church just stamp it out or something?' Adam asked. 'I mean, I thought the Catholic Church was hot on that sort of thing.'

'Good point. The answer is they did try a rear guard action by banning Aristotle's work on "natural phenomena", but only after the whole faculty in a Parisian university decided that Aristotle was right and the Church was wrong. Then a clever fellow called Thomas Aquinas came up with the idea – a very Greek idea at that – of separating the Church's sacred moral teaching, "the book of Scripture", from the study of the natural world, "the book of nature". And thus it has ever been: an uneasy peace – two classrooms, Mr Houston.'

The professor talked for some time about the great divide before a boy at the back raised his hand.

'I remember,' said the boy, 'when I split up with a girl last year and she said that she always wanted to be friends. Well, it never happened.'

'Yes, thank you. A very apt analogy.'

'So that's it, then,' Adam said, sounding triumphant. 'Science developed the truth and the Church stayed in the Dark Ages.'

'Poor child,' the professor sighed. 'A thought that gives solace, no doubt, to many little scientists and little followers of science, but it is not part of this lecture and I see that our time has gone.'

'What will we do next time?'

'I don't know. Poke your heads outside your goldfish bowls and bring me something interesting, and we will discuss it together.'

'How do you just log all this stuff?'

'Young man, before you were born I was teaching this in the great universities of Moscow and St Petersburg, in the days when all men were only allowed one bowl to live in.'

The bell rang and Will stayed behind to thank the professor and ask after his friends and family back in the valley. After a few minutes' small-talk he was left alone and walked down towards the Great Hall.

The corridor was empty now, his footsteps clicked and echoed off the parquet floors and around the oak panels. As he passed the door to the toilets, Will was grabbed from behind by three strong pairs of arms, one round his neck and the others round his arms. He tried to cry out but he kept his air in his lungs, feeling the grip so tight that he did not know if he would be able to get another breath. Will kicked his legs and twisted his body in vain, but before he knew it, he was in the urinal area facing the Black Prince and a large group of Dragoons, many of whom he recognized from the first XV rugby team. Will saw that the Black Prince's forehead was heavily bruised and he was removing his jacket. The Prince passed the jacket and a half-drunk wine bottle to a boy on his left by the door. It was Brummell.

Coburg said, 'Mr Houston, the great philanthropist – how delighted I am to see you again sir! Or should I call you William or "Our Billy", so you might feel more at home?' Coburg's voice seethed with a mixture of inner rage, and deep seated pleasure in inflicted pain '– so you might feel you're back with the rest of your dirty scouse mates, in your dirty scouse comprehensive in Liverpool, preparing yourself for a dirty scouse life, sponging on benefits that you'll get from people like us, from schools like this, where we study to improve ourselves and society. Perhaps you will remember *that* when you interfere with us again. Today, you will receive a lesson in manners from these people; tomorrow, you will ask your plebeian parents to remove you from this school; and the day after, we will wave you goodbye and you will go back to whatever hole you came from.'

He grabbed his riding crop and pointed it at Will's head. 'You'll find here that only the strongest survive. You want to live by the sword? Well, that's fine by me! Get his jacket off!'

Will was stripped, not for a fight, but so that his punishment might be felt. He was dragged into the disabled cubicle where the toilet had been blocked with tissue and was nearly overflowing. 'I realize that this will be less of a punishment for someone of your background, but tradition is tradition, and the bogwash is the tried and tested procedure for people who forget their manners. We've all urinated in it, and just to show you it's nothing personal, I've added something solid for you to chew on as well.'

'No, no, you can't do this!' Will struggled against the three pushing him forward toward Coburg's long, curling, soft turd. 'No, Brummell, help me!'

'Stop winging, you coward!' the prince said. 'Get him in!' There was no help from Brummell or anyone else. Within seconds, Will's face and hair were plunged into the tepid ammonic filth of the toilet, where he was held amidst the jeers. He clenched his mouth tight so as not to let anything in but they held him down so long, he thought he would explode. Then came the lashes of the whip, which fell hard and merciless, each stroke sending spikes of agony into his body.

After a minute he was pulled up and gasped, 'No, please, not again …' He spluttered, nearly vomiting, as the taste entered his mouth and nostrils.

'Get him down again!'

'Come on, Prince. He's learnt his lesson.' It was Brummell's voice.

'Get him down!' Coburg shouted, grabbing the back of Will's head himself now and ramming it into the water. 'Eye for eye, bruise … for … flipping bruise.' He slammed Will's forehead into the back of the pan until everything went black.

When he awoke, Will found himself in a small study that reminded him of the prefects' one in his house, though this one was somewhat larger. In front of him were three older boys whom he did not recognize. Brummell stoodby the door. Brummell nodded at another boy before leaving. Thinking he was again in the hands of the Dragoons, Will struggled from his chair to fight, but he was reassured by a softly spoken and handsome Irish boy: 'Steady on, Houston. You're in no harm here.'

'Where am I?' Will clutched his throbbing head.

'You, my young friend, are in St Oswald's house, under my protection,' said the tallest and plumpest of the three boys. He was forceful, yet impish at the same time. 'Sherry?'

'No, no thanks; not allowed to drink.'

'Well, rules are rules,' the boy smiled wryly. 'I'm only sorry I don't have anything stronger to offer. Burke, be a good fellow and get Houston some water.' The Irish boy filled a glass from a decanter and handed it to him.

'Here; drink this.'

Will downed it in one gulp, but the foul taste in his mouth did not go.

'Who are you?' he asked.

The third boy, who was lean and had a pinched face, took his glass to refill it. 'We're the prefects here; Brummell brought you to us. I'm Payne, he's Burke, and the fat one is Fox. Have some more.' He handed Will another glass of water.

'Thanks.' Will took a swig. 'I've heard of you – you're the radicals.'

'Radicals!' Fox said. 'I should hope not! Payne might be, but you'll find us merely less fascist than the other stiffs in this place.' He sat back in his leather armchair with his sherry. 'No, nothing radical about wanting to reform an outmoded system so that it embraces modern times and –'

'And the rights of those like you,' Payne said, who don't want to be bogwashed for standing up to bullying.'

'Yes, thank you, Tom,' said Fox, 'but unlike you, most of us see there's no need to overturn everything. Anyway, a clean bogwash never hurt anyone, and it does help preserve discipline. As usual, our illustrious monarch took it too far.'

Will squinted. 'So you have levels of these things?'

'Naturally. Most offences just get you a clean flush, and then off you go to lessons. Yours, however, were not considered like most offences.'

'That's very comforting. So, if not bogwashes, what on earth do you want to reform?'

Burke spoke up. 'The way we elect prefects is the key to the whole system. At present, the outgoing prefects, like us, plot with the headmaster and housemasters, and they always pick the same sort of people, ones *they* can rely on.'

Payne interrupted. 'It's totally undemocratic; it's obvious that it's every boy's privilege and right to vote on it.'

Will sighed. 'Right, sounds riveting.'

'Oh, and we want girls here too!' Fox added with a twinkle.

'Fine, fine,' Will said with irritation, 'and yet I was told you still hang out with people like Coburg and his cronies.'

'Dear boy, we all have to live together. The prince is a useful ally on occasions. We work from within, slowly, slowly. We don't want to become like a French state school. No, no – even Coburg's not so bad after a few pints.'

'Well, he won't be when I find him.'

Fox leant forward. 'If you will pardon me for moralizing – not something I'm prone to – I had taken you for a religious man, from what I had heard.'

'So?'

'So … I doubt your Jesus would condone you baring the other fist and not the other cheek … and we can't support vigilantism.'

Will looked into his glass in shame. 'Well, I'll go to the police then – I've been assaulted.'

'Yes, I dare say that's a convincing bruise you have, but I hear you had already given Coburg one too. If I know anything of lawyers and politicians, I would advise against even thinking about the law; they'll string you up without any difficulty whatsoever.'

'Well, what can I do, then?'

Burke spoke up. 'Do you have a fag yet?'

'No, I can brush my own teeth and warm my own bog seat, thank you. Why?'

'Yes,' Fox said, 'very good, Ed, very good. Well, you see, Houston, we have a rule that allows one senior to challenge another in the gym to a duel if his honour has been, um *soiled* … as yours has in more ways than one.'

'Oh, come on! Pistols at dawn?'

'Good Lord, no – they banned pistols here in 1811! No, no, now we box. Are you handy with the gloves?'

'I don't know.'

'Well, you'd better be, because Coburg is not bad at all.'

'Oh, so what's that got to do with fags?'

Fox's eyes gleamed. 'That's the best bit: if you win, you'll get to keep his.'

'But I don't want a fag, particularly his – he's a trouble-maker.'

'Oh yes, what do you mean by that?'

'Well, nothing I can talk about really,' Will said, realizing his mistake. There was already a reward out for the scalp of the 'Invisible College' vandal, and Will was not about to incriminate Ben.

'Fair enough,' Fox said. 'Dare say he's no more of a rebel than his brother was.'

'His brother a rebel? Thought he was the head boy.'

'Oh yes, you'd be surprised; old Pitt was more of a freethinker than any of us before all that dreadful business in our first year.'

'What business?'

'His friend did himself in at the circle,' Fox said.

'Percival. Percival was Pitt's friend?' Will said with surprise.

'Oh yes, best friend, though Percival was never really one of us – something the prince would never let him forget, sad git. Anyway, Pitt never really ever got over it. He lost all his reforming zeal, made him an ideal candidate for head boy.'

'So Coburg had it in for Percival too?'

'Oh yes, never happier than when he was "teaching him manners!" Made his life hell. Little wonder he topped himself. Anyway, enough of that. D'you want me to organize you a duel with Coburg or not?'

Will agreed, and he was helped to the washroom by Burke's fag to get cleaned up. It seemed that the young lad knew 'Pitt the younger', as he called him, quite well and said that news of a duel would be all through the school by dinnertime. Will washed his hair and put some antiseptic cream on his bruise which was, fortunately, well within his hairline and not really visible. Back in his room, he changed his shirt and examined the marks left by the riding crop on his back; they were sore but not bleeding. He washed his face again and cleaned his teeth four times before going to dinner.

As he entered the dining room a great hush fell over the other boys who were waiting for the housemaster and the prefects. Will expected to see Bede arrive through the door at the other end, but then he realized that everyone was looking at him. There were nods and smiles, some disapproving comments, and, after Bede had come in and all were seated, Clarkson and Thornton launched into Will with question after question. It appeared that everyone knew what had happened and everyone was talking about the duel.

'They're running a book on the event,' said Clarkson.

'Yeah,' said Thornton. 'I got three to one with one chap in Oswald's, and having seen you lay Coburg out once, I'd say it's money well spent.'

'Thanks for the vote of confidence, but as far as I know, boxing is way different from anything I've ever done before.'

'Nah, don't worry! I hear Dundas is going to second you and give you some tuition.'

'Have they fixed a date for the fight?' Will asked.

'It's not a fight,' Thornton said. 'Gentlemen are sportsmen: they don't fight. They spar and then shake hands.'

'Oh, save us your old-school rubbish, Thornton! They weren't so sporting when three of them held Will's head in the bog! Now, have they got a date or not?'

'This Friday, after games.'

'Well, there you go, Will. Plenty of time to sort out your footwork and right cross.'

After dinner Dundas summoned Will to his room. He sat at his desk, resting his ink pen against his temples. 'I don't want to know the details, Houston, but who in heaven's name put you up to this?'

'No one! Well, I was at Oswald's and –'

'Oswald's! It was Fox, wasn't it! Should have known.' He cast the pen across his desk.

'He mentioned it, but –'

'He used you, you idiot, to help Coburg – don't be so naïve.'

'What d'you mean, help Coburg?'

'He knows full well Coburg's unpopular but he's a sneaky pugilist, and the spectacle of Coburg flooring you is the sort of cheap stunt Fox would pull.'

'But, I don't get it …'

'The prince's – and his family's – support for Fox's reform is crucial if he's going to change the system; it's the only reason he keeps in with him.'

'But why is Fox so fixed on changing something, when he leaves the school in a few months' time anyway?'

'Because, Houston, Fox fancies himself in politics, and if he manages to prove himself and change things here – or anywhere, for that matter – his name will be known in London and they'll all want him, you see.'

'Oh, right, so he set me up to fall.'

'Fall! You'll do no such thing to shame your house! No, I'll train you this week and, though you may be beaten, I'll see to it that you will not disgrace St Alban's by going down in front of the whole school.'

'And do I get help? I mean, I'm two years younger.'

'No, you fool – you challenged a senior prefect to a duel. The fact that you're younger makes it all the more despicable; everyone apart from your house will want to see you take a lesson. Now I suggest you get to your room and do a hundred press-ups. We'll meet every morning at 6.45 a.m. and I'll give you some training.'

'Yes, Dundas, thanks.'

'Not doing it for you, lad, so no need to thank me.'

7

THE FIGHT

B limey, boy, you're in good shape! No wonder you can hammer out those press-ups!'

Will sprang back up off the sand and grinned at Dundas. 'That's rock-climbing and hay-baling for you.' Good as his word, Dundas jogged with Will up and down the coast as the pale sun rose on the cliffs. He drove Will in a punishing regime of press-ups, skipping and sit-ups on the beach.

'Whatever. Now let's see how fast you are.' They both put on some ancient-looking leather gloves and circled round. Dundas was swift, agile, and in top shape himself. Will moved in and out but found little to hit at.

'Now, Houston, I'm fighting like Coburg does. He may look out of shape, but he's quicker on his feet than me and has a sneaky little left uppercut that you've got to watch … like that –' his left fist connected with Will's right temple '– so for heaven's sake don't be sloppy with your guard, or he'll be all over you like a cheap suit.'

The tide was out and they sparred for twenty minutes on the sandy beach with the Druids' circle looming over them from its rocky promontory.

'D'you think Coburg was responsible for Percival's death?' asked Will.

Dundas' eyes opened wide for a moment. Then they hardened again as he gave Will a sharp jab to the kidneys. 'Still on about that, eh? Well, forget it; what's past is past. If you want my advice: leave well alone.'

'I hear that a lot.'

'Yeah, well, you're too like him; he could never leave well alone and just be a team-player. Now come on, let's see that one-two-three jab again. Good. Again. Tight and straight from the chin now. Good. Come on; twist those wrists, land 'em square or you'll risk breaking your bones. That's better, again. That's it; use your left as the range-finder.'

Will ducked and planted a right uppercut under Dundas' rib. 'Tell me about the Invisible College,' Will said.

Dundas weaved and moved in with a one-two, knocking Will off-balance. 'Something stupid we did when we were young. Move your head, you cretinous mollusc; it's a sitting target.'

'So you were in it? What was it?' They both ducked and weaved, the odd jab being exchanged.

'That's all history now; and Percival's dead because of it, case closed.' Dundas started landing stronger punches.

'So what's this secret society got to do with Percival's death?'

'I said –' Dundas slammed a one-two-three-four on Will's body and head and sent him right back '– it's history, right, all of it: the Invisible College, Percival's death – and if you mention either in my presence or in my house again, I'll drag you to the Senate myself.' He turned to look away from Will and inadvertently up at the Druids' circle, where he caught sight of a lone figure and two dogs looking down. 'So it's true. He's back, the devil,' he muttered under his breath, spat to the side and then said more loudly to Will, 'Come on, that's enough now. Let's get back to the house.'

Will watched the man wander along the cliff-edge. He never did mention these matters again to Dundas, but nevertheless, from that point on, he could not get out of his mind that perhaps the mysterious Mr John and the even more mysterious Invisible

College held the key to Percival's death, and that it had been no suicide.

The week passed quietly. Dundas trained Will every morning, and every evening Will worked out with his feet and hands until he was moving effortlessly. He passed Brummell in the corridor several times but he did not speak to him. On Wednesday, as Will headed for the house match practice, he noticed Adam getting into a taxi round the side of St Alban's. When Will later questioned him about it, Adam told him to mind his own business. On Thursday night he was alone with Adam. Will was writing, and young Elliot brought in some coffee.

'I've done your shoes, Rawkins. Can I go now?'

Just then there was a knock at the window. Will quickly opened it and Ben Pitt scrambled in. 'Dodgy drainpipe! Ought to get it seen to!'

'I know,' Adam said. 'And who are you?'

'Hello, Pitt. Fancy you turning up!' Elliot said.

'It's young Pitt, the cause of all my trouble,' Will said to Adam.

'Well, he's very small; doubt he'd be a good fag.'

'I don't want a fag, and if I did, I certainly wouldn't want one who pees on his senior's toothbrush!'

'He did what!' Adam said.

'Well, you've no idea how wicked he is,' Pitt said in defence.

'I really don't care,' Adam returned. 'Don't you get any ideas, Elliot.'

'Okay, so what are you doing here anyway?' Will asked Pitt.

'I came to warn you: Coburg plans to have someone get you tomorrow in rugby so you'll be injured before the fight.'

'He's going to do what?'

'I overheard him on his mobile.'

'I'd be flattered, Houston,' said Adam. 'Sounds like you've really got him worried!'

'Anyway, I've got to dash,' said Pitt. 'Hey, Elliot, just think: this time tomorrow, I could be free of the prince and we could be working together for these two!'

'That's only if I want you, you little runt! Now get out of here before you get us into trouble.' Then Will remembered the hammer. He opened his top drawer and held it up. 'Wait a minute – I think this is yours. Before you scramble off, tell us about the Invisible College.'

The boy's eyes widened in surprise, 'You were the ones in the passageway!'

'That reminds me, Elliot, go and fetch Clarkson and Thornton, will you? They'll want to hear this too.'

When they were all assembled Pitt began. 'Last summer I found my brother's first-year diary – you know, from '96 –'

'So what?' said Adam. He chewed his gum loudly and didn't bother to look up from the copy of *The Donor* he was reading.

'So they were all part of it – the Invisible College – most of them who are now prefects.'

'Yeah,' said Will, 'but what was it about? I mean, what did they get up to? Drugs maybe?'

'The diary doesn't say exactly, but it was something to do with science, something the school didn't want them to find out ...'

'Sounds like some kind of pseudo-intellectual conspiracy with secret societies,' Adam sneered. '"Something the school didn't want them to find out" – please!' He turned a page and dug his head deeper in.

'Something,' Will continued, 'that ended in Percival's death at the Druids' circle, Rawkins. This is no joke; I mentioned it to Dundas, and I've never seen him lose it as he did then. Told me never to mention it again to him.'

'Well, my brother would never talk about it either,' Pitt said.

'None of them will,' Will mused, 'but what about that Mr John, eh? He's the one that started it, that's what your brother said, Clarkson.'

'Well, yeah. Whatever they were getting, they were getting from him.' Ben Pitt glanced at Adam, who was now looking up. 'Don't know what it was, but it must have been –'

'Dynamite!' interrupted Clarkson. 'Well, can't you see – this guy's starting a secret society with a bunch of vulnerable kids, filling their heads with stuff – who knows what, maybe drugs? – and one ends up dying in suspicious circumstances in the middle of a stone circle. I'd say someone had something to answer for, but the school covered it up and shipped him off – and, perhaps more to the point, he may have had accomplices who remained silent!'

Pitt's mouth hung open. 'But you mean – my – my brother could be ...'

'Don't listen to Clarkson. He's full of it.' Will tried to reassure the young boy. Pitt's brother must have been that best friend who was first to arrive on the murder scene.

'But he was never the same after that summer – his whole personality changed, Mum and Dad said. Now he hardly smiles. He's never had any close friends since. I mean, perhaps ...'

'Perhaps nothing; it's just too soon to see right now,' Will said. 'But are we agreed that we should look into it?'

'Speak for yourself,' Thornton said. 'I'm not going up against the entire prefect structure on a whim of yours. I want a future outside this place, you know?'

'I'm not talking about a revolt; I'm talking about a bit of subtle investigation, a bit of surveillance. Nothing stupid – just a sniff around until we have something more solid. In fact, the prefects had better never know we're doing anything at all. Now what do you say?'

The younger ones agreed immediately and at length even Adam and Thornton agreed under certain conditions. As the others left and Adam went back to his book, Will didn't entirely trust him. *He's not a grass. Besides, if we're about to start uncovering mysterious things to do with science, who better to make sense of them than Adam?*

Will knew where to start and, after training next morning, he told Dundas that he would do one more quick circuit to the circle before breakfast. Sure enough, he spied Mr John on his morning ritual visit. Keeping downwind of the dogs, Will followed Mr John at a distance when he left to walk beyond the circle and along the rugged coastal path in the opposite direction from the school.

After twenty minutes, when he had lost sight of Mr John for a little while, Will arrived on a promontory overlooking a crystal inlet. In this sheltered bay surrounded by steep rocks nestled a lone fisherman's cottage, with a jetty and a narrow winding access road descending sharply from the heathland above. Mr John crossed the beach below the promontory, his stride steady and sure on the loose stone. Will watched him dry the dogs, then carefully remove his boots on a bench outside the cottage, before finally entering. With a plan forming in Will's mind, he ran back to the school in great excitement to his friends.

At rugby that afternoon, Will paced up and down the touchline trying to steady his breathing. He glanced this way and that for his would-be attackers. He had thought of pulling a sicky, but it felt dishonest, and he hated backing down from anything. It was house match practice again and Dundas had agreed to a friendly with St Oswald's. Fox stood with a brutish-looking friend of Payne's at the far end of the pitch, a boy called Cobbett. Brummell talked to two heavyweights from their own house, Grenville and Canning. Will cast his eyes to the side as Brummell directed their gaze to where Will was standing, but he knew what it meant. Ten minutes later he was running with the ball near their twenty-two yard line when he saw them both descending on him. A spasm of cold fear caused him to throw the ball away needlessly before the lad on the wing had a chance to get close enough. The ball fell and it lost them ground. That was not the only time. Wherever he went on the pitch they were never far behind, like wolves stalking their prey, lingering just outside his field of vision, as if waiting for the right time to attack.

After half-time the ball broke from the scrum and was passed down the line to Will. He started to sprint past the halfway line, and immediately, both Grenville and Canning thundered down on him. Will dummied two forwards as he made his desperate attempt to get clear of his hunters. His heart thumped at the ribs, each breath sounding more and more like a desperate cry as he sped on. He dodged one player after another, glancing over his shoulder on the odd occasion, eyes wide with terror. His pace brought a cheer from the onlookers, but his pursuers closed in as Will reached the last quarter. It was only then that Will saw the brute Cobbett cruising in from the side as well – a total pincer movement on three sides. Will cursed himself for not having been more vigilant, and closed his eyes a split second before impact.

But the impact did not come, for Grenville blocked Cobbett with his shoulder and both went sprawling. When Will turned and saw Canning, he noticed that he had a smiling, if exhausted, expression. 'Go on, Houston, take it to the line, man!' How about that? Will thought, as he dummied the fullback and glided onto the turf between the posts. They were guardian angels all the time! Canning helped Will up. 'Eyes forward next time,' he advised.

Will handed the ball to Brummell for the kick, but Brummell gave it back to Will. 'Take it yourself; it's easy enough.'

Will watched his face intently. 'Thanks, Brummell.'

'What, after a sprint like that? You've earned it.'

'I mean – not just that.'

'What, those two? Well, there is house loyalty too. Now take the kick.'

Will positioned the ball right in front of the posts; it was an easy kick. But as he swung in, the ball did not connect properly with his boot and the resulting slice sent the ball miles too far to the right. Will looked for a moment in disbelief, the redness in his cheeks rising further and further at the groans from his house on the touchline.

When the whistle blew at 3.30 p.m. Dundas walked Will over to the gym on the Black Path, made from bits of crushed tarmac. 'Don't worry about the match now, we can work on your kicking if you survive the next hour.'

The next hour! Will thought, a cold sweat spreading over his back. *That's a long time being hit by a big lad two years older than me.* At the end of the path, under the high eaves of the asbestos cement roof, boys in muddy rugby gear converged like ants, the smell of unwashed humanity and mud steaming out of the unheated gym. The boys parted to let Dundas past. Will tried not to look but he couldn't mistake the eyes hungry for blood. Inside, the atmosphere was dank and fusty. The strip lights were turned on to reveal a further two hundred boys already assembled. They began to chant 'Fight! Fight! Fight!' as Will's feet passed the threshold. Then the boys stamped in rhythm on the hollow boards, sending thunderous echoes that shook the ground beneath his feet. Will cast a baleful eye around the confusion. He cursed. No adults. No one to help. No rope. Just faces, bloodthirsty faces, and him, Coburg grinning all over. The noise grew in intensity and volume, as Will tried to control his breathing, and an overwhelming urge to run away, anywhere.

'Houston! Houston!' Dundas called above the din and led him to the centre. 'Remember what I taught you. Don't disgrace the house.'

Dundas led him to shake Coburg's hand. The prince leered at him. 'I dare say you'll find the way gentlemen fight rather too sophisticated for your guttural tastes, but I'll string it out as long as I can to entertain the boys!'

Will looked on with a dead-pan expression and simply returned to his stool.

As head boy, Pitt the Elder was referee. He quieted the crowd and said, 'There has been a challenge made upon a principle of honour –'

A boy behind the prince's corner shouted, 'The honour of a yob! Give me a break!'

'Silence, or you'll be removed! The challenge came from St Alban's, from Houston.' Boos and obscene gestures burst from five Dragoons from Aiden's holding back the mass of boys. 'The defendant is Prince Von Coburg of Aiden's.' Elliot and Ben Pitt cupped their hands around their mouths and booed, but the sound was drowned out by the cheers of the other boys. 'It will be settled after our usual manner. There will be no fouling, no punching below the belt. May the best man win!' The boys erupted with cheers and stamps of feet in unison until the floor shook as if there was an earthquake. Sheer adrenalin had Will trembling.

Dundas secured his gloves. 'Come on, breathe, man. That's better. Now watch him: bob and weave like I told you to, and watch for that left. Focus! Breathe, I said. Again, good. Now go.'

The bell went, and Dundas gave Will the gum-shield. As Will circled the prince it did not feel real; it was a savage dream. The prince was quick, and his jabs took all Will's concentration to brush off. He tried a few rash shots, more in panic, but the prince's head was never still for a moment. Instead he came back, bam, bam, bam – ribs and head. The tingly, deafening thud. The roar of the crowd. Will shook it off and dodged as best he could to the opposite corner, stumbling as he went.

'Come back here, Houston, you coward – I've only just started,' Coburg shouted.

He sprang in again, this time feigning a head shot but subtly planting a power punch on Will's stomach. Overcome by another series of attacks, Will spent the rest of the first round on the defensive, with little to show for his effort. The crowd loved every minute of it. When the bell went Will returned to his corner with slumped shoulders and aching ribs.

Dundas handed Will his water. 'What on earth do you call this? It's a fight, Houston – a fight, not a ballet dance!'

Will was gasping. 'Sorry. He's just so quick.'

'I told you he was fast, but he's not fit, so he should slow down as time goes on.'

'What can I do until then?'

'You can stop walking round like a stiff. Loosen your shoulders, move your head and, for heaven's sake, drop a leg when he sends in those head shots; that way you'll be ready to spring up and give him something back in return when he's reaching for you.'

The bell sounded again. Will tried hard to steady his legs as he got up. *Come on,* he urged himself in desperation. *Focus.* He followed the advice and on four occasions the prince completely overreached in his lust to get in a second or third punch. Will dropped down onto his right leg and then powered several massive uppercuts into the prince's midriff, using the added force of his rising body. After the fourth of these, the prince was winded but seemingly undiscouraged. He recovered his breathing for the third round and used all his remaining speed to drive Will towards his corner. Will assumed that he was trying something similar to the tactics he had used in the first round, so he swiftly moved aside, sending one-two-three jabs all the time to avoid been set upon.

After a few failed attempts to pin Will down, the prince appeared to stumble into Will and, in so doing, drove him right into the crowd. There the prince's Dragoon friends, Tarleton and Clarendon, helped him up. They were so thickly surrounded that no one saw the five or six bare-knuckle punches that each boy laid into Will's kidneys and side. Will could barely stand for the rest of the round, while the prince went for his head with everything he could muster.

Pitt was keen to call the fight off and spoke seriously to Dundas before round four, but Will would not have it.

'Look, Houston,' said Pitt, 'if this is about house honour, it's all right: you've stood your ground, you've done three rounds. It's not safe now – let me just throw in the towel for you.'

Dundas grabbed Pitt's sleeve. 'Never mind that, Pitt, look at the mess Tarleton and Clarendon made of Houston's ribs when they picked him up. This is outrageous!'

'Hmm,' Pitt said, scowling back to the Aiden's corner. 'I'm not surprised one bit, but it would be a hard thing to prove, and even harder to link their behaviour to a specific instruction from Coburg. It's up to you, Dundas. I can call a foul, but the school will just say that your man is a sore loser and made it up.'

'Don't you think he's tiring?' Will asked, panting through his gum shield.

'He's panting like a fat dog after that little lot you landed on him. Why?'

'I think I could take him still.' Will winced as he pressed his side.

'Take him?' Pitt said. 'You are really bruised, maybe broken! You'll do well to limp back to the house.'

Dundas' face lit up. 'No, shut up, Pitt. Perhaps he can; his arms are still fresh, and he's as fit as a butcher's dog. If he can keep Coburg away from his ribs and pin the rat down, he could have him. Why not?'

Pitt frowned. 'Sure you're not letting the house honour get to you, Dundas?'

'No, but maybe he is,' Dundas said.

Will looked straight at Dundas. 'I just want to win.'

So the bell rang and the two boys faced each other again.

'Are you back for some more, Houston?' taunted Coburg. 'Hope you like the taste of my gloves, 'cos there's plenty more where that came from.' As expected, the prince zeroed in on the bruised ribs and Will soon found that, no matter what ruse or jab he gave, Coburg was irresistibly drawn to go in low. Will counter-attacked as if never believing anything other than the prince's final intent. This edge meant that Will was always hammering the prince's head when he started his duck. With each hard right, Will twisted the ball of his foot just as Dundas had shown him, and he was thereby able to bring the weight of his full torso into each punch. The ones that glanced off Coburg's ears were payment enough, but the few that made full contact had Coburg wheeling back, stunned. He swore violently, but Will silenced him by feigning a left-ranging jab, withdrawing it three-quarters in and replacing it with a full-on right thrust, which knocked Coburg's blocking gloved hand straight into his mouth.

Coburg's head went back for a fatal moment, and Will was on him like a rash, left, right, left, right; the punches fell thick and fast. *My only chance!* Bam, bam, bam. The prince struggled to counter, but Will forced him back, back, back into his own corner with a relentless barrage. Bam, bam, bam. Will twisted and slugged like his life depended on it. *Coward,* bam, *bully,* bam, *cheat,* BAM, BAM. Coburg held his gloved hand against his face. *Got you!* Will did a left uppercut into his ribs and then, seeing Coburg hunching forward, brought up his strong right, catching him under the chin and sending him flying back into his Dragoon friends.

The prince was covered in blood and screaming for help. His nose was broken, and Will's last punch had split his lower lip wide open.

'I'll kill him!' He swore. 'I'll kill him – filthy working-class pleb …' he shouted as Pitt examined his lower lip.

'No, you can't go on with these injuries – you've lost. Go and see Matron, and mind your language.'

Dundas held Will's hand up and there were loud cheers, though mainly from the boys of St Alban's.

'Well done, Houston! That was a spectacular bit of footwork! Done the house proud!' shouted Dundas over the din. Fox, standing near the door, smiled with good grace and left. The prince was not so composed, still fuming and cursing at Will as he passed. 'It's not over yet, peasant, so watch your back!'

The boys of St Alban's returned victorious to their house and, as was their custom, carried the victor on their shoulders. From his perch of adulation, Will observed the sunken shoulders of Aiden's boys behind Coburg slinking to their house too. What form would the prince's revenge now take? *Find out soon enough, I suppose.*

Back inside the house, Will was sent by Dundas to the laundry room where the matron was running her surgery for the house. He trudged up the stairs clutching his sides, leaning on the bannisters every now and then to hiss with pain. Another boy was just leaving with his medicine when Will arrived. The matron, a tall, thin woman in her fifties, pushed her long, thick grey hair to one side as he limped in.

'All right, so what's this, then?' she asked, examining Will's bruised face. 'More masculine heroics?'

He lifted his rugby shirt to show his ribs. 'Just a bit of bruising – wondered whether you had anything?' He hadn't the heart to admit to boxing; she was already disapproving enough.

'Pathetic men and their silly games! Let's look at them.' Matron reached into her bag. 'They train you for rugby on Monday, army cadets on Tuesday, and then release you to rule the world on Wednesday –' she pasted a gel in stabbing movements onto his skin with her bony fingers '– and so we have wars, famine and pollution, and we are surprised!'

'Ouch, ouch, ouch!' exclaimed Will. 'What is that?'

'Arnica with other herb extracts. When you've been treating bruises at this ridiculous institution for as long as I have, you know what works – though I've found no cure yet for the male ego. Right, put your top down.'

'You've been here a while?'

'Thirty years. They get less for murder,' she said.

'You never left?'

'For something better?' she said, screwing the top onto the pot of cream with controlled ferocity. 'If there's ever something better, then it's usually found where you are. You make it yourself. Right, that should take the swelling down. Come and see me at the dispensary if it still troubles you during the week, all right?'

'Yeah, thanks.'

Will left; he was only too glad to.

8

THE MYSTERY OF THE INVISIBLE COLLEGE

First piece to Master Houston here.'

Hands helped Will into a chair at the top table next to Dundas, Will was awarded the first piece of toast and as much butter as he could spread on it. Afternoon tea was not a proper meal attended by the housemaster; neither was it even a particularly civilized one. Rugby boots were not allowed, but everything else was in a display of mud-covered hormones with low blood-sugar levels, shouting and squabbling. After a shower, Will found his fresh clothes laid out ready on the bed and his shirt ironed, shoes cleaned, and even the bed made.

Adam looked up from his book. 'Ah, the conquering hero returns, didn't kill you after all!'

'Just look at this shirt!' Will said.

'I know, sickening! Elliot can't get a collar half as good as that. Mind you, mine are Savile Row; expect yours are polycotton or something awful like that.'

'Get lost! They're cotton. Anyway, I never sent for him – where is he?'

'Left a few minutes ago; said he would see you later.'

'Hey, did you see the fight?'

'I was reading.'

'Oh.'

Adam looked up at him. 'That's why I'm more intelligent than you: I put things into my head, not have them knocked out in some draconian public-school ritual.'

'Binge-drinking screws up brain cells too.'

'That's different,' Adam said, pursing his lips and pulling his book slightly closer.

'Oh, yeah, why?'

Adam slammed his book down. ' A, because I've got plenty to lose, and B, because it's none of your blasted business.'

Suit yourself. Will tried to fit his arms into the immaculate sleeve without causing his sides to ache, which proved impossible. He let out a few hisses and groans before he finally got his hand through, but also noticed what he thought were tears in Adam's eyes. *Wonder what's up with him? Suppose that would be none of my business too.*

After the afternoon lessons, Will saw Ben Pitt in the Great Hall. 'How's the shirt?' Pitt asked, as other boys milled around, one or two slapping him on the back and others congratulating him in the corridors. 'Nice one Houston.' 'You showed him mate.'

'Shirt's fine, but I don't want any more of this stuff. You're not my fag. I don't need one, you're free – you don't owe me anything.'

'But if I'm not your fag, Coburg could have me back, and he'll make my life hell again!'

'He'll do that anyway. Besides, I've got my own back to watch. You heard him. He's determined to get me out of this place.'

'Well, then, we'll watch each other's backs.'

'Look, no offence, but I don't think you'll be a great lot of help the next time they have me in the toilet block.'

'Oh, right. What you gonna do?'

'I'm going to start praying. Suggest you do too!' Will meant it.

Ben was silent for a second before saying, 'And the Invisible College, Mr John and all that – you'll still need help there; I mean, we're in that one together already, so what if you let me just appear to be your fag while we work on that mystery?'

'Umm, I'm not sure what help you'll be but … okay, fair enough. Actually, that reminds me: I found out where he lives.'

'Oh, the old fisherman's cottage?' Ben said.

'You knew that?'

'I know lots of things. Like I say, you'll find me useful.'

'I think we should go over there and take a look around,' Will said.

'Good idea! When?'

'Sooner the better. What you doing tonight?'

'*Well,* I was going to do my hair,' Ben said with a broad grin, 'but as your fag I could be over at Alban's after prayers to do your boots and games kits or – *something*.'

'Okay, you're on, but don't be late.'

After prayers that night, Ben arrived as promised.

'Let's do it,' Will said. 'And keep an eye on the time. We've both got to be back at eleven when the house prefects come round to check our beds.'

It was a windy winter's night, but the stars were bright and occasionally the moon came from behind the clouds. They walked with brisk steps up the coastal path and took the narrower fork along the rocks to the Druids' circle. The moon cast great shadows from the stones that reached out their giant fingers to envelop the boys as they approached.

'This place is evil,' Ben said, walking closer to Will.

'I don't think things can be evil – only people … or beings.'

'Whatever. But my hair's standing up and I don't like it.'

'Me neither. Look, that's where he stands each morning, near that central stone.'

'Why d'you reckon he does it?'

'Dunno. It's like he's willing them to come back to him, perhaps.'

'Willing who?'

'Your brother's lot – the Invisible College, even Percival. Who knows?'

Suddenly their whispers were shattered by the most bloodcurdling howling noise. The boys spun round to see two huge dogs on the cliff above them, howling at the moon. They both nearly jumped out of their skins, but Will pulled Ben behind a stone. 'Shush, he must be up there somewhere.'

'What d'you think he's doing here?' Ben whispered, clutching Will's coat.

'I don't know. Perhaps he hunts juniors with his dogs and sacrifices them to pagan gods!' Will playfully grabbed Ben's neck from behind.

'Stop it. Be sensible, will you? It's not funny!'

Will spotted Mr John on the dark horizon, and the boys followed him using the lower path from the circle. They watched him descend to the cove, just as Will had done that same morning. They scrambled down to the cove and approached the cottage, keeping to the grass at the edge of the beach so as not to leave footprints. From the high dune grass they observed the cottage for a few minutes before finally getting up the nerve to move closer. They slid under the sitting-room window and peered through it. A very old man sat by a fire in a rocking chair, a book on his knee and his head nodding gently in sleep. Will craned his neck to see where Mr John was. He got a view through to the back kitchen. The back door opened. Will shuddered.

A guttural and fearsome growl sounded behind them. Both boys turned in terror.

'What are you doing here? Who sent you?' Mr John stood between his dogs. He held something that glinted in the moonlight. It almost looked like a small sword.

'Nothing. I mean, nothing. We're just from the school,' Will stammered, raising his hands in the air.

'Names!' snapped Mr John, raising the blade towards Will's face. 'Give me your names!'

'Houston, sir.'

'Pitt, sir.'

When Ben spoke Mr John lowered the blade. 'Pitt? Come out of the shadow, boy. Let me see you.' Pitt stepped forward, trembling. 'My, but – lad, you must be Willie's brother. You're the spit of him …' Mr John lingered for a moment as if distracted, but then spoke harshly again: 'Now what on earth are you doing here?'

'We came to find out about the Invisible College, sir,' Ben said, bold as brass.

'And what do you know about that then, eh?'

'I – I found my brother's notebook and …'

Will stepped forward between Ben and the blade. 'And we know you were teaching those boys some dangerous stuff that the school is trying to hide and –'

'I see, I see. And what's your share in all this, Mr Houston?'

'I found a trail of clues in Percival's desk and science textbook –'

'Very exciting for you …'

'They led to your book on local history, but it had vanished from the library before I could read it. We thought that –'

'You thought wrong, both of you. There are no clues here for your childish games. Now, get the –'

Just then the front door opened and they turned to see the old man standing on the porch. 'Who's that, dear boy? Has someone come to see us?'

'No, Father. Just two boys from the school, on their way home.'

'But I thought I heard someone mention Pitt, and I should so like to see young Willie. Such a lively little fellow. But my, there you are; it is you! Won't you come in for a drink?'

'No, Father, they must be going. It's late, and you need your sleep.' Mr John tried to usher the old man inside but he shook him away.

'But I'd like some visitors, and I thought I heard someone mention the Invisible College and –'

'Father, you are apt to mishear things. Now come on inside.'

Will seized his moment. 'We were hoping to find out about the Invisible College, sir.'

The old man leaned forward to examine Will. 'And you strike me as the sort of fellow who is interested in the truth, are you not?'

Will thought he meant about the conspiracy, so he said, 'Yes, sir,' at which the old man's face sprang into an ecstatic smile.

'Good! There, you see, John, there are still some left, like Houston here.'

'Yes, Father, but they are leaving,' Mr John said.

'You knew my name?' Will asked the old man.

The man winked and whispered, 'I was listening at the window …'

'Come on, Father, you're getting cold.'

'Yes, yes. Can't have that now, can we?' The old man shuffled off but then glanced back at Ben. 'Don't you worry, young Willie. I'll talk John round.'

'All right, enough of that.' Mr John pushed the boys away. 'If I see you two again, I'll call the school. Or the police.'

They said goodbye to the old man. He waved them off, but as they headed up the hill, they saw him watching out his window. 'And what do you make of that, eh?' Will said with a swagger as they passed the circle. 'He's up to his neck in it and the senile old man nearly let it out of the bag.'

'I don't think he was senile Will, not really, but yeah, there is something going on there all right.'

They sneaked back to their respective houses and called a meeting of their friends for after lunch the following day – Saturday when they would have all afternoon to talk through the details.

'This just gets better and better,' Clarkson said when they had gathered.

'Yeah,' said Elliot, who was handing out the teas. 'Wonder what else he's hiding up there.'

'Now just stop it, all of you.' Thornton threw up his hands. 'Have you gone completely bonkers? He said he'd contact the school and the police. Another stunt like that and you'll be expelled – or worse.'

Their conversation had barely dipped in volume or fever before the late post brought a letter addressed to Mr Houston Esq. He opened it while Ben rehearsed again the moment they were set upon by horse-sized dogs and the mad pirate of Smuggler's Cove. Will read his letter quickly then hushed his friends:

'Listen to this, you guys; it's from the old man, Mr John's dad:

> Dear Mr Houston,
>
> I am pleased to inform you that my younger son will be only too delighted to receive you this Friday evening to discuss the items you raised at our first acquaintance.
>
> You may wish to invite other trustworthy friends if they be seekers of truth in like manner to yourself.
>
> Yours sincerely,
> George E. Hanover, Senior.

'"… In like manner to yourself." What does he mean?'

Clarkson seized the letter. 'Give it here. It's obvious – he wants to lure us in, maybe flush us all out into the open, and have us busted by the school!'

'Or worse!' added Thornton. 'I mean, come on, Houston. It could be a trap! I don't fancy ending up like Percival.'

Adam looked up from the book he was reading. 'No, I think you should go. Mr John can disembowel the lot of you with his cutlass, and then I'd get some peace in my own room.'

Ben took the letter. 'What d'you think, Houston? The letter could be forged by Mr John.'

'No, I don't think so,' Will said, remembering that he had felt strange when they had talked to the old man. 'Look at the handwriting: it's shaky, like you'd expect, and, besides, there's something about that old guy that I trust.'

'What, senile old George?' Thornton exclaimed. 'My father said he was a tyrant of a headmaster when he was here, unless you were one of his favourites.'

'Yeah, well, perhaps your dad wasn't one of his favourites – I don't know! All I do know is, we're not going to be able to find out any more unless someone goes to the cove on Friday.'

After a pause Ben spoke. 'Well, I'll go, but not on my own.'

'He's right – there's safety in numbers. Count me in,' Clarkson said.

'I'll come, but I haven't got a torch,' Elliot said.

'That's all right, Elliot,' said Will. 'You can share with Thornton.'

'What!?' exclaimed Thornton. 'I've got a load of essays to write next week and –'

'Shut up, you coward!' interrupted Clarkson. 'You're coming, or I'll see that you never live it down!'

'Well, all right, but we must all swear to secrecy, 'cos if this ever gets out …'

'It won't – now, chill out!' Will said. 'What about you, Rawkins?'

'Are you serious?' Adam said.

'Yes,' Will replied.

'You want me to join the Famous Five at Mystery Cove? Get a life, will you!'

'Okay, just thought I'd ask.'

'Well, I'm touched – truly! But if Julian, Dick and Anne have finished their little meeting, perhaps they wouldn't mind shoving off somewhere else so I can read.' The others started to go anyway, but Adam called back to Elliot, 'Except you. I just saw the state of my suit trousers. You miserable cretin – do them again!'

Elliot carried the trousers out to the laundry with slumped shoulders, leaving Will and Adam alone. Will walked to his desk, shaking his head.

'What are you stropping about for?' Adam said. 'Elliot's a lazy cretin, deserves everything he gets.'

'You don't need to speak to him like that, that's all.'

'We can't all live in your little egalitarian religious utopia.'

'And what's that supposed to mean?'

'It means, the real world's painted red with tooth and claw, in case you hadn't noticed, and it steps on weakness to build something better. That's you, Elliot and me – everything.' Adam slammed his heel against the end of his bed, knocking his table and the books that were on it.

The sudden display of rage caught Will off-guard. 'Nice vision of the future. Bet you can't wait!' For once Adam had no come-back, and for all Will knew had not even heard him. Adam just looked away to one side, staring out into blank space, his mouth open and his jaw slightly forward. Will noticed that he had scratched the number 8000 another five times into the plasterwork.

They hardly spoke after that until Wednesday when once again, Will observed Adam leaving from the side of the house in a taxi and not returning until teatime. Will came back from games and found Adam sitting on the edge of his bed and staring at the wall with such intensity that Will asked him, 'What are you staring at?'

Adam did not look round but exhaled. 'The future.'

'All right. How does it look?'

Adam gave no answer, but shook his head slightly. *Oh, he's in a mood,* Will thought. *He'll get no sympathy from me, the way he treats Elliot.* Will stripped off his games kit and reached for his towel. As he left for the shower he heard Adam mumble. Will paused at the door and poked his head back round. 'What's that?'

Adam looked straight at Will for a moment, but it wasn't Adam at all as Will knew him; even his voice was different. 'I'm through, Houston, I need answers.'

Will came back into the room and shut the door. 'What?'

'I need answers. Can't you understand that?' Adam seemed so defenceless for once, so vulnerable.

'I guess.' Will leaned forward and said the only thing he could think of: 'Come with us on Friday night.'

'Huh, no – not those sorts of answers.' Will saw there were tears coming.

'I know, I know – but I think there's more to it – in fact, I'm sure of it.'

'Another hunch, Columbo?' Adam tried a smile as his eyes glazed over.

'Say you'll come, mate.'

Adam bit his lip and looked up at his books on the shelf on the wall and said, more to himself than to Will, 'God? Why not? Been everywhere else.' He carried on staring at his books. A few seconds passed as they just sat there.

'Are you okay? Wanna talk?' Will asked him. It must be something to do with the taxi rides.

Adam wiped his nose, sniffed and said, 'Yeah, I'm okay. Go, get a shower. You stink!'

'All right you lot, look lively,' Will whispered across the library table. 'We're being observed; Truncheon and Greaser at five o'clock.'

It was before prep on Thursday, and the five had met in the library – Adam not being present – to find out what they could about Mr John from the school year-books. The others turned to see Brother Brendan watching them through slit eyes and muttering to Brother Reece. It took them ages to go through the various year-books, but eventually they found Mr John and his brother in the one for 1958. The shock was: he and the headmaster were in the same year. 'They were twins!' Clarkson exclaimed.

'Still are, stupid!' Thornton replied. Will looked at the pictures. The two boys were identical apart from their haircuts. George looked serious and superior, John mischievous. While Will was still thinking about them, he smelt the powerful body odour of Brother Reece at his shoulder.

'The "No talking" signs are not for our health. Now, what are you lot doing?'

The boys made their excuses but Will later noticed Reece spying on them more than once. Eventually he appeared again at their table and through his shrew-like mouth said, 'All right, names, you lot.'

'What!' exclaimed Clarkson. 'For looking in the year-books?'

'No.' Reece hesitated. 'For – for creating a disturbance in the library. You first: name and house!' They each complied, and watched as Reece reported back to Brother Brendan.

On their way out Brendan blocked their exit. 'I don't like disturbances, not of any sort. Your names are logged, so tread carefully; next time I will not be so lenient.' The boys went their separate ways, but not before making their plans for the following night.

Friday passed so slowly it seemed as if Conlon's double English lesson would never end. Will felt that his work was getting better despite constant criticism. He was receiving extra tuition with a pretty young blonde teacher called Miss Moore, who seemed little older than himself. He looked forward to these extra lessons, partly because they added a sense of normality to the otherwise surreal masculine world he now inhabited, and partly because she made him miss Hannah even more than he already did.

The bell finally rang, and Conlon grudgingly dismissed the class. After prayers that night, the boys braved the drainpipe and dashed into Monks' Wood to rendezvous with Ben. He waited at the end of an expansive grassed walkway inside the mock Greek temple, exactly as they had planned. The boys crouched low and jumped the wall one by one at the far end, running with part terror and part exhilaration and delight along the coastal path to the circle.

Elliot would not walk inside the circle, but Will pulled him through it as kindly as he could. When they were out at the other side, Elliot asked, 'Where's Pitt?' They looked round. Pitt stood in the centre of the circle, alone.

Will ran back and the others joined him. 'Come on, Pitt, what's the matter?'

As the others gathered round him he said, 'We must promise …'

'What?' Clarkson asked.

'We must promise that, no matter what happens, we don't ever betray ourselves.'

'Oh, come on!' Thornton replied.

'No, I'm serious – we must promise.'

'He's right,' Will said. 'We don't know where this will end, and we can't end up like the prefects, I mean, like the last Invisible College –'

'Oh please! Spare us the theatrics,' Clarkson said.

'Well, supposing they did somehow betray Percival, it could be one of us next. I think we should agree to stick together, whatever we're about to find out.'

Adam spoke for the first time that night: 'Well, come on, let's just do it and get going before we die of old age. I solemnly swear not to betray any of you, so help me God.' The others followed in turn and were soon walking on the white sandy beach in front of the cottage, the warm light from the sitting-room window drawing them to the front door.

It was Mr George Senior who answered and brought them inside. There was no sign of Mr John or the dogs. Mr George wore a green flight suit. 'A memento from my days in the RAF' he explained. 'Runs on 9 volts – just plug it in here.' He pointed to a car battery at the side of his chair. 'Then there's no need to heat the house when John's away. But this blazing fire, eh?' He pointed his stick at the grate where driftwood sparked and crackled. 'Can an old man ask for more than that at my age? That and some company.'

The boys introduced each other in turn and sat awkwardly by the fire while the old man made enquiries after Thornton's father and grandfather. 'Fine fellows indeed, and big shoes to fill, I dare say.' He leant forward. 'Umm, but you look like a good fellow – bit fearful, perhaps, though I should think it will pass as you get older.'

Will wondered whether he should say anything but the old man, seemingly anticipating him, said, 'My son has just taken the dogs out and will be back soon. Tea, anyone?' The boys nodded and the old man turned to Adam: 'Perhaps you would oblige us.' He pointed to the kitchen. 'The kettle is here on the log-burner, my boy. Just make up a tray, there's a good chap.'

Elliot looked at Ben and grinned. Adam scowled but went into the kitchen. The old man called after him, 'There are some Jaffa Cakes in the cupboard – always a favourite of the Invisible College.' He winked at Will. 'It's the taste beyond the chocolate they liked – ah, I think that's John now.'

The front door opened and the dogs came in, though John was still in the porch hanging up his coat. 'Perishing out there, Father.

I covered up the leaks. Sure there'll be a frost tonight.' He came in and stopped dead as he saw the boys. 'What the dickens is this? I thought I told you two to –'

'Whisht now, son. I invited them over for tea … and Jaffa Cakes.'

'What? But, why – what?'

'Because, if I'm not very much mistaken, these boys need your help.'

'Father, we've been through this already! I'm not going to –'

'John, you can't hide forever! You've got to move on.'

'HOW CAN I!' Mr John shouted, and then said more softly, with tears starting in his eyes, 'How, I – I can't, Father, you know I can't.' He half reached out his hand, then walked through to the study, shutting the door behind him as he said again, 'I can't. Now please, send them away.'

The boys sat stunned, but the old man seemed unmoved. 'Well, boys, shall we have tea? Master Rawkins, have we the tray, sir?' Adam reappeared. 'Good, good. First rule of the Invisible College: If any man would be first, he must be the servant of all. Now, let's see, ah yes, hot water. Now, use the cloth to grab the kettle; the handle gets very hot.' Adam poured the tea, making no eye-contact as he handed Elliot the cup.

'Thanks, Rawkins,' Elliot said.

'Ah, now, the second rule of the college – one that my son will insist on when he joins us – is that we use first names only.' Thornton looked shocked. 'Just as you would for brothers. Perhaps Mr Thornton has forgotten that there is a wide world beyond the school walls, and tonight he is far beyond them, and so old names will not do. Let us start again and introduce ourselves as brothers.'

And so they did, and the effect was magical; by this one thing more than any other that would happen later, as the boys used their Christian names and shook each other's hand, the atmosphere changed and the tension left their shoulders – for all, that is, except Adam, who looked unimpressed. Beowulf came to where Adam sat in the corner and rested his head on his knee. Adam stroked his long grey fur and gazed hard into the dog's eyes.

'Capital, capital. Let me hand out the Jaffa Cakes and see I have you all: Master William Houston, Master Adam Rawkins – don't think I knew your father, no … ah, Master Pitt – Ben, isn't it? Have a cake, my boy; and Henry Thornton, and Eddie Elliot, Master Tom Clarkson. Good, capital, right! Well, you may call me Father George, and my son, Mr John, and, before you ask it – yes, age still applies!'

Ben spoke between nervous mouthfuls: 'Do you really think he will join us … Father George?'

'Gracious, yes, my boy, everyone knows Jaffa Cakes are his favourite – even through all this awful business, he still loves them. I always kept a few packets in the cupboard for when he came back from abroad.'

'Where did he go?' Will asked.

'Oh, now then – where did he say it was?'

The study door opened and Mr John walked back in. 'Nowhere that concerns them, Father!' Grendel went to him as the boys sat upright.

'Good – John, my lad, I've saved you your chair by the fire. Jaffa Cake?'

Mr John brushed his grubby nails on the edge of his coarse woollen cardigan and let out a huge sigh. 'You know I told George I wouldn't do this again.'

'John, I love you both the same, but it's time you took your seat, son.'

Mr John stood sideways a while longer looking this way then that, before picking up a mug and sitting down. He looked each boy in the eye and took a sip of his tea. 'Oh, for heaven's sake, who made this muck?'

Adam raised his hand. 'It said "Tea" on the tin.'

'That stuff! Father keeps it for when the school governors visit.'

'Keeps them away!' the old man said, with a cheeky grin.

Seeing Adam's face, Elliot sprang forward. 'I'll make some more, sir.'

While he was in the kitchen Adam asked the question they had all been burning to ask: 'Look, time's getting on and, well, we were wondering what you teach at this Invisible College – and they're all dying to know what happened to Percival.'

Will did his best to glare at Adam, who took no notice. Mr John looked at his father but the old man motioned for him to speak. Mr John looked at his boots for a moment and then straight at Adam, 'Spencer Percival was a brilliant student here: sensitive, intense, as prodigies often are, but an extraordinary keen intellect, amazing potential. He was a member of the Invisible College in 1996 and I, perhaps – no, blast it, I did – I did overload him ...'

'You can't be sure,' the old man said.

'I can; I gave him access to information that drove his already overactive mind into some sort of breakdown and – and the rest we all know.'

'The school blamed you?' Will said.

'Hang the school! They had their man to blame; it was all they cared about. No, it was the parents. I hope you never have to see two former friends look at you as they did me.' He paused. 'Anyway, as Father says, 'tis done now, and we'll not bring him back; life goes on. Or it's supposed to, anyway.'

Mr John looked into the flames and rubbed the back of his head. Ben leaned forward during the painful silence. 'So – so my brother didn't do anything wrong, sir?'

'No, lad – What? No, apart from caring enough for his friend to go and look for him, nothing at all. They tell me he's never recovered, poor Willie.'

'He – he does not laugh, sir. And he will not speak of it – or of you,' Ben said.

'Nor Dundas, sir,' Will added.

'They were saved from expulsion by –'

'They betrayed you, Johnny,' Father George said.

'They were children, Father; they were confused, upset.' Mr John held his head in his hands for a moment. 'My brother made them make certain pledges: firstly, that they would never again speak of me or the Invisible College, and, secondly, that each of them would sign an affidavit –' He stopped and stoked the fire, his bottom lip trembling as he fought back the tears.

'Laying the blame with John,' the old man said. 'Rather put him in the soup, I'm afraid. Led to his dismissal.'

'But was that all that was wrong?' Ben said.

'They were your age, their lives were in turmoil, they were threatened with expulsion – and my brother can be very persuasive.' Mr John put the poker away and looked up. 'No, I don't blame them; I let them down. It was right for me to go.'

'And your brother?' the old man prodded.

Mr John smiled for a brief moment and then said, 'Yes, well, George was not sad to see the back of me and my *negative* influence on the school's rising reputation for scientific excellence.'

'Why?' Will asked. 'What were you teaching these guys?'

'What?' Mr John looked up sharply. 'Hasn't Father told you?'

'We were waiting for you, dear boy,' the old man said.

'Oh, well, I taught them the true history of science, of course; first in regular history lessons until the school forbade me in '96, and then in the Invisible College, with the boys who didn't want to stop learning.'

'And that's when it all happened,' Will said, finally piecing it together.

'Yes, I'm afraid so.'

'Wait a minute: what do you mean, you taught them a revisionist history of science?' Adam put his mug down and grabbed his scarf. 'You're telling me that all this is about science?'

'Well, no one's forcing you to stay; in fact, I'm in two minds whether any of you are interested in anything beyond the intrigue of the suicide.'

'Adam!' Will said, and then added under his breath, as he was sitting next to him, 'You said you'd tried everywhere else – please stay.' Will then turned to Mr John. 'We want to know what you know, sir.'

'I see.'

'Well, all right,' Adam said, 'but what's this big secret take on history that's so controversial with the school?'

'All right, then, I'll tell you,' Mr John said, as Adam's challenge brought a new light into his eyes 'Who would like to pour the tea?'

9

THE SCIENTIFIC REVOLUTION

Will did the honours with the tea as Mr John was introduced properly now to each boy. That done, he reclined in his chair and, pinching his brows, started to transport the boys through the pages of history.

'Where on earth do we start? How far back, I wonder?'

Will was eager to show off the scraps he had learned from Professor Inchikov's lecture. 'Well, we know that the Greeks started it, sir.'

'Yes, if you like – if you separate technology from science, then yes, the Greeks started it, but despite some advances in maths and astronomy, they failed to progress with science.'

'What!' Adam said. 'How can you say that? They gave us everything – I mean …'

'They gave us philosophy and democracy, so everyone felt gratified that they were in charge, but they failed with the scientific method; they stood on the threshold of the scientific revolution for four hundred years but couldn't go in.'

He seemed about to go on but the old man cut in, 'Don't speak so generally, John; spell it out for them, my boy.'

'Well, imagine if they had been able, at a cultural level … if they had started with certain other precepts then – well … then they could have had the scientific revolution before the time of Jesus!'

'Sure, and the Celts could have had mobile phones! So is this your big theory?' Adams asked.

'No, not at all; it's an accepted academic debate. Even Francis Bacon said it; they made a vestal virgin of science and couldn't expect to get children. I only mention it, Adam, because it would take mankind fifteen hundred years to regain what was lost at the final destruction of the great Library at Alexandria.'

'Yeah, but that's when men turned from superstition and finally got on with the job!'

"No, no, no! Not in a million years! Atheism doesn't give you lenses in which to view the natural world in a meaningful way that could ever lead you to do science. No, it was firstly men like Copernicus and Galileo who challenged the Greek thinking that had poisoned the Church of Rome.'

'Excuse me, sir,' Adam said. 'I'm not bragging, but some of the best-known scientists in the world come for dinner at my parents' house. There are a lot of atheists there and they're doing just fine.'

'But, Adam, that's because they were handed the scientific method on a plate. I mean, the actual procedure of inquiry. If they had not been given the tools and shown the value of that way of thinking by someone else, they would never, and could never, have thought it up themselves ... no more than an ape, say, would invent a motor car. Yes, he might use technology if it helped his base needs, like using a stick to get ants out of a hole, or a log to hit someone with – but that's technology, not science.'

'Fine, I'll concede my father's mates are primates, but who are your supposed heroes giving us science, then?'

'Sorry, I didn't mean to imply anything by the analogy,' Mr John said.

'No – it's quite all right. There's no need to apologize; you've obviously not met them!'

'Well, as you wish, but see here now. The scientific theory de-rives from two traditions: first, monotheism, that is, there is only one God and there can be a single, unified understanding of Him.' Mr John glanced about at the boys' faces. 'Umm, now you may need to think about that but, basically, Christian monotheism – the belief in the God revealed in the Bible – gives you an understanding of a God who has an ordered mind, who makes laws and who has designed a logical universe, one capable of being explored and tested. Do you see that, boys? It's not random, illogical and reason-less – a universe governed by capricious, squabbling deities – no, there is purpose and design; all absolutely essential stuff, this, for even beginning to bother to explore the universe. I mean, if I threw some sticks on the floor in a heap, none of you would waste time studying their shape or construction. Why not? Because you know they are a random mess with no significance or meaning.'

'Like Clarkson's clothes drawer,' Will said.

'Yeah, okay, very funny, Will. So, a logical, law-making God; and second?' Clarkson said, getting more animated as the Jaffa Cakes went round for a second time.

'And second, that we, as a product of this God's creation – or his imagination, if you will – are fitted by God to be compatible with him and with creation. We are designed with faculties or abilities to check it out, or, as Kepler said, "to think God's thoughts after him". Or, as Solomon says in the Bible – he was the first-recorded scientist, by the way – "God has put eternity into men's hearts." Solomon says that science, the desire to acquire knowledge about our world, is "the weighty task that God has given the sons of men to do, that they may learn to speak" or, as one translator has it, "to sing".'

'Sorry, sir, you're losing me,' Elliot said. 'Why does the second thingy help?'

'Well, obviously, the created order is reliable because the Creator is reliable – or "faithful", as the Bible would say. The creation should therefore conform to certain rational principles: underlying laws, underpinning how its cogs operate. In the west the

Greeks couldn't go far in science because they did not have this thought. For most of them creation was eternal and depressingly cyclical – it had no loving Creator. The unruly Greek gods cared little for us or for the world, and their philosophers like Plato emphasised escaping it for the next world. Why? Because this world, including all matter, was essentially evil. In the east they were at a similar dead-end, as their philosophy taught them that there was no creation – basically, that physical things don't matter. Other parts of the east believed the universe was one great morphing organism, but in either case, not something worth studying to the extent that Christian civilisations started to do.'

'Okay, so how does this God get us to do science?' Adam recrossed his arms and leaned back.

'Are you kidding? We're made for it! What child doesn't show curiosity from day one about their environment, and how do they do it – anyone?' Mr John pointed to his eyes, ears, nose, tongue and hands.

'Their five senses?' Will said.

'Of course. And that essentially is what science is.' He reached for a wooden ruler from a pen cup on the mantelpiece. 'We can measure things, then use logic or reason to make deductions, but, if you really think about it, that only takes us so far. These are limited tools; they can't tell us things like how the world first came into being, how old a rock is, or why a mountain looks as it does. We can make guesses – good guesses. We can write our guesses in books and appear on TV, but, with only five senses, that is really all we can do.'

'But if you're going to be like that, then you contradict what you said before,' Adam said. 'You make out that there's this Creator; that we're given the tools to search out what he made; but now you say that we can only go so far. You've shot yourself in the foot!'

Knowing Adam's capacity, Will understood that the least hesitation here could lose Mr John a lot of ground. But the man showed not the slightest concern. Instead, with a smile, he said, 'Very good point; and you would be right if there were only five senses.'

'Oh right – a sixth sense!' Adam said, half mockingly.

'But of course! Socrates and Plato knew there must be; Aristotle too, until he turned to the dark side – probably Epicurus' influence.'

'Epicurus? Never heard of him,' Adam said.

'You should have! Your father's as much his disciple as any. "The universe is just matter and energy"?' Mr John raised his eyebrows. 'Come on, this is key to everything. The Epicureans said, "Only what our five senses can find out is true." Therefore, only what is material is real, which in itself is a neat piece of circular reasoning; a big circle, I grant you, but a perfect argument if, say, you wished to exclude the possibility of another interpretation of the facts.'

'I get it, sir,' Elliot said. 'You mean, like, if someone beyond our other five senses breaks in and tells us stuff. That's the sixth sense, isn't it?'

'Exactly, lad. Call it revelation, call it inspiration – but that's exactly the sense which the modern Epicureans force secular governments to exclude from your education, but it's like trying to walk on rocky ground with one eye shut; it's all two-dimensional; you keep tripping up.'

Adam leant back with his hands behind his head, letting out a chuckle. 'I'm sorry, sir – I mean, I like the idea of following this to see where it goes. It's nicely heretical –' Adam's eyes were alive with mischief '– and, hey, I'm a slave to novelty. Who isn't? But I can't think you'll be right. I mean, I've never heard anyone dis the Greeks before.'

'Thank you for being so frank – I don't mind a challenge. History has no fear; in some ways, it's already dead. And maybe what you've been told is true in part – but it's not the whole truth. Like journalism, no history is ever value-free. We all bring our own angles when we create the past. Doesn't mean it's unknowable, just that we have to be aware of our weakness for bias. I can give you the history of some of the great scientists of the last five hundred years, but it will be with my intentions, my editing, to highlight what I feel is important. If you disagree, you must say so; there's no bullying in the Invisible College, lads.'

'Why the name, sir?' Elliot asked.

'Hah, you must wait until later tonight, if we have time.'

'You've not told us yet who these supposed greats are either,' Adam said.

'Ah, well, they are the Invisible College's silent members, the secret cloud of witnesses who will teach us how to truly think, truly live – for their life stories, their witness, their discoveries are really what we live for here, to talk about them, to devour them.'

'Stories about scientists! Doesn't sound like the stuff of epics, sir,' said Clarkson. 'I mean, everyone knows that scientists are, well, you know, boring nerds.'

'Perhaps, but not these men; they were revolutionaries who defied the world – or, more importantly, defied the stranglehold that Greek thinking had on the Western world. Something that could not have happened without the Reformation.'

'Henry VIII!' Thornton said. 'I thought he was just into wine and women!'

'Thank you, but no, not the English Reformation – that was something different – but the continental Reformation. People went back to the Bible, *ad fontes*, *sola scriptura* and so forth. It set their minds free from the fear of challenging the Church of Rome and particularly that Greek stranglehold on science. It was a new breeding-ground of proper science, not just philosophy or misconstrued dogma.'

'But the abbot said the other Sunday that the Reformation was the worst thing that happened for science.'

'Ah, well, like I say: no view of history is value-free; perhaps the abbot has his own reasons for believing that. In fact, you will find that, whereas some Greeks went into naturalism – i.e. the universe is just matter and energy, as Aristotle and Epicurus taught – others went the other way and became pantheists, and so it is in this school. You'll find your teacher Mr Gibbs a good example of the first, and my brother and the abbot follow a woolly Christianized pantheism – you know, that God is present in all of his creation.'

'No way!' Ben nearly spilled his tea. 'That's what he said on Sunday!'

'Well there you go then. So remember, the re-establishment of the Bible as the sole authority apart from the dogma of a Greek-minded church gave men a way of looking at the natural world that countered their inherited Greek mindset; it's these Bible-minded men who are the giants of the Invisible College.'

'Bible-minded! You're not suggesting that a literal take on the Bible is friendly to science?' Adam asked, his top lip curled at the corner in disgust.

'No, I'm suggesting much, much more. I'm saying that we could not have even had science as we know it today without a literal take on the Bible!'

'What?!' Adam almost choked on his Jaffa Cake. 'This will be interesting. I mean, how are you going to prove it, eh?'

'Simple. We look at the fathers of each branch of modern science and see what they believed.'

'That's it?' Will asked, remembering all the dark suspicions about the Invisible College.

'That's it. Then you can make your own minds up.'

'But surely –' Adam folded his arms and frowned. 'Those were the men who insisted on a flat earth and a stationary earth at the centre of the universe!'

'Nonsense! The flat-earth myth was created in the eighteenth century by Washington Irving to popularize his books on Columbus. No one – absolutely no one who had any education, from Greek times onwards – thought that the earth was flat. And as for Copernicus or Galileo being the great heroes of science against religion: that's another convenient myth for modern scientists to joke about, a piece of pure revisionist history. Men like Copernicus, Kepler and Galileo were not in conflict with the Bible – which, by the way, they all believed – but they were in fact in conflict with Aristotle's cosmology, which the Catholic Church adhered to. And as for a stationary earth; the Bible uses the language of appearance in the same way as the weatherman does when he talks about the sun rising. To use it as an argument against the Bible is very childish.'

Will looked about the fire at the boys' faces, shiny-eyed and eager. It was right to come. He caught a twinkle in old father George's eye.

'I say,' the old man said, 'this fire is getting a little low. Why not take the young bucks onto the beach, and get us some of that driftwood that's come ashore after the last storm?'

'Yes, why not,' Mr John said. 'Come on, you lot, get your coats on.' The dogs sprang up and barged their way to the door, almost taking out the tea-tray. They were soon all on the beach where the boys searched the tideline for wood. Adam was off on his own, Will and Ben stayed near Mr John, and Clarkson hauled out a log too big for the fire. After five minutes however, because the heavens were so clear of cloud, Will found it hard to do anything other than look up at the constellations glittering as they did, like so many diamonds, from east to west.

'Totally awesome, isn't it?' Ben said.

'Sometimes you get a glimpse of the size and it just, like, blows your mind!' Will said.

'Yeah, but don't you feel, well …,' said Elliot, 'we're, like, so small compared with it all!'

'I know what you mean,' Will said, still staring up. 'I think it's in Psalm 8 where David says he looks up and sees how vast it all is, and then asks, how can God be bothered with us?'

'You read the Bible, Will?' asked Mr John.

'I just started reading it last summer, sir.'

A shooting star tore through the sky from one corner of their vision to the other.

'Wow! I've never seen such a massive one as that!' Thornton exclaimed.

'That was quite something! Anyway, come on, lads. Wood's down this end of the shore,' Mr John said. 'It is majestic, to be sure; they've had men intrigued from earliest times, those stars have. The apostle Paul told the Greeks in Athens one day that God had placed us here so we would seek him out. I doubt there's a man alive who's never looked up there and wondered about the big questions.'

'Sir, talking of star gazers, I know about Galileo and Copernicus –' Adam said.

'Who believed the Bible!' interjected Mr John.

'Yeah, yeah, I got that bit too, but you mentioned another guy, Kep-something – I don't know him.'

'Johannes Kepler. Now he'd make a good candidate for our consideration. Hey, you lot, gather round and hear about this man; you'll like him, but he's the kind of Protestant that our abbot would not like much, mind.'

'A rebel! I like the sound of him already.' Clarkson leaned on the huge log he had found.

'Yes, but he was only a rebel against ignorance. He was an outstanding astronomer. He was born in Germany in 1571, a sickly child with an unpromising start in life.'

Elliot rubbed his arms against his scrawny body to keep himself warm. 'Oh, a bit like me, then.'

'Shh, Eddie. Don't interrupt,' Ben said.

Mr John laughed. 'Tush, Ben, you can interrupt if you have a helpful observation, contradiction or question, or some such. Now, where was I? Oh yes, baby Johannes was frequently ill and narrowly escaped death after a severe smallpox attack at the age of three. His father was a mercenary soldier away from home, so his mum sent him to his granddad, who just happened to be a dedicated Christian. He not only encouraged Johannes in his faith but also sent him to school. His education, however, was stunted by his father's return from war. Mr Kepler wanted to run a pub, where Johannes was needed as free labour. But God has his ways, and even with all this against him, Johannes was accepted at a university on a scholarship.'

Will lay back on the pebbles so he could look up more easily. He breathed deeply. *Wow, talk about a local boy come good. Thought I had a rough start.*

Mr John saw Will on the gravel and sat down too. 'He loved maths, but he also wanted to be a Lutheran pastor. When he was offered a position to teach mathematics, he saw God's hand in it and took the job. It was here that he became the district mathematician, which led him into the areas of "calendar making", which, in turn, meant understanding the lunar cycle. In those days there was confusion as to where astronomy stopped and astrology started.'

Adam put his few sticks on the pebbles and sat down. 'Even my mum wouldn't throw away the paper without reading her horoscope. Drove my dad potty.'

'So little has changed!' Mr John added. 'Back then almost everyone held the superstitious view that the planets' positions affected the lives of men and women. Kepler questioned these views by his detailed study of astrological charts. Of course, he found that it was all twaddle and so published a controversial book scientifically refuting astrology as superstition.'

'Bet that made him popular ... *not!*' Will said.

'Exactly. Even today, six out of ten men and seven out of ten women read horoscopes! It's always been a big deal and big business.'

'So that was his big achievement?' Adam said.

'Heavens no – no! Over the next twenty years Kepler made colossal breakthroughs in the area of planetary motion that were to revolutionize astronomy forever. Working with Tycho Brahe at an observatory in Prague, Kepler used his mathematical and creative genius to unravel a riddle which had stumped so many great minds before him.'

'And that was?' Thornton drew his collar up about his ears.

'Why, planetary orbits, of course.' Mr John bent down and drew a large circle in the sand. 'Now, he referred to God as the architect of the world which he founded "according to order and rule and measured everything", just like any human architect would. That is, Kepler knew that there was order out there and that it could be measured. And that's why he plugged away at his research until eventually making his great breakthrough: Mars ran an elliptical orbit, not a circular one!' At this point Mr John drew an ellipse around the circle.

'Oh, right,' Ben said, his teeth chattering with the cold. 'Now I remember where I heard the name: Kepler's laws.'

'That's exactly it. After that he went on to formulate the three rules of planetary motion which would become the foundation for Isaac Newton's work on universal gravitation. He also made contributions to mathematics, optics and other areas of astronomy. He even wrote the first science-fiction novel!'

'Wow, watch out, George Lucas! Sounds like a charmed life,' Thornton said.

'Well, not exactly. Remember, Henry, these were turbulent times. Johannes Kepler had his share of hardship to endure, including the death of his wife and three children in childhood. He suffered religious persecution, for, as various squabbling Protestant factions demanded brand allegiance, Kepler refused any label but "Christian", which got him in a lot of trouble! So he now had even more in common with his great friend Galileo! Anyway, come on, let's get this lot back and get a brew on. It's perishing out here!'

They dragged their finds back to the cottage, asking more questions about Kepler on the way. Mr John told them about Kepler's faith as a Christian and the three great books he wrote. As they got to the porch, he dropped his logs, whereupon old Father George opened the door. 'Oh good, more wood, and did I hear you mention Kepler?'

'Yes, sir,' Elliot said, his toothy grin visible to Will in the moonlight. 'Mr John says he was very famous as one of the great founders of modern science.'

'Ah, very true, though of his own fame he said something like "Let my name perish if only the name of God is thereby elevated." Something like that; he wanted to be a theologian, you know, like John here. I always thought he'd go into the church – but what else did he say? Kepler, I mean. Ah yes: "But now I see how God is, by my endeavours, also glorified in astronomy, for 'the heavens declare the glory of God.'"'

The boys broke up some of the wood and brought it into the sitting-room. Father George sat back in his chair with a glass of whisky. Will took hold of Beowulf's thick leather collar and dragged the dog off the low, deep window seat. *Like trying to shift a cow with teeth!* After a few tugs he succeeded in winning the seat for himself and Adam. As they watched the bleached timbers send up a furnace of orange flame in the inglenook fireplace, Mr John brought a huge pan of steaming cocoa to the hearth.

'Now then, this will warm us up. Come on, Adam, you first; you look half-stiff, lad.'

'Thanks, yeah. I mustn't get cold either, really.' He held his earthenware mug forward with a slightly trembling hand. Elliot offered Adam a chair near the fire and he took it without argument. The others got their cocoa in turn and soon everyone was sitting still.

Mr John picked up a comment that Adam had made on the beach. 'Adam was right to point out that Kepler was not the father of astronomy – of course not; but I want you to see that by his breaking astronomy from the Greek, Babylonian and Egyptian superstition, he did something very significant indeed.' Mr John got a rug from under his chair and put it over his father's knees. The old man's eyes were closed and he began to nod his head slightly. 'Poor father – that'll be him for the night.' Mr John gently took the whisky and sipped it as the old man slept on.

'Now, the next man we'll look at is the founder of modern chemistry, Robert Boyle – though I did hear a French writer wrongly say it was Lavoisier, even though he lived almost a century later.'

There was a rumble from the old man: 'What would you expect from the French? Ungrateful people. Now, where's my whisky?' Without opening his eyes he reached out his hand to find his glass.

'Father, you're asleep.'

'Nonsense! I'm resting! Pass it over.'

Will and Adam laughed, and Mr John relented.

'All right! Now, Robert Boyle was the fourteenth child of the first Earl of Cork, who, though one of the richest men in Britain, did not want to bring his sons up as spoilt aristocrats so he sent them to St Columba's.' Clarkson chuckled. 'No, actually he let tenant farmers raise them when they were between the ages of six months and four years! Now, young Robert turned out to be a child prodigy, speaking Latin and Greek by the age of eight, which, by the way, was when he was sent to Eton.'

'Boo, hiss!' cried Elliot, Thornton and Ben.

'Poor guy!' said Will. 'I mean, on a farm till four, then off to Eton at eight – was he ever at home?'

'This was during the reign of Charles I. Times were different then. At the age of twelve, Robert travelled through Europe with his tutor to study the work of the great scientists. Now that was when he became inspired by the "experimental approach" of Galileo, which was something that greatly influenced his whole life and work. Robert also had a dramatic, personal encounter with God one night during a thunderstorm, and he committed the rest of his life to serving him. When he arrived back in England, Robert went to Oxford, where he founded a gathering of like-minded buddies, and guess what he called them?'

'Boyle's Buddies?' Clarkson suggested.

'Not quite: the "Invisible College", whose motto was *Nihil Auctoritas* – which means "Nothing by authority".'

'Oh, so that's what it means! But why "Nothing by authority"?' Clarkson asked. 'Were they rebels or something?'

'Oh yes, but not the average sort. You see, almost all the other scientists thought the answer to scientific problems could only be found in ancient Greek manuscripts, but Boyle and his maverick friends would now no longer just "take someone else's word for it"; they were going to prove it for themselves by experimentation. It was these guys that Charles II officially recognized in 1660 as the "The Royal Society of London for the Improvement of Natural Knowledge".'

'Wow, you mean the Royal Society was founded by a Christian?' Thornton said.

Adam folded his arms and shrugged. 'Yeah, but wasn't, like, everyone a Christian in those days anyway?'

'No – and certainly not like Robert Boyle, as we shall see.'

'So what kind of stuff did the society do?'

'Working with his practical friend Robert Hooke, Boyle created a pump that could suck the air out of a glass jar. By doing this he was able to conduct experiments that, amongst other things, proved Galileo right: that a feather and stone would fall at the same speed without air resistance; also, that sound does not transmit without air. This in turn led him to experiment with gas pressures, known today as Boyle's law.'

'Oh yeah – even I've heard of that,' Will said. 'Was that good?'

'Oh yes. For one thing, it helped Boyle reject the Greek idea that there were four elements – earth, fire, air and water – replacing it rather with his own theory: "We may conceive that God originally created matter in very small particles that were too small to be seen individually." Of course, he was right, and, though it was impossible for Boyle to observe creation at an atomic level at that time, he did go on, using his thirty-part chemical-analysis system, to identify what many of the real "elements" were. When he published his findings in a book called *The Sceptical Chemist*, he made many alchemists angry because they had, with a mixture of chemistry, witchcraft and astrology, made a living beguiling the masses while also secretly looking for a way to make gold from other substances. Boyle's objective research overcame their superstition by clearly showing that gold was, itself, an element and could not be reduced, or therefore made, by any means! Once again, like Galileo and Kepler, Boyle found himself battling against entrenched Greek philosophy and occultist superstition, but, as time showed, Boyle's insistence on scientific experimental processes overcame them all and endured.'

'Oh right.' Will sratched his temple. 'So that's what all those symbols and things are that Fizzy Fortesque goes on about.'

'That's right, Will. An element is something that cannot be reduced – bit like Father's homemade bread!'

'I heard that!' the old man said. The boys laughed.

'Now, that was his legacy to science,' continued Mr John, 'but I think his legacy as a Christian was even greater, for he also left behind an impeccable example of a Christian life. His generosity and character were universally acknowledged, even by his enemies – particularly when it was discovered that he had secretly financed humanitarian aid for London after the great fire. When that became known, he was repeatedly offered peerages and other honours, which he turned down, preferring rather to be known simply as "Mr Robert Boyle, a Christian gentleman". Think of that, eh? This man was a giant if ever there was one, and his insistence on "experimental" understanding didn't stop with chemistry; no, for he used it on the Bible, too!'

'The Bible?' Clarkson said.

'Sure; he learned Hebrew and Aramaic and used to get very irritated by preachers who spiritualized or allegorized the plain meaning of the Scriptures, like our abbot does!'

'That's right,' Clarkson said. 'Blow me if that's not exactly what he did that Sunday about the first chapters of Genesis!'

'That's right, lad, and, as the good book says, if you destroy the foundations, what will the righteous do?' Father George said, stirring himself.

Mr John looked very serious. 'If you want my opinion, I do not believe the materialists like Gibbs pose the biggest threat; but rather theistic evolution does: presenting a religiously inclined public with a third way.'

'Explain why, John – be specific!' Father George insisted.

'Well, obviously, for one thing, can you believe in a God who creates by death, savagery, annihilation, and then looks at it and says, "It is very good"? I mean, what kind of God would that be? He certainly does not square up with the God of the Bible, the one revealed in the Old Testament or the New, in Jesus. And, as for it being allegory, Jesus talks about the Genesis account as factual, telling the stories of real people and real events, not as an allegory. If you think you know better than Jesus, you're welcome to gamble your future on it; but I'm not clever or inventive enough to do that.'

The boys nodded. The point was clear.

'Now,' continued Mr John, 'To finish this off: Boyle wrote numerous Christian books, and supported missionary work in

America, India, Scotland and Wales. Out of his own pocket he paid for an Irish Bible to be translated, printed and distributed. He also paid for some parts of the New Testament to be translated into Turkish and Arabic. It was not surprising, then, that he was often offered many high positions in the Church, though he turned these down as well, preferring rather to serve God as a man of science, always affirming that "From a knowledge of his work, we shall know him". He never married, and he died on 30 December 1691. In his will he left money for annual lectures – not on chemistry, mind, but, prophetically, on the defence of Christianity. The "Boyle Lectures" are still given today. So then, lads, what do you think of that life?'

Clarkson nodded enthusiastically. 'Cool dude, sir. I mean COOL dude! That was a life well lived.'

Mr John ruffled the embers with the poker. It was more than just embers in the grate coming back to life. Mr John puckered his lips and let his greying beard bristle his nose, and then said, 'If you liked Boyle, you'd have loved Newton, but I fear the hour is late.'

Will detected the irresolution in his words. Not wanting the magical evening to end, he pleaded, 'We're not in a hurry, are we, lads?' The others quickly agreed, all, that is, except Adam, who stared silently into the dying fire.

Mr John turned to him. 'And you, Adam – want one more story?'

Adam didn't look up. 'I'd like more wood on the fire.'

'I'll take that as a yes.'

Will beamed at his roommate, then grabbed Thornton. 'Come on. Lets break up some more wood.'

Once they were back inside, Mr John apologized for having to get out his old notebook from his study: 'Sorry, lads, I'm a bit rusty on Newton after all these years.' While Will stacked the fire, Mr John skimmed a few pages and then said, 'Okay, let's do Newton.'

'Einstein never doubted that Newton was the greatest scientific genius of all time. He had pictures of him, Faraday and Clerk Maxwell on his office wall. The other two we'll deal with another time, but they are all Bible-believing creationists. Newton calculated the tides and the eclipses; if we were to send a space shuttle to Saturn or Jupiter tonight, then Newton's laws would be good enough to get it there. It's hard to overestimate the jump that this giant made. And yet, for all that, he said of himself –' Mr John looked down at his notes '– ah, here it is: "I do not know what I may appear to the world, but to myself I seem only to have been like a boy playing on the sea-shore, diverting myself in now and then finding a smoother pebble or a prettier shell than ordinary whilst the great ocean of truth lay undiscovered before me." To-day, the plaque on his grave in Westminster Abbey says this: "He overcame the world by genius"; yet this man was born the same as you and me, and was much poorer, and sickly too.

'How poor, sir?' Clarkson said.

'Yeah, and how sickly?' Elliot said, letting out a cough.

'Isaac was born a sickly, premature baby on 4 January 1643. He had to be a fighter to survive infancy. His father had died three months before his birth, and his mother was left to care for her sickly child as well as their Lincolnshire farm during the turbulent years of the Civil War that ravaged England. Mrs Newton later married a vicar, which introduced young Isaac to one of his future great loves: books, particularly the Bible. He was not sporty like the other boys –'

'Sounds a bit like Thornton, I mean, Henry, sir!' Clarkson interrupted.

'Speak for yourself!' the other replied with a punch to Clarkson's arm.

'Ah, well, there's hope for you both! Now where was I? Oh yes; he was not sporty, but chose rather to make working models of carts and windmills in his leisure time. When he was fourteen, his mother was widowed again and Isaac was forced to give up his education so that he could run the farm and care for his three young siblings. But, impressed by his Bible knowledge, The King's School, Grantham, awarded him a scholarship, and Isaac eventually made it all the way to Cambridge, where he paid his way through his studies by being a servant at the college. Now, I'm sure Ben and Eddie think they have it hard as fags, but as a sizar at Cambridge, Newton literally had to eat the scraps that fell from the richer students' tables!

'During the 1665 outbreak of Black Death, Newton returned to the family farm, where he worked on his binomial theorem, light, telescopes, calculus and theology. He later made a six-inch telescope that could magnify forty times! His work on calculus caused a revolution in mathematics. It was also at this farm that he is believed to have been pondering what invisible force tied the moon into orbiting the earth, when the famous apple fell in front of him. So he thought, "Gravity! Yes, gravity must be it!"

'Although a devout Christian, Newton was at odds with the Church of England in some areas, and his conscience would not allow him to become an ordained minister. This was a problem as, by law, anyone teaching in the University had to be an ordained Church of England minister. Supported by his friends at the Royal College, he managed to get a special dispensation from King Charles II to teach without being ordained. Now that was a major, major deal, as he was the very first to do this!

'Of course, he lived in the same days as Boyle and, like him, Newton struggled vehemently against the Greek philosophical stronghold that dominated university training and left many modern discoveries unrecognized. Superstition still dominated science; for example, the appearance of a comet was seen as an evil omen of coming judgement. Basically, the majority of scientists still held that the laws governing the planets were totally different from those we experience on earth. Newton, on the other hand, was adamant that, if God created both the other planets and the earth, then it was a reasonable hypothesis that they were governed by the same laws. Listen to what he says here about our solar system: "This most beautiful system of the sun, planets and comets, could only proceed from the counsel and dominion of an intelligent Being. This Being governs all things – as Lord of all."'

Thornton edged closer to the fire and held up his hands to the light. 'It's like you were saying before, about one God being the starting point.'

'Exactly Henry, well spotted, and in 1684, he started his work on "universal gravitation", or the "inverse square law", which basically proved mathematically that the same laws apply throughout the solar system. Once again, Newton's faith had pointed his scientific mind in the right direction and his landmark book *Principia Mathematica* was published in 1687.'

Clarkson placed his cup back on the table and took the last Jaffa Cake. 'If no one else is taking?' Adding quickly, 'But sir, could people understand his stuff? I mean, wasn't it a bit way out, like Einstein's stuff?'

'Exactly so, I'm afraid. Poor Newton endured battle after battle trying to get his work validated by the scientific community, though he never became bitter. He went on to serve two terms in Parliament, to reform the Royal Mint (coinage) and bust a counterfeiting ring, and he even found time to write Christian books! I read somewhere that he wrote more about theology than science, so there you are! He was elected as president of the Royal Society *every year* for the rest of his life, and in 1705 he was recognized by the nation for his work with a knighthood. He died in 1727 aged 84. Now, of course, today, we can see that any one of his contributions in physics, mathematics or astronomy would have earned him that epitaph I mentioned earlier.'

'He overcame the world by genius!' Pitt exclaimed.

'Well remembered, Ben, but he himself was a modest man. You know what he said? "All my discoveries have been made in answer to prayer." And, mark this, "I have a fundamental belief in the Bible as the Word of God, written by those who were inspired. I study the Bible daily." Get that? He says that the men who wrote the Bible were inspired, that the sixth sense of revelation was crucial to his discoveries. On the theory of atheism he said, "Atheism is so senseless. When I look at the solar system, I see the earth at the right distance from the sun to receive the proper amounts of heat and light. This did not happen by chance."'

'Wow!' Ben said. 'I never thought of physics as interesting, but that is way cool! He really believed the Bible?'

'Yes, and a good thing for us that he did, or he wouldn't have bothered to reach out like he did – or pray for answers. Just think what any of you guys could establish if you prayed like Newton. And, by the way, haven't you asked your Mr Hill about some of this stuff? He'll tell you a thing or two.'

'No, sir, we're doing kinetic energy,' answered Will. 'He's a nice guy and all, but I think he sounds as bored as I feel.'

'Oh well, I'm not surprised after the sort of things he was studying for his Ph.D. at Oxford.'

'What was that?'

'Just get him on cosmology at the start of a double lesson and you'll see a different man. Bet you ten to one, he'll talk non-stop for an hour and – if you can keep up with him – he'll blow your minds.'

The boys chatted for twenty minutes afterwards but eventually Will noticed Elliot yawning and so he ushered the lads to the door and down the beach. At the Druids' circle he felt a sudden clamminess all over his body, and tremendous quickening of his pulse. He was bringing up the rear alone, and as he passed those dark stones, now shining with a silvery glow in the moonlight, he couldn't shake the feeling that someone was there nearby, watching and waiting. He wanted to look behind at every step but resisted the urge. *Probably nothing, relax you idiot.*

10

Father Kentigern and the Druids

'Elliot! You snivelling amoeba, I don't know which bucket you crawled out of, but that Sunday shirt is as crinkled as your granny's flippin' backside!' Adam reached down from his bed, and threw a shoe at the bewildered first year as he entered. 'And don't gawp like an idiot at Houston 'cos he'll not help you. His head is too far stuck in that stupid Bible of his.'

'Er hello?' Will looked up from his desk. 'What's with you, Adam, bullying and sneering? You're worse than you were last week.' Will shook his head and went back to reading. 'Thought you'd mellow a bit now you've heard what Mr John had to say.'

Adam went back to his own book, clutching it before his eyes like a last defence, 'Everyone has a right to be heard; whether that gives them a right to be taken seriously is another matter.'

'Oh, so the jury's still out for you, then?'

'Hardly even sat! Look, Will, I'll keep going because it interests me, but don't take me for some spineless, intellectual retard, who jumps on every bandwagon. I'll look into what he says, but don't get yourself all worked up – and don't go forcing that Bible of yours down my throat.'

'As if! Anyway what you reading now?' Will said, trying to change the subject, though he noticed that Adam had been reading this particular book every spare minute since he arrived.

'What, *The Donor*? Excellent book – it's about a cleaner who's more ugly than Clarkson and you put together.'

'Thanks a lot. Anyway, it sounds riveting.'

'Oh it is. He's got awful acne, worse than Sidmouth, and also has a degenerative disorder that means he knows he'll die fairly young. So, when he graduates in biochemistry, he goes against his parents and gets two part-time cleaning jobs in two clinics.'

Adam's face was brimming with malevolent, wide-eyed mischief as Will tried to look interested. 'Right, great – a cleaner.'

'Wait – you see, they are IVF clinics, and what he does is go round with his cleaner's master key, and he replaces everyone else's sperm with his own. After ten years he's busted, but by then he reckons he's fathered about twenty thousand kids, so he's happy!'

'Urgh, that's nasty! So not a traditional happy ending then.'

'No, not like the nice little books you read, I bet.' Adam laughs through his teeth. 'There's a public outcry. In court, he defends himself. It's class, man, I tell you, gotta read it.'

'Why, what does he say?'

'Well, they keep up all these questions – you know, why d'you do it? It's wrong, it's evil and stuff, bla, bla, bla. And he just sits there and knocks them straight back.'

'But how could anyone defend it?'

'Oh easy – just depends where you start. He shreds them with Darwin's book *The Descent of Man*, and *Selection in Relation to Sex*, which is about human evolution. He says morality is a natural outgrowth of instincts that were beneficial to animals living in social groups. So he gives it right back to them. They say it's wrong; he asks, "Who says?" They call him a monster; he calls them hypocrites, teaching everyone from infancy that they are no different from other animals and that their sole job is to pass on their genes, but then they turn around to someone who's doing just that and get all hot and bothered! Like I say, it's class!'

'And you agree with him?' Will said, astounded.

'That they're all hypocrites? Absolutely. Dad's always banging on about it. Says we're a hundred years overdue for an overhaul in ethics. They need a good clean-out.'

'Flippin' heck! Hope I'm not around to see it!'

Adam smiled and went back to the novel. 'Like I said, I'm not a spineless, intellectual retard. The world's the hell-hole it is because of inertia. Billions live in misery 'cos no one can make decisions.'

Will pointed his RI folder at him and said, 'If I thought for a moment that you were serious about that, I'd clobber you with this!'

'A very Christian response, I'm sure.'

Will's RI lesson was held in a small classroom at the top of a rectangular tower attached to the Great Hall. Father Kentigern was a sinewy monk in his early fifties, over six foot four, with greased back grey hair that had nicotine yellow streaks in the whiter parts around his ears. He was universally feared by the boys for his strictness and total lack of humour. Will had already come to blows with Kentigern in his second week by pointing out that the school's embracive ecumenism seemed wide enough to fit anything apart from anyone who had a literal interpretation of the Bible. 'That,' Father Kentigern had replied with considerable venom, 'is because fundamentalist intolerants cut themselves off from the community of faith!'

He taught by rote, and his lessons were painfully dull, though in this day's lesson he made a comment that startled Will and caused him to comment without even putting his hand up first. 'Sorry, sir, could you repeat that, please?'

Kentigern turned round to Will and craned his head high to a suitable position from which to look down at his pupil. 'I realize that it may be difficult for you to exercise restraint, but it is our custom to show courtesy to the class and master by placing your hand in the air when you have a question.'

'Sorry, sir, but you said something about the Millennium not really being this year.'

'I did; by the new dates we have for the death of Herod the Great, our present calendars are four years out. What of it?'

'I don't know; four years which way?'

'Forward, boy, *forward*, and if you won't listen, I don't see why I should repeat m –'

'But that means that the real Millennium was 1996!'

'I congratulate you on your maths. Would you like to share with all of us why this makes you so excited?'

Will observed the master's tightening brow and piercing gaze – grey blue eyes, dark purple veins in the yellow balls, unblinking, unflinching. 'Well Houston?'

Will began to realize that he might have exposed his thoughts, and he quickly looked back down at his book and started scribbling. 'No reason, sir. Just didn't know it.'

For a moment Kentigern was silent, two forefingers caressing his thumb, and then he craned his wiry neck higher and higher, as if assessing some great matter. Will did not look up but was possessed of terrible thoughts, feeling the tightening of his stomach and knowing one thing: *I must find out, once and for all, whether there really is still a secret Druidic order in the school and, if so, were they really the guardians of a Millennial prophecy? Supposing they really thought that only a human sacrifice could stop the cosmos descending into chaos?* The thought sent a cold shiver throughout his body. The fountain pen slipped from his sweaty fingers, and he reached a now trembling hand to retrieve it. Once more he found himself momentarily staring up at Kentigern's eyes, and the thick hair in his nostrils, which widened as he spoke. 'Oh Houston, reaching with tremulous hands for things that are quite beyond you. Beware.' He smiled, jackal-like with his teeth for a moment before returning to his scripted lesson.

When it was over, Will stayed behind in the tower a while to finish his work. Kentigern again watched him constantly through narrowed eyelids, though, after scribbling some notes, he too finally left the room. Will followed him down the angular stone steps of the tower some minutes later. The smell of nicotine and incense was faint but constant as he descended to the bottom. He did not really think about it until he entered the library, but then, quick as a flash, it dawned on him where and when he had smelt that combination before.

Inside the library Brothers Reece and Brendan were snapping instructions at old Arthur, who was fixing up some new shelves for them. Will googled 'Druids' and took down some notes about the supposed sect structure. First there was the Druid, who, it was reckoned, had twenty years of training; an Ovate was a lower-ranking Druid; then there were priests or priestesses – for women were equal with men in religious and political matters. If you fancied interpreting the convulsions of sacrificed animals or humans, you might choose to be an Augur, though you would need twelve years of training even for that. Then there were the Bards, the poets who apparently survived into Christian times as minstrels, as did their songs, which were written down by, surprise, surprise, Celtic monks. But even here, many articles said that the Roman accounts – such as that of Julius Caesar – could well be merely 'conquest' propaganda; apart from these accounts, almost nothing was known.

Will visited modern pagan web sites but there was no listing for any group meeting in their local area. He read blogs of modern would-be Druids on other web sites but found, despite their claims of an ancient spirituality, they could not found their modern practices and knowledge on anything other than speculative archaeology and the Roman accounts. The brand of New Age religion that Will saw here seemed to be more '70's flower-power-paganism than anything else; in fact, exactly what he saw in his kindly art teacher. In the absence of history and fact, this sect appeared at a glance to be an amorphous mush, 'blendable' with every religion, 'even atheism', one web site claimed – which made Will chuckle.

He logged off and went to say hello to Arthur. Having greeted the old man, Will dumped his files on the desk and leant against the wall while Arthur worked away steadily at his shelves.

'Well, Master Houston, and how are you, lad? Little bird tells me you're getting quite a reputation.'

Will explained about the bullying and the hook-wedgy, and how he had stepped in. Arthur looked down and pointed the screwdriver at him. 'Ay, lad – well, you did the right thing. You keep your integrity in those little things and it'll be the surest guard that you'll not back out when the big 'uns come.'

'Don't mind if there aren't any bigger ones,' Will said, though he took courage from the old man's comments.

Someone was logging onto the computer he had just been using. *It's Brother Reece.* Will scanned the library. *There are half a dozen other computers available. Why has Reece waited for that particular one?* 'Anyway, I'd better leave you to get on. Looks like you've got your hands full with your two taskmasters!'

'Ay, lad. Ay, too true.' Arthur looked down and chuckled. 'There's plenty in this spot what talk, but if aught wants done, it's old Arthur they call for. You'd think, with all their book-learning, that there'd be one or two who'd know how to use a wall plug and screwdriver, but no.' He laughed again. 'aught needs done, I's the one that does it round here.'

Will laughed too, and as he left, he pledged to call in for a brew at the old man's shed one afternoon that week. His cheerfulness was turned to gall a moment later when he passed near to Reece on the computer and saw him looking up the computer's search history: Druids, Modern practices, West Cumbria. He passed quickly and unnoticed, clutching his tightening stomach. *Oh, boy, this isn't good. This is not good.*

Once outside in the Great Hall, Will steadied himself against the wooden lockers, and took big breaths. Next he knew, Will heard Sidmouth calling after him. 'Houston, Houston!'

'Yeah.' *What can he want? And why was he following me out of the library?*

'A point of etiquette. I mention it as a kindness as someone like you probably wouldn't realise – but we do not talk with the servants – the gardener chap.' Sidmouth's acned cheek wrinkled with a condescending smile. 'It's not that we're snobs or anything, but it sets an abominable example to the younger boys.'

Will, who saw Arthur as about the only slice of normality in the whole school, said, 'Might do them good to meet different people.'

'I dare say you feel more comfortable around your own sort, Houston, but I warn you: there is a right order to be maintained here, and you step out of line, you'll hear from the prefects.'

Will shrugged, and Sidmouth walked off, joining the house prefect, Liam Wordsmith, at the top of the steps. Wordsmith stared down at Will as if he was weighing a great matter; his arms were folded, and a bony right index finger caressed his chin and lip.

'Look at the prat!' The voice came from behind Will.

He turned to see Elliot with his friend Gordon, the first-year who had admired Will's kicking.

'You heard, then?'

'What, not to associate with the lower orders?' Gordon said. 'Yeah, typical of him. Even Wordsmith now.'

'Gordon! Not so loud! He's still looking,' Elliot said.

'Well, it's true! Afraid that, if there's no working class to govern, there'll be no jobs for them when they leave here.'

'Oh, and as a titled Englishman, you'd be the man for the people?' Elliot said.

'Okay, shut up you two,' Will said. 'Gordon, why did you say "even Wordsmith"?'

'What? Haven't you read some of his older stuff from the *Rad Rag*?' Will shook his head. 'Well, I suppose you've only just got here. Wordsmith started the *Rag* himself – you know, the school's first really radical magazine – him and Sam Taylor, when they were first-years. Those guys really saw stuff as it was and weren't afraid to say it: anti-class, anti-church; I tell you, they were Rads all right. Of course, the school tried to gag them.'

'And did that work?' Will asked.

'No, made them more anti-establishment, but, eventually, I think they must have sold out for position. I mean, look, they're all prefects now – somebody got to them.'

That night, Will noticed Wordsmith watching him during prayers. Later he asked Clarkson, 'That Wordsmith guy is a strange one, can't quite make him out.'

Clarkson closed his room door and drew close. 'Sure, Wordsmith used to be a radical, but he got one of the servants pregnant!'

'Pregnant!' Will almost dropped his tea.

'Shush, not so loud, it's still not widely known. My brother told me, so don't go blabbing.'

'So that's it,' Will said. 'He's in disgrace and they let him stay on if he damped it down a bit?'

'Sort of, but not just that. You see, it was also the time when that riot happened at that public school in Yorkshire a few years back.'

'I don't remember that,' Will said.

'Yes you do – it was all over the TV. A hundred-odd local yobs from a nearby comp got beered up and baseball-batted their way through the school, left two nearly dead, one in a coma, and wrecked the spot.'

'Oh yeah, I remember that,' Will said. 'So, the *Rad Rag* stopped after that?'

'No way – it's still going. They cut out all the Leveller stuff, made it more spiritual.'

'What d'you mean, spiritual?' Will asked.

'I don't know, weird stuff – God in the trees and man, and nature and stuff,' Clarkson said. 'Gordon and his mate Shelley from Oswald's are taking the *Rad Rag* on next term just before Wordsmith leaves; keeps telling everyone he's gonna put the "Rad" back in the *Rag*! He's so full of rubbish.'

Will made good his pledge to young Gordon after Friday lunch before games, and, the more he listened to him, the more he agreed with Clarkson: he really was full of it.

That afternoon, Will had another 'test' kick in a friendly against Aiden's. He had been kicking well with Brummell, but something about the pressure of doing it in front of an expectant crowd always made him erratic. It was the last quarter of play. He lined up his ball, trying not to be distracted by the lads who were ogling at a young woman passing by along the road. Will saw it from the corner of his eye, but did not look round. *Come on, breathe. Must make this a good one. A conversion here will equal the scores. Can't cock up again.* He squared up to the ball and paced backwards, but miscounted by one step because he was too busy wiping his sweaty palms on his shorts. One last unsteady breath, ten steps. He started down the short path toward the ball, and to yet more gut-wrenching humiliation. His foot was high and the ball dribbled along the ground 'like a snot', as Dundas elegantly put it a moment later. The groans of St Alban's were only drowned out by the jeers and laughter of Aiden's.

On the way back for tea, the shouts of 'Totty alert' were increasing from the boys. Will caught sight of the girl standing near a Ford Fiesta.

This was just one more thing that made Will laugh at the whole set-up. *Haven't they ever seen a girl before?* But on this occasion, he recognized the girl the boys were whistling at. She was wearing jeans, a jumper and a suede jacket with tassels; he didn't recognize the jacket at first, but the deep auburn hair was unmistakable.

Leaving Dundas and Sidmouth, he ran across the grass to the road, where she was standing in a pool of dying winter light, like some vision from another world that had never heard of St Columba's.

'Hannah! I don't believe it! Why didn't you tell me?' He went to embrace her but then stopped because of the mud on his games kit, but he did venture one kiss, which left mud on her jacket and cheek. Knowing that his friends and enemies were looking on, Will felt more embarrassed to do this than she did, for Hannah had other things on her mind.

'I was missing you, and you hadn't written and ...' She clenched her fists and gave a little jump of excitement. 'I passed!'

'Of course! I clean forgot – the driving test! That's incredible! Well done!' There was an awkward pause which Hannah soon followed by describing every little mistake she had made, or thought she had made. While she was talking, Thornton and Clarkson came to introduce themselves as the ones who 'looked after' Will. They talked for a while and then all went up to the house for tea. Without really giving it much thought, Hannah went into the house and sat at the top table in the refectory, with the rag-tag huddle of muddy boys, all eager to meet a real girl and feed her tea and toast. Will had never seen such civility among them. It was as if Wendy had come among the lost boys. Hannah, in turn, also seemed to have a great way with them, partly due to her being the older sister of a very lively younger brother.

The spell was only broken when Dundas appeared. He introduced himself but then said apologetically, 'I'm dreadfully sorry, but the house rules don't permit us to entertain girls.'

'Girls!' she said. 'You sound like my father! I mean, I am flattered, but I'm also eighteen, you know – hardly a girl!'

Dundas blushed, and the boys stared at Will with an even greater reverence now. Somewhere off in the nerd's corner Will heard someone say, 'Man, to actually have a girlfriend is cool, but one two years older than you and who can drive is cooler than Brummell, man!'

Having made her point, Hannah got up with good grace. She apologized to Dundas, he apologized to her, and Will apologized to both of them. That done, Dundas showed her through to Father Bede's study, where she could be properly entertained by the prefects, and Will went to shower.

'Don't worry, Houston,' Dundas said, with the pink still very evident in his cheeks, 'there's really no way you could have known that rule; we've not had a girl in the dining-room all the time I've been here.'

Having showered and dressed as quickly as he could, Will was about to dash out of his bedroom door when Adam said, 'You know, Houston, you're blessed with an optimistic temperament, an archaic religious worldview that makes you happy, and now, it seems, you also have, by some miracle, found a beautiful girl who's not ashamed to be seen with you.'

Will grinned. 'Yeah, miracles still happen mate. Even for people like me and you.'

Adam lay back down on his bed and dismissed Will. 'Oh, get out – I'm just in danger of hating you more than ever.' He threw a cushion in Will's general direction. 'Go on, Romeo. Run along to her. It'll be lessons in twenty minutes.'

Will found Hannah coming out of Father Bede's study surrounded by the attentive prefects; even Sidmouth was smiling, something not really pleasant to see. Will took her to the beach so they could be alone. He introduced her to Arthur as they went out through the gates. Arthur docked his cap and seemed as enamoured with her as any of the boys. Matron was also there, just coming out from Arthur's shed with some cuttings. 'Ah, yes, Houston – how's that bruising?'

'Much better, thanks. That stuff was magic.'

'Of course.' She eyed him carefully. 'And this is …?'

He introduced Hannah, and after making pleasantries Matron left them. She did not acknowledge Arthur with more than a nod, which Will thought strange, though when he looked at the old gardener there was nothing in his eyes but pleasure.

'Go on, you two,' Arthur said, smiling and picking up his wheelbarrow. 'You want to be alone, not talking with an old fella like me – go on, get to the beach.'

They laughed, made their excuses and left him. Once alone they talked of all that had happened over the previous weeks, and how Will was looking forward to the Easter holidays, now only a few weeks away. But as he talked about Percival, Mr John, the Druids, and the monks he suspected, he noticed her eyes disconnecting and her hands fidget. Changing tack he said, 'So what do you reckon to the lads?'

'The boys are darlings, and the prefects – well, I like Dundas; he's honest. Sidmouth's a creep – you know he tried to hit on me? Brummell's just lost on himself – can't make him out at all.'

'And Wordsmith?' Will prompted.

'Yes – a strange one. You know he's big into the outdoors?'

'Well, I had heard he helps out with the junior house Scouts,' Will said.

'Oh yes, says that nature is the only purifying thing about the school, being so close to raw nature. He's quite definite that it's the best thing for kids – get them away from computers and everything. I told him you'd agree. Actually, I told him that you were a great climber and you'd love to go out with him sometime.'

'You didn't!' Will exclaimed.

'Why not? Think you could do with getting away from all those web sites and books and conspiracies.' Hannah looked up at the

Druids' circle and then back at Will. 'You know, blow the cobwebs away.'

'He's into weird stuff – or so I've heard – and knowing what we now know, its just possible that someone like him might be part of all this stuff with Percival.'

Hannah flared up. 'For goodness' sake! I've come all this way, we've got a few minutes together, and all you can talk about is this – this – obsession with Percival and Druids!'

'Hey, wait a minute! It was you who said that you got bad vibes from Father Bede.'

'Yes I did – all that unanchored mystical monastic stuff gives me the creeps, but your witch hunt – that's another matter, Will. You accuse this one and that one as if the fact that they differ from you in theology makes them all obvious murder suspects. I mean, you should hear yourself! These are human beings, not perfect maybe, just muddling along like the rest of us. I'm worried, baby, you're in danger of becoming judgemental and hard-hearted about this – I realise you've had pressures here but I think the sooner you get a break from this place, the better.'

Will stopped himself coming back with a defensive reply. Instead he nodded slightly, gazed out across the ocean and said, 'Okay, maybe I've been a bit obsessive. Sorry.' He glanced at her with his puppy dog face. 'Still get a kiss?'

As Hannah's freckled face broke into a slight grin, she nudged him in the ribs. 'Come here, looking at me like that, supposing you can get round me like I'm some sort of soft touch.'

'No girl can resist *the* look!'

'It's a good thing then there's no other girl about.' She kissed him and he saw her to her car.

Hannah ground the car's gears as she drove away and, with one more embarrassed look and a half-blown kiss, she sped up the hill, out of Will's strange new world for another few weeks.

He envied her for the freedom age gave her, and he ran to his double geography lesson feeling, for the first time in weeks, quite homesick.

Will liked physical geography – he always had. They were studying glaciology and erosion. Mr Geoffroy was a good teacher, and he insisted they copy his cross-sectional diagrams into their books. Will, ever the artist and visual thinker, loved this way of learning; it was pictorial, simple and 'pin-downable'. But as he was accepting more from the Bible, Will now saw a huge gulf opening between the small time scales mentioned in the Bible and what his teacher was saying in terms of vast geological ages.

Secretly Genesis' young earth was Will's biggest hurdle for, as even he looked around at the mountains and the cliffs, he could not see how the earth could be so young. He knew better than to stick his neck out in class again by even asking about it, especially when he was so uncertain himself.

After prayers, Will's friends assembled once again in his room, ready for their next Invisible College meeting. The school's stand-ard-issue navy duffel coats were extremely dorky but, as Clark-son pointed out, 'They're excellent for moving about at night. We'll never be seen, and … we get hoods, just like the monks … Wooooo!'

At 8 p.m., Will led them out of the window and up into the woods, where Ben waited. Along with the rest of them, he found it hard to keep down their giggles. They stole through Monks' Wood and over the high wall to the freedom of the sea, beach and cliffs, whispering jokes with barely concealed laughter. Will watched anxiously as Ben and Elliot ran in circles on the sand. 'Come on you two,' he hissed, 'let's get there.' His own heart pounded with excitement as he clambered over the rocks in the moonlight. For Will particularly, for these brief hours it seemed that he was be-yond the system, beyond the rules and the doctrines of the school.

Here, the Invisible College motto, 'Nothing by Authority', captured his imagination as if, for the first time in all his life, he was allowed out of the goldfish bowl that Professor Inchikov had talked about. Finally, among likeminded peers, he was able to walk and think as a man: expansively, imaginatively, daringly.

He grabbed hold of Clarkson as he came off the beach: 'Boo!'

Clarkson hardly jumped, for he was looking ahead to where Adam was picking out his way up the path all alone. 'I don't get him at all, you know, Houston.'

'No, me neither,' Will said. 'It's like some massive cloud's hanging over him.'

'D'you think he's just been indoctrinated by his dad's lot for so long that he can't see the wood for the trees?' Clarkson asked.

'No, that's not it; you saw how he shredded the Gibbon. The guy's eyes are wide open – I've never seen an adult who knows half the stuff he comes out with. I mean, he really wants the evolution thing to be true. It's as if a God out there would be the worst thing in the world. I don't get him.'

'Rumour has it, he got kicked out of Eton for punching the Dean; maybe he just hates religion?' Clarkson said.

'No, it's got to be more than that. It's God he's afraid of; I'm sure of it.' Will stopped suddenly and grabbed Clarkson's sleeve. 'What's that?'

'What?'

'Up there on the cliff, the skyline. There's someone standing there.'

Clarkson followed Will's finger. 'What, no. Just another tree. Why're you so jumpy?'

Will looked toward the others making their way noisily toward the circle, and then back to the empty cliff.

11

SECRETS OF THE EARTH AND SEA

C ome in, come in, all of you; leave your coats and boots in the porch.' Father George pottered back to his chair. The boys filed in and took their seats. Adam took a window seat out of the circle. Thornton and Clarkson went to the kitchen to bring the tea-tray, and after a few minutes Mr John appeared from his study in a long, coarse, woollen dressing gown over his clothes.

'Welcome, boys! Forgive my attire; I'm starting to feel the cold but, unlike Father, have not found a flight suit that fits me.'

'It's not your age, boy,' Father George said. 'Your blood's thinned after all those years in –'

'Perhaps that's it. Now, shall we get started?' Mr John cut his father short with such force that the boys started.

'Oh, of course, the great secret,' the old man said, arranging his blanket. Clarkson shot Will a look.

They spent ten minutes recapping about Copernicus, Galileo, Kepler, Boyle and Newton before Mr John read them an article about Nicolas Steno, a believing Christian who lived in Boyle's day and became the father of geology.

'I mention him tonight because, chronologically, he fits in with last week's lecture, but his field of study fits with tonight's, chaps. Tonight I want us to travel two hundred years, right from the reign of Queen Anne to that of Queen Victoria, to see the men who gave us, amongst other things, botany, palaeontology and oceanography.'

The dogs stretched themselves before the fire with long yawns and Father George said, 'Perhaps a top-up of tea before we start?'

The tea was poured, and Mr John opened his notes and began to read.

'Carl Linnaeus, 1707–1778, the world's pre-eminent botanist and information architect who created the Latin binomial system still used in biology today. Discovered God's secret logic of biological creation, as Newton had done with physical mathematics. His father was a Lutheran pastor and amateur botanist in Sweden. He was the eldest of five children and had his own botanical garden which, young Carl would say, "inflamed my soul with an unquenchable love of plants". By the age of twenty, he was studying medicine and science at Lund University and later Uppsala University.' Mr John peered over his spectacles at the boys. 'Now, see here – interrupt if you want to ask anything, all right?'

'Come on, boy, on with the story!' Father George said impatiently.

'By the age of 23, Carl was made lecturer of botany and then, three years later, of geology as well. After some foreign expeditions, Carl settled down, becoming the personal physician to the Swedish royal family at the age of 29. He became convinced that many illnesses were caused by bacteria, or, as he called them, "living particles". This was a hundred years ahead of another Christian, Louis Pasteur, who would prove his theory. Linnaeus developed a revolutionary new cure for tuberculosis and was soon back at Uppsala as professor of botany, while also lecturing in zoology, geology and medicine, a position he held for the rest of his life. When he was 40, he published his medical and botanical research, and later was appointed chief royal physician.' Mr John took a sip of his tea.

'So what was he the father of: TB cures?' Clarkson asked.

'No – though if you got TB, Tom, you'd be glad he lived. No, his great legacy to science was his system of plant and animal classification. At the time there was an overwhelming glut of new species being discovered, and he was able to create a "branching", or "box within a box", catalogue system based on his understanding of Genesis chapters 1 to 3, where we are told that the plant and animal species created "reproduced after their kind". When he published his *Species Plantarum* and *Systema Naturae* in the 1750s, Linnaeus became the father of modern taxonomy and systematic biology.'

'So this is the start of Darwin's great tree, like the posters in the lab?' Elliot asked. Will glanced at Adam who still looked down, arms folded.

Mr John stretched his legs towards the fire and rested them on Grendel. The dog sniffed him and lay back down. 'No, not at all; it's totally different. Darwin probably got his from Aristotle; Carl got his from Genesis. You see, evolutionary thinking was already making a come-back in science, and this nearly a century before Darwin, but Linnaeus strongly refuted it, based on his research. In fact, his "biblical" classification system only became as popular as it did because it fitted species into categories and not into a continuum. In all his long years of research, he had never witnessed any species transitional to their kind and –'

'Excuse me, sir,' Thornton interrupted him. 'Transitional?'

'You know, where one kind of organism changes into another: like a cat becoming a dog, or a lizard becoming a bird. But that does not mean that Linnaeus, the Bible or other modern creationists argue for the fixity of species. They do not. Linnaeus started out thinking that way but subsequently rejected fixity of species and argued that speciation within a kind can happen in a limited way. Now, of course, this was 1750 –'

'Yeah,' said Adam, looking up. 'That's before there was a fossil record.'

'Yes, yes, quite so – but I doubt that, if he were alive today, Linnaeus would accept the scant offerings of two centuries of fossil-diggers.'

'So there are transitional fossils, then?' Clarkson asked.

'Well, there are fossils showing speciation within a kind, but claims of fossil transitions between kinds are often disputed, even among evolutionists themselves.'

'Okay, well how many – like a thousand or something?'

'Heavens no. No, if you put them all together, they would all fit on a dining-table. But we'll come to that when we do the father of palaeontology in a minute.'

'But, sir,' Adam said. 'What about transitional forms in plant fossils?'

'The same story as for animals; the latest research by two evolutionist scientists, Margulis and Schwartz, now suggests – as Linnaeus could already have told them – that not one phylum, which is a major category of classification, like arthropods, mollusks, etc. – is either ancestor or descendant of another.'

'But how do they make their tree of life work, then?' Clarkson said.

'Oh, that's easy; when they get stuck with something, like a Giant Sequoia, they say: of course, it's descended from progymnosperms.'

'And what's a proggy-whatsit?'

'A mythical linking species that must exist but they haven't found yet!'

'What? Please tell me you're joking!' Will said. 'I mean, please don't tell me that they give fancy Latin names to plants that don't exist in the hopes that no one will notice?'

'No, I'm sure everyone on the inside knows, but, of course, if you know – or should we say, *believe* – the theory is right anyway, why not? But come on, let's finish this chap. What I want you to see is that Linnaeus always felt that his work should have a practical outworking and so, for example, his research into the food chain had beneficial spin-offs for Swedish agriculture in pest control. And he was not just a scientist; he is also celebrated as one of Sweden's greatest writers, poets and thinkers. He received a knighthood in 1761 and a state funeral when he died of a stroke seventeen years later. He left behind his wife, Sara, and three children, one of whom replaced him at the university. A fourth child had gone before Linnaeus, having died in infancy. His long academic career was astounding, but see here: he never lost his boyhood wonder and love of the natural world, though he always kept it in perspective. He once said, "Let us … not set aside God's works, but, guided by them, revere the master." Well, that's him done. What do you think, boys?'

'Sounds like Thornton, sir!' Clarkson said.

'What, our Henry?' Mr John replied.

'Well, that fetish with organizing things; Henry's just like Linnaeus. I mean, you ought to see his sock drawer – all laid out just so!'

'Shut up, Tom. We can't all be slobs!' Thornton said, giving Clarkson a kick.

'Yes, all right,' Mr John said. 'But can you see how Linnaeus was fulfilling God's command to be a steward of creation? I must admit, I'm probably more like Tom there; but the first part of caring and valuing something is usually taking stock of what's there. I couldn't say how many pairs of socks I have – they're in singles all over the place, but that's because I don't value them highly – well, perhaps not as highly as Henry, anyway!'

They spent a few minutes talking about Linnaeus, looking at reproductions of his drawings. Will was in awe of the detail and craftsmanship, handling the books with reverence. *Wow, really shows the guy cared about this stuff.*

'Hey Adam, you wanna see these? They are amazing?' Adam shook his head.

They also talked about John Dalton, another Christian who at a similar time was working on the atomic theory, the laws of partial pressures, meteorology and atomic weights. 'But if you want to know more, lads, you'll have to look it up yourselves later, for we must go on to look at a most interesting man: Georges Cuvier, the father of modern palaeontology.

'Born in 1769 in a small French-speaking town in the Duchy of Württemberg adjacent to France, Georges was initially educated at home by his devout Lutheran mother, who immediately saw his interest in zoology and botany.'

'He's just like Linnaeus,' Elliot said.

'That's right, but who doesn't dream of a little place in the country with a few animals and a vegetable garden, what author John Steinbeck called "earth longings"?'

'My mum called it "Eden longings".' Adam's voice came from the window. Will turned to see him speaking with his right hand pinching his brows. 'Used to sing the Joni Mitchell song "Got to get back to the Garden" just to annoy my old man.' Adam sighed and shook his head. 'See the thing is – ah, why is this so hard – the thing is, I was like Linnaeus and Cuvier, wanted to be Gerald Durrell when I was growing up. I loved all that stuff, collecting beetles, even had a few lizards. Could spend hours with them, just, just with them.' His right hand came forward as if he could still touch them.

Will saw that his eyes were tearing up. 'So what happened, mate?'

Adam paused, then snapped back, 'I grew up, didn't I. What's your excuse?' He closed his eyes once again, this time with both hands massaging his temples.

Mr John spoke through the silence that followed. 'Well, I think we'd best move on, lads, continue with young Georges?' The boys nodded and Mr John placed the spectacles back onto the end of his nose. 'Well, then – where were we … ah yes. Georges was schooled primarily to become a civil servant – ah, like you again, Henry!'

There were some chuckles but Thornton rose above them. 'You may pick on me tonight if you want, but don't expect mercy if it's your turn for ribbing!'

Mr John continued. 'He was schooled to become a civil servant, but, when no jobs were forthcoming, Georges became a private tutor, then a town clerk in Normandy, where he devoted all his spare time to studying plants, animals and marine invertebrates. When he was 26, the famous agriculturalist H. A. Tessier recognized Georges' unusual ability and so recommended him for the position of assistant to the Professor of Comparative Anatomy at the National Museum of Natural History in Paris. But – and mark this, lads – Georges soon came to loggerheads with Anaximander and the like in their Greek evolutionary mindsets!'

'Hang on, what were those dead guys doing in France?' Clarkson asked.

Mr John smiled. 'Don't ask me, lad, but they were alive and well, though their names had changed to names like Buffon, Geoffroy Saint-Hilaire and Lamarck.'

'You're saying that they were teaching evolution in France half a century before Darwin?' Will asked.

'Sure; these guys were copying another countryman, Maupertuis, who had been, despite Linnaeus' system, trying to fit all living creatures into a great chain of being. Lamarck also believed that the fossil record contained prehuman ancestors of humanity.'

'Excuse me, sir,' Thornton said. 'You said "a great chain of being", and that kinda rings a bell with me.'

'Yes, well it should if you've been listening; it was Aristotle's idea, and if you're stuck for an original theory, just as those guys were, then take something Greek: it will always give you a ring of authenticity!'

Father George shook his head. 'Frenchies!'

'Wait a minute, Father, it wasn't just them. In Britain too, evolution was already rife. Around this time, James Burnett wrote not only of the concept that man had descended from primates, but also that, in response to the environment, creatures had found methods of transforming their characteristics over long time intervals. Of course, there was John Locke a hundred years before that, using the Hindu or Brahmin doctrine of reincarnation to formulate his own theory of evolution. In fact, Locke's theory received the support of the male members of Darwin's family. In 1794 Charles Darwin's grandfather, Erasmus, wrote a book entitled *Zoonomia*, which marked out his theory of evolution. Being a Freemason like Locke, there is little doubt that Erasmus could see how neatly the theory dovetailed with the Masonic occult doctrine of "becoming". Of course, when you read *Zoonomia*, you could think you were reading something from ancient Greece: "all warm-blooded animals have arisen from one living filament". In his 1802 poem "Temple of Nature", he resuscitated another Greek idea: that of the rise of life from minute organisms living in the mud to all of its modern diversity.'

'But hang on – that sounds like Charles Darwin's big idea!' Elliot said.

'No, no. Darwin popularized this same Greek idea half a century later using natural selection as the agent.'

'But I saw a documentary about Darwin's Beagle voyage, and it made out that he went off with a clean slate and was struck by the evidence.' Ben's voice rose to a pitch of excitement that roused Father George out of a momentary slumber.

'None of us is quite as logical as we like to think. None of us has a clean slate. And you can certainly see an intellectual plausibility structure given by Darwin's own family into which his thinking naturally ran, can't you? He once wrote that he could not see how "anyone ought to wish Christianity to be true; for if so, the plain language of the text seems to show that the men who do not believe, and this would include my Father, Brother and almost all my best friends, will be everlastingly punished. And this is a damnable doctrine." I think that's what called presupposition!'

'I think, my son,' Father George said, 'this is called a digression. Were we not at a university somewhere in France?'

'Yes, so we were. Young Professor Cuvier was being clobbered by Lamarck and other professors who supported the idea that an animal could be classified from the "simplest to the most complex", and what made it all happen was time and the "use versus disuse" of body parts. It was only natural, therefore, for Lamarck to believe that the fossil record showed the ancestors of modern-day animals, but Georges asserted that this evidence pointed strongly to extinct animals, and that the fossil record was actually, therefore, damning proof that Lamarck's theory of evolution was without foundation, as no evidence could be found in the fossil record for intermediate or transitional forms. Of course, if evolution were true, there would be as many "in-betweenies" as there are other fossils, but there were none. Even Darwin admitted this. "The number of intermediate varieties, which have formerly existed on the earth, [must] be truly enormous. Why then is not every geological formation and every stratum full of such intermediate links? Geology assuredly does not reveal any such finely graduated organic chain; and this, perhaps, is the most obvious and gravest objection which can be urged against my theory." Two hundred years and billions of fossils later, there are still none that are not disputed. Lamarck believed not only in evolution, but also in the "spontaneous generation of life".'

'The what?' Clarkson asked.

'I know, it sounds ridiculous, and actually it is, of course, but it's another very important bit of daft Greek philosophy that you ought to understand if you are going to see how the world would ever swallow a theory like macro-evolution, that is 'goo to you', or 'rocks to rocket scientists' evolution. It's something we'll discuss another week when we look at Louis Pasteur, but suffice it to say that, when the Greeks saw maggots "magically" growing on meat, or insects coming out of swamps, they got all excited and said, "Look, look – life can spring from non-living matter! Hey, I bet that's how everything originally came into being." And so on.'

'Didn't anyone tell them to stop being silly?' Clarkson said.

'Well, yes, but remember that this was the current of scientific thinking that Cuvier was standing against. We're still over sixty years before Darwin's book, remember, and here was a young man on the ropes against his older peers just for basing his science in divine creation. Again, don't believe all that about poor Darwin, the humble original against the whole world; it's piffle! Macro-evolution, as a doctrine, was looking for an exit point onto the world stage.'

'Yes, sir, we've had all that ominous personification in our philosophy lecture,' Adam said, looking up and jiggling his leg as he did whenever he was irritated. 'But how did Cuvier answer "spontaneous generation"? Did he throw Bible quotations at them or something?'

'No, Cuvier pointed out that, and I quote "Life has always arisen from life. We see it everywhere transmitted and never being produced." In fact, he rarely referred to his creation worldview, preferring to keep his argument against evolution on a purely scientific basis. Cuvier also *refuted* the notion that the similarities of human and animal body structures – for example, a human arm, a horse's leg, a dog's leg and so on – were conclusive evidence of evolution. He said that this was rather a good argument for a common designer. Later on, the evolutionists thought they really had Cuvier on the ropes with vestigial organs. For the uninitiated here, *vestigial organs* are the bits of our bodies that seemed to have no apparent function and therefore, the evolutionists said, must be evolutionary hangovers from our animal past. One example is the "tail-bone", which the eminent men of the day said must be the remains of either our fishy or our monkey past. Cuvier was bold enough to stand on his biblical hypothesis that "they all must have their own reason for existence", but he was also humble enough to add, "even if we are ignorant of it". Of course, recent science has confirmed his faith, as over a hundred of these supposed "vestigial" organs have now been found to have significant roles.'

'Poor man, sounds like he spent valuable time arguing with the Greeks!' Father George said.

'Oh, he managed to get some work done too. For example, Cuvier went on to update Linnaeus' branch-classification system by starting to classify animals by their nervous systems. That, along with his encyclopaedic works, still greatly helps biologists to this day in classification – although the system has understandably undergone many changes. Cuvier also managed to classify many fossils and thereby establish palaeontology on a firm scientific foundation. And he refuted "uniformitarianism".'

'Woah, big word alert!' Clarkson said.

'Thank you Tom, but it's quite simple. Uniformitarianism basically means that the landscape we see has come about by small changes and is therefore billions of years old.'

'Right, so big word equals long ages.'

'Correct. Cuvier was adamant that the fossil record proved that "catastrophism", i.e. big catastrophic events, like the Genesis Flood, were the predominant influence on how the earth appears today. He went on to hold many national academic, religious and government positions, bringing in huge academic reforms in France, Holland and Italy. His wife, Anne Marie, previously a widow with four children, bore him four more, three of whom died in infancy. Georges was made a baron by a grateful nation and he died one year later in a cholera epidemic, though his reputation as one of the most important anti-evolutionary figures in the history of biology still lives on today.'

There was a small round of applause, and Father George prodded the fire. 'Jolly well done, Master Cuvier! I revise my opinion of the French. But look here, I will have to plug in my flight suit to the car battery if no one gets me more firewood!'

Mr John stretched. 'You must excuse Father; he has very fixed ideas on national characteristics, it is –'

'It is the province of old men and retired teachers,' Father George interrupted. 'It helps us to rest easy. What did Livy say? The Spaniards are unreliable, like all foreigners; the Carthaginians treacherous; the Nubians overly amorous; the Gauls fearsome but easily discouraged; the Thessalians restless and given to rioting; and the Athenians – yes, mark you, the Athenians – "easily suggestible", a factor, no doubt, which helped them to swallow bad science and pass it on to us. Now, what of my fire?'

The Invisible College disbanded and headed to the beach in search of wood. They spent twenty minutes hauling it back to the cottage, and all the while Will kept looking at the huge strata in the cliffs as the moon now half lit them, now left them in darkness, while the tide ebbed and flowed around the jagged rocks of the headland. Will found Mr John staring intently up at the cliff head. 'Everything all right sir?'

'Er, yes, think so. Just thought I saw something. How can I help?'

'Well sir, it's the strata on these cliffs. I mean, they look pretty old to me.'

Mr John's white teeth grinned in the darkness. 'All right you lot, gather round, anyone who hasn't a head for heights can go back to the cottage – there's no shame. The rest follow me out along this rocky shelf into the ocean.'

They all followed Mr John far out along a rocky ledge usually covered at full tide. Just metres below them, the great surging currents of the ocean lunged and swallowed, thrust forward and receded. The constant motion and power caused even sure-footed

Will to occasionally take a handhold to steady himself. 'Now then, the age of the earth is a contentious issue even among Christians so I don't want you to get hung up on this, or fall out with people who think differently. And if your study of Genesis and geology leads you to a different conclusion than mine, then we can still be friends. But having said all that, let me give you my take on it, okay?'

'That's fair,' Will said.

'Right then. I preface with this point that I really want to make clear: My starting point in objecting to an old earth is theological. What I mean, lads, is that if we have death, suffering and disease before the fall of man, then we have a different sort of God in charge of the universe – one who called death and suffering "all very good" and who even used death and suffering to create. And all that stuff in the Bible about death being God's judgement on sin, and the last enemy Christ came to destroy is all rubbish.'

'Wow,' Will said. 'Never thought about it like that before.'

'Exactly. You couldn't class a God like that as *good*. But that aside, I want you to imagine you had never had that thought, the thought already placed there by your education, *that it's all so very old*. Imagine that I said, "Now look here, Will, these cliffs are the direct result of catastrophic events that happened quickly, and there is overwhelming fossil proof and many modern-day observable comparisons." You'd just say, "Okay, thanks." Right?'

'So there's plenty of proof?' Will said, trying not to sound sceptical.

'Sure; rapid burial is almost a must if you want a good fossil.' Mr John gave examples of how rapid the events must have been. 'A fish dug up in Caithness was still in the process of swallowing another fish when it was fossilized. Then there was a large marine reptile called an Ichthyosaur, which needs a lot of mud to bury it rapidly. Well, one was dug up in Germany, and it was in the middle of giving birth: I mean a baby was just coming out!

Another specimen found had three babies in her ribcage and one already born. And then there was the classic: a Velociraptor and a Protoceratops fighting, found in Mongolia.'

'Oh yeah, I remember raptors from *Jurassic Park*,' Thornton said, at the same time holding tightly onto Will's coat, as the ledge started to thin out into a narrow finger of rock jutting far out above the swell.

'Yes, well, in this case, the raptor had just jumped onto the ceratops' back when they were both deluged by mud; that has to have been a split-second event. I took the original Invisible College up to Carlisle Cathedral in 1996. In the choir of the cathedral is a fourteenth-century bishop's tomb set into the floor, and on the brass-surround edgings you can see various reptiles engraved. Among them are what might be Apatosauruses, maybe even a Shunosaurus or Vulcanodon. Whatever they are, they aren't anything alive today! And the world of archaeology is littered with these images.'

'Yeah, but come on – that doesn't mean they actually saw them; they probably just saw the fossil remains,' Adam jeered.

'It's a possibility but I don't think so. This was four hundred years before people were digging up fossils. Also, there is one detail that no one knew until recently. You see, in the cathedral engraving for example, the beasts have their tails off the ground like cantilevers. Now, if you look in your older textbooks or comics, their tails are trailing behind them on the ground. No, I think those creatures were still alive in folk's memories, and, besides, the Bible talks of the same creatures!'

'The Bible talks about dinosaurs?' Will said with amazement.

'Of course it does! Read the book of Job. There's a huge creature mentioned there called Behemoth. His tail is like a cedar tree, and his power is in his loins. Now, that's a very accurate anatomical and mechanical description of dinosaurs. And we can argue back and forth about the engravings, but the recent findings of soft dinosaur tissue and DNA should have shaken the long agers to their very core. This is very big, I mean big. Collagen in protein could survive, in ideal lab conditions of zero degrees centigrade, for a maximum of 2.7 million years. But at twenty degrees centigrade, that dinosaur tissue would only last fifteen thousand years. To say these T-Rex or Hadrosaur tissues are eighty million years old flies in the face of known scientific data.'

'Perhaps. Dunno about all that,' Adam said, and Will heard Adam's scoffing laugh above the noise of the spray. 'But what of these supposed catastrophic geological deposits?'

'There have been plenty of examples in our lifetime, like the 1929 Grand Banks earthquake, which sent a two-foot-thick layer of mud onto the Atlantic floor. That mud slick travelled five hundred miles in just thirteen hours, and covered a hundred thousand square-mile area.'

'But how could they possibly calculate that?' Adam asked.

'Because of the times when three transatlantic cables were snapped. Now, I'm not saying that geology is a straightforward business by any means – it's complicated; but I would say this: first, you don't have to commit intellectual suicide to believe in a young earth. There are plenty of evolutionist scientists who will agree with what I've just said: that the strata we're walking on now seem to have been laid down in similar catastrophes.'

While Mr John stamped his boots on the strata, Will asked, 'But how do they then get millions of years if it's not done gradually?' Will said.

'They say that millions of years must have elapsed between the layers.'

'And is that observable?' Will asked.

'No, quite the opposite; a fresh layer left for months or years will show it by signs of erosion or burrowing creatures. For example, Hurricane Carla in 1961 left a layer of sediment that was almost completely gone twenty years later."

'Yeah, well okay,' Adam said, 'so there's physical evidence, but what about historical evidence; I mean, is it just the Bible that bangs on about a global flood?'

'Not at all and that's just it. There are more than 138 flood accounts from around the world. Okay, so some have obvious elements of fantasy and local colouring, but throughout, and almost without exception, there are four basic themes they share with the Bible. First, there was a moral cause for the flood, either because of the sin of men or the misconduct of the gods. Second, they all agree that either a god or an animal gave one man advance notice of the flood. Third, and again without exception, all agree that the flood destroyed all of mankind except those warned and that these survivors are the progenitors of the present world population.'

'Wow, that's freaky,' Will said.

'You're telling me, but there's more,' Mr John said. 'The fourth similarity between the accounts is that animals played a significant part by giving warning of the flood or by indicating that the flood waters had abated and that dry land had appeared. In addition to these big four things there are also a great many accounts that imply that eight people were saved while almost all say that some kind of vessel was used to house the survivors. Now given this, what I'd call an overwhelming oral and historical tradition, wouldn't you think rational, scientific men might want to interpret geology with that in mind? But of course they don't, and what's worse, you can't even teach this sort of stuff in school nowadays; it's plain heresy.'

'But why not, if that's where the evidence leads?' Clarkson asked.

'Well, that's my second point: you absolutely need, at all costs, to have millions of years if you're going to make evolution believable. Men like James Hutton and Charles Lyell gave the evolutionists in Cuvier's day, like Darwin's grandfather, these understandings. Again, it's all borrowed from the Greeks and the Hindus, surprise,

surprise, but there you have it; teach otherwise today in a school geography class, even alongside a long-age view, and you'll lose your job. But anyway, as I said, it's a complicated business. Even creationists have always been divided about Flood geology – and even about the age of the earth, but I'll not pour any more oil on that unhallowed fire.'

'But you believe in a young earth?' Will asked, partially relieved.

'I'm not clever enough to think any different. Besides, there's plenty of evidence, and I'm stubborn, and suspicious of people who tell me that I've got to accept an argument that is so crucial to propping up their theory of my origin.'

Mr John reached the end of the jagged spit and turned, just in time for Will to hear Adam mutter under his breath, 'My thoughts exactly.'

If they had all felt giddy before, now even Will was finding it hard not to hold onto someone.

'Now, boys,' continued Mr John, 'I've brought you out here to introduce you to our next member of the College: Mr Matthew Maury. Now, you see this mighty ocean? Does she not fill you with dread and wonder? Do you not wonder about what secrets she holds? The Greeks had that same feeling you are having now, and they suggested that surely life came from the oceans. Stanley Miller thought the same, but I wonder: have you ever thought what secrets the deeps would really yield to a man who looked at the sea with biblical lenses? Well, tonight you shall meet the father of Oceanography. But let's get back to the fire before one of you falls in.'

As they started to go back, Mr John turned to Will. 'I'm going to take the cliff path with Beowulf; you take Grendel.'

'Is everything all right?'

'Yes, yes. I'll be back in five minutes. Grendel, home!'

Mr John disappeared up the nose of the cliff and Beowulf followed. The boys were back by the fire minutes later and Mr John came in not long after that. When they were all settled with a hot drink, Mr John rubbed his hands and spoke. 'Well, now, fire all right, Father?'

'Yes, quite all right, dear boy. Pray continue. I must to bed soon.' The old man patted his son's wrist and then pulled the blanket up over his legs.

'Good, good. Matthew was born in Virginia, USA, in 1806, the descendant of a Huguenot family that had originally fled religious persecution in Europe. His parents brought him up to believe that the Bible was the true Word of the living God. That's what my brother and the abbot would call a Bible-belt fundamentalist, Adam! Yet no matter, the world would later thank Mr and Mrs Maury for the narrow way they raised their son, as we shall see! At nineteen he joined the US Navy and, virtually self-taught from the ship's library, he graduated in his navigation exams six years later to become a warranted midshipman. His next post was that of sailing master; basically he was in charge of navigation.

'Now, here's the interesting bit. You see, Matthew was sure that when the Bible talked of the "the paths of the seas" in Psalm 8 verse 8, it was not just religious or allegorical spiel! No, he had understood by that verse that the sea must contain currents which act over great swathes of the oceans, like global conveyor belts. But when he tried to locate information charting these currents, he was amazed to find that there was none! So, while other men, like Darwin, carried forth the theories handed down to them by their forefathers, our young hero decided he would benefit mankind by putting into practice what he had learnt from his. Basically, almost single-handedly, Matthew went on to chart the ocean currents that God had revealed through the Bible! He also found that another scientific hypothesis based on Ecclesiastes 1:6 was similarly true about the winds. That's the verse that talks of the wind which blows south, then turns north in a continuous cycle. You see, although it is true that the Bible was written by men who sometimes used the language of appearance, just like we still do, there are also times when God reveals in it things that cannot otherwise be known, like the currents; or he anoints a man with special wisdom to scientifically discern things, like the winds. Solomon, like our Matthew, had access to this wisdom, and the results would make Matthew famous and revolutionize shipping for all time.'

'You're generalizing again, John. Tell them how it changed things,' the old man said.

'Well, for example: a ship's journey from New York to San Francisco was cut by nearly a third (fifty-one days!), and a journey from England to Australia cut by over twenty per cent. He published his *Wind and Current Charts* in 1847 and soon became the leading authority on the subject. The Navy put him in charge of the Hydrographical Office and the US Naval Observatory. Under his direction, top-class work was done in the field of astronomy, particularly on comets. He also discovered a plateau on the ocean floor after taking depth-soundings of the Atlantic Ocean, and found that there were no significant currents at great depths – which would prove extremely useful in years to come, when another Christian, Samuel Morse, invented the telegraphic system, making it possible to connect the USA with the UK. This could not have been done without Maury's research, nor without the help of the great British physicist Lord Kelvin, who was himself an enemy of evolution – but we'll talk about him next time. Suffice to say that, when he carefully studied the seas, Matthew Maury said he fully expected to "perceive the developments of order and the evidences of design", which is exactly what he did discover.'

'Wow, that's quite a story, sir!' Ben said.

'And that's not the end of it, Ben, it's just the beginning. You see, Maury could see that, to really benefit mankind, international cooperation was needed to consolidate the meteorological and oceanographic data required, so he organized an international conference in Brussels in 1853. It was a landmark event – no pun intended – that set a new precedent in international cooperation in science, and many remember this as his greatest legacy. In 1962, an international symposium on Antarctic research was named after Maury in recognition of him being the "pioneer in cooperative international studies on the oceans, the atmosphere, and the polar regions". After the American Civil War, he became a professor of physics, established the Virginia Polytechnic Institute and organized meteorological stations for the collation of accurate weather information, something that became a great help for agriculture and commerce. He died in 1873 in Lexington, Virginia, aged 67. In his lifetime he was honoured by the governments of many nations, including Britain, Russia, Belgium, Germany, Denmark, Portugal, France and the Papal States, though he remained a humble man, always giving glory to God for his achievements. Of course, as the old saying goes, "The flea does not know whether it is on a giant's shoulder or one of ordinary size", and many attacked him for using the Bible as if it could have "authority in matters of science". Maury was understandably indignant. "I beg pardon!" he once said. "The Bible IS AUTHORITY for everything it touches. What would you think of an historian who would refuse to consult the historical records of the Bible because the Bible was not written for the purposes of history? The Bible is true and science is true and therefore each, if properly read, proves the truth of the other!" There, I think that sums it up, don't you?'

The boys agreed fairly heartily, except Adam, who sat once more brooding by the window. They talked and asked questions for another half-hour before Mr John drew Will aside.

'I'm going to come back with you all tonight as far as the circle. I want you to bring up the rear and keep the others close.'

Will's face dropped. 'Why? What's the matter?'

'I can't tell; Grendel wasn't happy on the beach earlier. Are you sure you weren't followed here?'

'I don't think so – I mean, I thought I saw something but wasn't sure.' Will's face grew downcast. 'We weren't really watching. Sorry.'

'No matter, lad. It's probably nothing.'

Will glanced at Mr John's eyes. *You don't believe that for a moment, do you?*

12

THE DRUIDS' WARNING

While some of the boys helped to clear away the mugs and others humoured Father George, Will went with Mr John to comfort Grendel, who was whining by the front door.

'Easy there, girl,' Mr John said.

'Mr John, there was something I wanted to know,' Will said.

'Yes?'

'About that book you wrote on local history and the Druids' curse.'

'Hah, 'twas no curse, boy, just a runic prophecy about the Millennial solstice. There's a lot of that sort of medieval witchcrafty mumbo-jumbo around. Made a good titbit for my book! Anyway, what of it?'

'Well, what did it actually say about the solstice?'

'Oh, well, I've lost my copies of the book. I can't find them, though it's not for lack of trying. Mind, it wasn't very well written. In fact, I went to a publisher in Whitehaven to see if they'd do another run, but they told me the strangest thing. Said that I myself had sent a signed letter telling them I was changing publishers, and that all the proofs should return to me straightaway!'

'And, and you never actually wrote it? That's a bit weird!'

'Yes, I know. The chap was a bit off-hand, and seeing as they all thought I was an oddball anyway, I just left it there and walked out.'

'Yeah, but the prophecy – what can you remember about it?' Will asked.

Mr John stroked Grendel's shaggy neck. 'Oh, something like the world would know a great new era of peace and tranquillity if blood were offered at the Millennial solstice, but, if not, it would descend into chaos – or something like that. The carbon dating said it was fifth-century but I don't rate carbon dating. It was found in a Norman tomb, so I'd say it was medieval, not really Celtic, and it's not unusual for the period, but I doubt if anyone took it seriously anyway.'

'What about the Druids in the school? Do they really exist?' Will said.

Mr John hesitated, then looked at his father, who nodded. 'Yes, sadly. They've been there for centuries as far as I can tell, but, if I had to place my money on it, pantheists of the modern era are really too interested in nice woolly experiences to be bothered with anything as mundane as history. Mind, it's snowballed in the last thirty years and picked up all sorts: feminists, New Agers, environmentalists and the like; but as I say, they're more keen to establish a system of righteousness based on their carbon foot-prints, than to actually treat history seriously.'

'Father Kentigern said that the Millennium solstice, if it was dated by the death of Herod the Great, was, in fact, in the summer of 1996!'

Mr John smiled automatically, then stopped stroking the dog. His eyes strayed to the floor and there was a dreadful pause. The air itself seemed electric, and Will felt the hairs on the back of his neck stand up. Mr John looked up at Will with his mouth open and then, clutching his chest like a man who'd been shot, he quickly pushed past him to get to his study. He left the door ajar, and Will heard the sounds of Mr John riffling through his books and papers

and cursing simultaneously. 'You idiot – stupid imbecile – idiot!"
Eventually all noise ceased and a moment later he appeared in the
doorway with a 1996 diary opened in the middle. As he staggered
through the door he let the diary fall onto the floor of the study.
He walked past Will but did not look at him, though he did speak
in a low, tremulous voice. 'Who else have you told?'

Will stood dumb for a moment, face drained of colour.

'Blast it, Will! Who have you told about this date?' He almost
shouted.

'No one, except some of these guys.' Will's eyes watered and
his mouth felt suddenly dry.

'Kentigern?' Mr John snapped, still looking towards the fire at
the other side of the room.

'No. I mean, I don't think he understood my meaning when
we talked.'

'Better hope not; from now on, you mention it to no one,
understood? And that goes for the rest of you.'

Will was about to say 'yes' but Mr John quickly spoke again.
'Right, you lot. I'm taking the dogs out. Be ready to leave with me
in one minute.'

They got their coats, and Will observed Mr John in his study,
sliding a long cutlass-like knife and scabbard under his coat. 'All
right, let's be gone, and not a sound, anyone.'

It took until halfway across the beach for their eyes to read-
just to the dark. Mr John walked swiftly, looking inland towards
the woods. Will did his best to hurry the others and keep them
together, but they were all so jolly following their night out that
it was hard to stop their whispers rising to chat. Ben whispered
to Will, 'Is everything okay?' But he was stopped from getting a
reply when Grendel broke into a low growl.

'Stay, Grendel, stay here. Beowulf, come to heel, sir.' Mr John's
voice was stern and low. The dogs obeyed and the other boys
quietened instinctively as they mounted the cliff path to the circle.

From this point, there was a clear view of the cliff above, which, in turn, led gradually on to a wooded knoll. It was here that a large walled cemetery, the necropolis, was sited. As they came to the circle, Will felt more uneasy than ever as he thought back to the solstice night of 1996. What might it have been like; hooded figures, incantations, Percival struggling, the knife, the screams. His mind raced on but each time he also heard Hannah's voice calling him back to normality. *Am I really becoming obsessed about it all, just like Percival did? Have I not more grounds now than ever to be suspicious? Can scarcely see any other interpretation, mind you; it's all getting a bit weird now and I'm not so sure of anything in this place.*

While he tried to rein in his mind, he heard Grendel's low growl again, this time breaking into the most ferocious, blood-chilling snarl. Mr John quickly silenced her but was not quick enough to stop Beowulf darting off into the darkness beyond the stones. He blew his whistle but there was no sound. 'Stupid dog! Listen, all of you: get back as soon as you can – do not stop for anything and don't, for God's sake, go into Monks' Wood tonight.'

He brushed away the questions and, turning briskly to Will, whispered, 'See to it that Ben gets to his house all right, d'you hear?'

'Yes, but –'

'Just do it. Go!' Mr John slipped Grendel onto a lead and disappeared beyond the circle into the great darkness. The boys did as they were told, their joviality evaporating and their footsteps hurried. Will's palms and forehead sweated hot then cold as he imagined he could see watching monks in every shadow. Twenty minutes later he was glad to be back within the stone confines of the school, but, as he lay awake, he turned it all over and over in his head.

'Pssst. Adam, you awake?' No response but Will had just heard him scratching another '8000' into the wall with the end of his compass. 'Pretty weird night, Mr John got pretty jumpy. Freaked me out.' No response. 'I don't think we're very safe right now; need to look out for each other, especially Ben and Elliot.'

'Houston, will you shut up with your Famous Five rubbish and let me get some sleep.'

'What, Elliot! What's going on?'

Elliot stood over Will's bed with Adam's newly polished shoes in his hand.

'Wake up, Will. It's the phone for you.'

Will went downstairs in his pyjamas. 'This'd better be good,' he mumbled to himself. 'Yes, hello?'

'Will, it's me – are you alone there?' It was Mr John. The line was bad; he must be on a mobile.

'Of course I am! It's probably 6 a.m. or something!' Will said grumpily.

'No, it's 7.10. Meet me in the necropolis in ten minutes, and be quick.' Mr John hung up.

Having dressed hurriedly, Will half jogged, half walked across the pitches and up the track to the hillside and its wooded knoll.

The necropolis, as it was called, was not old, dating back only to the great plague of the seventeenth century, when there was a need for fresh graves away from the monastic buildings. It had been added to over successive centuries, and so the tumbled-down tombstones and small shrines, statues and mini-mausoleums occupied a three-acre site. Windblown sycamore trees surrounded the enclosure, bowing like great guardian angels, leaves tatty like old rags. Will had never been here before; few boys had. Occasionally, those with bottles of gin and the like would come to evade detection, but that was only the younger boys who had no rooms of their own. For the most part, the necropolis was a desolate, eerie memorial to death, clearly seen but equally ignored by all but the desperate.

Mr John met Will by the north gate. He looked tired and care-worn. 'Anyone follow you?'

'Don't think so. You look wrecked!'

'Been up half the night looking for the dog. I had a few hours tossing and turning before I thought of looking here.'

Will noticed dried blood on Mr John's hands. He started to feel agitation rising in the pit of his stomach. 'What – what did you find?'

'You'd better come in, lad.' Mr John turned and walked through the gate. 'Welcome to the underworld, Orpheus. Follow me.' Will followed him through the archway, half-covered with ivy, and along past the graves and sarcophagi to the central mausoleums.

'I hope you're not squeamish,' said Mr John. 'I found him just like this before I called you.'

'Where's Grendel?' Will asked, not sure what else to say and not really wanting to follow.

'Sent her home – but she knows.'

At first Will could see nothing but the wrought-iron railings around a double grave-site. A weathered stone bust stood at one end of this enclosure, but there was little else to alert Will as he drew close. Dark markings of spilled blood glistened on the outer stones. Will stopped and looked away.

Mr John, now by the railings, turned and saw him. 'It's okay, Will. You don't have to come any closer if you don't want to.' But at this, his eyes welled up with tears and he kicked the railings hard. 'Scum, cruel butchering pagan scum – I'll make them pay for this!' He grabbed the railings with both hands and hung his head and sniffed.

Will walked forward, irresistibly drawn to look. At first he did not understand what he was seeing; only after he had finished gagging on a mouthful did he fully realize. Beowulf had been laid on his back, cut right down the middle and stretched out, his ribs splayed wide, his four paws tied tight to the railings in a giant X shape. His organs had been removed. They lay near him, some cut up, as was the intestine.

'Arrgh,' Mr John sighed in pain. 'Don't worry, lad. I was sick too, and you'd think an archaeologist would be used to seeing this sort of thing.' When Will had finally recovered and finished clearing the acrid taste of vomit from his mouth, he stumbled away. 'Why – ? I mean, what … ?' He sniffed it out of his nose, holding his sleeve up against the stench and the flies.

'It's a warning shot,' Mr John answered.

'But how do you know?'

'Look at the headstone,' he said, motioning with his hand.

Will looked at the words written beneath the statue and read, '"Harold Hanover esq., 1836–1900" – but that's your family name, sir.'

'He was my great-grandfather, headmaster here long ago, and an evangelical Christian who publicly withstood Darwin's theory and …' Mr John looked up and pursed his lips.

'And what?'

'He also tried to speak out against the Druidism in the area.'

'Oh great. How did he die?' Will wasn't really expecting an answer.

'Had a fall while walking on the cliff-top near here,' Mr John said.

'How near?'

Mr John pointed to the cliff-edge some four hundred metres away to the west. 'Just there. They recovered his body below that point.'

'But that's got to be near the …'

'Oh yes, I know, lad. Coroner's report said his broken corpse was found just outside the stone circle on the rocks, and I confess I thought nothing of it really until this morning. Of course, people gossiped at the time that the evil eye had been put on him, but that's what superstitious people always say.'

'But now, after Percival and the dog?' Will said.

'I dare not think, Will. That's the truth. Only suppose that the prophecy was known before; suppose that the school – the monastery, whatever – was the guardian of it and perhaps other secrets; the more I think that, the more I think Percival died for what he had discovered.'

'But what did Percival tell you?'

'Argh, been so blind!' Mr John took several steps away from the grave and faced seaward, taking several large breaths of the salt air before continuing. 'He came to me the evening before his death. He said a whole lot of things about the Druids and the prophecy. It seemed mostly nonsense to me and I told him to "think on whatsoever is good and excellent" and not lose sleep over what the wicked do in secret, etc., etc. Anyway, we prayed together and he left more settled. I was the last person to see him alive – though now it seems perhaps not the last.'

'I really think we should go to the police,' Will said.

'I agree, but I'm worried to do that right now,' Mr John said. 'We only have speculations at present, but that's not the main thing.'

'No – what is?'

'I perhaps can't expect you to understand this until you've been through it, but I am very much afraid we are up against clever people here, and people in authority, working together. When I lost my job four years ago, the whole establishment closed in on me like a pack of wolves. It was more mechanical in its efficiency; it felt like a set-up. In fact, it was so effective that it took me in too, and I've lived with this guilt for Percival's death ever since.'

'What, and you're afraid that, if you go to the police –' Will said.

'Exactly, the power behind the throne might have me set up for it.'

'And who's that?' Will asked.

'Pah, I don't know! My brother, Malthus, any of them, all of them; I've never really cared until now. But I tell you one thing: I want to know, and I'd like to see Percival's autopsy file too; that would be a start – though how, I've no idea.'

'Wait a minute,' Will said. 'My dad's brother is a forensic crime-scene investigator in London; perhaps he'd help us.'

'I doubt it, but it's better than nothing. Try him. Also look into Druidic ritual killing. I've got no Internet at the cottage. Oh, and find out when else Druids are likely to meet.'

They agreed that it would be too risky for the Invisible College to meet in the foreseeable future. As Will helped Mr John untie the remains of the poor dog and bury them, they talked together of many things – anything to take their minds off the grim task in hand. As they parted Will said, 'Well sir, really sorry about all this.'

'Not your fault Will. No need to apologise.'

'Suppose. Well sir, you take care.'

'Don't want to be melodramatic lad, but right now I'm more worried about you and your friends.'

Will did not see Mr John again for a month, until after the Easter holidays, though they were often in touch about what they had discovered.

Will's Uncle Phil in London was a large and loveable cockney copper and, surprisingly, at ease and helpful. 'Yeah. All right old son', he bellowed down the phone. 'I'll send you 'em autopsies by post. Ain't no problem as they're just hospital records. Ain't a forensic pathologist's report, or anything top secret, or I'd have to kill'ya first. Anyway, that do'ya? Sweet as a nut mate.'

'Wow didn't think it'd be that easy. Thanks.'

'Well, it's a straight suicide, innit? The police ain't bothered if the next of kin don't request it. Anyway, I'll send what I can get to you, but just don't flash them around, right – you know, burn after reading.' Will heard his aunt shouting in the background, and then his uncle said. 'D'you hear that? They can usually hear your aunt in Watford. She says, why don't you come down and see us soon? Your cousin made some good money doing relief postal work leading up to Christmas; he could get you in if you want. Besides, we'd like to see'ya, seeing's now you live in God knows where – back of beyond!'

Will thanked him and said he might be interested in the job as he was saving for a motorbike.

The next Sunday Will studied his suspects in church more closely than ever: Malthus, Bede, Kentigern, Reece, Brendan and the others. They all looked guilty of something, and the more he watched them, the more he imagined they all knew something, or even everything that had happened, and were all laughing at him and plotting against him. Along with the Gregorian chants and swirling incense encircling them like serpents that did not uncurl, the mesmeric effects in his already overloaded and tired mind were almost hypnotic. He closed his eyes to it all and prayed quietly.

The next two weeks were full of house-match fever. And fever it was. Will had nothing to compare it to from all his other school experiences. It was all that was talked of. Wordsmith collared Will one day after lunch as he was putting on his boots.

'Ah, Houston, hard at it I see. Dundas and Brummel training you up are they?' He didn't wait for an answer but went on at length about his disapproval of the time and energy wasted on 'such a boorish sport'.

'Sorry Wordsmith, but I'm going to be late for practice.' Will stood to go.

'Yes, very well Houston, but if you fancy doing something more honest and manly in the summer term on the rocks on the headland above the sea, I can recommend some good "mod-severe" climbs under the circle that I've not done since I was your age –

what do you say, give our bodies to the wind for an afternoon?'
Stuck for a way of refusing without giving offence, Will agreed.

Although he was young, Will was placed on the reserves list
in the house senior team and brought out for the odd match.
He did reasonably well; he did not score any tries but, more
importantly, neither did he show any weakness or otherwise let
the house down. The house did well and made the semi-finals
without too much trouble. Here they were pitted against their
mortal foe, St Oswald's. Fox's boys had some dashing bursts of
brilliance and speed but, in the end, Dundas' disciplined training
regime paid off and Brummell's golden foot carried the day with
a series of precision punts that kept St Alban's at the right end of
the pitch for the second half, and also two stunning drop-goals
from oblique angles.

The finals were against St Aiden's the following Friday, the last
day of term. This was an event that most parents came to view as
a yearly highlight. Will was still on the reserves list, and he called
his parents to make sure that they, and Hannah, if possible, could
be there.

All the lessons went on as usual. Will kept his head down
during RI and biology, though things were not at a standstill for,
it seemed, there was a noticeable, perhaps even coordinated, prop-
agation of media in the school aimed at discrediting the creationist
sentiments that were still evident from earlier events that term. It
was not the big guns this time, for the abbot and headmaster had
fallen silent on the issues, but quietly and steadily, snide comments
were made in lessons, articles were placed on school noticeboards,
and even appeared in the *Rad Rag*, reporting the moral fall of
creationist apologists in America.

Even Mr Gibbs was 'given' a brand new PBS documentary to
show all his biology students; it featured the famous Pennsylva-
nia test case in which the Intelligent Design lobby were defeated

by evolutionist scientists in a dramatic court-room drama over whether anything other than evolution could be taught in the science classes at US high schools. Will sat and watched in horror as the 'Christian' school governors were seen to be dishonest, the Intelligent Design lobby were exposed as nothing other than creationists by another name, and, worst of all, the ID experts were slaughtered on the stand, though little of their argument was told by the biased documentary makers. Assuming that most involved were Christians, Will was ashamed by the time the credits came and he tried to avoid Gibbs' swaggering stance as he switched off the TV.

Meanwhile, Adam started a half-hearted clap. 'A stunning piece of objective documentary making!' he called out.

Gibbs smiled callously. 'Ah, didums. Don't like it when the boot's on the other foot, eh, Rawkins?'

'As far as anyone can see, sir, we've no idea if the first boot could talk; the film-makers only gave us one side of the argument.'

'We heard the side that matters, the winning side. The judge has spoken: ID is another label for creationism, and it is false and not to be rammed down children's throats any more in school.' Gibbs looked around at the class to survey the liberated minds.

Adam shook his head and bit his lip, saying under his breath, 'Stupid, mindless, arrogant piece of –'

'What's that, Rawkins?' Gibbs said.

'You don't get it, do you? You just can't grasp anything beyond the walls of this lab.'

'Rawkins, you dare cross me again in this class and I'll have you –'

'But, sir.' Keats stood up, placing himself between the antagonists. 'I think Rawkins might have meant that the judge merely said creationism was by definition not something observable by science and was therefore really only a religious proposition and not one allowed in American science classrooms by their constitution.'

Now Clarkson spoke up as the bell went. 'It doesn't mean it's not true; it just means it doesn't suit our classroom arrangements. Anyway, I read one study on the Internet that said that thirty-one per cent of UK teachers want creationism to be given an equal status in the science classroom, and seventy-three per cent of science teachers want it discussed openly in their classes – but they are not allowed. Sounds a bit like a secularist dictatorship to me – I mean, what are you all so afraid of?'

'And you can sit down too,' Gibbs said. 'Modern science has no fear of scrutiny, as you fancifully imagine – that idea's just in your heads.'

'Hmm,' Clarkson said. 'In the same article it said that the Royal Society sacked one of its top staff for even suggesting that if a teacher was asked in a class about creationism, they should at least give a courteous reply. I mean, that's how uptight the establishment are!'

Gibbs dismissed them. 'Yes, because the science is settled. The whole world says that creationism is not science; it's false. In fact, I'd go so far as to say it is child abuse to force it on children!'

'But that's just it: this man in the Royal Society, he wasn't a creationist, he just said that, if someone asks a question, a science teacher should be able to answer it!'

'Yes, sir,' Adam said, 'as you do, so well.'

'I see, I see – we're all in smart-alec mode again. Well, if you persist, remember it will be worse for you all. I'm warning you!' Gibbs stood for a moment, hands on his hips and breathing fast, and then said, 'Anyway, get along with you all – lesson's over.'

Will had gotten to know Keats quite well by this time and had learnt that he had lost his mother and sister from an inherited disease. While walking to their double physics lesson, they talked together and, though it seemed that Keats had leant towards a woolly New Age spirituality to see him through his troubled life, it was clear to Will that he had a genuine, serious searching heart. *I'll have to ask Mr John if he can come to the Invisible College when we resume summer term. If we resume summer term.* Will sincerely hoped they would.

Mr Hill was rubbing down the whiteboard ready for the usual lesson when Will remembered what Mr John had said about the latest discoveries in cosmology. As Mr Hill wearily opened his book, Will asked, 'Sir, a friend told me that new discoveries in cosmology really challenge the atheistic status quo in the science classroom.'

'Ooh, I see, very interesting point Master Houston, thank you. Thank you indeed.' He spoke quickly, his dark eyes flashing this way and that with the very real excitement that pulsed through his mind as he reached out to bring the galaxies closer to his pupils.

'Yes, excellent! Well, the two queens of science, maths and physics, produce mathematical physics.'

'Like you marrying Ms Sykes, sir!' Clarkson said.

'Oooh,' Mr Hill pulled a tight, pained expression. 'Not quite what I imagined – anyway, where was I? Ah yes, the triumph of applying maths to the universe, a big leap in science, as the universe is written in maths, or spoken, even. Well, anyway, you should know that things have really moved on apace in the last fifty, yes, even twenty, years in astrophysics – and I do mean apace; light years, in fact. I tell you, boys, what we now look out into through our telescopes is a universe that will blow your minds a thousand times more than anything the first astronomers could have imagined.' He took a swig of water from his cycling bottle. 'All that we find, all the seemingly arbitrary laws and constants of nuclear physics, have something quite startling in common.'

'What's that?' Will asked.

'Well, that it's all been fine-tuned to support life; even the astro-physicist Sir Fred Hoyle had to admit that it looks like someone's been monkeying with the physics! I've just finished my Ph.D. and I'd go even further: I'd say that the evidence overwhelmingly points to our planet being at the very centre of the universe's purpose!'

Adam shouted out, 'Come on! You could just as easily argue that we're here as a product of random laws, surely?'

'Right – the old chicken and egg thing. Well, I'll leave that for you to decide, but I'll give you the physics if you want it. If you arrived on the moon and saw a big biosphere pod there and you went inside it and found machines keeping the air humidity at fifty per cent, the temperature at seventy degrees, the oxygen levels just so, food production, energy available, waste-disposal systems and a hundred other things to support life, and then you saw it all controlled from a series of dials, what would you think?'

'That someone's designed it?' Clarkson said.

'Exactly! Now listen, I'm from an atheist background original-ly, right, so I'm not shoving anything on you. This stuff was not available to my parents – these are new discoveries, but, basically, the tuning on each of the dials for this universe is staggeringly fine. In fact, there are many physical constants which have to be just right in order to have life at all.'

'Such as?' Will said, seeing that Adam was silent.

'Like the electromagnetic coupling constant, which binds elec-trons to protons in atoms. If it were smaller, fewer electrons could be held; larger, then electrons would be held too tightly to bond with other atoms. Then there's the ratio of electron to proton mass, which is, hmmm...' Mr Hill walked back to his desk and picked up a piece of paper from his folder. 'Ah yes, 1:1836. Again, if this were larger or smaller, molecules could not form. Another: carbon and oxygen nuclei have finely tuned energy levels.

'And then there is our sun. Did you know that because the electromagnetic and gravitational forces are also finely tuned, our sun can be stable and the right colour; any redder or bluer, and photosynthetic response would be weaker. Our sun is also the right mass; if it were larger, its brightness would change too quickly and there would be too much high-energy radiation. If it were smaller, the range of planetary distances able to support life would be too narrow; the right distance would be so close to the star that tidal forces would disrupt the planet's rotational period. UV radiation would also be inadequate for photosynthesis. Our distance from the sun is crucial for a stable water cycle. Too far away, and most water would freeze; too close and most water would boil. Need I go on?'

'Yes please,' Adam said, looking up briefly from his book where he'd been taking notes.

'Well, we could be here all day, but I'll give some headings to look up, Adam, if you're taking notes; how about the earth's gravity; axial tilt; rotation period; magnetic field; crust thickness; oxygen/nitrogen ratio; carbon dioxide levels; water vapour and ozone levels – all of them are fine tuned to allow life. Alter any of the dials and you have meltdown. These are just right. They are clues that demand an explanation. It's no wonder that eminent physicist Sir Fred Hoyle said, "Common sense interpretation of the facts is that a super-intelligence has monkeyed with physics, as well as chemistry and biology, and that there are no blind forces in nature." He was an atheist who came to believe in God because of studying physics. For him and for me, it was the only logical conclusion. Right, Adam?'

'Yeah, I guess. Never really thought about it before.'

'Well, you should do; the people who work on things like inflationary cosmology do – all the time! As one bloke said, "These are inflationary times; the cost of atheism has just gone up!"' Individual boys laughed gradually as the joke hit home.

'And, of course,' continued Mr Hill, grabbing his blow-up globe, 'that's all just the beginning of what astronomy is now telling us. We were brought up to think that the earth's an unremarkable planet in an average solar system, but now we find that's a load of baloney too – pardon my French! We're amazingly in the right time and in the right place; and something else: it looks very much like we're here for one purpose, at least …'

Adam seemed to snap at the word "purpose". 'What purpose? What on earth do you mean?'

'It now appears to many that we have been placed in an optimal position in the cosmos for observation and discovery. This is something that has troubled me too, Rawkins, for many years; human beings, so obsessed with purpose, have been told by scientists that they inhabit a universe where there is none.'

This blinding thought seemed to send Adam's mind all over the place, but Mr Hill barely stopped to breathe. 'Now, I have a young daughter, and we leave her in her playpen; but we put toys for her to discover inside the playpen, and we also put the playpen near the garden window so that she can look out and see the clouds and birds and so on. Well, that's a good picture of us, guys; a very uncommon earth and very exact location.'

He talked on about the different types of galaxies, and the stupidity of beaming messages to globular clusters, as they had done when he was a boy. He talked about particle radiation, gamma rays, X-rays, heavy particles, all the time narrowing down and down the suitable places where a habitable planet could be sited.

'We're only just finding out how even the things we take for granted are all essential to our existence. Take the moon for example! Did you know that the moon is exactly four hundred times smaller than the sun, and that the sun is four hundred times further away than the moon, making the best place to view an eclipse the only place where there is someone to see it – that is, Earth? Coincidence? A bizarre one, surely! And because it only just covers the sun in an eclipse, it means we can accurately study the sun's corona, which was important for lots of things. It's only small, our moon, but we discovered in 1993 that it stabilizes the tilt of our axis, making life here possible. You see, it's like a cosmic dancing partner; it has just the right size and position to give us enough tidal range to create circulation of heat and nutrients in the oceans; any bigger and we'd be stuffed!'

'So, you see,' he summarized, 'habitability is one characteristic of this planet's position and composition; but that's not all, for with this habitability also comes "measurability". You see, I told you earlier that I not only gave my daughter toys to play with in her playpen, but I also put the playpen in a position so that she could see outside; and that's what we find with Earth. It's fine-tuned for discovery, as if we're placed at the window of the cosmos.'

He talked then at length about the transparency of our atmosphere, our advantageous location away from the centre of the galaxy, and many other chemical and biological observations.

The boys were reeling from the implications, particularly given the current tensions and what Will thought had been a definite smear campaign. Adam was the one to speak as the bell went, though no one moved or showed the slightest inclination to leave. 'Okay, I admit that this stuff is not my thing, really – I'm more of a biologist – but don't you worry about the implications of what you're teaching us?'

Mr Hill laughed. 'Don't you get it, Rawkins? Physics has always been light years ahead of biology, and the last few years have changed the whole ball game; we're looking at stuff with new eyes. What people outside this classroom make of it is their business. Physics has cut man free, and biology needs to get used to it – or catch up, at least!'

Mr Hill gathered his papers and quieted the boys. 'But listen seriously now: here's a quote from the godfather of astrobiology, a guy called John A. O'Keefe. He says, "We are, by astronomical standards, a pampered, cosseted, cherished group of creatures; our Darwinian claim to have done it all ourselves is as ridiculous and as charming as a baby's brave efforts to stand on its own feet and refuse its mother's hand. If the universe had not been made with the most exacting precision we could never have come into existence. It is my view that these circumstances indicate that the universe was created for man to live in." Did you get that?'

He put his papers down. 'Listen, if you're staring down a black hole in the biology lab, you're not in physics. I've been there; it's an ugly, bleak place; no design, no purpose, no evil, no good – nothing but blind, pitiless indifference. Hey, I've got a family now, and it makes you ask questions, and this stuff has been a pathway of hope for me out of atheism. So what if parts of the science faculty don't like it? They head-hunted me; they can fire me if they want and find someone else to teach the ABCs. I reckon I need to be back in research anyway – there's a universe out there to explore!'

13

THE BIG MATCH

Will did some covert research in the library during that last week of term. He sensed someone behind and turned to see Ben Pitt staring over his shoulder. He was frowning and looking at the news clippings of Percival's death. 'What are you doing with those? Will, what's going on?'

'Erm, nothing.'

'Is that why we can't have the Invisible College anymore? Because of Percival's death? Because there is more to it?'

'Shhh, not so loud.' Will moved Ben into a side cubicle beneath the stern gaze of a statue of St Kevin and there told him almost all that had happened, everything except the names of those suspected. Ben's eyes grew wider and wider, uttering 'no way' every now and again.

'What we need is evidence, see? We need to know where they'll meet and when; we need to find out who they are, and gather what evidence we can. Now look, it says here that the word "Druid" means "Knowledge of the Oak" and that Druids meet in stone circles – well, we know about that; but it also says that they meet in oak groves. Are there any round here?'

'Yes, of course!' Ben said with surprise.

'Well, where?'

'Don't you know? Hello? The Monks' Wood is one big oak grove, and it's ancient, too.'

Will shuddered. 'Oh, and to think we've been there at night!'

'You've been there! Hey, it was me who had to stand there alone waiting for you!'

'No wonder Mr John said not to go there the other night.' Will looked at another piece of paper. 'Now, it seems to me that, apart from solstices, various of these bods meet any old time, but look at this: it says here that a full moon is a powerful time for magic, and that some meet then.'

'Ooh, sounds creepy! When's the next full moon?' Ben said.

Will glanced around the corner to make sure that Brendan and Reece were nowhere near. 'Twenty-sixth April, it says. That's just after we get back from the hols. I reckon if anything's going to be found out, that's our best chance. I'm sending these notes to Mr John, and I'd better get back to packing my trunk. Then just one more lesson – philosophy, I think – and no more work for a week or two!'

'I'll see you at the match, won't I?' Ben said. 'My bro's looking for a win, and you'll have to watch out for the prince; he's scrum half, and he's out to get you.'

'Don't worry about me. They won't call me from the benches on this one.'

'Elliot, you imbecile!' Adam barked out various encouragements for Elliot, who was packing his things. Will looked up from his own packing to observe Adam's frown. He didn't seem happy about the holidays, and even less excited about the house match finals that afternoon. He was what was known as a 'trainbug': boys whose parents, for various reasons, did not come to collect their kids but let them travel on their own. Will piled everything into his bags, mostly unfolded. For want of a better place, he put his bright blue soccer boots into his rugby kit bag, as they were still a bit dirty. Before he left for his last lesson of the term, he noticed again the rows and rows of the number 8000 written or engraved into the wall. *If that's not a cry for help, I don't know what is! Now isn't the time to tackle Adam about it, but I'll get to the bottom of it next term.*

'Welcome, William, Adam; come in, boys, you are not too late.'

Professor Inchikov stood by the whiteboard and stroked the stray grey wisps of his beard. 'Now then, welcome one and all to your last lesson of the term! You look so agitated that I think it will be a wonder if I should get anything over to you in this state! Perhaps we'll have some questions and answers, then?'

Will saw Adam put his hand up. 'Sir, do recent discoveries in cosmology prove that there is a God?'

'Thank you Adam. The answer is possibly, though some might think that, if there were a God, he would never provide total proof to arm-twist belief; that would spoil the game, wouldn't you say?'

'Yeah, okay. Well, can philosophy give us answers on it?' Adam pushed his pencil across his desk.

'I doubt that too. I can teach you reason, though, and that might help you to ask the right questions. Have any of you heard of the Kalam cosmological principle?'

The boys all looked blank.

'I am not surprised, though I dare say you all know how to march in formation at your soldier games! Really, I don't know what they teach you in these schools.'

He approached the whiteboard and wrote on it 'John Philoponus of Alexandria' and 'Al-Ghazali'.

'This piece of philosophical and mathematical deduction was first used by Philoponus. He was a Christian in the fifth century. The second man carried it forward some centuries later.

'The Kalam principle has three parts: first, whatever begins to exist has a cause; second, the universe began to exist; and third, therefore, the universe has a cause.'

While the professor was still writing these on the board, Adam spoke. 'But I thought everyone believed in an eternal universe at that time?'

'Yes, everyone except Jews, Christians and – a century or two later – Muslims, and, before general relativity, few scientists would have talked about Kalam but –' he spun round '– here we are at the start of the century, and Einstein might have done that one thing he didn't want to do; namely give the theists big smiles all over their faces.'

'But I can't imagine the premise goes unchallenged?' Adam said.

'Of course not; that's how people make a living. But just how high will you put the bar for proof?'

'So why couldn't there have been nothing before the beginning?' Adam asked.

'Well, now we are into philosophy, but it is not complicated. "Nothing" might be a misnomer. You must understand the concept of nothingness, for to say that something came from nothing is really worse than magic. In the case of a rabbit coming from a hat, at least you have a hat – and a magician, for that matter!'

'So, science now proves that time had a beginning?' Will said.

'Yes, I suppose so; both laws of thermodynamics would suggest such, but the past could not be eternal in any event; philosophically, perhaps, but mathematically it would be an absurdity: it would demand an infinite number of past events, and how could that be?'

'But how can God be eternal, then?' Will said.

'Aha, you move me on apace, Will, but for the sake of this class, we still must call him "the first cause", not God, for that would be politically incorrect. The first cause, the thing that made it happen, must, by necessity, exist outside space and time; it must exist in an eternal state, it must *not* consist of matter as we understand it, it must itself be causeless, and it must possess enormous creative power to act according to a free will.'

'Pah, this is just special pleading for God! You defeat yourself by your own argument,' Adam said. 'Everything has to have a cause – what about your first cause, then? Who made God, eh?' Will discerned a genuine hint of disappointment in Adam's voice and eyes.

The professor held up his hands slightly. 'I can forgive this in you: you are young; but I must say that I did read of two eminent scientists saying exactly the same thing, and for them it is inexcusable folly. The first premise of Kalam is that whatever "begins" to exist must have a cause; the first cause of space, and therefore of time, must, by necessity, exist eternally to have been that cause.'

'Okay, but why does it have to be one God? Why not many?' Adam said.

The professor shrugged. 'Kalam cannot tell you that, although another piece of scientific philosophy called Ockham's Razor says that you should never multiply a cause beyond that which is necessary for the effect. In this instant, a single cause, or creator, is sufficient for the effect – but of course you are welcome to draw your own conclusions.'

'But it could be an impersonal, unconscious force, like a New Age deity?' Adam said.

'No – think about it. For one thing, a pantheist deity cannot be the first cause because it exists as a part of their conception of creation. That's fine as an argument in an eternal universe, but not in a universe that had a beginning. Can you see that? The first cause therefore must be personal.'

'How?' Adam asked.

'There are explanations; they're quite simple. One's scientific; the other's personal.' He walked across the room and raised the window facing the quadrangle, letting in a fresh flush of warm spring air.

'If you ask me "Why is the window open?" I could give you a scientific explanation about the laws of gravity and friction. I could talk about the use of weights and sash cords and such things – that is a valid explanation, is it not? But there is also a personal explanation: that I opened the window to let in some air, because someone on the front row passed wind!'

The boys laughed, and the professor smiled and scratched his beard. 'Now then, because science cannot take us beyond the first state of the universe, the explanation has to be personal. The other reason is something I have already alluded to: the cause must be immaterial, that is, it must not be a physical reality, and there are only two things that we know of like that. One is numbers, or mathematical entities – but, of course, we know that abstract entities cannot create things; so the other is the only probable conclusion.'

'And what is that?' Adam drew to the edge of his chair, his mouth slightly ajar.

'Some sort of unembodied mind, of course.'

'God?' Adam whispered, his face draining of colour.

'Call it what you wish; my job is to teach you to reason, seeing that no one else seems to have bothered.'

'A personal God?' Adam repeated, slumping back in his chair as if winded.

'Nothing is more probable. His personality you will have to discover yourselves. Our time will be gone soon, and I see one or two of you already anticipating your freedom from my presence.'

Will glanced pensively toward his roommate. *Poor Adam looks so sad, so lost.*

'Whoa, they don't mind spending a bob on their motors!' Will and Clarkson were on their way to the playing field for the house match finals. Flash cars were already arriving, and parents were setting up their picnics along the bank that flanked the first XV pitch. Champagne corks popped and friendships were renewed as they mingled and talked of business in the city and all that they had achieved. The wives dutifully passed around the smoked salmon sandwiches from the backs of their Range Rovers, and bemoaned the price of food, school fees and skiing holidays. Many of the older generation complained about how school standards were slipping and how much 'new money' was in evidence, while others, less truculent, were just glad that their kids were in – for that was the big thing: just to be there, on the inside, invited to the party in order to at least have a chance of getting on in life. It wasn't hard to spot Will's parents' Ford Mondeo, and he took Clarkson to meet them. Hannah had come too. She squeezed his hand, 'Your big match! How do you feel?'

'The house has done well to get this far, but don't expect me to make a burk of myself again – I'm just on the subs bench today.' At the sound of the whistle, Will gave them a quick nod and sprinted off to join the team on the bench.

The teams were evenly matched, and Pitt's team worked hard to harass St Alban's. The prince was their scrum half and he won every scrum and line-out he served. The crowds chanted and sang traditional songs, and the ball went back and forth, in and out of touch. Dundas broke their line early on with a stunning solo run down the left wing. Brummell tucked the ball over from the corner to hysterical stamping and deep-throated roars.

The prince frequently disputed the decisions made by the team captain. Pitt never backed down although their fragmentary team spirit was evident for Dundas to exploit. The first XV props, Grenville and Canning, drove the scrum for Dundas but it was clear to Will that their hooker was limping badly just before half-time. At half-time Dundas said to Will, 'He's sprained it, Houston, you'll have to step in.'

Will's throat was dry. 'Yes, Dundas.'

'Now, I know you can do this – I've seen you.' Dundas wiped the mud and sweat from his right cheek. 'Dig in and get us that ball from the ruck, eh?'

Will nodded and when the whistle blew, he forced his trembling legs to jog after the others. *Come on, come on now. Don't let the guys down.* Grenville's shovel-like hand slapped his back and ruffled his hair. 'You'll be all right – just stick close to me.'

After two minutes' play, a scrum was called. The prince stood with the ball as they went down. 'Hello, Houston. I've been looking for you – unfinished business.' Will did not reply but stretched his arms around the props' mighty shoulders, and they went down with their opponents, creating a dense thud. Will recognized both the other props as the Dragoons Clarendon and Tarleton who had held him for the bogwash and roughed him up at the boxing match. Their faces, at first all smiles, quickly turned as solemn as stone when they went down into the scrum. Inside there was heaving, puffing, mud, saliva, all suffused by the smell of dank, dirty and sweaty sports gear. The opposing hooker had not shaved and his bristly cheeks ground their filth into Will's face. The second rows dug their feet in as the ball was tossed in. Then came the tremendous surge and, as the titans routed each other, all that energy, all that heavy mass, now seemed to pivot on Will's own shoulders. The prince spun the ball, and the other hooker neatly heeled it back.

The second row lingered with the ball as they tried to maintain their footing against the Grenville and Canning thrust. Will saw his chance and brought his whole body forward. Held up only by the props, he slithered his legs right inside the other pack and grabbed the ball with both feet. The prince shouted at the others, but, though they kicked and scraped, Will dragged the ball back into his own side. Dundas soon had it out down the line to Brummell, who did a drop goal. As the crowds went wild, Brummell shook Will's hand. 'Nice – but watch your neck in there.' Will observed the prince looking on and taking counsel with his Dragoons.

There were more tries on each side. St Alban's were two points behind as the second half rolled on to a close. Will saw the pressure on Dundas' face, trying to brave the last plays for the house's sake but knowing Aiden's would win. Will looked for another opportunity in the scrum. He read the prince's smile as nothing more than that of a gloating winner. The scrum went down; the ball came in and, again, lingered with the second row. Will lost no time in craning his body forward and grabbing the ball between his feet – but then it happened: the Dragoons closed ranks and sandwiched Will's hips between their thighs.

'Come on, Houston, let's have the ball,' Dundas shouted.

'Can't – stuck,' he spluttered, his head crushed forward onto his chest.

It was now that the Dragoons started, as one man, to collapse the scrum by taking the weight from their legs.

'Aargh, aargh, my neck!' Will screamed, as it was forced to bend further. 'Help me! Hel – !'

He could see the prince peering in at his crumpling mass of flesh. He was smiling.

Will could not even call out. He had to shut his eyes to prevent them bulging out of their sockets. He desperately tried to twist his head any way other than the way it was going.

He heard Dundas' voice shouting, 'Quick, blast it, push or he'll be killed!' But Grenville and Canning had their work cut out just to hold up what was left; they were trembling and hissing like engines fit to burst. Suddenly, like a rush of charging bulls, the scrum, now powered by some of the centres, such as Brummell, joined Dundas in shunting the scrum forward until Will got his body back, and the other team were literally under their feet.

For a minute Will lay still on the ground. 'Let's have a look at you,' Mr Gibbs, the referee, said, almost compassionately.

He examined Will's eyes. 'Survival of the fittest isn't just a nice idea, lad! How many fingers am I holding up?'

'One, sir,' Will said. *I think.*

'Think you can play on?'

'Yes, sir.'

'Well, if you wish – though it's hardly worth risking your health with so little time left.'

There was just one minute left, with very little hope indeed for Alban's. Pitt's team had them pinned down near their own touchline as the seconds ticked quickly by. Brummell, chancing all, punted the ball skywards and charged it. Will was close behind, and the pair of them tore through the enemy line as the ball plummeted down, bouncing favourably and now moving fast to the halfway line.

'Who's with me?' Brummell screamed at the top of his voice. 'Who's with me?'

'I'm right behind you,' Will shouted.

'Let's do this,' Brummell shouted back, as the ball jumped and he reached out his hand to take it. It was a bounce in a million, and in that split second it looked as if Brummell had done it. Will felt the surge of disbelief and utter thrill combined: they would make it, they would charge like cavalry together and win the day!

Thud. Crunch. Clarendon and Tarleton took Brummel out from the side a split second before he could bring the ball back in. He went down with both of them covering his body, ploughing a slimy furrow of groans in the mud. As Will came up, the prince was also descending on Brummell, letting the full weight of his elbows crush Brummell's ankle.

There was a snapping sound, like broken celery. Brummell let out a wail of agony as the other two went for the ball. Will arrived to hear the prince talking in a low voice: 'That, Brummell, is a little payback for going against me and ours in regards to Mr Houston – or did you think I didn't notice?' He left off to chase the ball as Will skidded in on his knees. 'Stop play! He's hurt! Stop the play!'

And then turning to Brummell: 'I heard what he said – it was deliberate! We've got to tell –'

Brummel grabbed Will's top. 'No one, *no one* must know, d'you hear? Just mind your own business. Aargh!' He curled up, clutching his foot, his golden kicking foot.

'But why? What on earth would make you –'

'I'm keeping in the game,' Brummell muttered between clenched teeth.

'But you can't play like this!'

'Not this game! Who cares about rugby, you idiot!'

Gibbs, Pitt and Dundas arrived, and Will was pushed away. Brummell, true to his word, said nothing about what Coburg had done. Gibbs had awarded a kick to St Alban's, but was all for calling the game off. 'There's eleven seconds left; let's just call it a day, eh, men?'

Dundas covered his mouth at the sight of his friend. Brummell said to him, 'You could get a kick over from here.'

'Don't be stupid! You could barely do that on a good day, and I'm certainly not going to attempt the impossible in front of the school and the parents.'

'Get Houston to do it, then,' said Brummell, as the stretcher arrived.

'What! He's hardly got a ball over in any match I've seen.'

Brummell grabbed Dundas' sleeve. 'Give it to him!' He gritted his teeth. 'Please, just give it to him.'

Dundas looked at him steadily for a moment, then at the crowd, then at Will and finally back at Brummell. Dundas shook his head and smiled. 'I must be mad, I must be flippin' mad!'

Dundas turned to Will as Brummell was placed on the stretcher. 'You just toe it, Houston, d'you hear? Toe it square on, with everything you've got.'

'I can't do that!' Will said in panic. 'You saw how I screwed up at the house trials.'

'Listen, Houston,' Dundas said, 'no one expects a miracle! Just do your best, there's a good man.'

'No, you don't understand: I can't do it with these boots,' Will explained.

Dundas' face dropped. 'No, you're not suggesting –'

'I can't kick in these! I'm not used to them, even now; you know that.'

'Houston, I will not have any man from St Alban's walking out in front of them all with football boots on!'

Brummell spoke one last time as he was carried off: 'He's right.' Dundas and Will looked at him as Brummell continued, 'He could never kick with them – give him his own stupid boots if you want a chance.'

Gibbs came back from the line. 'Okay, Dundas, are we blowing the whistle on this or not?'

Dundas looked at Will. 'Okay, then, but you'd better make this worth our while, because otherwise we'll be a laughing stock for years to come.' Will grinned and sprinted back to the subs bench to get his football boots out from his kit bag. He fumbled with the laces but soon he was running back out into centre field, hands trembling like a drunk. No one seemed to notice until a small ginger-haired boy shouted, 'Eyup, the comp lad's got his footy boots on!' Clarkson was nearby and thumped the boy hard. Will ran past the prince, who spat at him. 'Filthy little pleb! What on earth are you trying to prove?'

Will didn't look up.

He paced three steps back from the ball and looked down the pitch. The posts. The team. Dundas. The crowd. *What am I trying to prove?* The ball. Ten foot of ground. The crowd. *God help me. Just want to do this for my captain and the house. Mostly anyway. Breathe, one, two, three.*

The crowd fell silent; only the sound of the birds could be heard now above the thumping of his heart. He started forward and heard Gibbs clicking the stopwatch: one pace, two paces, head down, the ball, the blue boot, the ball, thump, it's flying, but no, it's too low, surely, not again?

But he was wrong this time, and if an error in trajectory was made, it would be all to his advantage now as, at this great distance, a low trajectory was essential. He thought he heard the whole field breathe in as his heart pounded in his chest, while the ball flew and spun and approached the post. The crowd started their usual, 'YYYYEEEESSSSSSSSSSS!' But no.

'It's too far to the left,' he said out loud, clutching his temples – and it was; it glanced the right post but, by some miracle, still dropped over! The crowd erupted in cheers, but Will didn't move. 'No, no, I don't believe it!' Tears rolled down his face.

Dundas was quickly at his elbow. 'Oh, I do, Houston! I blooming well do, and I'll frame those blessed boots above the top table, I will!' Dundas broke into a great roar of ecstasy, and, for the second time that term, Will was hoisted high on the shoulders of the boys of St Alban's and returned to the stand in a triumphal procession. As the schoolboys swarmed onto the pitch, no other boys save those from St Alban's were allowed near the team.

Will's parents were there with Hannah to see the presentation, and soon after Dundas had been awarded the house cup, he made Will take one handle and lift it up high with him. Will did his best to direct the applause to the rest of the team, particularly to Canning and Grenville, who had both sustained neck injuries in the process of saving his, but they pointed and shouted at him all the more. 'You're the man, Houston, you're the man!'

A special tea was given in the cricket pavilion for the winning team and their families. Brummell was there, resting up, as was his father, who loudly toasted St Alban's as the 'finest house in t'school' with champagne, or 'bubbly' as he called it, which he himself had provided for the occasion. He was a large, ebullient character who wore all the right clothes but whose accent betrayed his Lancashire roots. Will liked him very much, and he and Hannah spent some time with him, his wife and their beautiful daughter. Others, though happy to neck the Moët & Chandon, were less pleased to associate with 'the nuevos', as they were called, even complaining amongst themselves that it was not Bollinger's. Sidmouth, invited as a prefect, though not a player, talked to Will's parents, though showing on every possible occasion that he would rather be somewhere else. His lofty indifference made Will's mother speak all the more to fill in the pauses. And later, before the speeches began, Will overheard Sidmouth say to someone else, 'It's not that they won't stop talking – more that they won't allow you to stop listening!' Will felt the shallow laughs that followed this comment, as did Brummell, who, sitting alone in a corner, gazed across the pitch crunching his jaw.

Will took a chair near him. 'Thanks for earlier.'

'Oh, it's okay – I knew you had it in you. It was some kick.'

'How's your ankle?'

Brummell looked out the window again. 'It's the end of the rugby season; it's my last year – what does it matter? It's probably bust. Dad's taking me to A & E later.'

They talked about what Brummell would do when he left. His grades were probably not high enough for Oxford or Cambridge, unlike most of the Dragoons, but he hoped to make it in the rugby team. 'They can't resist the golden foot, Houston,' he said, patting the ice packs. Will got up to go and Brummell, still looking at his foot, said, 'Don't worry about Sidmouth – he's a non-entity. Just be your own man.' Will wanted to say, 'What, like you?', but he hadn't the heart; besides, Brummell wasn't stupid, whatever else he was.

The Easter holidays were a very welcome break from the tensions of that term. Will split his time between working with his dad on the house and tripping out with Hannah and her brother, Richard. One day they went climbing in Borrowdale; another day they rode on the fells above Lorton; and a third day they kayaked along the swollen river Cocker that ran through their land. But there was an unending demand for menial labour at the barns and money to earn. Both Richard and Will were saving up for motorbikes, so they spent as much time as they could at the site. The planning was through, the building regulations approved, and the soft strip of timbers complete. Will's dad, having spent years at the office-end of property development, was now loving the nitty-gritty of site work – double wrapping the old asbestos corrugated roofing sheets, removing the two-hundred year old oak roof perlins. High on the scaffold, he, Rick and Will worked together building the wall heads and labouring for Uncle George's mates, who did the first-fix joinery. The rough-sawn joists were tremendously heavy, but Will relished showing his dad how much he could lift. He and Rick were also allowed to tighten the bolts on the roof timbers, which meant some hairy balancing nearly ten metres above the ground on a single scaffolding plank. 'Don't tell your mother' became a regular phrase.

On some evenings, Will pored over the plans with his dad. They talked of different ways to create greater space, fewer passageways and a greater flow of light. Will loved to look at the little square on the plan which represented his new room. He dreamed about it: where he would put his bed and desk, where his stereo would go, the view he'd have. He wondered whether he'd ever live there one day with Hannah and raise a family among the hills. As he looked at the electrical diagrams and waste-management systems, he was also constantly reminded how much thought and design were involved in creating a relatively basic place to live. More than ever, Mr Hill's and Mr John's words came back to him. Things he had never noticed before, like garden birds, became things to look at, sometimes for minutes at a time. Had he never realized how beautiful they were? Perhaps he was getting new eyes after all?

Rick and Will received their pay on Friday afternoons and Will, who had promised Hannah a romantic day to make up for his absence, took her for an afternoon and evening in Carlisle one Saturday. She drove, but he paid for the fuel and the dinner at the suave Pizza Express. They visited the cathedral, and Will got an old war veteran called Joe, who was a steward there, to show them the dinosaurs on the tomb. At first, Joe did not know what Will meant, but he showed them the bishop's tomb which was under a heavy rug in the choir. There, sure enough, were the dinosaurs, with tails aloft, exactly as Mr John had said. Will proudly pointed out these details to Hannah and some passing tourists. He tried to explain what it all signified, and they smiled and nodded sympathetically. Hannah, however, was thrilled and made Will stand there while she photographed him with his mobile phone. 'Come on Indiana Jones, pose a bit for your Invisible College friends, and then let's hurry or we'll miss the theatre.'

They then hurried through the shopping precincts to the Sands Centre, where they had mid-row seats for *Les Misérables*. They drove home talking about what they would do at half-term and listening to Van Morrison on Radio Two.

Hannah dropped him off at the farm, and Will found his grandfather tying flies for the forthcoming sea-trout season. It reminded him of Father Bede, and when Will asked his grandfather about him the old man said, 'Nice enough fellow – ties a mean fly, and's a cunning fisherman.'

'Do you know him well?'

'No – just a bit of fishing and shooting. Used to have a great little bitch of a pointer – would send Nelson into raptures, eh, boy!' He patted the terrier's head. 'Yes, nice enough fellow, though I wouldn't show him your eggs, that is; I wouldn't trust him.'

'Grandpa?'

'Well, I never trusted any of those SOE boys – they're shifty.' After more questions, the old man explained about the Special

Operations Executive in World War II: their espionage training, their silent killing, but also some of their great successes, like the heroes of Telemark. 'Don't get me wrong, lad: we all learnt and saw things we wished we hadn't, but some lads always gave you the impression that they didn't want to unlearn them after the War. Bede's one of those. Oh, by the way, a parcel came for you this afternoon. It's on the stairs.'

Will took the parcel up to his room and, sitting on his half-packed case, he opened it. His hands retracted momentarily and he stopped breathing; the word 'Autopsy' was in thick type in the right-hand corner. It was the report from his Uncle Phil in London. Much of it confused him greatly; and what didn't made him sick.

14

GAME'S AFOOT

Hannah drove Will back to school the following Sunday evening. They dropped the autopsy report off at Mr John's and stayed there for a cup of tea. Having had his room searched once, Will did not feel it safe to leave the report in St Alban's. Father George was delighted to meet Hannah and monopolized her conversation, which left Will to discuss the details of the report with Mr John.

'There's not even a specific time for death: 9 p.m. till 8 a.m. is eleven hours,' Will said.

'Oh, yes, well,' Mr John said, poring over the third page, 'it's only pathologists in crime novels and on TV who can pinpoint the hour. No matter; more significant is the fact that there are no other signs of bruising or struggle mentioned.'

'And you thought there would be?'

'Yes; I would have thought it almost impossible to murder someone without leaving some sign of force on the victim. Anyway, let me see, page four: contents of stomach, blah, blah, blah, pocket contents, card with "Ignis Sacer" written on it – hmm, curious; look into that, will you? And page five, pictures … oh!' Mr John slammed the book shut and took a deep breath. 'Look, I'll go through these later and we'll discuss it on Friday.'

'You mean the Invisible College is back on?'

'Well, Grendel's not sensed anything suspicious over the last few weeks, and, anyway, what are we hiding from? If you lot are still interested, we could have it on Saturday afternoons instead; the nights are too light for sneaking around now anyway.'

They also agreed to invite Keats, but Mr John was quite adamant that now, more than ever, they needed to keep their cards close. 'Bring him up to speed with what we've covered but apart from that, trust nobody with what you know. Many of those monks and teachers were themselves prefects in the school, and there is no reason to suppose that the Druids do not select some of their number from among the schoolboys themselves.'

Before they left, Will and Hannah went for a last walk along the cove. She was still worried about his obsession with Percival's death and kept glancing anxiously at him.

'You know my mind babe, from what I can see, nothing in the autopsy suggests anything other than a troubled boy driven by school bullying and conspiracy theories to a grisly end.'

'Yeah, but Mr John says...'

'Mr John!' She exclaimed, dropping his hand and turning to face him. 'He doesn't exactly look like a man at peace with himself. I mean, I'm glad he's giving you all this information about science, but involving you in all this other stuff is just unhealthy. The last boy he was close to topped himself and frankly, sweetheart, I'm worried.'

Will tried once more to fob her off with one of his cute looks and a cheeky kiss, but her words struck home. *Perhaps she is right; but what about the date of Percival's death? Was that just a coincidence? And then, what of the dog? A little more than school politics.*

Later that afternoon they stopped at Arthur's shed as they passed the main gates. The old gardener was overjoyed to be remembered by her and equally happy with the present of biscuits and tea bags – 'to replace the ones Will has when he calls,' she explained.

Old Arthur chuckled, finished washing his hands and speaking in his broad dialect jovially announced, 'Young 'ens is welcome anytime at my laal spot, Miss Hannah, especially your young fella.'

As they drove past the priory, Will noticed the matron in the monastery garden talking to three monks. Hannah dropped Will off at St Alban's, staying to talk with his friends for a few minutes before leaving. He waved her goodbye amidst the teasing from the upper windows.

Will received his house colours for rugby that evening at dinner. This was a navy tie with the thin yellow stripes of St Alban's: quite ugly, really, but not to Will. Adam seemed as glum as ever, perhaps even more so at the news that his own father had agreed, for a large fee, to speak at the headmaster's lecture on Midsummer's Eve. The lecture, attended by the boys, the teachers, parents and members of the public, was the supreme display of the school's academic prowess. One or two had been televised, and this one probably would be too: a thought that made Adam even more disconsolate.

'Nice.' Will pointed at a new mini-fridge Adam had placed near his bed. 'For milk or beer? And what's with the padlock?'

'Mind your own business.'

Lessons were as usual, and Will did his best to concentrate, though all the time he was aware that any one of his teachers might have been complicit in a murder, or at least in part of the school's best-kept secret.

Saturday came soon enough and the Invisible College, now including Keats, took their packed lunches from the kitchen, and headed for the beach. This was not unusual for a hot spring day; many other boys were doing the same thing, as the area between the circle and the northern cliffs was within bounds. Will led the others to the rocks under the circle, and, when they were sure they were not being observed, he scrambled up the far side and walked to the cove. Mr John was in his small ribbed inflatable, chugging back from a yacht now anchored in the bay. A fire was lit on the beach, and Father George sat with Grendel under an umbrella, handkerchief on his head and trouser-legs rolled up, his feet bare and half-buried in the warm sand. He was introduced to Keats and motioned that they should sit. 'My, boys, this is the life, what? Blazing hot spring weather – makes a man forget it was ever winter at all!'

Ben grabbed a nearby stick and began toasting his cheese sand-wiches on the coals. The others joined in.

'Is that Mr John's yacht?' Will asked.

'One day, perhaps it will be. George seems to have lost his taste for the sea these days. The *Argonaut* is a family treasure. We sailed right up to Scotland in her when the two were boys. John's taken it a lot further recently, of course.'

'Where?' Clarkson asked.

'Oh, Greece, Alexandria and such like.'

'Egypt? He went all the way down there?' Will said.

'Oh dear, I wasn't supposed to tell anyone.' The old man looked down at his feet. 'See here, not a word to anyone, all right? His work there is very hush-hush and all that.' The boys agreed, and when Mr John did come, bringing fresh mussels, they had other things to think about. The mussels were boiled up in a pan of milk and wild garlic. Will put the first one in his mouth while they looked on. 'Hot, but hmm, nice.' The other boys ate them – all except Elliot and Thornton, who were suspicious of seafood.

After lunch Mr John explained to Keats all about the Invisi-ble College, concluding, 'So, you see, we follow in their spirit of independence, not swallowing everything that the establishment forces on us; in fact, the more they force it, the more we hold it to scrutiny, examining the history of scientific endeavour through the lives and creed of the men who gave it.'

Keats pushed the rims of his round glasses further onto the bridge of his slender nose. He nodded and smiled, the pinks of his cheeks telling Will that their newest member was engaged.

'All right then lads, let us start today with the founder of modern computing. Charles Babbage was born in 1791, the first of four children, though two of his brothers died in infancy. Charles survived childhood illness and showed great promise in mathematics, to the point that he was sent to Trinity College, Cambridge, at the age of nineteen. It was here that he pored over maths books, even some in French!' Mr John raised an eyebrow.

'French? What was wrong with that?' Keats asked.

'Oh, the Napoleonic Wars were in full swing, and it was considered very un-PC, you know – unpatriotic. But Charles was shocked that his tutors knew none of the breakthroughs happening across the Channel in France and Germany by men like Blaise Pascal and Gottfried Leibniz. And so, forming the Analytical Society in 1812, Babbage teamed up with the outstanding astronomer John Herschel, another devout Christian and mathematician, and George Peacock, to flout the "lemming style" intellectual blockade of foreign texts, and to yoke their hungry minds with the leading brains of Europe. They may have been labelled "liberals", but these men went on to be very influential in the reformation of maths, teaching in English universities, though Babbage's reputation led to him being refused by the Church of England as a minister! On balance, that was probably a good thing for us.'

'Yes,' Father George added with a knowing look, 'and you take note, John: when God closes one door, another will open.'

Mr John looked up from his notes, gave a resigned smile, nodded and carried on. 'Babbage was elected a member of the Royal Society at the age of 26, and though he made contributions to algebra and the theory of functions, it was his great desire to put maths to use: to make it work and have practical applications.

And so it was during this period that he began to work on his "analytical machine".

'A computer?' Keats asked, sitting up from a reclining position on the pebbles.

'Of sorts, yes. Of course, various calculating machines had been used throughout history, from the Chinese abacus, Napier's bones and machines by Pascal and Leibniz; but Babbage took them to a new dimension. They were now smaller and could calculate and print twenty-digit calculations and mathematical tables. The Society was impressed, and the Government enthusiastically funded another larger, more complex version, which he called a "difference engine".

'Groovy! He must have been chuffed to get Government funding,' Clarkson said.

'Well, yes and no. Of course, the potential commercial benefits for Britain were enormous, but insufficient funding and red tape hampered the development to the point that Babbage put his own money into his new four-part "analytical engine", which turned out, in design and essential components, to be a model of our modern computer.'

'What, it had RAM and processors?' Clarkson said, trying to get a laugh.

'Yes, of a kind; there was the "store", i.e. the memory, then there was the "mill", or the processor; then the gears and levers that transferred the data from the processor to the memory store, where up to a thousand numbers with fifty digits each could be stored!'

'Wow! That sounds better than my dad's old IBM!' Adam said.

'Well, perhaps not; but just think of it: fifty thousand digits, in the reign of George IV! But the project was dogged by financial and manufacturing problems; it was not only extremely expensive to build but also, as time showed, it was impossible for the engineers of the day to meet the accuracy required.'

'Poor bloke,' Elliot said.

'Yes – a man a century ahead of his time. He was heartily disappointed, and it was only when his notebooks were discovered in 1937 that people realized that his designs were in fact totally sound. With the help of the technology of the 1940s, they became a reality. Not only that, but it now also appears that Babbage conceived how software programs should be written.'

'What a shame, sir,' Will said, throwing a pebble into the gently lapping sea. 'I mean, it sounds like quite an unfulfilled life.'

'No, not at all. I've only told you one part of what he is remembered for. One thing that might interest us, as we are now within the years when evolution will finally be able to emerge as pseudoscience, is that it was in this era that Babbage began to be alarmed by the lack of scientific zeal in the nation. He wrote about the "decline of Science in England", which he controversially laid at the door of the Royal Society, as only one hundred of its 650 members were then practising scientists. Now, by any standards, that's an awfully high proportion of men sitting around, detached from the real world of scientific endeavour.'

'Why's that dangerous?' Adam said.

'Well, it's just a footnote really, my own pet theory, but that's exactly the situation in the library at Alexandria in ancient times. Science became unmoored from the world of practical application and so stagnated – a little simplistic, perhaps, but a theory.'

'I think that what my son is hinting at, boys, is that idle hands are easily put to work. What did the apostle say? The Athenians lived just to discuss every new idea.'

'Yes, thank you, Father. That's it exactly. I have a clipping here from *Nature* magazine. The article is by two well-respected evolutionary scientists, Birch and Ehrlich. Listen to what they say: "Our theory of evolution has become … one which cannot be refuted by any possible observation. Every conceivable observation can be fitted into it. It is thus 'outside empirical science' but not necessarily false. No one can think of ways in which to test it.'"

'Wait a minute,' Keats said. 'Gibbs said evolution can be observed. I mean –'

Adam interrupted, 'No, Keats, I mean Jack, don't get confused. Microevolution – what some call speciation or adaptation – can be observed – you know, small, limited changes; that's not an issue here. We're talking about whether natural processes can add significant amounts of new, beneficial genetic info. This is what's needed to turn microbes into men, but it's not observed. In fact studies of speciation and adaptation indicate that these kinds of changes arise through processes that are either informationally neutral or downhill.'

'Oh, right. I see.'

Mr John continued, 'Yes, that's it, but I'm not finished yet. Here's the bit I particularly wanted you to hear. Birch and Ehrlich go on: "Ideas without basis or based on a few laboratory experiments carried out in extremely simplified systems have attained currency beyond their validity. They have become part of an evolutionary dogma accepted by most of us as part of our training." There!' he said triumphantly, looking up and tossing a stick onto the coals. 'D'you see that? "Currency beyond their validity"; you could almost sum up the last 150 years of evolutionary science under that heading, in fact I read another biologist lamenting that the supposedly essential theory of evolution has no bearing whatever on any field of science beyond its own sub-set in biology called, surprise, surprise; "Evolutionary Biology" – which probably tells you all you need to know about it.'

Will looked at Adam and saw from his furrowed brow that he did not disagree. Keats was stirred. 'Yeah, but you still said that microevolution happens. I mean, if I saw my sister off at Penrith on a south-bound train to London, and the train went round the first bend, I'd have no reason to suspect it wouldn't get to London, given enough time.'

Mr John gave an impish grin. 'But the train's not going to London; it's north-bound, going to Glasgow!'

'What do you mean?'

'Well, we probably shouldn't use the word microevolution for the misleading impression it gives. As I said before, microbe to man evolution would require an uphill process in terms of information and complexity. Observed cases of speciation and adaptation – what some refer to as microevolution – generally involve downhill changes. You can't go upstairs by walking downstairs.'

'But there are selection advantages,' Adam said.

'Certainly, but only of the order of a man who's born with one arm and can't, therefore, be handcuffed; that's a very different thing from a protozoon getting lungs, fins, feet and so on.'

'Okay, I get it: the train's going the wrong way; but back to Babbage: you say that the bulk of the scientists in the Society were sitting round, drinking sherry, chatting about new ideas. What did Babbage do?'

'Yes, it's a shame; Robert Boyle would have barely recognized what he and his friends started all those years before. But Babbage didn't sit around bemoaning the good old days, he actually went on to be a founding member of the British Association for the Advancement of Science in 1831 and the Royal Statistical Society in 1834. Oh, and I forgot to mention that he had also helped found the Royal Astronomical Society in 1820.'

'Not a guy to sit around! I expect that kept him busy.' Clarkson said.

'Certainly – that and other things. You see, he also compiled the risk tables for insurance companies, reformed the modern postal system, and designed a stunning array of inventions to help medicine, mining, railways, architecture, bridge construction and the manufacturing industry. He also, with those financial struggles fresh in his mind, went on to be a great champion of the need for "operations research", writing a book on the subject and constantly petitioning the Government to increase funding for scientific research. All the while he was a family man too; he married Georgiana at 23, and they had eight children, though only three of them survived to adulthood. He was tragically widowed at only 36.'

'Poor bloke. But you say he was religious?' Will asked.

'Yes, absolutely. Listen to what his biographers say: "Charles believed that the studying of the works of nature with scientific precision was necessary and indispensable to the understanding and interpreting of their testimony of the wisdom and goodness of their Divine Author." And with that mindset he went and wrote the *Bridgewater Treatises* in 1837 "on the power, wisdom and goodness of God, as manifested in creation". Another biographer says, "Babbage came to believe that the scientific method pursued to its uttermost limit was entirely compatible with revealed religion, and he wrote the *Ninth Bridgewater Treatise* to prove the point." So there you go; a good chap and, as you say, quite a mover.'

Seeing that the heat was getting to the boys, Father George suggested a swim in the sea. At first, the boys laughed off the suggestion, not having trunks with them; but when the old man chided them, 'But good Lord, don't you wear underpants?' they soon got the idea. Clarkson led the charge and even Adam eventually went in. The water was icy cold but refreshing. They laughed and splashed each other as the sunlight reflected off the white sandy bottom. Will and Ben swam out around the *Argonaut* and dived down among the rocks along the spit. Twenty minutes later they were all back on the beach, and Mr John brought cold lemonade from the cottage in huge, bubbled glass tumblers.

Father George was lying asleep on the rug and the boys sat drying out on the rocks sipping their drinks as Mr John continued his stories.

'Well, lads, on such a hot day it seems appropriate to discuss James Joule and Lord Kelvin, the fathers of thermodynamics.'

'Thermo-whats?'

'It's the study of the transfer of energy, a very important development in science, as you will see, and one which flies in the face of evolution.'

'Oooh, sounds juicy,' Clarkson said.

'All right, here we go.' Mr John grabbed his notebook and sat forward. 'James Joule was born in 1818, the second of five children, to a wealthy Manchester brewery owner. He was home-educated to the age of fifteen, at which point he went into the family business. His father's illness meant that he had to spend more and more time at the brewery, and so he missed going to university for a formal training in science, which had been his great desire. This desire sprang chiefly from his thirst to know the God of the Bible, for, as he wrote, "It is evident that the acquaintance with the natural laws means no less than an acquaintance with the mind of God." Now –' Mr John looked up. 'Tom, tell Jack what kind of men can give us science?'

Clarkson grinned at Keats. 'Easy! They must have a "one-God" worldview, and they must believe that we're made like God.'

'Yes, thank you, Tom; but why? Anyone?'

Elliot spoke up. 'You said it was because it was only then that we would bother to look into it.'

'Exactly; as Newton says … anyone?'

'"To think God's thoughts after him", sir,' Thornton said.

'Excellent, Henry! Science was born by asking very narrow and particular questions. To do that, these narrow assumptions had to be in place first. That's it. And see young James here – not able to go to university because of family pressure, but with this sincere heart to be "acquainted with the mind of God" through scientific discovery – how could God resist such a lad, eh?'

'So what did he do?' Clarkson said.

'Well, at the age of 21, James started experimenting at his home laboratory. This led to him writing a paper entitled "*On the Production of Heat by Voltaic Electricity*". He sent it to the Royal Society a year later but it, and others subsequently submitted, failed to impress the scientific community, which was wary of amateurs and also doubted the accuracy of Joule's measurements. Oh, and also, of course, because it challenged the prevailing "Calorific theory", which stated that heat was a fluid substance. Now this particular theory was not kosher for our James – because he held that some aspects of it contradicted what the Bible said; but there you go.'

'Right, so the sherry drinkers don't dig his work. What did he do?' Adam asked.

'You're right. The Society was not in good shape; but there were three other Bible-believing Christians who saw that Joule was onto something big – and I mean big. Michael Faraday and George Stokes were two, and the third was a brilliant young physicist who, although only 23, was already Professor of Physics at Glasgow University. He was none other than William Thomson, later to be Lord Kelvin, and he saw straight away that Joule's work fitted in with the unifying pattern that was beginning to emerge in physics. With their help, Joule's paper on "The Mechanical Equivalent of Heat" was published by the Society in 1849, and he was elected to their ranks. He had been the first to demonstrate what would now be the new branch of science: thermodynamics.'

'Sorry, sir, I still don't get what it – thermowhatsits – is?' Clarkson said.

'Well, basically, Joule was showing empirically that work can be turned into heat, and vice versa. The first law of thermodynamics is that *energy can neither be created nor destroyed, but it can be changed from one form to another*. In other words, the total amount of energy, including matter, is constant. This, by the way, shows that known science indicates that universes do not create themselves – Big Bangs notwithstanding. He went on to be the first scientist to estimate the velocity of gas molecules, or the kinetic theory of gases, which was later extended by others, like the eminent mathematical physicist James Clerk Maxwell.'

'Wait,' Adam said, shivering near the fire. 'Don't tell me – he was another Bible-basher.'

'You're getting it, lad, he was, and we'll study him later. Joule also pushed for standardization in the measurement of electricity. The work on this was overseen by Maxwell and units of measurement were later called *joules* in recognition. In 1852 he started a decade's work with William Thomson – Lord Kelvin, remember – in which he was to take the humbler role of experimenter. This he did not mind, being more concerned with benefiting science with accurate results than making himself famous. It was a fruitful period for them both, and what one lacked, the other had in abundance! Tragically, Joule's wife died in 1854 after only six years of marriage, leaving him to raise their children. As Darwinism was sweeping the nation, Joule was one of only eighty-six fellows of the Royal Society who signed a declaration of confidence in the Bible's account of creation.'

'Wow, that's not many if there were 650 members!' Adam said. 'What's that – something like 15%?'

'It's 13.3%, if your figures are correct,' Father George said from under his straw hat. 'You could hardly say that Darwin was a lone crusader: 86.7% of the Royal 'sherry-drinking' society doubted the Bible even then.'

'Yes, Father, quite. Now then, let me finish with this. From the age of 54 until his death seventeen years later, Joule did little research because of declining health. Work, though, had never actually been his first priority, as he said that "after the knowledge of, and obedience to, the will of God, the next aim must be to know something of his attributes of wisdom, power and goodness as evidenced by his handiwork", and he certainly did that!'

The boys agreed, and Clarkson proposed a lemonade toast to him. Most of them then lay down on the sand, or on the pebbles. They were now partially dry, and all felt every bit alive and fresh from their swim, as a gentle sea breeze cooled the effects of the afternoon sun. Keats put his glass back on the tray. 'I'm sorry I missed the other meetings. But what about the other bloke Joule worked with – Thomson?'

'Ah, well, William Thomson is a real all-rounder. He was born in 1824, the son of a maths teacher from Belfast. His mother died when he was only six years old, and when a short time later his father got a job at Glasgow University, William and his brother James were home-tutored by him in all the recent mathematical innovations. Basically, the lads had a great head start in the maths department, and they were good at it.'

'How good?' Clarkson asked.

'Good enough for them both to get into Glasgow University when they were ten and eleven!'

'What? I couldn't even do long division by then!' Clarkson remarked.

'That's as may be, but young William went on to study the controversial work of the French mathematician Jean Baptiste Fourier. He had been applying advanced mathematics to explain how heat flowed through solid objects, though most scientists rejected his work. But this didn't put our young hero off! And so, when he was your ages, lads, he not only published two papers showing that Fourier was right, but he also started to think of using the same principles to study the flow of electricity and the motion of liquids.'

'Wow.' Thornton was sitting up, arms around knees. 'Sounds like a bit of a maverick. I like the idea of someone who thinks maths are cool for once!'

'Yes, he was. His ability, at such a young age, to recognize Fourier's work, when others refused to, is much to his credit, and it would not be the only time he did something like this, for he would also publish a paper in support of James Joule's work when he too was overlooked. William graduated from Cambridge University a few years later and took a job as head of Physics at Glasgow University at the tender age of 22. He would stay here for the next fifty-three years, even though he was offered other positions. Through his studies of the flow of electricity and the motion of liquids, William – let's call him Thomson now – established their mathematical relationship, and soon he was articulating the first two laws of thermodynamics.'

'Hang on, sir. Didn't you say that was James Joule?' Keats said.

'Yes, that's right. Joule is rightly seen as the father of thermodynamics, but William Thomson's genius was to accurately articulate the laws and establish it as a branch of science.'

'Sir, you mentioned the first law of thermodynamics earlier, and you've just said there are two laws, so what's the other one? I mean, could we understand them?' Thornton asked.

'Yes, these two laws are absolutely fundamental to the universe and, by the way, are not easy bedfellows with evolution or the Big Bang theory.'

'Oh, great, this I have got to hear!' Clarkson said.

'Right, well, as I said before, the first law of thermodynamics is that "Energy cannot be created or destroyed, only changed from one form into another". So, the total amount of energy, including matter, is constant.'

'Oh, I remember: you said the universe cannot create itself!' Clarkson said.

'Yes, precisely; the structure of the universe is one of conservation and not innovation. The second law is the law of energy decay, or increasing entropy. The universe relentlessly moves towards a state of greater disorder'.

'Like my bedroom!' Ben said, and the other boys laughed.

'Exactly! And this doesn't just relate to your bedroom. Evolutionists believe that first life arose spontaneously from a chemical soup. But even the simplest cells require information and software to work, which is encoded in their DNA. The second law of thermodynamics indicates that this and the machinery they control could never arise without an intelligent input—even given the billions of years evolutionists think the universe has been around. Can you see that?'

Will leant forward, glancing to see if Adam was still listening. 'Yes, sir, but don't evolutionists just say that thermodynamics is a branch of science created by Christians? I mean, it seems to sum up the biblical idea of a fallen world in a nutshell.'

'Thank you, Will, that's very perceptive; but remember, thermodynamics existed before the fall of Adam in some form or other, because, for example, it helped Adam digest the fruit he was allowed to eat before he was tempted. Let me put it this way: the second law of thermodynamics is not Christian fiction, it is a law accepted by everyone because it is an observable law. Why should it surprise anyone if the evidence fits the biblical account? Paul says in Romans that "all of creation groans in anticipation" for the new creation that God has begun by raising Jesus from the dead. These things are as they are because ... they are!'

'So what else did Thomson do, apart from encouraging other people?'

'Well, yes, he was quite a Barnabas, I suppose, but he was amply repaid by his own achievements. His greatest contribution to science was really that he was foremost amongst a small group of scientists who laid the foundations for modern physics. He did this by showing the intertwined nature of magnetism, electricity, heat, mechanical motion and the motion of gases. It was a significant theoretical extension of what other Christians like Faraday and Joule had done, and it laid a great foundation for others, like Clerk Maxwell, to push off from, with his work on the electromagnetic theory of light. He also worked with the other two notable Christians, Maury and Morse, in laying transatlantic telegraph cables and other cables all over the globe, for which he got a knighthood from Queen Victoria. He patented seventy inventions and was given twenty-one honorary doctorates, was president of the Royal Society, and was even made Lord Kelvin in 1892.'

'Oh yes, Kelvin – that rings a bell,' Keats said. 'Isn't that a measurement of temperature or something?'

'Yes, minus 273 degrees Celsius is 0 degrees K or kelvin, as it was Thomson – that is, Lord Kelvin – who worked out that this is the lowest possible temperature at which all particles stop moving.'

'Cool dude!' Clarkson said, angling for humour.

'Thank you, Tom. That's almost funny. Well, let's finish off by saying that he was honoured greatly in his lifetime for contributions to science and humanity, and he was buried in Westminster Abbey. In his lifetime he debated long and hard with Darwin's so-called bulldog, Huxley, over the origin of life, saying that "the commencement of life upon earth … certainly did not take place by any action of chemistry or electricity or crystalline groupings of molecules." He also said, "With regard to the origin of life … science positively affirms creative power." Another quote, a favourite of Father's, goes, "Overwhelming strong proofs of intelligent and benevolent design lie around us … The atheistic idea" – that's what he correctly called evolution – "is so nonsensical that I cannot put it into words."'

The boys laughed and chatted around the issues for a while. They pushed Mr John to go on and tell them about Faraday and Clerk Maxwell, but he would not. 'No, boys, you've heard enough for one day. Go away and double-check that I've told you the truth about these men. We'll do the others next weekend, God willing.'

As the boys were leaving, Will briefly drew Mr John to one side. 'Sir, there'll be a full moon on Thursday next week.'

His eyebrows rose. 'I see, then we shall have to make our plans.' He looked out to sea for a moment and then turned back to Will. 'I'd dearly love to speak to Ben's big brother about the fatal night, find out what he knows.'

'Perhaps sir, we could bring Ben into *the know*. I don't think his brother will speak to you.'

'Good point, see what you can do.'

Twenty minutes later Will was approaching Alban's, full of thoughts about the coming week. *Supposing we discover someone I like is a druid, what then?* His eyes caught a movement. *What's that?* The curtain in the housemaster's study. He looked discreetly from under his brows but saw nothing. *Stupid mutt, imagining things again.* But something made him look up one more time as he got closer. Back in the shadows was a spectacled face; immoveable, resolute. *It's old Bede. He's been watching all the time.*

15

MIDNIGHT IN THE CRYPT

'Yes, gentlemen, you heard me right.' The headmaster thumbed his lapels like some latter-day Victorian schoolmaster, announcing after church on Sunday the glad tidings of the prestigious speaker for the headmaster's lecture that term: 'Of course, we have sent letters to your parents. It is an enormous privilege to have Professor Rawkins among us, talking about the need to "Redefine Ethics for the Modern World"; jolly engaging subject, good exposure for you, good for the school, for us all.'

Adam sneered under his breath, 'Naïve cretinous mollusc; hasn't got a clue.'

That Sunday night Will had a terrible nightmare. He was being stalked by hooded men in black robes. Having made it to his old home in Liverpool, he banged on the door as the shadows drew upon him. Hannah opened the door on the chain and chided him for his paranoia. Alone outside, he was dragged away by six faceless reapers and was sliced open. He awoke shouting in terror, to find Adam putting something in his padlocked fridge. After he had calmed down, he questioned Adam about what he was doing; but Adam merely said, 'Mind your own business and go to sleep – and no more shouting, please.'

During prep the next day, Will went again to use the library computers. *I have to put faces to those wraiths*, he said to himself over and over again. When Ben saw him in the Great Hall, he came over with an eager expression. *Some good news perhaps.*

'Will, there you are! Listen, I did speak to my brother, and guess what he told me …'

'Not so loud, Pitt, come on, let's find a spot in the library.' They went in and were just in time to get a computer station in a secluded part of the study area. Will noticed, out of the corner of his eye, that Brothers Brendan and Reece were watching them as usual.

Ben drew his chair in close. 'We'd almost finished talking, right, when Willie just let slip that Percival had been looking forward to the summer; that they always went to France with this other family and he had been saving up for a ring for one of the daughters.'

'You mean, he was engaged?'

'Maybe – maybe it was just a lover's gift; but don't you see the significance, Will? He wasn't, like, this desperate, bullied nerd, filled with conspiracies and mentally unbalanced; he was looking forward to something, and, more importantly, he was making plans for the future, buying the gift.'

'Yes, yes, I get it; not your typical suicide guy.' Will scratched his cheek and logged onto the network. 'But everyone seemed so convinced. I mean, the police and everyone thought that he was capable of it.'

'Not surprised, are you?' Ben said, pulling his chair up to the computer. 'The other options are pretty unthinkable.'

'Well, let's think them.' He googled 'Druidic sacrifice' and soon found Iron Age 'bog bodies', human remains from peat bogs in Europe. One in particular caught his eye; it was Tollund Man. As he scanned the page, there was one word that kept cropping up, a word that he had seen before, in the autopsy report. 'Ignis Sacer,' he whispered out loud. 'Ignis Sacer or ergot was once a ritual drink in a prehistoric fertility cult akin to the Eleusinian Mystery cults of ancient Greece.'

'What does all that mean?' Ben said.

'I swear I saw this mentioned in Percival's autopsy report. There were traces of it in his stomach.' Will clicked on the Greek link. 'See here, Kykeon; the beverage consumed by participants in the ancient Greek cult of Eleusinian Mysteries, might have been based on hallucinogens from ergot.' He went back to the original article and Ben read out in a whisper the first paragraph.

'Okay, slow down, what does it say? "The body of Tollund Man was found in 1950 in a Danish peat bog, where it had been preserved since the first century BC. Tollund Man was about 40; he was stripped naked and garrotted before his body was laid to rest in the bog. Examination of his stomach contents found a wide variety of different grains, suggesting a ritual last meal. There were also traces of ergot, a highly toxic mould found on rye. If Tollund Man was the victim of ergot poisoning, 'ergotism', he would have suffered convulsions and hallucinations. It may be that this ergot-induced trance state was part of a ritual sacrifice …" Ritual sacrifice, blimey, that sounds evil.'

'Never mind that, Ben. Look at the bottom: it says about a classical historian called Diodorus Siculus reporting on the scenes of human sacrifice by the Druids. Listen to this: "When they attempt divination upon important matters they practise a strange and incredible custom, for they kill a man by a knife-stab in the region above his midriff." Oh boy …' Will's voice trailed away and his hand fell limp.

Ben put his hand over his mouth. 'Holy moley, Will, that's exactly what happened.'

'Not so loud,' Will said, seeing Brother Reece leaving his desk. 'That's not all; look here. After the sacrificial victim fell dead … "they foretell the future by the convulsions of his limbs and the pouring of his blood". This is serious – we've got to get this to Mr John fast.'

'Never mind Mr John. You've got to get to the police fast! I'm frightened.'

'I know, I know. Keep it down. At nine o'clock I'll call Mr John and we'll take it from there.' He closed the Web pages and erased the history on the browser before Brother Reece arrived.

'What's all this noise? You causing mischief again Houston?'

'No brother, just leaving.'

Will found a quiet spot in the priory graveyard, glanced about to check that no one was watching, then dialled Mr John's number with a trembling finger. *Breathe, come on, breathe.* It rang three times and then Mr John answered. Not waiting for pleasantries Will blurted out, 'Sir, we've got to talk.' He quickly shared the information in excited bursts, slightly garbled but mostly accurate.

There was a brief pause on the line then Mr John said, 'Ignis Sacer, Ergot, of course – and me an archaeologist, and I didn't put two and two together!'

'So you've heard of it, then?' Will said.

'Of course, ergot-contaminated grains have historically been blamed for poisoning humans and animals. There were epidemics from ergot-infected grain in the Middle Ages. Mind you, they also used it in medicines – headache cures, I think – and they used to give controlled doses of ergot to induce abortions and to stop maternal bleeding after childbirth.'

'But why didn't the bloke doing the autopsy pick it up?' Will said.

'Don't know; you can probably still get it in wholefood rye breads. Anyway, I doubt they were looking for a Druidic sacrificial victim; it was a hospital pathologist doing this, not a forensic one.

He was only delivering a narrow set of observations, he wasn't looking for anything behind them.'

'Oh, a bit like some modern scientists,' Will said.

'What? Oh, right – well, there's no time for digression now. We need to make a plan.'

'Go to the police?' Will said.

'Yes, certainly we must but …' Mr John hesitated. 'Let's wait till after Thursday night. We might have something more concrete in the suspect department by then; otherwise it might be me the coppers go gunning for.'

'Yes, I see; I just wish it could be sorted, that's all,' Will said.

Mr John seemed not to have heard. He talked quietly, as if to himself. 'Yes, if only we could prove who possessed that manuscript – or, more to the point, who had been possessed by it. Motive and means, that's what we need.'

'Is it true that it was written on human skin?'

'Perhaps, lad, perhaps. I felt it soon after it came out of the crypt, still rolled up, still fairly soft,' Mr John said.

'Soft, not cardboardy?'

'No, soft; they used to boil up pulverized brain to tan skins; just paste the stuff on. It does wonders.'

'Oh, gross! This whole thing just gets worse!' Will glanced left and right to check he was still alone.

'Maybe,' Mr John said, 'but whoever was responsible for that lad's death will pay – by God, they will; I owe that at least to his dad.'

'Yeah, but we're not going to take the law into our own hands, right?' Will said.

'No, certainly not – but it would be good to have something more definite to give the police, that's all.'

Will agreed. As he ended the call and put the phone back in his pocket, he noticed the gravestone. He was standing where the grass was cropped and fresh roses were arranged in a water pot at the base. 'Private Chris Nicolson, Royal Armoured Corp, Killed in Action, during Operation Iraqi Freedom, 16th January 1991.' *Must be Arthur's son,* Will thought. *Poor man, how do people survive something like that? And Percival's parents too – how do you move on?*

While he was thinking about this, he heard the rustle of material and steps on the gravel. When Will stood up, he saw to his horror the abbot over the wall in the monastery vegetable garden. Father Malthus sat alone in one corner under a mistletoe bush, with crook in hand. Will lingered for a moment to observe him, but, like a flash, the old man's eyes sprang open and his gaze shot right through Will. For a moment Will was unable to move, his feet seemed rooted into the earth, his mind whirling in inertia. Eventually the abbot closed his eyes and Will's strength returned. As he reached the graveyard gates, he trembled from head to foot, and he was glad to get back to the house.

Thursday night came horribly quickly. Ben turned up after supper on the pretence of cleaning Will's cricket gear. Adam, obviously not wanting to be outdone by their secret escapade, announced, 'I'm going to the pub, it being quiz night.'

Will looked at Ben, then said, 'Adam, I don't think that's a good idea.'

'Why, Houston, you puritan rascal, if you want to come another night and do homage to Bacchus, why don't you say? I don't mind company.'

'No, it's not that; it's just that it's a full moon tonight, and the Druids might be meeting and –'

'Oh, you're still on about that! Come off it, if they really are out there, I'd think they'll be too busy having gooey feelings to notice the pub-quiz genius coming home.'

'Yeah, that's if you make it! Last time –' Will said.

'Last time, I rested a little en route; tonight, it's not dark until nine, so I'll only get two hours to get hammered before chucking-out time, so I should be sober as a judge for the trip back. Don't fret.'

It was useless to talk further, so soon after nine o'clock, all three left: Adam went up the hill and the others went into Monks' Wood, where the remaining light cast gnarled shadows in the oak groves. The woods were still and silent, their secrets of long ages tightly kept. Will felt the displeasure of each tree, each rock. Tonight they were about dark business, and the very place seemed to come alive as the darkness crept on.

'You afraid Will?' Ben whispered, as they crouched behind a holly bush.

'Yeah. You?'

Ben nodded, his curly locks bobbing in the halflight. 'But we shouldn't back down. Besides, what harm can come to the good guys?'

Will tried to smile at his naïvety, 'Yeah, just hold that thought.'

At 9.45 p.m. Mr John texted, "In position at the Necropolis, all clear here". At 10.04 p.m., the clouds broke and the full moon made silver and black of all that lay beneath it. Will glanced over towards the priory.

'Look Ben, down there. Four figures coming across the cloister to the priory door. Game's afoot, Watson.'

'I see them.'

'They're going in, wonder why? Will's fingers twitched and fluttered. *I've got to know what they're up to.* 'Wait here,' he said to Ben, 'make sure you've got your phone on vibrate; I'm going down there.'

'What – why?' Ben said.

'A hunch, that's all.' Will scrambled down the banks, keeping to the shadows and stopping every now and then to make sure he was not being followed. Creeping low under the monastery windows, he entered the cloisters and sprinted towards the shadow under the Great East Door. He looked around again, panting through flared nostrils, his heart thumping so fiercely it was almost jumping out of his chest. *Nothing – good.* He opened the heavy iron door latch without making a sound and crept in. The curtain was drawn across the entrance, and in the darkness Will listened and weighed his options. *No sound, nothing at all – so where are they?* He sneaked a look through the crack between the curtains. *Four of them should be making at least some kind of sound. This isn't good.* He listened harder, though it was difficult to trust his ears above the thumping of his heart. *Nothing. They've vanished.*

Then his eye caught sight of the distant crypt door. It was open, though no light was on. *Of course, the crypt. It would have to be the one place I'd rather not go! I wish I'd brought Pitt now. Breathe lad, breathe. One. Two. Three.*

Will slipped through the curtains and, keeping low, crept among the pews and traversed the nave. Still no sound, no movement. He double-checked all the shadows: each one for a face, an arm, a weapon. He wiped his eyes with sweaty hands; the adrenaline was almost overwhelming. *Come on, focus, breathe.* He moved out to the wall, listened at the small doorway: nothing, just the beckoning silence. He must go down, of course he must; where else would any secrets be?

The steps went straight down for about three metres, then they turned to the left. There was no light now, just blackness all around him. He dare not even use his phone as a light; suppose he gave himself away? He lingered at what appeared to be the bottom. He felt that nothing was worth this, nothing at all; he wanted to go back. It was like some horrible Greek mythic place. He battled in his mind with minotaurs and Medusas that came out of the darkness at him. *Stop it, stop it, get control of yourself, boy.*

He reached behind for the wall, but it had gone. In his panic he was about to get his phone when he suddenly saw a light far down the crypt. He dropped to a crouch. The air was noticeably cooler and damp down here, just as he imagined the underworld should be.

The faint light barely lit up the crypt, but it was enough to give him his bearings. *Whoa, the place is massive, must be larger than the priory above even. Goes on further than I can see anyway. Need a plan, a plan. Breathe. Let's go.* Everywhere there were round sandstone arches partitioning the spaces into little rooms, chapels, alcoves, tombs, sarcophagi. These were not all obvious at first, but as Will crept towards the light at the far end, he passed them, hardly daring to take his eyes from his target. Halfway along, he started to hear muffled voices, low and reverent. *One sounds like a woman. Is this it? Is this the Druids' meeting?* He approached the last arch. *Okay, okay, this is it, slowly, slowly, now.* He crouched and peered around the corner, and there, to his astonishment, caught the glimpse of one hooded face. *It's Matron!* She was standing above three kneeling figures, all similarly hooded but with their backs to him. She handed them scrolls from an alcove and turned away from them to do something that he could not see. There was the noise of moving stone, and then the three appeared to be getting ready to leave. Will sank back into the alcove behind him and hoped they would pass without stopping. He heard Matron's voice again, this time so close that he could hear her lips open: 'Come, the others will be waiting at the sacred grove.'

They came out and turned past Will. He held his breath and closed his eyes. He felt the movement in the air, smelt them: *tobacco and incense – Kentigern.* The hooded figures kept walking, and darkness was soon restored.

Will did not move for a minute as he tried to process his thoughts. She's a priestess, he thought, possibly in charge. *Okay, think now. They have scrolls, they get them here, they're kept here; they come at night, because the scrolls are a secret; they're a secret because what they contain is incriminating. There are more than four of them; there are others, they are meeting at the grove … the grove – Pitt! I must warn him!* He texted, "Pitt, keep low, many druids coming, matron and Kentigern have taken three scrolls from crypt, stay low." He copied the message to Mr John, who replied a minute later, "Meet you at woods, hurry." There was no reply from Ben, though.

By now Will was already at the top of the crypt steps and surveying the priory. The hooded figures had gone; all was still. He retraced his steps up the hill, where now the light of a bonfire could be seen reflecting in the tree canopies.

The steep sides of Monks' Wood had been carefully terraced over the ages. The first two terraces were graveyards, the third was expansive and lawn-like, and this one was where the small temple-style gazebo was located. But it was the fourth, the highest and most unvisited terrace, where Will saw flames rising as he approached his original hiding place.

Ben wasn't there. *Perhaps he's gone to the final terrace to get closer.* Will moved with speed up through the undergrowth. *Perhaps he's been discovered – or taken!* Will's heart pounded. *He shouldn't have gone without me.*

Will could now hear the chanting of many voices. He scrambled up the final bank under the cover of some holly trees. The dead leaves crackled, but for once it did not matter; the noise of the chanting was getting much louder. He reached the terrace about fifty metres from the fire, and he now saw twenty or so figures standing in a circle. There was no sign of Ben, so he climbed an oak tree to get a better view. The fire threw elongated shadows of the hooded figures far out into the woods and up the trees. There was still no sign of Ben. Where was he? The more Will looked towards the fire, the more his night vision went, but there was no sign, no movement; only the rhythm of the guttural chanting and the shadows – everywhere the shadows.

The chanting faded and a tall figure stepped towards the fire, holding out a flapping bird; it was a chicken. Another approached with a knife. *It's a woman, Matron perhaps – yes, there was her face.* She dug the knife in to the bird, and the tall man poured some of its blood onto the ground and then laid it down. Another tall figure came forward slowly. The poor bird convulsed and jumped, then fell onto its side and scraped its way round in a circle for a few moments while the others looked on. When it stopped, the second tall figure stooped down, produced another knife – it's upwardly curving blade glinted in the fire. A fish-gutting knife. Will had seen that before – on Father Bede's desk with his fly gear. *It's him all right; see the way he hunches, the broad forehead shining in the light, the rimmed spectacles – yes, he's the Augur.* Bede presented something to the other two: the innards of the bird. They conversed for a moment and then Bede raised his hands to the sky and they all bowed. He threw the bird onto the fire, and another figure came forward to wash Bede's hands. A fourth presented a wooden staff to the other tall man. *It's an abbot's crook, Malthus.*

Will's stomach began to churn and his mouth filled with saliva, not so much because of the bird or even the place, but more because of the unmasking of naked paganism, and perhaps – even worse than that – the inescapable thought of Percival and all that had befallen him. The circle now reformed, and all the figures raised their hands and chanted 'come' – very slowly at first, almost like a passionate whisper, but then getting louder and longer. It made Will weak, just as he had felt weak the afternoon he had been locked by the abbot's stare – like in the bad dream when he had turned to run but could not. 'Come … Come … Come to us …' Will held on to the branches with his locked arm, not trusting his trembling hands.

After what seemed like an age, a dreadful sound cut through it all. It came out of the darkest part of the wood, out beyond the circle of orange light. It was the hideous voice like that of some awakened creature. 'Aaaaaaaargh! See, I have come to you.' The Druids dropped to their knees. A figure descended into the light from the far bank. Will thought he was in some nightmare, but here it came, slowly, staggering as if not used to human limbs.

Will hid behind the trunk as the creature spoke again: 'Yes, I have come …' The Druids were still bowed low to the earth, one or two stretching their hands out, though keeping their heads down. The figure walked past the circle of prostrate bodies and into the centre. Will opened his eyes and braved one more glance; there was something familiar about the figure who approached the fire. 'Yes, here I am. Now, any of you weirdos got any booze, 'cos I'm dry!'

Will's eyes almost fell out of their sockets! *Rawkins!* A moment later one of the hooded figures flung his hood back and exposed his face. 'What the devil? It's a boy! Get him!' It was Brendan. Adam quickly gave him two fingers, said he'd see him in class, and sprinted past the others and out towards Will's tree. The circle disbanded and another figure broke from the shadows and followed Adam. *Ben!*

Seconds later, Adam passed the tree laughing and shouting, 'Morons!' and then disappeared off down the bank. Ben, not so fortunate in his timing, approached Will's tree with three hooded figures gaining fast on him. Will braced himself; he let Ben pass, then the nearest figure in pursuit, and then he jumped from his branch onto the second pursuer. The man was sent sprawling, and Will wasted no time using him to cushion his own fall. The third man stopped for a moment in shock, but then grabbed Will with a grip that almost dislocated his shoulder. 'Right, got you, little devil.' It was the voice of Brother Brendan. Will dealt him a sharp blow to his windpipe with the side of his hand. Brendan let go and reeled back, clutching his throat. Will heard Ben cry and he turned to run, but the other man now had his ankle.

251

'Not so fast,' he said; it was Reece. Will stamped on his fingers and kicked him in the stomach. Reece howled in agony, and Will darted into the bushes.

Others, seeing the fight and hearing the cries of pain, were dispatched. Will ran in the direction of Ben's voice and soon came upon a shadow dragging him out of the bank. 'Come on, what's your name, eh? Name and House, quickly.' Will ran as quietly and as fast as he could, catching the attacker on the kidneys with a full body-blow. Ben was released instantaneously, as the figure fell back, clutching his side. Will pulled his hood off and drew his fist back to punch the Druid's face.

'Wordsmith?' he exclaimed, letting him drop back and grabbing Ben. 'Come on, quick.'

Down on the next terrace and panting hard, Ben said, 'It was – it was – Rawkins up there!'

'Who else would be stupid enough? Come on, there are more coming!'

Will glanced back to the upper terrace as they descended the bank. He could not see anybody. They went down and down, sometimes tumbling, sometimes falling right over, but never stopping. By the time they reached the bottom terrace, they thought they would make it, but it was here that Will discerned moving shadows. The tomb stones seemed to move as one and then five more figures stepped forward to block their escape. 'Quick, Ben, they're trying to trap us – use the other gate.'

They turned and ran, and the six came after them – just shapes, no noise. They were quick, very quick. The lower gate of the necropolis was in sight, but Will could almost feel the breath of the hunters upon him as he approached it. He was almost tempted to turn and fight it out, but six of them? *No, the gate was almost there – if only … Just a few more seconds …*

A shadow moved at the gate and a broad figure stepped forward to block them. The glint of cold steel flashed in the moonlight; *a sword!* But then Will heard the words, 'Quick, through here, I'll cover your escape.' It was Mr John, with Grendel by his side! Will and Ben shot through the gate as they heard Mr John bellow, 'Stand where you are, all of you cowards, and turn around, or she'll tear you limb from limb, I swear it!'

That was the last Will heard. He saw Ben safely through his common-room window, and then he got back as quickly as he could to his drainpipe. He was up it like lightning and back into the room, where Adam was rolling a joint. 'Rawkins, what were you thinking? You almost got me and Ben busted with that stunt!'

Adam laughed. 'Chill, dude! Didn't know you were there, but anyway, I couldn't resist when I saw the bonfire. Oh, that was funny, I tell you!'

Hands on knees, Will shook his head and smiled. 'You idiot! Made me jump out of my skin!'

'Never mind, Houston. I managed to score some dope tonight! Hey, we can get high, man, and get what those suckers can't.' He lit the joint and took a long drag.

'Oh, right, so this is you, the biologist, the great materialist, getting stoned?'

'Hey, don't label me, dude. I'm coming to the conclusion that there might be something spiritual in here after all.' Adam pointed to his head. 'Just needs a little unlocking.'

'Well, not in my room,' Will said, grabbing the joint off him.

'Hey, you not having some, man?'

'Had enough … *man* … at my last school, and if you want to do this sort of thing, you can do it somewhere where you won't get me expelled!' He threw the spliff into the sink. 'I swear, Rawkins, I do not get you at all.'

'I didn't ask you to.' Adam jumped up and retrieved the joint from the sink. 'And neither should someone who is such a hypocrite always be so ready to cut off the only crutches I've got left.' He sat on his bed, looked at the soggy spliff, swore and threw it at the wall. Will tried to ignore him, but when he did look, Adam sat, pensively chewing his knuckle with tears running down his cheeks.

'Rawkins?' Will said, more gently.

'I'm dying, you stupid cretin, I'm dying, and I'm bricking myself – that good enough for you?' Adam broke down, and Will went over and sat next to him.

'What – what do you mean?'

Adam wiped his nose, sniffed and then steadied himself. 'I'm HIV positive.'

'But – but how? I mean …'

'Does it frigging matter? Maybe I'm queer, maybe I got it from a needle or a whore – it doesn't matter, I got it, and I'm going, like the other 8000 each day.' He pointed to his wall and wiped his eyes. 'I'll be another anonymous statistic in the march of natural selection – ironic, eh?'

'But you're wrong, Rawkins. They can do stuff now. I saw a programme –' Will said.

'Sure, with people who get in quickly and don't dick around with their antiretrovirals like me.' Adam stood up and went to lean on the window ledge.

'What does that mean?'

'It means my count got low, I developed immunity to one lot of drugs, and there basically ain't no paddle for the creek I'm up.'

'And your family?'

'What about my family?' Adam said.

'Have you told them?'

'I don't want them to know – I don't want anyone to know.'

'And God, is he still not a viable alternative?' Will said, reminding Adam of their first conversation outside the biology lab.

'I may be a little sketchy on Christian theology, but I think we're all pretty definite that AIDS is God's judgement, so, hey, let's not go there. Oblivion's not much of an option, but I'd take it over facing your God any day.'

'Hey, you got it all wrong Adam, dead wrong.'

'Enough, I'm tired of it all, all the words, even my own.' He sighed, sniffed. 'Just, just leave me be. And if you want another roommate I'll understand.'

Will put an arm around Adam's stiff shoulders. 'I'm here man, just don't use my toothbrush.' Adam smiled slightly, so Will went back to his shelf and took a Gideon New Testament off it for Adam. 'Suppose you know what this is?'

Adam looked to the side, 'Suppose I do: bit late for a Bible-bashing don't you think?'

'No,' Will placed it on Adam's bedside table, 'and if you'd stop being such a smart alec for once, and actually read it, you'd see – well, you'd see for yourself.'

Will received a text just after midnight: 'Back okay, will arrange to meet police after Invisible College on Sat. LET JUSTICE BE DONE THOUGH THE HEAVENS FALL.' Will switched off his phone, glad that all had turned out all right and hoping that neither he nor Ben had been identified. Adam was another matter entirely, having walked straight out in front of them all.

Still jittery with nervous exhaustion, Will lay awake for at least another hour, trying to imagine a full-scale murder investigation going on in the school. The heavens might fall indeed; at least now they had suspects.

16

REGAINING CONSCIOUSNESS

Will avoided all eye contact with Father Bede or Wordsmith that next morning during prayers and breakfast. He was not summoned anywhere, and neither – which was perhaps stranger – was Adam. Dundas showed no signs of doing so, and for the moment all looked well. Friday lessons were uneventful, though a note on the library door said that Br Brendan was on sick leave due to a 'sore throat', and research matters should be referred to Br Reece.

On Saturday the boys went to morning lessons as usual. Mr Gibbs droned on about how far science could now see and how nothing was beyond the abilities of the great men in white coats.

After break Will and Adam sat in front of the professor for their monthly philosophy lecture. One boy moaned to his friend on the way in: Why did they have to sit through such obscure lessons?

'Because, young man,' the professor replied, 'the greatest un-explored territory is under your hat, though in some cases it may be all desert.'

As the boys took their seats, Adam said, 'So you wouldn't agree that we are meat computers, and that soon computers will achieve consciousness?'

The professor took his chalk to the board. 'Do you think that?'

'I dunno; maybe, but then I sometimes think there may be something more than neurons ticking away.'

The professor wrote on the board. 'Cogito ergo sum. René Descartes again: "I think, therefore I am." I am sure you have heard this, but of course the big question is, where does the brain stop and mind start?'

'And you reckon we have a mind?' Adam said.

'I reason that I have more than a brain. What you may call the other is another matter entirely. The mind, the soul, the conscious self, whatever you like; but whatever it is, it is the most important part of our existence after physical life itself.'

'How do you reason that there is more than meat, sir?' Clarkson asked.

'Because I am able to reflect on your question, give a subjective answer, even consider internally whether it is worth answering.'

'And will you answer?' Adam said.

'I have free will to do so, or not to do so. Now if, for example, I had just a physical brain, if I was just a material being, I could have no such free will.'

'Why not?'

'Because a purely natural world is governed by natural law. A cloud, for example, does not decide where it will go, who it will rain or not rain on. Do you see?'

'And my question?' Clarkson said.

'He's answered it, you idiot,' Adam said.

'Well, is there no way to experiment?' Clarkson insisted.

The professor smiled. 'You have reached the boundaries of science, my boy. For those little men in white coats, your mind is as far beyond the reach of their measuring instruments as is the beginning of the universe. How do you measure what is out of reach, what is sentient, immaterial?'

'But surely there is something,' Adam said.

'Perhaps. Two things spring to mind, but they only highlight another barrier to science. First, the work done by Professor Penfield, the father of neurosurgery. He electrically stimulated different parts of the brains of epilepsy patients. He found that he could turn their heads and eyes, and move their hands and legs. But in every case they would say, "I did not do that" – you see?'

'But they did do it, if their legs moved!'

'No, their brain moved their legs, but each person was conscious that their will did not initiate or permit the action. Their brain, if you like, had acted without the mind's permission.'

'I get it – I am more than my brain,' Clarkson said.

'That'll be a relief to your mother!' Adam said, and the class laughed.

'Very funny. But, sir, what about the other thing Penfield found?'

'Ah, well, I'm sure you've heard of rapid eye movement?'

'Sure. It happens when you dream,' Adam said.

'How do you know?' the professor said.

'Because, well, because …'

'Because they woke the person up to ask them, of course; because their instruments can only measure eye-movement and brain activity. The mind and dreams are private.'

'So what about computers having a form of consciousness one day?' Adam asked.

'What?' The professor reeled. 'For inanimate bits of micro-processors to become sentient beings?'

'Yeah, like Terminator!' another boy exclaimed.

'Well, perhaps in Hollywood and for some vacuous technologists.'

They talked further about what the mind might be and also the logical reasons for how it might reasonably have come into existence. Then the bell rang; the weekend had begun.

The members of the Invisible College met up and took their packed lunches to the beach as arranged, though this time they separated to avoid detection, converging just past the circle. It was a stormy afternoon, and thunder could be heard far off. Will looked down on the bay where the *Argonaut* strained at its moorings as a gale started. 'Come on you lot, before the rain hits.' They raced down the coastal path and crossed the beach. Suddenly, to their right, a jagged streak of lightning struck the western seaboard. The boys stood aghast, in awe at the spectacle. A thunderstorm was something Will had always found irresistible: the power, the random suspense, the noise.

The thunder rumbled and rolled as Father George welcomed them to the fireside and insisted they toast their sandwiches. 'Here's my crumpet fork. Take it in turns; we have pickle in the fridge if you'd like it – made it myself.' Hot coffee was also brought out by Mr John. Will got up to help him. *Wow, he looks tired, and why is he constantly looking at the clock?* Grendel stretched out all alone on the rug, and Adam sat on a seat near her and fiddled with her ears. Will glanced up. Poor Adam, looked as lost as ever.

After a preamble Mr John introduced his topic for the day. 'We'll have to be quicker than usual, lads. I have visitors coming at 3 p.m., but that'll still give us enough time to look at two devout men who were undoubtedly two of the most profound contributors to science since Newton. Their names are Faraday and Clerk Maxwell. In fact, when Einstein was once asked about whether he saw himself as standing on the shoulders of Newton, he was quite definite: "No, I am standing on the shoulders of Maxwell". Yet I dare say that some of you have not even heard of him.' Keats and Adam said they had, but the rest looked blank.

'Good, then you need educating. Now, for the ones who hate maths, it might encourage you to know that Michael Faraday could not do even the simplest of sums! He was born in 1791 in South London. His father was a blacksmith with poor health, and he and his three siblings grew up in relative poverty. In fact, Faraday only got two years' education before he went to work as an eleven-year-old errand-boy.'

'That would suit me, sir – just two years,' Clarkson joked.

'I doubt it, Tom, but anyway, that's all he got, and then, at the age of fourteen, like you, Ben, he became an apprentice bookbinder. That's when he got to read interesting books and developed a passion for science, particularly chemistry. His big break came after attending the lectures of an eminent scientist. That man was Humphry Davy, and Mike took very precise notes, bound them and actually gave them to Davy. Davy was so impressed that he took Faraday on a two-year lecture tour of Europe. Davy also took along his newly-wed and very haughty wife, which, as you can imagine, dampened things for Mike.'

Father George chuckled. 'Some honeymoon!'

'What did she do to him?' Thornton asked.

'Basically treated him like a servant: "Do this, do that." But he learned to put up with it and enjoy the trip. And there was plenty to enjoy for, with Davy to learn from, Mike was with a mobile one-man university! He even got to meet the eminent men of European science and looked through Galileo's telescope. They were magical days for a poor blacksmith's son, days he would look back on and describe as times "when my fear far exceeded my confidence and when both exceeded my knowledge"! Later on, back in England, he got a job at the Royal Institute as a technician, making many advances in chemistry, particularly in steel alloys and in liquefying chlorine and other gases. Actually, it was this that would eventually lead to refrigeration. He also discovered benzene, which became invaluable in the manufacture of nylon, plastics and dyes, things we could not live without nowadays.'

'But I thought he had more to do with electricity or something,' Will said.

'Yes, of course; his next great discoveries related to electricity, and these are what most people today associate him with. Scientists knew that electricity produced magnetism. Faraday's creative mind wondered whether it would work the other way round. He was absolutely right, of course, and he invented the first transformer and the first electric generator. His work on electrolysis would also benefit industry and manufacturing.'

'Electrolysis? Isn't that something to do with women's legs?' Clarkson said.

Mr John raised his eyebrows. 'My dear Tom, I doubt whether, even if it were, you would be old enough to talk about it.'

The boys laughed but Mr John continued, 'One of the loveliest things about this wonderful, humble man was something that captivated all of Victorian London.'

'Oh?' Will said.

'His Friday night lectures. You see, he felt it was his responsibility to share his passion for the knowledge that could so easily have been denied him by birth and situation. He felt so humbled that he, a poor blacksmith's son, had been gifted to look into the eternal laws of the universe. How could he not share these insights with his fellow men? There was no pomp; as the clock struck the hour he would appear on the stage as the audience waited. Men like Dickens and Darwin attended and were rapt as Faraday dazzled them with his own brand of theatrical experiments and "easy-to-understand" approach. At the end there was no one asking for a vote of thanks; the clock struck the hour, he would simply leave and everyone would burst into spontaneous applause. And all this from a humble, unshowy man who looked after his old mother and who might then go off to visit one of the church widows on his way home. The Friday lectures, which still continue today, are hailed by many as an achievement in themselves for the popularizing of science, which, of course, is so necessary.'

'Wow, sounds like a charmed life – rags to riches and all that!' Thornton said.

'Well, not exactly; of course, he did become internationally famous. Mind you, his local church, which very strictly followed the New Testament, made sure that he lived as humbly as any other member. In fact, Queen Victoria was petitioned by others to give him a charitable place to live for his retirement, as he had no savings.'

'Wow, that's hard-core Christianity!' Will said.

'Yes, and once he got into trouble at church for missing a meeting because of an invite to take tea with the Queen! The elders put him under discipline and disallowed him from preaching for a while.'

'Sounds like a friendly bunch! I hope he left,' Clarkson said.

'No, it was just like with Davy's stroppy wife; Faraday, famous though he now was, submitted under the littleness of others without getting bitter. In fact, you could say it was a hallmark of his character, that he lived for God's glory, not his own, and certainly not to seek redress for personal slights. He got better, not bitter. He even managed to patch things up with his old mentor after Davy used his position as chairman to block Faraday's application to join the Royal Society!'

'I thought he was the guy who had given him a leg-up in the first place?' Keats said.

'Yes, but it was a bit of a Saul–David thing; Faraday's star was rising.'

'Right,' Clarkson said, 'and Davy was a bit green over Faraday's discoveries?'

'Yes, basically, though it was a bit more involved than that. Anyway, they were friends again later, and Faraday went on from strength to strength with his work.'

'What, there was more than the electric stuff?' Clarkson said.

'Oh yes – the man who used the five talents got five more, remember? Faraday's most important, and virtually unknown, work in theoretical physics was about to begin.'

'Theoretical physics?' Keats said. 'Sounds a long way from an electric motor.'

'Well, it doesn't do to pigeon-hole people; in fact, this was a natural extension of his work on magnetism. It's just that he went big with it.'

'How big?'

'Basically, he radically challenged the ideas of physicists before him and ended up making the greatest breakthrough in physics since Newton!'

'Wow – so what was that?' Keats asked.

'His genius theory was "the notion of field". Basically, it was the idea that the field of a magnet went beyond just its immediate vicinity, that there was something greater, something in between, something huge and powerful, out there in the ether – possibly something that mankind could tap into and harness. It was a mammoth conceptual breakthrough.'

'And now we have the mobile phones and other electronic stuff, all because of him?' Ben said.

'Yes – him and a few others; but see here, Faraday gave us three great theorems that revolutionized the world, but Clerk Maxwell – who was he, Henry?'

'Oh, right, yeah – he was another one of those right-on, Bible-believing fundamentalists that your brother likes so much!'

'You've got it; and he gave us four of the most beautiful equations to explain Faraday's theorems.' Mr John examined his nails, gave a half chuckle and then explained. 'If Davy was something of a Saul towards Faraday, then Maxwell would be his Prince Jonathan; it was a match made in heaven. Remember that Faraday couldn't do maths, so God provided him with one of the most gifted mathematical geniuses of that age – or any age.'

'How gifted?' Father George said. 'Tell them, my boy.'

'Put it this way: as a young guy, he was the only one to enter a competition to theorize what Saturn's rings were. No one else had a clue! He proved mathematically that they must be ice, and it was only a few years ago, nearly 150 years later, that we found out he was right! That's how hot he was! I mean, his electromagnetic theorem was the foundation for radio, TV, satellite communication – this man was a real giant. He and Maxwell laid the foundations for Einstein's theory of relativity.'

'How so?' Keats asked, blowing the steam from his tea.

'Well, in effect, Einstein, like everyone else, saw that Maxwell's new equations and those of Newton were at odds. Most people thought that Maxwell must be wrong, but Einstein wondered whether Newton's theory was just too limited – and, well, the rest is history. Einstein published a book, knowing that only twenty people in the world would understand it, and he blew everyone's minds forever! I hear that some of you have already asked Mr Hill about breakthroughs in astrophysics and how science brought him back to God; well, it was Maxwell who said, "Almighty God, you have created man in your own image … Teach us to study the work of thy hands." And God certainly did teach Maxwell; and he taught mankind, and your Mr Hill got saved out of atheism because of it.'

Adam, who had said virtually nothing since they had left St Alban's, spoke gently as he looked into the fire. 'And then they died.'

'They're not dead,' replied Mr John. 'That's to say, yes, their bodies have gone, but they're still alive. God's the God of the living, not the dead.'

'Okay, how did their bodies die, then?' Adam said.

'Maxwell broke off his work to nurse his young wife, who was ill with the disease that would kill her. He then got the same disease, and though he was often in great pain with abdominal cancer, he told no one about it, and only complained that it prevented him from personally caring for his wife. He went to God young – just as she did. Faraday, however, lived into his late seventies. In fact, a reporter asked him one day about his speculations about the afterlife, and he said, "Speculations? I have none; I am resting on certainties." He then went on to quote the Bible: "I know whom I have believed, and I am persuaded that He is able to keep what I have entrusted to Him unto that great day."'

'Certainty. I envy them that,' Adam said, still not looking up from the flames.

'All mathematicians and philosophers, from Archimedes and Euclid right up to our day, have been concerned with one thing,' Father George said. 'Certainty, assuredness, surety. But men like Faraday didn't find it in science; they got it from the God of the Bible, and used it in studying what they knew God had made.'

'Oh yes, the Bible.' Adam picked up the poker and prodded the ashes.

Father George leaned forward. 'My dear boy, there is assurance enough in that book for anyone – even you. What does John say? "I write these things that you may be sure that you have eternal life"; and Luke, "I have made a careful investigation so you may be certain" of these things.'

'Yes, yes, I read all that yesterday,' Adam said.

'All of it? The whole New Testament?' Will said.

Adam nodded. 'Some bits twice.'

'And what about the prodigal son?' Father George said.

Adam's eyes were filling with tears. 'Five times; it's just all too good to be true. God! If only it were.'

There was a pause. The other boys sat silently and looked at the adults. Father George took a Bible from the table near him. 'There is, I believe, the most significant scientific hypothesis found in Hebrews 11 verse 6. I dare say that you read it yesterday. Now, where is it ...' He thumbed through the tattered pages unhurriedly, looking up occasionally above his spectacles and smiling at Adam, who was himself now looking up too. 'We have already seen that science went forward by right-minded men asking the right questions and then verifying those questions by experimentation. So let's see whether we cannot do the same with the Bible. Ah, here it is: the letter to the Hebrew Christians in Rome. "Anyone who wants to approach God must do so with confidence that He is really there and that He'll reward those who scrupulously reach out for him." My paraphrase, there you are.'

'Yes but ...' Adam said, though lacking his usual conviction.

'No buts, Adam, you've been spoon-fed from Plato's fountain like a lazy fool for long enough; it's time to stir yourself, boy! Remember our motto: "Nothing by authority". What do you think we've been doing here – telling stories?'

'That's not what I meant.'

'It's time for you to stop whining, and do some experimentation yourself. Get on your knees; perhaps one day you'll make the *real* Royal Society.'

For once, Adam had nothing to say. He looked around, turned down the corners of his mouth, rolled his tongue in deep thought and finally said, 'Well, I'll read it again.'

At 2.45 p.m., Mr John disbanded the group, but drew Will aside. 'You and Ben wait behind. The police are coming at 3 p.m. to take your statements. Don't be worried, just tell them what you saw.'

The boys followed Mr John into his study, where he started to dismantle a loaded shotgun that was lying on his desk.

'Been hunting?' Will asked.

'No – just a little extra protection. The six hooded goons from the other night.'

'Did you have trouble with them?' Ben asked.

'Not as such, but they said that they knew where to find me, so I've been expecting company the last two nights. Still, better get the gun away before the police come.'

'Yes, suppose so. Do you think they recognized Pitt and me?'

'Don't think so. What about in the crypt, Will? Did they know you were there?'

'No.'

'Good, then we can safely assume they have been put back. Now listen, we need to keep the locations of those scrolls a secret,' Mr John said, boxing his gun and stowing it away behind the desk.

'Even from the police?' Will asked.

'Yes, especially from the police, if the Druids are anything like the Freemasons round here. We need to get back to the crypt and find what we can before anyone gets spooked.'

'Well, I'd rather not go alone, thanks,' said Will, hearing a knock at the door.

Inspector Peel wore a squeaky faux-leather bomber jacket that he would not take off, even when invited to do so. He was in his mid-forties, thickset, nervy and suspicious. Father George went off for his afternoon nap and Ben served tea as the four sat down to discuss the case. Will told the inspector about the inscription he had found on his desk, the lost book, the intruder in his room, the ancient prophecy, and the recalculating of the date for the Millennium. Mr John then told him about the discovery of ergot in Percival's autopsy and the method of ritual killing that matched historical accounts. He finished with a list of people they had identified in Monks' Wood two nights before. All the while, the inspector took notes and said nothing.

'So, according to your testimony, sir, we have the abbot, Kentigern, Bede, Brothers Brendan and Reece, the matron, and this lad Wordsmith, plus about fifteen others to find and interview in connection with the possible ritual murder of young Percival.' He tapped his notebook with his pencil. 'It's going to be hard to make it discreet; they won't like it – the school, I mean; it'll be a proper witch-hunt.'

He pursed his lips. 'And your brother – he's the head, isn't he, sir?'

'Yes, but I don't think he's involved.'

'Oh – sure about that, are you, sir?'

'George is a bit pompous and naïve, perhaps, but he'd have to have dropped a long way to be party to such idiocy.'

'Really, sir? Well, we'll see.' Inspector Peel's beady eyes darted about the room. 'Lots of books sir. Big reader are you? The wife's a reader, but not me. I generally trust my own eyes and ears. Second-hand sources can be unreliable. Got a copy of this prophecy then have you?'

Mr John looked at Will. 'Certainly, officer. I'll dig out a copy for you. And another thing you might do is –'

'Thank you, sir, but we'll take it from here. You just find that prophecy.' He stood to leave. 'I must caution you, though: if the occasion arises that you and the kids are in possession of information that is materially relevant to the case, don't be tempted to take the law into your own hands.' He walked to the door, and Mr John went with him to his car.

As they were talking Will overheard Mr John say, 'And you understand why the boys' anonymity is paramount?'

'I can see that it might make things a bit tense for them at school, sir, but sooner or later –'

'No.' Mr John lowered his voice. 'The other Millennium solstice is now only weeks away.' Will's stomach tightened. *Another Millennial solstice. Of course.*

'And you think they might try again?' Peel said, sliding into his seat.

Will went to the cottage door to listen more closely just in time to hear Mr John say, 'If the last victim didn't bring in a new age of peace and fertility, what would you do?'

Peel closed his door and wound the window three-quarters down. 'I see, sir. Well, I'll be in touch. And remember what I said.'

As the car sped up the track, Will came outside. 'What was that about?'

'That? Nothing.' Mr John shrugged and smiled. 'But we'd best be after those items from the crypt before things break loose in the school. How about 7 p.m. while certain characters are occupied at Vespers?'

'You mean while they're all above our heads at prayer in the choir stalls?'

'It's the only way we can be sure they're all busy.' Mr John bucked Wills chin up. 'Come on. What could possibly go wrong?'

17

DANGER ON THE CLIFFS

Clarkson was in a state of near ecstasy. 'It's really hitting the fan now, boys. The Police are calling in the monks one by one. Old Malthus is blazing about it.' He shut Will's door behind him. 'Word is, they've taken all the computers from the monastery, library and like everywhere, man. The place is in meltdown.' He slumped onto Will's bed. 'Where's Adam?'

Will put his pen down. 'Come in. Make yourself at home, why don't you? Adam's out and I'm trying to concentrate on this essay.'

Not one for subtle hints, Clarkson carried on. 'Hey, old Bede's face was a picture at dinner. Thought he was going to hit someone. Wouldn't surprise me, all the teachers are well uptight. Most of the lads think it is to do with drugs.'

'Good. Let's keep it that way, Tom, okay? No blabbing about me, Percival or anything else. Had enough trouble this year.'

'Sure. You seem jumpy, mate. Everything okay?'

'Yes, just a lot on my mind right now.' He glanced to the window. The Vespers bell was sounding mournfully across the valley. Summoning him to the crypt.

Will reluctantly went as arranged to the rendezvous with Mr John. He slipped into the priory via a side entrance. Glancing back through the half-open door, he noticed a lone hooded monk approaching the priory building. He looked round the gothic vaulted passageway and listened. *This place gives me the creeps. Can't escape the feeling I'm being watched.* He moved silently down the passageway and, as he and Mr John had agreed, slid into the shady anteroom just off an ambulatory that connected the priory to the monastic buildings. It was cold and damp, with the familiar smell of mould in the stonework and peeling plaster. Will looked back to where he'd come, but he could see no one there. *Good.*

After a minute he heard a door shut. He looked again into the passageway, and there was the monk he'd seen before. The monk glanced about and walked towards Will. He was holding what looked like a body sack. Will took a big breath and then moved back towards the toilets. The windows were barred, no way out. He checked the passageway: the monk was ten metres away. He was coming. *Think, think. What do I do?* Will moved back into the room. There were no weapons; in any case, he needed space if he was going to fight it out. He waited as the steps came closer.

The door opened. Will waited breathlessly behind it, flat against the wall. The black form moved into the centre of the room, then turned to shut the door. Will was preparing to strike when he saw who it was.

'Mr John –'

'Good, there you are! Here, take this.'

'What is it?' Will held the habit Mr John handed him; it was heavy and smelled of sweat.

'Your disguise. Come on, the monks will be assembling in the cloister in two minutes.' Will put the habit on and pulled the hood over so that it covered his forehead. The two of them ambled piously to the cloister. They waited in a doorway as the column of hooded figures passed. Mr John and Will joined at the back. Led by the abbot, they marched slowly and solemnly to the priory for Vespers. They entered by the East Door and turned across the chancel towards the choir stalls.

The line of monks passed the crypt door en route, and when their turn came Mr John and Will slid out of line and down the steps. A minute later the chanting started. Reaching the bottom of the steps, Mr John switched the lights on.

'Oh, there were lights,' Will whispered in surprise.

'We're not in the Dark Ages! Now take me to the spot.'

Will wandered down the arched corridors. All the arches looked the same. He was only able to narrow the bays down to about five.

'It must have been one of these ones. Sorry, it was just so different in the dark.' They searched each one, trying the stones where Will thought he had imagined the matron standing, but they found nothing: no loose stones or anything to indicate that they were in the right place. After a frustrating ten minutes, Will stepped back into the corridor and looked around: had he come too far, or not far enough? As his frustration grew, he looked up. A plaque on the column nearest him demarcated the bay. He walked forward to examine it. 'P. LVII,' he read aloud.

Mr John said, 'What was that?'

'Nothing. Just reading the letters on this column.'

Mr John joined Will and examined the plaque. 'Oh yes, we marked them back in '86 when we did the excavations. These are the foundations of a massive Roman villa. The columns were originally around the courtyard, or peristyle – hence the P.'

Will saw it quick as a flash. 'Hey, in your book, what page was the Druids' prophecy bit on?'

'Oh, quite near the end – well into the 300s, I'd say.'

'But not page 66?'

'No, definitely not! Page 66 was barely out of the introduction! Why?'

'Because Percival somehow knew about this place and left a record inscribed on that desk: "P66".'

'P66 – of course, it's a bit further this way, come on.'

They quickly ran further up the corridor, counting the columns, and eventually found the right one: PLXVI. Will immediately recognized where he had hidden, and they both went behind the small altar to the alcove at the back. Mr John examined the floor carefully.

'Look, someone's been here recently; the dust is disturbed on the flags – and see here, in the alcove, this square indentation in the dust surface, it looks as if someone placed something here.'

'A stone?' Will said.

'Too right,' Mr John replied, running his hands over the brickwork. 'Like this one.' He slid a stone out from the wall and got out his torch. Shining it into the hole, he said, 'Bingo! Hold the torch, and I'll grab what I can.'

Mr John put on some rubber gloves and then slid his hands into the hole. He carefully brought out three dusty parchments, putting them into a plastic bag. Shining the torch into the hole again he said, 'Hello. There's something else at the back.' He pulled out an ancient-looking greenish dagger. 'Hmm, bronze, Celtic, possibly sixth century; look at the decoration and jewel inlay. It's definitely a ceremonial dagger, not for buttering toast.'

'To be honest, that's not what I'm thinking about,' Will said.

'I know. Percival; it's very likely that this is the one that was used.' He paused for a moment, holding the bag up. 'Poor lad. Anyway, we can't hang around here; it'll not be long before they finish up there.' Mr John placed the bags into his satchel and wrote out a note to put back in the hole, speaking aloud as he wrote: "'I whet my glittering sword, and mine hand take hold on judgement; I will render vengeance to mine enemies, and will reward them that hate me" – there, a bit of Deuteronomy for them to choke on; should set the cat among the pigeons! They'll probably start blaming each other.' He gave Will a cheeky grin and put the stone back. 'I'll get these to the police. You tell Ben it's sorted – but don't say anything to anyone else. If word gets out about who did this, there'll be hell to pay.'

Later that week, rumours circulated that the prefects had been taken to the police station for questioning. On Thursday and Friday night, Will saw Father Bede coming back to the house very late with Wordsmith following him a minute later. Will assumed that secret meetings were taking place as stories were corroborated and backs were covered.

Wordsmith cornered Will on Saturday and insisted that it was a perfect day for a climb on the cliffs. When Will said he was busy, Wordsmith said, 'Busy? What on earth would keep you from a climb?' Will, realizing that he could not say that he was about to go out of bounds to an illegal meeting, agreed to go. They went to the Scout rooms after lessons to pick up the climbing gear they needed. There they met Mr Hill. 'Be sure you're off the cliff before high tide. The wind will be up.'

'Yes, sir,' the boys murmured.

On the way down to the beach, Wordsmith gave Will his theories about education and morality. He did not wait for Will's comments or encouragements but just kept on and on, happy with the sound of his own opinions. Cities were to blame, rote-learning, SATs and computer games too. Kids needed to be brought up close to nature, not pressured and squashed into educationalist moulds.

As they arrived at the rocky platform that ran out under the Druids' circle, Wordsmith dropped his rucksack and pulled off his jacket. His t-shirt got pulled up too, and Will noticed the severe bruising on his ribs.

'Right,' Wordsmith said. 'Here we are. The Bard's Buttress is a classic bit of rock; if you survive that, we'll have a crack at the Druid's Finger.' He pointed to some very severe-looking cliff faces to their left, and then, getting out his belt, said, 'Man, I've needed this!'

'Been a difficult week?' Will asked. 'A few late nights?'

Wordsmith looked up for a moment, but Will made an effort to avoid his stare.

'Here are your rock boots,' Wordsmith said. They got geared up and Wordsmith led the first pitch on 'the Bard', as he called it. After ten minutes he called to Will to climb. It started with an enormous overhang of about six metres, where the merciless Irish sea had undercut the cliff. Will was at the peak of fitness and jumped for the first hold and hung there for a moment to pray. The slack in the rope was taken in, but he did not dare trust Wordsmith. In the pit of his stomach he was sure that mischief was somehow determined against him. He eased his legs into the holds and, almost upside down, climbed the overhang to the buttress. He swung his right leg over the lip of the cliff and pulled himself into view of Wordsmith, who was positioned on a ledge.

'You made it – good; you'll find some good holds on your left.' Will could see that they were no way near as good as the ones on his right, but he took them anyway. All the time, Wordsmith was watching him, and all the time the sea thundered in, though not yet at high tide. They climbed like this for half an hour; the further they went, the more sparse the holds became. Wordsmith insisted they do Merlin's Nose while they were up there, though Will said that he was really quite rusty.

Merlin's Nose turned out to be another overhanging piece of crag in the shape of a giant nose. They ate a sandwich on the ledge beneath it, and then Wordsmith went around the far side and scrambled up. 'Hey,' Will said, 'aren't you going to do it too?'

Wordsmith looked back at him. 'There's no time if we're going to do the Finger as well.'

'Look, I'm not sure about this,' Will said.

'Nonsense! Just reach for the hold I told you about, and you'll be fine.'

A few minutes later the call came to climb. Will stood up on the ledge and felt giddy as he stretched out on tiptoes, letting his fingers run along the rock. *Breathe, come on, you can do this, breathe.* There was no foothold for the first three moves; he could use only his hands. He found the first hold and let his body swing out onto the precipice above the waves that were now fast approaching the base of the cliff. He swung his body this way and then that, eventually reaching for the right handhold, but all he could feel was smooth rock. 'It's – it's not there, I can't feel ... any ... thing.'

The voice came back from above. 'Nonsense! Try again.'

Will panicked, and, desperately trying not to look down, swung himself out again, for by now he was committed and there was no way he could regain the ledge even if he had wanted to. So out he went. The weight on his left hand becoming excruciating, but, again, nothing. He tried one last time before his left hand gave out. This time, reaching higher still, his right hand connected with something beyond the overhang. *It's nowhere near where Wordsmith said it was and it'll only take three fingers. I'll have to take it; there was no more time, arms won't take any more.* So, placing his thumb – the thumb having the strongest hand muscle – over his index fingernail, he said a quick SOS prayer and let go. His body swung even further away from the ledge. The wind caught him on the left, whistling through his hair and flapping his T-shirt. He could not wait for the blood to fully return to his left arm, for his right was now losing grip. He reached up with his right and mercifully found a good hold there. He eased himself up and swung his leg above the overhang and scrambled up the Nose towards Wordsmith, who all the while had been smiling. 'There, you see, easy as pie!'

'It was not as you said; the second hold was nothing,' Will fumed.

'Daah, stop whining! Where's that pioneer spirit, Houston? Imagine the Victorians: no ropes, hob-nailed boots, and no no-

276

tion of what was there before they let go.' He glanced at his watch. 'Good, we've just got time to do the Druid's Finger.'

'I don't know – those waves have covered where we started already.'

'Tush, man, we'll be fine; we don't need to go right to the bottom. I'll lower you on a rope to the overhang and you can do the Finger from there.'

'Well, I'll abseil myself, then.'

'No need. Just stick yourself in here.' Wordsmith offered him the rope. 'I'll lower you; it's all quite safe; you'll be miles above the waves.' They could not see the waves breaking at that point, for the overhang was still some fifteen metres below them.

Will looked over towards the Finger; it looked easy enough, so he agreed. The two traversed to the belay point and Wordsmith fixed the ropes. 'Okay, nice and easy then.'

Will clipped in but climbed downwards, for he barely trusted the rope.

'Houston, what are you doing? I said I'd lower you,' Wordsworth insisted. His voice was mocking.

'No, it's okay,' Will said. 'It's good practice for me. You know what they say: if you can't climb down, then you shouldn't climb up.'

Down he went, easily for the most part, but there was a very bare bit not far above the overhang and, for a few moments, Will put his weight on the rope as he slid down. At this point, he was not visible to Wordsmith. Will released his grip to tug on the rope, then all at once the rope went slack. His stomach was immediately in his mouth as he felt the air rush past his ears and his body plummet toward the rocks. 'H-help! Argh!' Will clawed the rock but he was too late: the edge of the overhang approached, and he shot over with accelerating speed, hitting his head twice on the way. His body swung in the overhang, his half-shattered helmet hitting the underside ceiling, battering his ribs and sending pain into every region of his body. The last thing he remembered before blacking out was the waves surging a mere six metres below him.

'Ouch!' he groaned. Will awoke when the crest of a wave clipped his head. *I'm upside down. I'm in trouble.*

Blood ran down his face and into his mouth. He didn't wait to see whether the wound was serious. What concerned him more was the position he was now hanging in. Three metres above the thundering waves, three metres below the edge of the overhang, with frothing walls of dark-green water approaching like battalions to crush all in their path. He could not reach the rock in time to climb up, and he doubted whether he could shimmy up three metres of rope. One thing was sure: any one of the waves rolling towards him could smash his body to pieces against the ceiling of the overhang.

'Oh God,' he cried, more out of sheer terror than anything else. It was then that the wind and spray caught his body and an idea came to him. He swung with the wind, and then back again – in again, then back. He kicked his legs and reached his hands out – in and then back – and his right hand found a hold in the overhang. He forced his whole body to cling to it.

He was only just in time, for cocking his head backward, he saw the first leviathan thunder in. The roller was a six-metre wave, the same height as the overhang from the sea. He waited for another second as it sucked the waters away below him like some great monster gathering strength, and then Will kicked out with all his might, swinging violently out towards the rising mountain of water that rushed in on him. His body went nearly 180 degrees and even though the foam now sprayed his back, he was swung clear. The turbid explosion of raw, liquid power rushed into every crack and then exploded above the lip of the overhang. Will was at once engulfed in white spray and then, in the next moment, ejected out of the abyss into the air with tremendous force. Up and up he went and then, in a moment, down he came again into the frothy destruction under his feet. His body slammed into the upper cliff, where he tried to reach out his hands for a hold. There was none, and the weight of his body wrenched his fingers back down the rock, taking the skin off. He cried out and hissed, issuing from his mouth those last syllables of despair, for now all strength and hope fled him. He slid towards the lip of the overhang once again, and, in what seemed the very last moment, his foot caught on the edge: it was a hold.

He rested there for one glorious second. He couldn't believe he had done it. *Now let's see if my hands still work.* Though nearly numb with pain, his right fingers held fast, and he took a long, juddering breath. Glancing behind, Will saw the next wave approach; it was even bigger. *Got to get clear of this place quick.* He swung his left hand up and then his leg. The waters below were sucked away again, and the wave rushed through. Will swung his body up and onto the higher rocks, getting as good a hold as he could. The noise was deafening as the waves pummelled rocks on the sea floor, and the swell erupted once again. He braced every muscle and sinew in his body as the huge burst of spray shot past him. It lifted his legs right up, but he grimly kept his fingers in the crevices. The white torrent rushed back, filling his eyes and mouth; his legs found the rock once again and he was left alone.

He looked back; more waves were coming. He heard Wordsmith calling his name. *No more,* he thought bitterly, *no more of your rope.* He drew his knife and cut it, throwing it away in disgust. His suspicions now seemed confirmed: he had been singled out for silencing, and Wordsmith was the executioner – though even now, it seemed unbelievable. So incredible, in fact, that once he had cut himself loose, Will decided to free-climb around the other side of the Druid's Finger to spy on his would-be murderer.

Wiping the blood from his eyes, he traversed the cliff face at forty-five degrees, beyond the reach of the next wave and out of sight of the belay point; all the while, shouts came from above. Will saw the rope disappear back up the rock face. Wordsmith's voice became more and more frantic, something Will thought odd for a would-be-murderer. When he was level with where Wordsmith was, Will peered around the crag. To his surprise, Wordsmith held the severed rope and cried out, his shoulders heaving uncontrollably. 'Houston … Houston …' Wordsmith's palms were red and swollen. Then Will knew it had been an accident all along.

'It's all right!' Will shouted. 'I'm here.'

'Houston! You're alive! I'm so sorry – I wasn't concentrating and I let go. I thought you'd gone! I did get hold again, but I thought I'd been too late.'

'Nearly were.'

'You're soaking and there's blood on your face, God I'm sorry! But how on earth did you get away from the sea?'

'How? Upwards, of course, with a little help!'

Thirty minutes later, they were back at the school and Will was at the dispensary, waiting to have his head looked at by Matron.

'Yes – you again?' she said as she registered who he was. 'What's it this time?' She folded her arms and raised her nose in the air. 'More macho pursuits, I suppose?' Will tried to explain, though he felt all the time that she was only half listening. She made him sit down, and she riffled through his hair. She found the cut at the top of his neck, just below the helmet line. 'So, the sea gave you back your life … ah yes, just a small cut. I'll use a Steri-Strip and … some of this to sterilize the wound.'

She reached into the very bottom of her bag and brought out an unmarked bottle. The thought 'ergot' immediately flashed through Will's mind. He tried to push it out, but it came back again: 'Ergot – she's going to poison you.'

Will dug his fingers into the arm of the chair. 'I don't want anything on the wound, the … the salt water's done a good enough job.'

He said it with such force that she hesitated, but then she said, 'Men are such babies when it comes to a bit of pain. Why, I remember iodine –'

'I'm serious! I'm not having that stuff. I'll have iodine instead.'

'But I don't have any,' she said, opening the lid of her bottle.

'There – there on the shelf, I can see it,' Will said.

Matron paused, and her lips tightened into a smile. 'Very well, as you wish.'

She applied a liberal dose of iodine to his head and fingers, sending Will into spasms of pain. She pushed hard with the Steri-Strip, not easing the pressure until she felt him wince.

'Now, you can't wash your hair for forty-eight hours or the wound will reopen. I'll change the dressing on those fingers next week when I'm at your house. Anything else? Any secondary dizziness, blurred vision, or anything like that?'

'No, I can see perfectly, thank you.'

Later that evening, Clarkson and Thornton barged in on Will while he was trying to stretch out on his bed.

'Heard you had a little mishap at the beach,' Thornton said.

Will showed them his wounds and told them everything. When he had rehearsed it all three times, he said, 'And you lot, what did you get up to today at the Invisible College without me?'

Thornton sat on Adam's bed, 'Not a lot; Leonhard Euler, the mathematician, and Samuel Morse, the pioneer of telegraphy.'

'Oh yeah,' said Clarkson. 'There was this dude called George Carver. He was a slave in America and God used him to save those Southern states from bankruptcy after the Civil War.'

'Yeah,' Thornton continued. 'He was adopted by his owner, who managed to find a Christian college that would educate him, and guess what? God showed him that the cotton fields – you know, the very place where the slaves had been working for so long – were clean out of nitrates and that they needed to rotate the crops.'

'Right,' Will said, stretching out his stiff limbs. 'Bet they loved being told that by a black guy!'

'Not exactly, but what else d'you do when you're facing starvation?' Thornton said.

'You eat humble pie, that's what you do!' Clarkson said. 'Or peanuts!'

'Peanuts?'

'Sure! He told them to plant sweet potatoes and peanuts, but that's not the amazing thing.' Clarkson waved his hands about as he did whenever he became excited. 'You see, just planting them wasn't enough, 'cos they grew so much of the stuff there was a glut in the market and it looked like he'd failed, unless he could find them a use for it all.'

'And did he?'

'Did he! Listen, he found hundreds of uses, and got trade laws passed to help the South to *really* rise again!'

'Must have been one clever bloke.'

'Well, I think Carver would have said it was more an answer to prayer. You see, he cried out to God in the midst of the crisis and asked him what the universe was for.'

'And I s'pose God answered?' Adam said.

'Yes, actually he said, "The answer is too big for you, little man." So then Carver asks what man was made for, and God says the same thing: "The answer's too big for you." So then Carver asks, "Well, what about the peanut, what's that for?" and then God says, "Right, I'll show you!" So he discovers three hundred uses for peanuts and a hundred and fifty uses for sweet potatoes. Cool or what?'

'The other irony, of course,' Thornton said, 'is that the Southern states claimed they needed the black population to make the economy work. If they'd educated them rather than whipping them, it could have worked a whole lot better for the previous hundred years!'

At this point the bell rang for prayers and the boys went downstairs. When Will returned to his room afterwards with Adam. He screwed up his nose. 'What's that smell? Sort of B.O., with something – oil?'

'Don't look at me, Houston.' Adam flopped on his bed. 'You're the one who comes in each afternoon stinking like a pig.'

Will sniffed again. 'No, that's old man's sweat. Someone's been in here while we were at prayers. Check your stuff.'

After five minutes checking their valuables Will sat at his desk and looked about the room, 'Weird, nothing's been taken.'

'Come on, Will.' Adam grabbed his toothbrush and pointed at him. 'You looked knackered. Need some sleep. Probably nothing.'

18

The Net Tightens

'My text is from Revelation chapter 11 verse 18: "I will destroy them which destroy the earth".'

Abbot Malthus stood erect and defiant the next day as he thundered forth his sermon from the altar steps. His thick fingers clutched and unclutched the gnarled staff as he railed against greed and irresponsible government, overpopulation and mass pollution. He spoke with such force that the headmaster, addressing the boys at the end, seemed quite demure in comparison. Mr George spoke of the recent disturbances and said that the school was cooperating with the police and that there was nothing for the boys to be concerned about.

That week Will saw Ben running up to him in the Big Passage. 'Hey Will, guess what; Ms Woolfe has got a lottery grant to build a giant wicker man as a "spiritual art project" to celebrate the Millennium solstice. What's the matter? You're as white as a sheet!'

'You don't know what they're for, do you?'

'No, what?'

'The Romans said that the Druids burn people alive inside them to appease the gods.'

'Oh, come on,' Ben said.

'No, seriously. Of course, there's no archaeological proof for the wicker men, but burnt human bones are not uncommon finds in

Celtic archaeology. Where d'you think we get the word "bonfire" from? It's a fire of bones. So, where's this one going to be put?'

'Apparently the abbot has given permission for them to have it in the woods at the back of the necropolis.'

Will's throat was suddenly dry and his pulse racing. 'Oh, really – how charitable of him!'

Will waited until Saturday to give Mr John the disturbing news. The other lads were assembled in the sitting room, squabbling over seats and biscuits. Mr John, who was in the study with Will, said nothing for a moment but looked out of his window up the hill, where the tops of the Necropolis trees could be seen.

'I wouldn't worry, Will. It's probably nothing. I know Sheila. She's up to her eyeballs in that stuff, but I couldn't think her guilty of anything more than misplaced enthusiasm.'

'I know what you're doing,' Will replied with a sigh.

'What?'

'Trying to get me not to worry. Well, it's not working. I accidently overheard what you said to Inspector Peel, and I think you're right – they'll try it again.'

Mr John scratched the side of his beard and blew out a long breath. 'Okay, but that was then, and now with the investigation in full swing, they'd have to be seriously crazy to try anything. Sure I'd be careful, Will, but don't let it get to you like it did Percival. The police will soon have the forensic reports on those artefacts, maybe even an arrest before the solstice. In the meantime look out for the others.'

There was a sudden commotion in the front room as they heard Adam announcing, 'Gather ladies and gentlemen, tea is now served.' Will and Mr John joined the others by the fire, as Adam continued. 'Now, I'll hear no grumbling from you, Tom, you peasant – this is proper tea, Earl Grey from St Petersburg. Yes, that's right, Russia, you pleb – not some snivelling sweepings off the floor of some grubby bobbin mill in Wakefield!'

'You seem rather more perky than usual,' Father George said, taking a cup.

'Well, let's just say, I'm feeling the effects of spring,' Adam replied.

Will shot a look at Elliot as Adam served him tea, and the younger boy beamed back.

Mr John put on a video for the boys, showing a digital animation of what looked like a futuristic city, though in fact it turned out simply to be a human cell. Little 'things' that looked like spaceships were docking at terminals, picking up things, transporting them, building, repairing; it really was like an alien colony. Will sat open mouthed, and when it had finished Mr John said, 'Let's be very clear, boys, no one – and I mean no one – knew anything about the complexity of the simplest biological cell until very recently. Darwin assumed that the further in you went, the simpler it would be, but the level of order, programming and complexity in the cell should be a massive wake-up call to modern man. It screams out, "Hello! design!" Today, we'll look at a few men who started to bring this to our attention.'

Mr John pointed at Will's finger plasters and said, 'It's especially relevant to young Will here. Even in the days of your great-great-grandfathers, medicine and surgery had developed little since Greek times. In fact, Will could have been dying this afternoon of septicaemia from his wounds if he'd lived back in the days before Louis Pasteur and Joseph Lister. These men changed things for ever for all of us.'

'So they're the ones we're doing today,' Clarkson said.

'Well, mainly Pasteur and Mendel actually, though Lister will be mentioned also. Louis Pasteur, the father of molecular biology, was born in France in 1822. He received such poor results in all his school tests, except for art, that many teachers thought that he would leave and join his father, who was a tanner.'

Clarkson feigned a cough: 'Houston!' The boys laughed.

'Hey, my grades aren't all bad.'

Mr John smiled and continued. 'Providentially, for mankind, another teacher saw that his desire for knowledge and his persistent, methodical approach might come to something, and so, at the age of fifteen, Louis was enrolled in a secondary school in Paris. Unfortunately, he got homesick.'

Clarkson coughed again, 'Thornton.'

'Thank you Tom, I think that's enough.' Mr John turned back to his notes. 'And so Louis went home, trying again later nearer to home at the Royal College in Besançon, from where he graduated at the age of 20 with a BA in science. Louis wanted to be a teacher and so he studied chemistry at the Ecole Normale in Paris, where he obtained a Masters at the age of 23. He then started a doctorate, choosing, for his thesis, to study the tartrate and paratartrate crystals and explain the difference between them.'

'What are they?' Ben asked.

'No idea, but it says in my notes that this was something that had been baffling scientists for years. Now, when Louis looked through his microscope, what he saw was evidence for a mighty Creator. He applied the same cautious and methodical correctness that had once been taken as "mental slowness" in his early schooldays, and he soon cracked the enigma. There were, in fact, two sorts of paratartrate crystals, one the mirror of the other. So he gained his higher degree, some modest notoriety among research scientists, and a job as professor of chemistry at Strasbourg University, where he spent five happy years teaching and starting a family. At the age of 32, he took on a huge challenge to set up a new "applied science" faculty at Lille. Now don't forget, this was in an age when the scientific community was still largely orientated around theoretical science, something that Louis had little relish for.'

'Right, another one who wouldn't just take it from the book,' Elliot said.

'"Nothing by authority,"' quoted Adam.

'Exactly, and what really got him going was making science work to benefit mankind. It was at this time, whilst studying fermentation, that Pasteur became the father of what we now call "microbiology". This research alone would have incalculable effects on the wine and food industries of his day. Every time you have a nice glass of milk that is not sour, or – when you're with an adult, I'm sure – you have a glass of wine that is not bitter, you must thank God for this man. For it was he who discovered that gentle heating or boiling of a substance would kill off microbes and aid preservation. If he had patented this one discovery, he would have been the richest man on the planet, but he offered it freely to mankind. Perhaps he felt that God had shown it to him – I don't know; but one thing I do know is that "to him who has received much, more will be given": this benefit of pasteurization would seem small compared with the other things he would discover.'

'Hey, I bet the scientific community were chuffed!' Thornton said.

'Ah, well, not everyone was – you see, this was the time when the theory of evolution was being dragged out of the cupboard again, this time by Charles Darwin and the lesser-known Mr Wallace.'

'But sir, I don't understand how pasteurized milk could threaten evolution. I mean, what's the big deal?' Keats asked.

'Ah, it's a very big deal, as you'd know if you had been at all our earlier lectures in the Invisible College. I put to you my hypothesis that evolution is like the dispersed seed from the flowers of Greek philosophy, sometimes lying dormant in the earth for generations and waiting for the water of occultist superstition or atheistic religion to eventually revive them. Kepler saw it, Boyle saw it, Cuvier saw it, Faraday, Joule and Babbage saw it, and so did Pasteur. For Pasteur burst wide open one of evolution's essential myths: "spontaneous generation" – another Greek idea that just would not die.'

'It kept springing to life?' Clarkson added.

'Very funny, Tom.'

'Yes, I remember this,' Ben said. 'When the Greek dudes saw maggots appear on meat or weevils appear in flour, they said, "Hey, look at that – life appearing from nowhere!" And then Aristotle and some others reckoned that's how life must have happened originally.'

'Yes, exactly, Ben, well done; but of course, as we now know, there were fly and weevil eggs there, too small to see with the naked eye – though Francesco Redi proved all of this in 1668.'

'Wait a minute,' Keats said. 'That's, like, over two hundred years before Pasteur, so why hadn't the idea just, well, died?'

'Because, quite simply, if you want to be an intellectually ful-filled atheist, then you need a mechanism that will explain away God totally! So what if it sucks – as the Yanks would say. If it's all you've got; it'll have to do! Either you have "In the beginning God created ..." or "In the beginning spontaneous generation just happened in a primeval soup". Pasteur proved to the world that microbes were never spontaneously generated and that they too "must come into the world from parents similar to themselves". Of course, evolutionary theorists have been banging away ever since, trying to prove Louis wrong but, guess what – a hundred and fifty years later, spontaneous generation has still never been observed. If I were a scientist or a government using tax-payers' money to fund this kind of research, I would think that a hundred and fifty years is plenty of time to try to prove it; it's time to move on, to try something else!'

'Wow, that's so lame! I'd no idea.' Keats sank back with wonder into his chair.

'Yes, well, people who don't know history will fall for almost anything they're told. Anyway, enough of that. Let's see what else Pasteur did. He saved the French silk industry by helping farmers identify and destroy diseased silkworm eggs. His pioneering work on microbes inspired the Christian surgeon Joseph Lister, who himself pioneered "antiseptic surgery", saving the lives of millions. He also extended the work of Edward Jenner, an English physician who discovered that people who had contracted cow-pox (which is not deadly) were immune to smallpox. Jenner sought to develop the idea of vaccination by taking advantage of this naturally occurring cow-pox vaccine. Pasteur, however, took the idea to another level by creating, through tireless, methodical experimentation, vaccines for chicken cholera and anthrax in sheep and cattle. The French government awarded him their highest honour, the Legion of Honour, though it had been a hard enough slog to get the scientific and veterinary profession to accept his work.'

'But why? I mean, how could they oppose the guy?'

'Many believe that the opposition he received then, and would get later, from the medical profession was partly because he was a chemist, not a medical professional – but also because of his stance on Darwinism and spontaneous generation.'

'But even after the results!' Keats exclaimed.

'Yes, even then. Remember the times, and don't be fooled by the image of nineteenth-century Europe being a bastion of Christian virtue. Basically, a religion of atheism was in the ascendant with the new priesthood.'

'I get it – the scientists!' said Clarkson.

'Exactly, it was the very spirit of the age: the great discoveries, the great machines, and, of course, most flattering of all, *the great men* – and they loved it. It's a long throw from what Charles II saw when he looked at his Royal Society; he thought Robert Boyle's eccentric ensemble of aristocrats existed merely as a gentlemen's club to provide interesting titbits for the royal fancy. Could he have dreamed that they would one day be the archbishops for the new religion?'

'Blimey, that sounds a bit freaky,' Thornton said.

'That, Henry, is the twentieth and now twenty-first century in a nutshell, and it's more than a bit freaky, believe me. But anyway, back to the man: Pasteur saw that spontaneous generation contradicted scientific evidence and, though he was opposed by some, he went on to produce a vaccination for rabies.'

'Well, good on him! I mean, where would we be without it?' Keats said.

'Actually, when a boy bitten by a rabid dog was brought to him, he was not sure whether the vaccine would actually work on humans at all, but, realizing that the boy would certainly die if he did nothing, he agreed to try it.'

'And?'

'And it worked! Later, aged 66, with failing health, he founded the Pasteur Institute, which continued this work of fighting diseases. He kept going even at the expense of his own health, suffering a brain haemorrhage and several strokes leading to partial paralysis.'

'Well, why didn't he just retire? I mean, he'd already done quite a bit!' Clarkson said.

'It may have been because he lost three of his five children to childhood diseases, and he had seen his sister grow up with great learning disabilities as a consequence of a childhood disease. Many would say that his work went on to save more lives from untimely death than that of any other human being in history; in fact, it is possible that not one of you lot would be here today without him, if you take into account the possibility of any of your great-grandparents onwards dying from a disease that we now vaccinate against, from dodgy surgery – or dodgy food, milk or wine for that matter!'

With that sobering thought they broke off to refill their mugs and fetch more Jaffa Cakes before Mr John called them back to the fire. 'Now, boys, I want you to take special note of this next man, for you might all have more in common with him than you know. He came from obscurity and died in obscurity, and yet what he discovered should have been enough to dissuade Darwin from publishing the third edition of his *Origin of Species*. Why? Because Darwin would have seen that it disproved his theory. Now, that's got you interested hasn't it? So grab your seats and listen to this.'

The boys shuffled round the dog and took their seats in anticipation. 'Young Johann,' began Mr John, 'was born in 1822, a few months before Louis Pasteur, in what is now the Czech town of Hyncice. His father was a poor farmer, and Johann learned a love of the land and growing things. At school he was seen to be sharp and therefore sent to a secondary school thirty miles away. It was a great financial burden on his family, who were not able to pay the full fees, which meant that Johann got only half food rations and he became run-down and ill. But he did all right, although, when he finished at the school, it seemed impossible to him that he would ever be able to go to university because he lacked the cash.'

'I know that feeling,' Keats said. 'Dad's always going on about the cost of the fees and whether he can afford to keep me in a private school another year.'

'Well, Jack, you're not the first to experience that, so take courage. God had his own plans and out of the blue one of Johann's two devoted sisters, gave up her marriage dowry to assist with his university fees. Remember, without that dowry she probably would never marry, so it was a big deal. It was a show of supreme love and faith in her brother's ability and destiny, although she herself would never see the full outcome of his genius; mind you, no one would until after his death!'

'Did God get her a husband anyway?' Will said.

'Oh yes, he did, and we know that Johann was actually able to pay for the education of her two sons. So you see, "cast your bread on the waters" and all that. But back to our man. First of all, listen to this: he failed on two occasions to get formal qualifications as a teacher, though he managed to be an excellent one for fifteen years anyway by being a "temporary teacher"! Secondly, he was refused his qualifications because of gaps in his scientific knowledge, but he did not pout and strut. Rather, he went to Vienna University and studied hard, particularly on how to conduct experiments, being so impressed by the mathematical approach of the physicists. He was refused his qualification again, but, in the economies of God Almighty, he had obtained all he needed to carry out his ministry to science and mankind. If I told you that he would become the father of modern genetics, you might, if you were up on these things, say, "But sir, I don't know of anyone in that branch of science who was called Johann." Well, that would be true enough, but that's because our young Johann joined a Moravian monastery at the age of 21 and took a new name: that of Gregor.'

'Ah!' Rawkins said. 'It's Gregor Mendel!'

'Bingo. He was the one who tirelessly studied heredity in peas on a scale that was so ahead of his time that his work, even when published, would go unnoticed for over half a century, and only be discovered in 1920.'

'But you said that Darwin probably read it,' Adam said.

'Gregor sent it out to forty leading scientists in Europe. Darwin was famous by then and Mendel had certainly read Darwin's books, so we may suppose –'

'That Darwin didn't let Mendel's exacting maths get in the way of a good story,' Father George said.

'Come on, Father, we can't say that; Darwin may not have understood the maths. You know that he didn't like to have it applied to biology.'

'Yes, and a great pity that was too.' Father George rattled his walking stick. 'It would have pulled him out of his fanciful stories. But, anyway, back to 1920, my boy. What happened then?'

'It was then that three other scientists simultaneously discovered the same thing.'

'And what was it, sir, this thing that he discovered?' Keats asked.

'It's a bit complicated, but by following successive generations of pea plants that he selectively pollinated and observed, he was able to see the dominant and recessive genes and therefore establish the laws of genetic heredity, now known as Mendel's Laws of Inheritance. Back then they were just his own scribblings, though he knew he was onto something, and predicted that it "would not be long before the whole world acknowledges it".'

'It was just an inconvenient truth at the time,' Father George added.

'Yes, an unfortunate pattern we've seen a lot of. Mendel sent his work to the most eminent biologist of the day, a man called Carl von Nägeli, but Nägeli disapproved of the methods used and doubted the findings. The same man would one day write a book on evolution, which also gives us a clue as to why he and the scientific community could not accommodate this humble man's research.'

'Sorry, sir,' Clarkson said, moving to the edge of his chair. 'Are you suggesting another conspiracy?'

Mr John laughed. 'Maybe; maybe not. But listen: Mendel established the stability of created kinds. Yes, "natural selection" is a law that determines the survival of the fittest in a fallen world, but it does not establish the "arrival of the fittest". The genes never merge to provide new information; they are always separate, inherited pockets of data that join others in various combinations. They can never create a new kind!'

'But, sir, what about de Vries?' Adam asked. The others looked blank.

'Ah, thank you, Adam! I'll come to him now if you like. De Vries asked in 1901, "What about random, chance alterations in genetic data?" Could that – what we now call mutations – be the agent of change? In a word, NO! Each of us is born with about one hundred mutations, so they are rare. They are rare, in the first place – to the tune of one in ten million – and then they are either harmful, fatal or what is called *near neutral*. And even if some could be classed as beneficial, they do not add further genetic information, and that is the important point, but that's the hinge of Darwin's theory. In other words, if you're relying on this method to transform one kind into another, you're going to need more faith than any Christian I know because the product and the process of Darwin's theory have yet to be observed. And yet, would you believe it, most evolutionary scientists even try to incorporate Mendel's laws within the "evolution faith system". Yes, I know, utterly astounding!'

Father George rattled his stick again. 'But as the old saying goes, "Keep your friends close and your enemies closer still".'

'Thank you, Father. Anyway, that is young Johann's story, lads: the story of how we started to realize that in each cell there was some sort of information-storage system – what we now call DNA.'

One molecular biologist said, "It is so efficient that all the information … necessary to specify the design of all the species of organisms which have ever existed on the planet … could be held in a teaspoon and there would still be room left for all the information in every book ever written." I mean, imagine boys if you landed on the moon and found a piece of notepaper with a message written on it. Surely your first deduction would be that some form of intelligence had written it.'

'Yeah, I guess.' Rawkins said.

'Well there you are! And so serious is the dilemma,' he continued, 'that, in an act of desperation, some scientists have even said they would *not* rule out aliens having seeded life on our planet. No, don't laugh. I'm serious! That's how far they'd go in their insanity – though of course they would rule out God, strangely.'

The boys nodded solemnly, even Adam looked as if he had learnt something new.

Father George rubbed his arms. 'Don't know where my summer has gone, but we need more wood, my boys. Would you oblige?' The little group ranged the beach and dragged in the previous week's offerings of timber brought in by the tide. It was here on the shore that Adam started to quiz Mr John over the differences between Darwin's theory and others that had gone before.

'In a word, Adam: Thomas Malthus. He was the missing link for both Darwin and Wallace.'

'Who was he then, a relation of the abbott?' Keats said, as he joined them dragging a log somewhat bigger than himself.

'Doubt it. The Reverend Thomas Malthus was an Anglican clergyman. He's still hailed today as the father of population genetics. His idea of man's "struggle for existence" provided the catalyst by which natural selection produces the "survival of the fittest". Darwin called his theory an application of the doctrines of Malthus, referring to him as "that great philosopher", and he wrote in his notebook that "Malthus on Man should be studied".'

'I see; and Wallace?' Adam said.

'Who's Wallace again?' Will asked.

'Alfred Russel Wallace. He proposed the theory of natural selection at the same time. He called Malthus' essay "… the most important book I read" and considered it "the most interesting coincidence" that reading Malthus led both himself and Darwin, independently, towards the idea of evolution.'

'Wow, so Malthus was an important guy. What did he say, exactly?' Keats asked.

'Well, basically, "Population, when unchecked, increases in a geometrical ratio. Subsistence increases only in an arithmetic ratio." Simply put, he insisted that society should adopt certain social policies to prevent the human population from growing disproportionately larger than its food supply. It was an over-simplistic bit of maths but people liked it, particularly Hitler, who, over a century later, would use natural selection, along with phrases from Darwin's book, as the perfect propaganda rationale for his own genocidal purposes.'

'Come on, sir,' Keats said, as they approached the front door of the cottage. 'You can't link a misguided English vicar with a maniac like Hitler! I mean, anyone can twist someone's ideas.'

'Oh, can't I? Well, you just listen to your English country vicar's genocidal recommendations, and, when I read you these, please remember that this man is still "respected" around the world as the father of population genetics.' Mr John went inside the cottage and grabbed his notebook. The boys kicked off their boots and followed.

'Now ...,' said Mr John, finding the page. 'This will shock you, I hope. Here we are. As you can imagine, his policies specifically targeted the poor. For instance, he writes, "Instead of recommending cleanliness to the poor, we should encourage contrary habits. In our towns we should make the streets narrower, crowd more people into the houses, and court the return of the plague. In the country, we should build our villages near stagnant pools, and particularly encourage settlement in all marshy and unwholesome situations. But above all, we should reprobate specific remedies for ravaging diseases; and those benevolent, but much mistaken men, who have thought they were doing a service to mankind by projecting schemes for the total extirpation of particular disorders." There!'

'Bet he wasn't one of Louis Pasteur's admirers,' Clarkson said. 'Think of it: Pasteur saves all these lives that Malthus would rather have dead; so there'll be enough grub for him and his rich mates!'

Will looked over to see Keats' nodding his head in disbelief, his face drained of colour. 'But that really is genocidal, sir! Wasn't his book banned?'

'Banned? No, the government of the day thought it a good excuse to tighten their purse-strings and change the Poor Laws. It is the *partial* rationale behind eugenics, abortion and euthanasia.'

'A brave new world indeed,' muttered Father George from his chair, as Will put the kettle on.

'Quite right, Father. What did Huxley's grandson say in his book? You know, the bit where he says about why the masses chose science, not religion.'

'Ah yes, dear boy, I remember. It was something like, "The older dictators fell because they could never supply their subjects with enough bread, enough circuses, enough miracles, and mysteries … Under a scientific dictatorship, education will really work". Sounds a bit like the way your brother wants St Columba's to be.'

Mr John threw a log onto the fire. 'I know, Father, but I can't interfere now.'

'Ah yes, but you can pray, eh?' The old man patted his son's leg with tenderness and Mr John returned his gaze. Eventually the old man beckoned them all back to the fireside. 'Come on, come on, you lot, draw up a seat. Who's hiding those Jaffa Cakes now?'

As the Jaffa Cakes were handed round, Adam said, 'give us your take on Thomas Huxley sir. He's always been a bit of a pin up for my dad and his mates.'

Mr John talked very generally about Huxley's life and anti-religious stance, and the debates with the Bishop of Oxford. 'Of course, Huxley knew jolly well, as anyone does, that if you take the bottom from a house of cards, the whole house will fall. Genesis is the bottom card from the house of Christian theology. If you say "Jesus quoted Genesis and believed it to be accurate" and then someone proves that Genesis is unreliable … Jesus too becomes unreliable. Can't you see that?'

'Yes, sir,' they said.

'Then listen to Huxley here.' Mr John again thumbed through his notebook. 'Ah yes: "I am at a loss to comprehend how anyone for a moment can doubt that Christian theology must stand or fall with the historical trustworthiness of the Jewish scriptures. The very conception of the Messiah, or Christ, is inextricably inter-woven with Jewish history; the identification of Jesus of Nazareth with that Messiah rests upon the interpretation of the passages of the Hebrew Scriptures, which have no evidential value unless they possess the historical character assigned to them." In other words, one card from the base brings the house down! There, boys, do you see it? It's not Genesis that the spirit of the age is after, it's Jesus Christ, the Jewish Messiah, that it wants to topple.'

'So,' Adam said, taking a deep breath, 'you don't believe that the theory in itself is value-free?'

'Value-free! Not on your life! Of course it is true that wicked men will twist any ideology to get what they want. Men have even used the teachings of Jesus for wicked ends, but we all know that they were wrong. Even a twenty-first-century atheist knows that – but how? I'll tell you: because they measure what is wrong or right – or at least they used to – by what Jesus or Jehovah said. Can you see that? It is indelibly engraved, to a greater or lesser extent, on the cultural consciousness of the West.'

'And that's not the same for this new theory of origins?' Adam said.

'Lord, no. Those naïve parents who argued with me at our school governors' meetings that Darwin should be the only thing taught in the schools won't have actually read him. If they even knew the full title of *On the Origin of Species by Means of Natural Selection, or the Preservation of Favoured Races in the Struggle for*

Life, they might think twice about where evolution is going to take us, our school, our society, our civilization.'

'Careful son.' Father George raised a finger. 'In *Origins* he is referring to plant and animal races, not humans.'

'Thank you, Father. That is a good point, but he does hint at the end of *Origins* that his theory might one day shed more light on human origins. Basically, he opened the door. In his next book, *The Descent of Man*, Darwin ranked races in terms of what he believed was their nearness and likeness to gorillas. Then he went on to say that "the civilised races of man will almost certainly exterminate and replace the savage races throughout the world" without expressing any abhorrence at the concept. If this were not done, he posited, those races with much higher birth rates than "superior" races would exhaust the resources needed for the survival of better people, eventually dragging down all civilization.'

'No!' they exclaimed in unison. Will noticed Keats' hands trembling, and his eyes blazing with incredulity bordering on rage.

'I'm afraid so. I've jotted down here Darwin's primary views on race. Basically he said that:

'Humans are divided into sub-species.

'The strongest live and the weakest die, which is good, of course, according to him. Marx and Hitler agreed: "Lebensunwertes Leben" – life unworthy of life. Get rid of the "useless eaters", as Hitler said.

'Blacks and Aborigines are not simply variants. No, they occupy a sub-species between apes and Caucasians. These sub-species Darwin tellingly calls "races".

'Therefore in terms of evolutionary progression, the extinction of blacks and gorillas (to advance the white "race") must be seen as good. He wrote

300

that different sub-species have different characteristics, such as mental capabilities (e.g. Irish are also
non-Aryan and couldn't support their offspring
and should be left to go extinct). A "race war" was
inevitable, the results would be that "…the civilized
races of man will almost certainly exterminate, and
replace, the savage races throughout the world."
Another passage in Charles Darwin, *Descent,* vol. I,
201, *Life and Letters* says, "What an endless number
of the lower races will have been eliminated by the
higher civilized races throughout the world."

'And, by the way, these were not dark, hidden sections of his
secret writings; they are in his books and autobiography!'

'Sounds ominously like the Germany I remember,' Father
George said, looking steadfastly and solemnly into the fire.

'Yes, Father, and no wonder; they drank deeply of these ideas,
which became the perfect justification for racism and Nazi-style
nationalism. This totally underpinned their "racial hygiene" department.'

'Oh, that is evil,' Keats said, his white knuckles gripping the
arms of the chair. 'Really evil.'

'In Hitler's own mind, he was doing the world a great service.
He had the backing of the new science and the benediction of a
new morality and ethics that flowed from it. "If natural selection
is true, then why not work with it and do something good for
humanity, instead of propping up a load of free-loading cripples?
Let's give nature a helping hand, be its agent not its subject etc.,
etc." So he started their sterilization programme, in which three
hundred and seventy-five thousand unfit people were stopped
from reproducing.'

'But that's sick,' Keats said, his face now livid.

'Hey, boys, it happened in America too, so don't go and get all anti-German! And Britain can hardly preach to anyone about humanity; besides, we handed this theory to the world on a platter.'

'Yeah, but the Germans ran with it, didn't they? I mean, they really believed it would make a perfect society,' Keats said.

'Sure they did. The swastika is a Hindu symbol; the word is from the Sanskrit for "well-being". That's what Nazism was about; evolution was not a side issue to empire; it was the issue. These guys were saying, "We see what evolution is and we are prepared to cut the ties with an outmoded code of ethics, to follow it through to its natural conclusion." You can search for the video on the internet tonight and see Nazi propaganda films using natural-selection dogma *ad verbum* to support the sterilization of anyone who "bled the country's strength and vitality".'

'And there's my dad spouting off that it's religion that causes all wars! Once, he actually blamed the Second World War on Hitler's Catholic heritage!'

'Nonsense; Hitler was totally against anything Christian. Listen to him here in a pre-war speech: "I do insist on the certainty that sooner or later, once we hold power – Christianity will be overcome and the German church, without a Pope and without the Bible."'

'What about Communism?' Will asked. 'I remember Professor Inchikov mentioning it last term when he spoke about this.'

'Did he, now? Well, I'd say that he knows his stuff, and that first-hand, too! Yes, of course, Karl Marx could see that Darwin had given validity to atheism, and he developed it with his political theories to give a purely naturalistic state religion. He would doubtless have agreed with Hitler: "Christianity is a rebellion against natural law, a protest against nature. Taken to its logical conclusion, Christianity would mean the systematic cultivation of human failure." So we have Stalin, Mao Zedong, Kim Il-Sung and Pol Pot, a hundred million deaths and about as much human oppression, misery and anguish as you can get. But it's just like Solomon said in Ecclesiastes 10 verses 12 to 14, "the philosophy of an atheist (literally; a fool) will bring destruction. He writes books and manifestos about how the future should be but because his starting point is all wrong his conduct will always tend to total madness."'

The boys packed up their gear at 4 p.m. and wandered back across the cliff. Their minds were jammed full, and it took them most of the walk back simply to adjust to normality. Adam was, for some reason Will could not fathom, chatty and in a buoyant mood, but Keats was fierce in his disgust about the lies he'd been sold for so long. He ranted at the top of his voice about it. Will cautioned him to be measured in what he said, but he took no notice.

As they rounded the corner by the circle, and were almost back in School bounds, they heard Sidmouth's nasal voice shout down from the cliff above, 'All right you lot, stop right there. You're busted, all of you, and this time you're going straight to Dundas – and to the Senate!'

19

BEFORE THE SENATE

Y ou did what!' Dundas shouted at Sidmouth, as he rose
from his seat in the prefects' study, where he had dragged
Will as 'the ringleader'. Brummell and Wordsmith looked
up from their books.

'Look, younger Pitt was with them, so I notified the duty prefect in Aiden's.'

'Oh, and the fact that it was Coburg didn't influence your efficiency, did it?'

'I followed school protocol. Pitt had been out of bounds, so
they had a right to know.'

'Ben Pitt fags for a boy in this house – you knew that! We could
have dealt with matters here and told his brother in private.'

'I really don't see that his connection to the head boy has any
bearing, and I don't think you should bend the rules to suit your
friends –'

'Don't lecture me, Sidmouth, or I'll smash those zits across
your ugly face! Now, get out of here and let me think. Houston,
you stay where you are.'

Sidmouth sulkily protested. 'Well, there's no need to be personal, I was just doing my j –'

Brummell grabbed him by the collar and flung him headlong
towards the door. 'OUT, sly git,' he said, 'and shut the door behind
you.'

When Sidmouth had gone, the three prefects talked quietly. Dundas pinched his eyes and groaned. 'I could kill him; he's been looking all year for a chance to undermine me like this, and now, Houston; you play right into his hands.'

Will raised his hands, 'I'm really sorry.'

'Shut up, Houston, just shut up.' Dundas pinched his eyes shut. 'I can't handle this right now, not with exam pressure as well.'

'So, the Senate will deal with it.' Brummell said. 'Speak to Pitt and a few of the players; argue for leniency.'

'Come on, Brummell, you know how unbending Pitt will be, particularly with your mate Coburg breathing down his neck. If anything, he'll play it more by the book than ever. No.' Dundas bit his lip and looked at the clock. 'They're going to be crucified for this, and there's nothing we can do about it.'

Wordsmith snorted. 'Don't be melodramatic! We've all been caught out of bounds! God knows I have.'

'It's not that! Don't you get it? They were coming back from Mr John's house; they've been having the Invisible College, even after what the headmaster said. And I doubt we'll be able to keep it from him.'

A meeting of the Senate was called after prayers that night, and Dundas escorted Will and the others through the Great Hall to the prefects' common room. Will wore the house colours in a vain effort to gain grace in Dundas' sight, though Dundas barely noticed the gesture when he passed him. 'Stupid cretin, Houston, why didn't you listen to me?' Dundas walked quickly so they could barely keep up. When they eventually reached a dark ante-room, he snapped, 'Wait here. Don't move. Don't speak.' Adam leant against the panelling and looked up with a smirk. 'What? You boys never been to a firing squad before? It gets easier each time, believe me.'

'Just shut up, will you. It's not funny.' Thornton's jittery hands were trying to straighten his tie. 'I knew it. I should never have let you talk me into any of this.'

Clarkson placed a comforting hand on his shoulder. 'Shut up, and don't be so wet.'

Elliot was quite tearful. Will steadied him. 'Come on, Elliot. They'll go easy on you. We'll just say that Rawkins made you go as his fag.'

Elliot started to sob. 'But is it true they can still beat you in there?'

'No one will lay a hand on you, Elliot. I promise,' Will said. 'Do they still, Thornton?'

'Of course not,' Thornton snapped. 'More's the pity. At least then it would be over and done with. Now they're left with fewer options and it could be a lot worse for us.'

'What?' Clarkson said. 'Might damage your chances of being a prefect!'

'Oh shut up, Clarkson. Why do you always have to be so "anti" all the time?'

Clarkson didn't get a chance to answer as Coburg approached from behind them with a few Dragoons in tow. He pushed Ben Pitt toward the others. 'Wait there and don't move. Oh, Houston, what a surprise! Seems like you didn't escape after all.' He leaned over so that Will could get the full impact of his foul beer-breath. 'I think I'm going to enjoy this more than cleaning our bogs with your head.' Will said nothing but stared intently at him until the prince broke off, leading his friends through the heavy oak doors.

A minute later they were summoned. Will went to go first but Ben Pitt held him back and talked quietly to him for a moment before entering, it was only a moment's whisper, but it was enough – and then they entered.

The prefects' common room was a bit like the prefects' room in Aiden's but larger and resembled more a gentlemen's club, or at least what Will had seen of them on TV. There were leather chairs in small groups around a huge fireplace, a billiards table, and a small kitchenette in the far-right corner. Straight ahead of them was a huge dining table, used once a term for special dinners. Great wooden boards hung on the walls with names and dates of former prefects. Oil paintings and framed photographs of old boys who had gone on to be men of particular note hung on the walls.

The prefects, all perfectly still, stood around the great table, facing each other. A door opened beyond them and Pitt came in, with Dundas behind. They took their seats at the table and the others sat. All the while, no one so much as acknowledged the guilty seven standing by the doors, which were closed behind them.

'Right, gentlemen,' Pitt said. 'Let's get started. The chair recognizes Prince Von Coburg, who has a matter to bring to our attention.'

The prince stood and, driving his index finger on the table to make his point, said, 'It was brought to my attention –'

'Cretin,' Adam half coughed, half whispered.

'– to my attention, by the duty prefect from St Alban's house, that these boys have been going to the cove to visit the house of the disgraced brother of our headmaster. In any event, you can question them yourselves, and you might well find that these visits have been regular events and relate to meetings expressly forbidden by the headmaster and abbot.' Coburg lingered, leered at Will and then took his seat.

Pitt spoke, remaining seated. 'We thank the prince for his diligence in bringing this matter to us. We also pass our thanks to the other duty prefect for his promptness and impartiality. The floor is open, gentlemen; your thoughts, please.'

Canning, who had been looking pensive, asked, 'Is it true, Houston? Did Mr John start the Invisible College again?'

'Yes, he did.' *Of course, most of these guys must have been former members.* 'He didn't want to, after you sold him out last time, but I persuaded him to.'

Canning stared at Will. His huge shoulders dropped and his eyes welled up. 'But they said –'

The Dragoon Clarendon sprang to his feet. 'I fail to see why you have got us here, Pitt. This is a school matter, quite beyond our powers. As the prince said, they have, by their own admission, been engaged in something prohibited by the head. This is no house matter.'

Pitt, who was looking down at the table, did not answer immediately. 'What? … Yes, I suppose. Anyone else have anything to say?'

Will looked the length of the table but there was either denial or triumph in the faces of those gathered. The prince looked again at Will and gave a wry smile; he had won. There was no way that Will could not be expelled for violating an explicit order. There was a silence as Coburg looked round to Pitt for the verdict. Pitt was looking steadfastly at his younger brother and Will saw him mouth "I'm sorry" to him. *It would not be good.*

Pitt stood, and the other prefects stood also. Pitt opened his mouth to speak, but Will blurted out, 'I, er, I appeal to the house heads!'

'Silence, you imbecile!' Coburg said. 'You have no right to appeal unless you're in the top year!'

'I appeal to the house heads,' Will repeated.

For the first time in the procedure, Dundas turned to face him, and then his eyes widened. 'Of course, those in the top years, but also those with house colours!' Will saw Ben give his older brother a wink and Pitt grinned back.

'Nonsense!' Coburg shouted. 'Never heard such rubbish!'

'I can assure you, Your Highness,' Fox said, breaking his bulk away from the table and walking towards Will, 'it's all in the rules.'

And then to Will. 'To the house heads you have appealed my young friend, so to the house heads you shall go … gentlemen?'

Dundas and Pitt started to go, but three of the other house heads, taking their cue from Coburg's frown, declined the privilege. Will followed Fox, Dundas and Pitt into the back room.

'All right, Houston, this'd better be good,' Pitt said.

'Oh, I'm sure it will be,' Fox said, impishly slumping down into a window seat and leaning back. 'Mr Houston lives only to add texture to the dullness of school life. Someone get me a drink.'

'Well, come on then, Houston, what is it?' Dundas said.

Will eyed the three of them. 'You must give me your word,' he said with faltering voice, 'that you will not breathe a word of what I am about to tell you.'

'For heaven's sake, Houston, that's enough theatrics! You're hardly in a bargaining position!' Dundas shouted.

'You see,' said Fox. 'Texture and colour!'

'You must swear,' Will said.

Pitt looked at Dundas and sighed. 'All right. Go on. But no more theatrics.'

'Has the head told you why the police are here?'

'He said they're working on busting a marijuana syndicate,' Pitt said.

Fox laughed. 'Naturally – that's why they spend so much time interviewing monks and teachers. Probably caught Brendan and Reece growing their own in the crypt!'

'Okay, Houston, so why are they here?' said Pitt.

'Because of Percival.'

'Percival's dead,' Pitt hissed, clenching the tail of his jacket with his thumb and forefinger. 'So what is all this about?'

'He was murdered.'

'Oh, for heaven's sake …' Dundas began, but Pitt cut in.

'What?'

'It wasn't suicide; it was murder.'

Pitt slumped involuntarily in the chair next to Fox, his mouth wide open. 'What? By whom?'

'He was ritually executed by the Druids at the Millennial solstice.'

Dundas was about to cut Will short but Pitt raised his hand. 'No Dundas. Let him speak. I knew it.'

'All right Houston,' Dundas snapped. 'You've got five minutes to tell us what you know.'

Will explained all he'd discovered and did his best to answer the myriad questions that they came back with. By then even Dundas was sitting, wide-eyed with shock.

Eventually Pitt looked about the room, as if gathering his wits. 'I bet it was Kentigern; he's an evil devil. I've always thought he was.'

'Steady,' Fox said. 'Let us hear what Mr Houston proposes before we jump to any conclusions.'

Will leaned over the small round table between them and whispered, 'Okay, I think there will be a repeat sacrifice on 21st June, three weeks tonight. It might be our only chance to catch the killers. If you blow the Invisible College thing now, then the guilty parties might close ranks and try to pin it on Mr John, just as they did before with the suicide.'

Fox puckered his lips and looked across to Pitt. The head boy didn't look convinced, so Will added, 'If nothing happens on the twenty-first, then fine: hand us over; but I'm sure the next victim has already been lined up. Come on, I think you at least owe it to Mr John.'

Dundas exploded. 'Now wait a minute, you can't use emotional blackmail on us; we were kids.'

'No. He's right.' Pitt softened his voice. 'We do owe it to Mr John. We were cowards and we took the easier way.'

'Oh fine – and the school rules? Our responsibility to the head-master?' Dundas said.

'My dear Dundas,' Fox said, 'if your Mr Houston is right, there won't be much of a school left after the police have finished, so I wouldn't overly concern yourself.'

There followed many thoughts and as many words. They forged a plan quickly and when this was agreed upon, they returned to the common room to address the other prefects. Pitt solemnly reminded them of the rules of privacy that governed meetings of the Senate. No one was permitted to tell a master or another boy what had transpired there. Coburg glared at Fox; Fox smiled. For once he was enjoying being on a different side.

Pitt delivered the judgement: 'Because of extenuating circumstances, the house heads have agreed to "gate" the boys before us and have them fag for the first XI cricket team this summer.'

'What!' Coburg hissed, glaring at Will. 'You can't – I won't let it.'

But he soon felt the shovel-like hands of Canning and Grenville on his shoulders. 'Shut it – or else,' Grenville said.

'Well, now.' A broad grin crossed Fox's sweaty face. 'I'm parched! Anyone for sherry and a game of billiards?'

The boys went out and were escorted back to their houses. 'Wasn't so bad after all,' Clarkson said, nudging Thornton who was grinning once more.

'Yeah, but thanks to you, Tom. What did you tell them Houston?'

'Never you mind. But tell me one thing, what in the world is it to be "gated"?'

'Basically to be put on permanent curfew,' Clarkson said. 'Only allowed from the house for lessons and games – no more.'

Thornton breathed a sigh of relief and added, 'And let that be an end of the matter.'

Will looked at his shoes, then up to the Necropolis woods half a mile to his left on the skyline, ignoring the hairs beginning to stand up on his neck. 'Yeah, let's hope so.'

20

Expulsion

Quick, Will, you've gotta get to the Big Passage mate. We're really up the creek this time.' Clarkson dragged Will from his maths homework down the corridor, and there hanging at one end of the Great Hall was a huge poster of Adolf Hitler with a speech bubble that read, 'The civilized races of man will almost certainly exterminate, and replace, the savage races throughout the world.' Another bubble underneath read, 'What an endless number of the lower races will have been eliminated by the higher civilized races throughout the world.' And then came the shock accreditation underneath for both quotations: "Charles Darwin, *Descent*, vol. I, 201. *Life and Letters*".

Will cupped his mouth. 'We've been betrayed. There's a mole in the Invisible College. Is this the only one?'

'Are you kidding, they're all over the school, plus whoever it is has hacked into the school's server and posted them there too; it's on the website which means the media, the parents, everyone will be reading it.'

As the boys swarmed and chatted around that poster in the Big Passage, more boys came shouting that there were others at the science labs, the geography classrooms and on the monastery noticeboards. Will and Clarkson followed the crowd down to the science labs, where they found a Monty Python-style poster showing Gibbs, with an ape's body, trampling on an Intelligent Design textbook and waving his finger, saying, 'No intelligence allowed;

Darwin has every answer for our department.' Underneath, Darwin was quoted saying, 'I am quite conscious that my speculations run quite beyond the bounds of true science' and, 'Long before having arrived at this part of my work, a crowd of difficulties will have occurred to my reader. Some of them are so grave that to this day I can never reflect on them without being staggered …'

'This is not good, Tom. Who do you think did it? Adam?'

'I dunno mate, but these aren't the most offensive, come to the geography noticeboards.' Will followed Clarkson down the steps and along the corridor where more cackling first years were pointing at posters pinned everywhere – doors, boards, walls – all the same. Will ripped one down and looked to see a caricature of Mr George and Abbott Malthus bowing before Darwin and reading an 'Origin of Species' Bible. Both caricatures had a look of shocked horror. The speech bubbles read, 'But, as by this theory, innumerable transitional forms must have existed, why do we not find them embedded in countless numbers in the crust of the earth?' Underneath was a picture of Mr Geoffroy, the school geography teacher, giving the modern update: 'Well, Gibbs, old chap, we're a hundred and fifty years on and still no change, but no reason to sweat: we know the theory is right, so there's no reason to change the textbooks just yet!'

In other corridors there was even a poster showing Adam's dad sporting devilish horns and a tail and telling Mr Gibbs, 'Now, remember: keep telling the kids that all the evidence points towards evolution, and if anyone says otherwise, we'll call them fundamentalists, okay?' Gibbs was depicted grinning and holding open a copy of *Origins* behind his back, which showed the following quote: 'For I am well aware that scarcely a single point is discussed in this volume on which facts cannot be adduced, often apparently leading to conclusions directly opposite to those at which I have arrived.'

On the monastery noticeboards and on every door were also A4 posters showing the abbot saying, 'Of course, Darwin wasn't against the Bible as a whole, just a fundamentalist interpretation of it.' Underneath, Darwin was seen holding a match to a Bible and saying, 'From its manifestly false history of the earth … [the Bible] was no more to be trusted than the sacred books of the Hindus, or the beliefs of any barbarian.'

Will sat on the stone steps, shaking his head, 'We are for it this time, Tom. No one is going to believe it wasn't us. But who would do it? Sure it wasn't you?'

'No! Can't draw, for one thing.'

'No, but Keats can!'

'Yeah. He can draw all right, Will, and he looked none too chuffed the other day after all that Nazi stuff we learned.'

Will stood up, 'The selfish little cretin, I told him to bottle it, but I knew he hadn't listened, and now we're all for the chop. How could he?'

'HOUSTON, CLARKSON!' The boys turned to see Gibbs advancing down the corridor, his face purple with rage. 'Happy at last are we? Well, you'll find the headmaster not so happy, and he's ordered you and your little gang up to his office double time.'

'But, sir.'

'Shut up, Houston. Think you're so smart? Well it's over. We won't be seeing you again, so good-bye and good riddance.'

By the time Will and Clarkson arrived outside the headmaster's office, the other five were already standing in line, silent, heads downcast and shoulders' slumped. Even Adam.

'Hello, Jack. Nice work,' Will whispered sarcastically, looking across at Keats who stared pursed lipped at the head master's door.

'Don't worry, any of you. I'll say it was me – stick it right in their faces. They can expel me if they want but at least they can never go back to pulling the wool over one generation of students' eyes.'

'I laud your faith in human nature, Keats,' Adam said, 'but you'll find most people – that is, people unlike your good self – are on a happiness search, not a truth search.'

'Rich coming from you Rawkins.' Keats pushed his spectacles up his nose, but did not take his eyes from the closed door.

'Just saying, mate. If the Invisible College has taught you anything, it's that people choose which truth they want to believe. Just build your hopes up, that's all.'

'ENTER!'

The boys jumped at the headmaster's voice, then Will noticed Keats licking his lips and starting to breathe hard. He reached over and placed a hand on Keats' slender shoulder. 'It's okay, Jack. We're all together. Right, lads.' Will tried the handle, but Keats pushed himself in front slowly but firmly, whispering, 'You've been a good friend Houston. I won't forget you.' He walked in ahead of them to where Mr George, stood in the window behind his desk, hands on hips, slowly shaking his head.

'Sir, sir, before we go any further I swear to you that I and I alone am responsible for the posters. These guys knew nothing of it until today.'

'Is that true Houston? Rawkins?'

Will nodded. 'Yes sir.'

'And my brother, did he put you up to this? Well, did he? Answer me.' Mr George's hands shook, his eyes wide with fury.

'Mr John? No sir, of course not. Why would he?'

'Ah, so you have seen him.' The headmaster's right eye began to twitch. 'Well, my brother is not a well man, and has the unfortunate habit of passing on his condition to impressionable boys with disastrous results.'

I'm not taking this. Will stepped forward. 'Sir, that is unfair.'

'MR HOUSTON!' Mr George exploded, shouted with such force that saliva flew across the desk. 'If I want you to speak, or advise me in any way about my family, or my school, or anything, I WILL ASK YOU. But until such a time you will remain silent.' He released his trembling grip on the back of his chair, leaving a greasy mark, and started to walk towards Keats. 'Right, Master Keats, help me understand your difficulties, so we can move on with the day's business, and I can get back to calling EVERY SINGLE JOURNALIST AND PARENT TO CONVINCE THEM THAT THIS SORT OF STUNT WILL NEVER HAPPEN AGAIN!'

Keats said nothing for a moment, not even meeting Mr George's glare. But after a pause he slid his glasses onto the bridge of his nose again and said, 'I expect you'll find that the parents will want to know when this school will begin to teach science without atheistic blinkers on.'

Mr George's face fell from grimace to open mouthed incredulity. 'You stupid, naïve boy. Did you really think any of the other parents or boys care about my brother's twisted theology and scientific conspiracies?' He took hold of Keats' lapel and pulled him back to the window and pointed down below to the school buildings. 'Right now the boys who laughed at your little posters will be learning their letters, and in an hour they will eat their lunch. In a few weeks we'll have Rawkins' father speak some sense to us, and after that they will forget that this morning ever happened – but you – you!' He spat. 'You are expelled, sir, and will never be permitted here again. And when you are festering in some back office after your state-school education, you will remember this day, and how you threw away your life on this – this misguided, religious side issue!'

Keats pulled his lapel free. 'A side issue, is it? I bet you never thought to wonder why a side issue needs such constant suppression, such dogmatic intolerance!' Keats fumbled for the notebook in his jacket pocket and, turning to the back page, said, 'As Martin Luther said. "If I profess with the loudest voice –"'

'Oh please spare me! Worse than my brother, and all his quotes.'

But Keats shouted above him, '"IF I PROFESS WITH THE LOUDEST VOICE and clearest exposition every portion of the truth of God except precisely that little point which the world and the devil are attacking, I am not confessing Christ, however boldly I may be professing Christ. Where the battle rages, there the loyalty of the soldier is proved, and to be steady on all the battlefield besides, is mere night and disgrace if he flinches at that point." Basically sir, what I will remember is that a living dog is better than a dead lion.'

'That's quite enough from you!' Mr George pointed to the door.

'No, it is not.' Keats stamped his foot. 'You say I've condemned myself to a back office. Well I say, I'd rather be a road-sweeper who knows how to view the universe than some jumped-up eunuch of a scientific system cut loose from its founders and its God-ordained purpose!'

'That's it, all of you, out of my sight. Go help Mr Keats pack for his new life, away, away from here.'

They didn't need to be told twice.

Will and Adam went back with Keats to help him pack. His father came before dinner. There were stiff goodbyes, but Will was glad to be there. Back at the house he explained everything to Dundas without being summoned, and Dundas seemed appeased.

For a week, everything seemed back to normal, almost as if nothing had ever happened. Even the police seemed less evident, and certainly Will heard of no arrests. Because of this, he was more careful than ever to always be in company; not because he feared physical assault, but so that he might always have witnesses in case of false accusation. He also made sure that the first XI cricket team had no cause to find fault with his work, which was endless. Oiling cricket bats and whiting pads and shoes were the least of his new chores, for he and his friends became the grounds-maintenance and laundry team too. It was a hard grind but Will, in a strange way, enjoyed the challenge, and there were perks even there. Many times, on long summer evenings, he would be called on to catch for the practices, and it was soon seen that not only were his feet golden, but his throw was pretty good too. This did not get him a place in the team that year but it was certainly here, bearing his punishment and in between his menial chores, that Will's future skills at the game were honed.

On Friday night, while the rains lashed his bedroom window, Will was on his mobile updating Mr John on his research about ergotism, as the effects of ergot poisoning were called. 'Yeah, the medical dictionary says pretty much what you said; "symptoms of ergotism, also called 'St Anthony's Fire' or 'Ignis Sacer' – namely irrational behaviour, convulsions, strong uterine contractions, nausea, seizures and unconsciousness – "' At first he did not see Adam's face but instead kept on talking about how some historians suspected ergotism of being a possible, undiagnosed factor in the French Revolution or Salem Witch Trials. It was soon after he mentioned the word Ignis Sacer that he noticed Adam fumbling frantically in his jacket pocket. Adam produced a little card, just like the one found on Percival's body. Will read the same spiky handwriting, *Ignis Sacer*. He almost dropped the phone. 'Wait a minute, Mr John – I'll call you back.'

Will stared wide-eyed at Adam, and tried for a moment to control his breathing. 'W…where on earth did you get this?'

'I don't know – I just found it in my jacket pocket.'

'When? It's really important – when?'

'Few weeks back. Why? What does it mean?'

'Means we'd better call the police, and quickly!'

21

THE ARREST AND THE LECTURE

Will and Mr John agreed to meet Inspector Peel privately in a quiet part of the school where they could talk unobserved. The investigation was now six weeks old, and Peel had turned up nothing solid to go on, so this was a very significant development.

Adam produced the card, and Will rattled on about this being a way the Druids marked their victims before murder and about Adam needing protection, particularly as the solstice was just a week away. Peel said little as he examined the card closely. Eventually he commented that it was a shame that they couldn't have had it sooner for the forensic people to look at. After asking a number of leading questions, he gave them both his mobile number and told them he'd be in touch when he had had time to think about it.

'And the Druids? I mean, you have their names.'

'These are strange times Mr Houston. Those Druids have every right to practice their religion, as do you. We've questioned them and if we push any more, the school solicitor told me in no uncertain terms that CID will be done for religious harassment. The knife is clean as far as forensics go, and the parchments tell us nothing to incriminate anyone. My Super ain't happy, and frankly, nor am I. I've one lead to work through, but I can't discuss it right now. My advice to you is to leave it to the professionals and not to agitate the situation.'

'Will, Will, they've got him!' It was forty-eight hours before the solstice. Will was between lessons in the Great Hall when he saw Ben running towards him, his face streaked with tears.

'What do you mean? What's the matter Ben?'

'They've taken him. Oh Will, they've got him!' His voice was shrill and desperate.

Will drew him into an alcove to protect him from the stares and whispers. 'Easy, Ben, not so loud. Now, what do you mean: taken who?'

'Mr John! He's been arrested for the murder of Percival. My brother just told me!'

'What? He can't have been. This is madness!'

'Apparently Peel has evidence! It will be all over the school tonight.'

Will found somewhere quiet to call Peel's mobile.

'Hi, it's me, Will.'

'You've heard, then. Well, it didn't take long. I was going to call you,' Peel said, his voice distant on his car's hands-free set-up.

'You've made a big mistake, sir. I don't know what this evidence is, but it's a stitch-up, you've got to believe –'

'Listen, Will, I don't have to believe anything except the evidence. You've done your bit, lad, now let justice take its course, eh?'

'But Mr John couldn't have done it!'

'Why not? You're a canny lad; I dare say, when you've had time to separate your emotions, you'll be able to look at the facts squarely. An unmarried man who attracts kids around him, a case history of instability and religious fanaticism, the last one to see Percival alive, the one who was likely up all night cutting up that dog of his to turn you against the Druids –'

Will gasped. 'No, he couldn't –' but Peel continued.

'The one who saved you from the hooded druids that chased you that night and managed to get away unharmed – and then there are his secret trips abroad, his arsenal of weapons. He was the one who planted the card in Rawkins' pocket, deciphered it and would use it to lure you out at the solstice on some witch-hunt to save your roommate, but which would, in fact, end in your death, with all the evidence pointing at everyone else who no doubt slighted him and had him out of his job – a powerful enough motive by any measure.'

Will burst out, 'It can't be, it's impossible, he couldn't –'

'Will, you've been taken in, and he's a clever blighter, I'll give him that. You just content yourself that you'll be alive this time next week. Anyway, look, I'm on the road – I'll call you later.'

He hung up and left Will reeling. For a full twenty-four hours he could not reveal the conversation to his friends, such were the depths of his confusion. Did he trust Mr John because he fit what Will held to be a sound Christian worldview about the compromised monks? Had he been seduced by his own religious bigotry? Certainly many things rang true: Mr John was obsessive about Percival's death, and Will had felt very frightened that morning with him in the necropolis. And then there was what Hannah had said. She hadn't liked the sound of him or the whole business from the beginning – but there were so many other things to consider and balance as well.

On Friday afternoon of 20th June, just twelve hours before the official solstice, Will saw Fathers Bede and Kentigern walking together on the playing fields, having just descended the hill from the woods behind the necropolis. Will knew that they had been to inspect the huge wicker man sculpture and were no doubt preparing for that night. His confused mind flared up with questions, and his stomach knotted up with his indecision.

As he stood there in desperation, he heard the rattle of old Arthur's wheelbarrow behind him and his friendly whistling. 'Now then, Master Houston, you do look deep in thought on this fine summer's day, most boys has only got faces like that during exam time, and your A levels is next year.'

Something in the genuine kindness, or perhaps even homeliness, of Arthur's voice drew out all of Will's emotion in a stream of tears, though he said nothing and did not cry out.

'Now then, lad, don't trouble yourself. You hold this here dove and come back to my shed for a brew.'

Arthur handed Will a fledgling collared dove from his barrow. The dove's wing was damaged and stuck out slightly.

'What happened to him?' Will asked with concern.

'Fell out of a tree. Mind, their mothers build such daft nests it's no wonder! Hold it close now, lad. It's still a bit skittish-like.'

They went to his potting shed for a brew, as Will had done so often over the previous months. Arthur rattled on about nothing in particular as he splinted and tied the wing up. Then, without looking up, he said to Will, 'And what's wrong with your laal wings, lad, eh? Breaking your heart like you were out there?'

Will, sensing that their meeting had been heaven-sent, poured out his heart to the old gardener while he tended the bird. 'And so you see,' Will finished, 'I'm so confused. I just don't know what to think or who to turn to. Perhaps it was Mr John all along, but perhaps not – and if not, well …'

Will trailed off, and Arthur, putting the bird in a box by the window, said, 'You're worried about your friend.'

'Yes, I am. What do you think?'

'Me? Well, for one thing, lad, I'll tell you for nowt: larl Mr John's done nowt wrong. I've known him since him and George were in short trousers. There's no harm in him, but the other lot – well, old Arthur's not the brightest pebble on t'beach, but I've eyes enough to see what them lot get up to –'

'So you know about them?' Will said.

'Ay, lad, more than they know, but I'll not let harm come to this friend of yours, I swear it.' Arthur bent down, leaning his elbows on the window-ledge, and looked towards the priory. 'Mind, we'll need a plan, and not just to protect your friend – we'll have to catch t'others in the act if we're going to help Mr John.'

Will and Arthur discussed various ideas for what to do that night and decided on a stake-out around the perimeter of St Alban's. Adam was going out for dinner with his father and the headmaster straight after the headmaster's lecture that evening. Expecting that he would be back and asleep from the effects of booze well before midnight, Will agreed to a rendezvous with Arthur shortly after that time.

'Aye, okay, midnight. Bring a torch and that fancy mobile, so we can call t'authorities if we need.'

Arthur also said he would bring tie wraps to serve as handcuffs, and told Will to bring his speed and muscle. 'I dare say, tackling Druids will be nay different from t'rugger lads, eh?' Will laughed at the flattery and left the shed, thanking God and feeling altogether more settled.

It was no surprise, after all that had transpired over the previous weeks, that the headmaster's midsummer lecture was the talk of dinner that night. Every boy was obliged to attend, but on this occasion there were few indeed who would have stayed away. This was not a debate, but the boys would be entitled to ask questions to a panel at the end of the lecture. The panel would, of course, include Professor Rawkins but also members of the school staff. The boys bolted down their suppers and most of the school was already seated in the auditorium at least twenty-five minutes before the lecture was due to start.

Will was pleased to see Professor Inchikov on the panel. He was flanked by Father Kentigern, the self-styled religious intellectual who was present, no doubt, to field questions of a spiritual nature. There was Gibbs, too, who had asked to be there. Many of the more local parents occupied the front rows, and the various personnel from the television company were milling around with cables and walkie-talkies. As the clock struck seven, Mr George introduced the speaker and Professor Rawkins walked to the lectern in the centre of the stage. He was balding, but handsome with it, the remainder of his hair being curly and black like Adam's. He wore a beige suit and blue shirt with no tie and was, Will thought, a lot shorter than he appeared on TV. Will was desperate to find fault and hate him from the outset, but he seemed so reasonable and witty, even winsome, that Will found this very hard.

'A very good evening to you all.' Professor Rawkins walked in front of the podium, nodding his head. 'We stand at the beginning of another millennium, faced with colossal challenges and, in my opinion, tremendous opportunities. Two weeks ago I was speaking to the United Nations about these very issues, and they agreed with me. Science has made strides in the last thirty years that were unthinkable to our fathers. In twenty years more, who knows? Maybe stem-cell research might cure all disease; cloning might bring back extinct animals, or even humans; advances in security might make the world safer from terrorists. My question tonight is, are you ready to be part of this great challenge, to embrace it, to carry it forward?'

He went on to speak of a world where the extremes of religious ideologies that had plagued mankind with so much misery would soon be replaced by a new tolerance, a common ideal. He spoke of the new ethical possibilities, the spread of a new technocracy, of planetary exploration – and many other new ideas that flattered and inspired. He rounded off by repeating, with open hands, his challenge.

The boys lapped it up, breaking into a spontaneous and ecstatic applause. Rawkins bowed and took his seat on the panel, where Gibbs shook his hand with sycophantic zeal and Kentigern looked as dour as ever. Professor Inchikov glowered at the table and scribbled with a pencil back and forth across the paper in front of him. Mr George, dapper in his best double-breasted suit, thanked the speaker and invited questions.

Adam was on his feet straight away, and having been acknowledged, asked, 'Does Professor Inchikov agree with our speaker, and this prevalent modern view, that all value is relative and merely subjective? And is this a philosophically supportable position for an advancing scientific age?'

Mr George looked at the professor. 'Perhaps a brief answer professor.' His hard stare was lost on Inchikov, who continued to wear out his pencil until the lead broke, after which he leaned towards the table microphone slowly and replied, 'There has never been a child yet who thinks he does not know better than his parent, and I suppose there has yet to be a generation of men who have not in some way felt themselves better than those who preceded them, but never –' he glowered '– never has there been a generation of men who have not given place to the cultural accumulation of traditional values.' He paused, and his eyes travelled round everyone in his bewildered audience. He continued, 'That is, *until this one*. And I would say this most sternly to all who would listen: the debunking of traditional value, as highlighted so vacuously tonight, is as illogical philosophically as it is ruinous socially, a ruin from which mankind will not, and cannot, recover, for it will be total.'

He leant back in his seat as the lightning bolt went out to his hearers. After a moment or two, a very ruffled headmaster asked for a response from his eminent guest.

Professor Rawkins smiled to reassure the audience and said, 'Objective value is just one more overhang of our ancestral heritage. That might have helped primitive societies develop, but, now that society has evolved to this degree, to cling to outmoded prejudicial viewpoints is harmful to us as a species. What is true for you may not necessarily be true for me, but, either way, we need to move on from this *old ground* to face the challenges of the new millennium. Surely the teacher on my right wouldn't keep these boys in the Dark Ages?'

Without being asked to respond, Inchikov leaned forward to the microphone. 'My name is Conrad Inchikov, Professor of Philosophy, and I tell you that objective value must be held as supremely valuable to us, whether our value base is Aristotelian, Stoic, Platonic, Christian, Muslim or Oriental.'

'What kinds of objective values?' Professor Rawkins said.

'Things like life being sacred, that children are delightful and old people venerable; these are universal values, not because we feel them emotionally, but because they are true. If you try, by your endless debunking and relativism, to reject what some may call "natural law" or "traditional morality", or "first principles of practical reason", "first platitudes" or whatever, by saying that they are just one of any number of value systems, you reject all source of future value. You cut the string forever. If you try to replace it, as you suggest, that will, in turn, be self-contradictory, for whatever presents itself as a new ideology will be just a lone fragment isolated from the old, swollen to madness and ridden to death.'

'So, now you are trying to uphold all the old superstitions and value systems?'

'I am not saying that they do not contain absurdities, but I am saying that you can no more create a new system of values, as you have proposed, than you could produce a new primary colour. I also say that you can only cut so far through the branch of the tree on which you sit before you realize too late which side you were sitting on as you fall.'

'Well, I'm sorry, I disagree; it's nonsense to suggest that to go on is to go back. That's just scaremongering.'

'Your image of infinite unilinear progression is understandable, but there are some progressions where the final step is *sui generis*, incommensurable with the others and, in fact, undoes the others.

It's like the man who found a particular stove so efficient that it halved his heating bill, so he bought another stove and reasoned that he could heat his house for free.' This brought a muffled laugh from the audience.

'This is ludicrous!' said Professor Rawkins. 'You would stop the necessary progression and efficiency of science to benefit the good of mankind by these vain hypotheses, these silly jokes.'

'Good of mankind? But who could decide that value? You talk of "necessary progression and efficiency", but necessary for what? Progressive for what? Efficient for what? What is this great end that you condition us towards? How will you decide this value? In the end, everything that claimed objective value will be cut away to leave one thing – yes, the one thing for which objectivity was never claimed in the first place: our own subjective desire. The mere impulse to scratch the itch, to pull to pieces what interests you. For when whatever says "It is good" has been done away with, whatever says "I want" remains. Whoever has the power to condition men in this future world you have spoken of tonight must necessarily have this alone as their basis for deciding out of what cloth to cut men from then on.'

'We thank you, Professor –' Mr George said with a nervous laugh.

But Inchikov raised his hand slightly. 'A little longer, headmaster, please, for the point must be answered and made clear. Professor Rawkins, the future you speak of will perhaps be more honest than the denial present here today, but it is altogether more terrifying. For in that world you will have a generation who have been conditioned to think that all moral values are relative; a generation who willingly defer to leaders, innovators, conditioners, scientists, whoever. They will have no remembrance of religious superstition, they will be quite different from anything that has gone before. They could torture and kill a baby or an old woman if there was a logical reason to do so. They could not see it as wrong, or evil in itself; those value judgements belong to antiquity, to superstition. Their utilitarian minds only feel and think what they have been programmed for. And once objective value has gone, it will go for ever – can you see that?'

'Well, I think it is plain enough to see that this is an anti-intellectual stance,' Professor Rawkins said.

'You may say what you will,' continued Inchikov, 'but in the old world, the world which you just now called "old ground", an intellectual would be marked out by his virtuous pursuit of truth, but what motive would there be in your brave new world for such a thing as this? Virtue itself would have been deleted as mere sentiment. No longer will there be a world of men transmitting manhood to their young, for Plato's desire for every child reared as an orphan in a bureau will have come true. No longer birds teaching the necessary skills to the fledglings, but gamekeepers breeding and moulding stock to be what they wish.'

'Again, this is pure speculation and supposition!' Professor Rawkins protested.

'It's not speculation. I am a Russian. The conditioners of my own country tried all this in a fashion and then wondered, where is the drive we conditioned the young Russians for? Where is the enterprise, the honour, the courage, the creativity? Where indeed? They had removed the organ but still expected the function. They had castrated the eunuch yet still bid him be fruitful.'

'Look, I'm sorry, but I've spent my life listening to this sort of thing – people who want our conquest of nature to stop short in some stupid reverence. In fact, as far as I know, every advance in science has had this sort of obscurantism to deal with. Always the threat of fire, judgement, damnation and catastrophe, always the fear-based, Luddite, knee-jerk reaction that stands in the way of progress. I dare say we'd still be pushing ploughs if the men of science had listened!'

'Your talk of the "conquest of nature" to benefit mankind sounds truly noble, but you are naïve, for in actuality what we call our "great power over nature" is nothing more than the power of some people over others, wielding nature as an instrument.'

'Oh I see. You would have us go back to a world without the aeroplane and the Internet!'

'No, not necessarily, but it is important for these young men to see technologies for what they are. We are as much the subjects as we are the possessors of these new things. The conquest of the air is, in reality, the ability of some people to make money out of air travel from other people and to exclude still others, or drop bombs on them. The Internet gives me access to more than the library at Alexandria, but I am also tracked, observed, profiled, advertised at and, in between it all, I am the subject of propaganda.'

'Each new power won by man is also, by necessity, a power over man. We are at once the conqueror and the conquered. That future master generation, controlled by an omnipotent State with an irresistible scientific technique, will remake people, by whatever form of prenatal conditioning or perfectly applied psychology it deems fit. That final generation, far from being the most liberated and freed from traditions and taboos, would, in actual fact, be the most restricted and conditioned people ever to live.'

'I'm sorry, but this is just a sort of anti-government conspiracy! Why on earth would you suppose that these future "conditioners", as you call them, will be such evil men?'

'You have missed the point. Have you heard nothing, or learnt nothing from history? I am not supposing them to be good or bad; they are not people at all, as we might understand it today. For they are the heirs of your philosophy and have sacrificed their share in traditional humanity in order to devote themselves to the task of deciding what humanity should henceforth be. "Good" or "bad" are meaningless words applied to them, for they are Plato's true "guardian stock", the ones who will decide what morality, or, for that matter, what conscience even, will be from then on.'

Professor Rawkins was shaking his red face with a weakening grin that told all. 'You are deluded, sir, you are warped. I cannot foresee any such abuse. If you knew the men that I know, in our Government, in the UN, in the World Health Organization, if you saw their dedication to humanity, you would be ashamed of this, this snapping at the heels of their great efforts!'

'Not at all; the mere fact that they, and you, are perhaps better than your philosophy will be of little consequence two hundred years from now to those who will inherit the fruit of it.'

'You may scoff as much as you like, but I know them, and it is their work, not that of the two-penny sophists, that will underpin and advance mankind.'

Professor Inchikov, absorbing the personal insult with a wry smile, glanced at the neoclassical pilasters that lined the auditorium. They were half-cylindrical columns in the Corinthian style fixed onto the walls to add grandeur. 'I dare say that some of the boys, when they were younger, thought that these columns held up the roof under which we now sit.'

'And your point?' The headmaster said, with an exasperated sigh.

'My point is that, on inspection, they are found to be only two-dimensional and hollow, and are, in fact, attached to the wall themselves and rely solely upon it for their own strength and position.'

Mr George lost his patience. 'For heaven's sake, man, don't speak in riddles!'

'Well, the point should be clear enough. Our speaker and his important colleagues may have a certain unconscious sense of value and reason which they inherited and enjoy without being aware of it. They appear to support the roof with their two-dimensional philosophy, when all the time they are enjoying the support of the very values their philosophy will obliterate for the future generations.'

'Yes, yes,' Mr George snapped. 'All very deep and meaningful. Another question please, anyone.' He tried to avoid seeing Will's hand as he surveyed the crowd, but when nobody else offered, he eventually said in a weary tone, 'Yes, Houston, what is it?'

Will was not about to let the issue be swept away. Professor Rawkins looked at him, willing him to make the question a good one.

'My understanding,' said Will, 'is that much early scientific advance came from people who held the Christian worldview that Professor Rawkins is keen for us to abandon. Would it be fair to say that a society that entrusts scientific power to people who do not share those values is like giving a loaded gun to a toddler?'

A few of the boys laughed, but Mr George glared at Will, who, in turn, stared back straight-faced. Mr George held Will's gaze and started to raise his hand towards Professor Rawkins, who leant towards his microphone. Will, remaining standing, said with as loud a voice as he dare, 'My question to Professor Inchikov, please.'

Held in that spot, Mr George had to pass the question to the man he was now quite determined to sack at the end of term. Professor Inchikov, still amused by the question, was a moment in answering but eventually leant forward, his elbows on the table, and gesticulated with his hands as he spoke.

'Yes, that's a very good question, Master Houston. Please let me say that I am not anti-science as such, and that I am also aware that many good and noble men brought the scientific method to mankind with no other motive than to "think God's thoughts after him", as Newton said. But let me also say that mankind's desire for science in general has been less than pure. Indeed, magic and science were twins, if we speak of the age in which they blossomed. And they were both born of the same impulse; but what magic could not do, science did, so magic died and science grew. But let us be clear: scientific knowledge is vastly different from the wisdom of preceding ages. The ancients pursued ways to conform their souls to reality through knowledge; that is, they knew there was something wrong with themselves, and sought to remedy this by the pursuit of virtue and self-discipline, whereas the objective of magic has always been – as it has for applied science too, to some extent – to subdue or bend reality to the will of men; very, very different. So you are correct to say that Christian men gave the advances at the birth of scientific branches, but do not miss the point that, though perhaps not tainted at birth, science was certainly born in an unhealthy neighbourhood, and that is not irrelevant to your second point.'

'Oh, there's more?' Professor Rawkins said, as he shuffled his papers together and looked at his watch.

Professor Inchikov took no notice but continued. 'At this moment of history, after science has subdued and manipulated every part of nature for four hundred years, we have sat here in this auditorium and discussed the final conquest of modern science's desire: that of humanity itself; to lay it bare and re-engineer it. I have tried to present you a purely philosophical and logical hypothesis, without reference to a religious viewpoint, of what must necessarily happen in the future to a relativist society. You ask me if it is a loaded gun and I say, "Yes it is." We may have gained something from every past conquest of nature – though, perhaps, we'd all admit that the price has been high, whether environmentally or socially – but when it comes to this final conquest I would plead with you to remember the stove; there are some progressions that undo the whole. Science is useful just as a window is useful. Science may help me see the world, just as the window helps me see the garden, but you cannot go on forever seeing through things. If I keep wishing to see through the garden as well, I will eventually make translucent the thing I had once wished to see, and a transparent world is an invisible world. By seeing through everything, I end up seeing nothing at all. The slow abolition of man by the loss of objective value has a final step just like that.

'You ask whether the loaded gun is in the hands of responsible people, and I say that the gun is in all our hands. Do not look at the speaker or me; we will, in all likelihood, be glad to pass out our days without being the subjects of the laws of euthanasia!'

'Oh please, spare us!' Professor Rawkins said.

'Ah, our guest thinks I am scaremongering! I tell you that, when I left Russia to come here, we were aborting 73% of all babies – 73%, I tell you! Now, which generation gave men such powers over an unborn generation? And which generation will decide that it is less wrong to murder a child who has no voice than an old man who has no strength? The steps are already in progress; turning from the precipice seems barely an option at this point in history. And, as I say, it's you – all of you – who hold the gun, for it will be you, and those like you, who will be given it. And when that day comes, I pray God that you will not forget the words of this old man.'

This last challenge was so sombre that everyone sat still for a few seconds; even Mr George gazed gravely at his tie. Eventually he looked up and thanked everyone for coming, asked for another show of appreciation for the guest speaker, and closed the gathering.

As Will followed the other boys down the aisles, his forebodings about the future of mankind were only eclipsed by his anxiety about the night's work ahead of him.

22

THE SOLSTICE

It was a mild summer's evening, and many stopped to talk in the courtyard outside the lecture hall. Will talked a good while to Professor Inchikov, but left him when he saw the headmaster striding towards them with a face like thunder. He was about to lambast the professor, when another figure approached first, walking with stick in hand; it was his father. Father George shook the professor's hand. 'A most excellent piece of deduction! Well done, sir.'

He went on at length to say that he had been there all the while, enjoying every minute of the question time. As Mr George came closer, the professor excused himself and left father and son alone on the edge of the crowd. Will lingered nearby.

Mr George spoke in a low but seething voice. 'He wrecks the school lecture, humiliates our guest speaker in front of the media, in front of the boys and the parents, and you stand there in public and congratulate him?'

'Your guest speaker needed putting right, as do you, my boy. As do you. If you had listened as you should, you'd have asked for applause for him instead.'

Mr George shook his head in disbelief. 'All my life, I've worked here to build something that you would be proud of. You know, perhaps once in a while it would be nice just to hear you say, "Well done, son" – just once – but no, it's never good enough. Doesn't matter what John gets up to, he'll always be the golden boy; and

I suppose you're sure he's innocent even now and it's all been a big mistake.'

The old man straightened up and took his son's shoulder. 'I am sorry if I have failed you. God knows that I have tried to love you both the same. George, George, look at me! Everything I have is yours – you know that. But I cannot support your stance on science, not while I love you. I just can't.'

'And John?'

'You don't believe any more than I do that your brother could do such a thing.'

Mr George looked down at his shoes. Will could see the tears in his eyes and the faint shuddering of his shoulders. 'I'm scared.'

'For John?'

Mr George wiped his nose. 'Yes, and the school; the whole thing's falling apart.'

'Have you prayed about it?'

'Yes, but it doesn't help.'

'Perhaps, George, after tonight, you might reconsider your position and try repentance first?'

'But –'

'No buts, my boy. I won't be here for ever, you know; sometimes I think I'm only still alive like the priest Simeon: just to see my prayers for you answered. Think about what I say, and, if you need me, I'll be at the cottage.'

Back in the house, Adam returned drunk, as predicted, but he was happy enough to get to bed. At 11 p.m., Will visited Clarkson and Thornton's room, 'Look after him will you, I need to pop out for a while.'

'Where?' Thornton asked.

'Best not to ask. Be back soon.'

At 11.55 p.m. Will checked that the coast was clear and climbed out the window. As he was halfway down he heard the front doors shut and the sound of footsteps: it was Father Bede. Will moved his body into a shadow by a bay window and waited. The steps came closer. Will held his breath as the steps passed right underneath him; he looked down and watched as Bede walked around the corner. After a few seconds Will dropped the remaining few metres and hid in the shadows for a minute. There was no sound other than an owl calling from Monks' Wood. Will ran along the shadows, past the priory and on to the gates, where Arthur's gatehouse and shed were situated.

The shed was dark, but the gatehouse lights were on and so Will went to the back door. He tapped gently and, as he waited for a response, he noticed dark figures appear from the priory and head across the playing fields to the necropolis wood. It was only then that he also noticed the light of a fire shimmering among the distant tree-tops. *It's the witching hour. They've begun.* There was then a noise behind the door and presently Arthur let Will in. 'Aye, lad, come in. Have you got your torch?'

'Yeah. Batteries are a bit low, though. I see there's some of them already in the wood,' Will said.

Arthur led Will into the sitting room. 'It'll likely be quite a do, I'd say. Your friend – all right, is he?'

'Sleeping like a baby. I've got some friends watching out for him, but I've not told anyone about all this, as you suggested.'

'Ay, well, there's no point getting them in trouble if aught goes wrong. Cuppa?'

'Well, okay, if you think we've got time.'

'Oh, plenty of time, lad.'

'Want me to make it?'

'No, you take a seat, young master. Old Arthur'll get the pot on.'

Arthur went through to the kitchen, and Will pottered around the sitting room. He went over to the fireplace. There were family pictures of Arthur's son and wife, knick-knacks on every shelf, rough wood carvings of animals, and some amateur attempts at taxidermy on the window-ledge. Will tried to peer past a lumpy-looking buzzard to see if anything was going on outside, but he could see nothing beyond the rowan-tree.

Arthur shouted to him from the kitchen. 'Eh, come on, lad, away from t'window, or it'll be my job gone if you're seen.'

Will drew the curtains and took a chair by the fireside. 'His favourite chair was that,' Arthur said, pointing to the small arm-chair where Will sat.

'Your son's?'

Arthur served up two big mugs and Will took a long sip.

'No, Percival's.'

'He used to come here?'

'Oh, ay, poor lad. He were homesick and tired of bullies and such; he'd often call in.'

'But you don't think he committed suicide?' Will sipped his tea again.

'No, he'd no more have done it than you would. Anyway, that's past now, and he's in a better place. We've all got to go sometime, the thing is to be ready, like.'

Will glanced at the clock. 'So we'll neck these and get out there?'

Arthur, as if not understanding, said, 'Oh, yes, ay, certainly.'

'He looks friendly.' Will pointed at the stuffed badger awkward-ly curled up by the fire and Arthur laughed.

'Not very professional, I know. All fingers and thumbs I am. Wife wanted rid of them, of course. Mind you, so does Sarah.'

'Sarah?'

'Oh, "Matron" to you, I suppose.' Arthur gave a cheeky grin. 'I'm old, but not past it, lad!'

Will downed his mug as quickly as he could for, though it was only 12.15 a.m., he was nervous about not being able to watch the house. Seeing Arthur looking at his watch Will said, 'Shall we go?'

'Ay, in a minute. Just let us finish me tea.'

Arthur sat in a chair opposite Will and talked about his wife and son, occasionally pointing out photographs. Will nodded, but after a few minutes he noticed Arthur's head growing to twice its size. The finger he used to point stretched out, sometimes to one or two metres in length, and touched the photographs. Will raised his hand to wipe his eye. No. He didn't. His brain told his hand to wipe his eye, but there it was still resting on the arm of his chair. *What is happening to me?*

'I'm not feeling well – I'm getting dizzy,' Will said. His voice sounded shrill and loud. 'I can't move.'

'Easy, easy, Will, lad; don't fight it or get worked up. Let it in.' Arthur's smile appeared to spread right up beyond his ears and meet round the back of his head somewhere.

'Your head is ... it's not right. I-I can't see straight – everything's going strange.'

Arthur hovered forward. 'Ay, that's right. Now tell me what you see.'

The paralysis seemed permanent, but the hallucinations came in waves. A hot flush rushed through his body, and when the cold sensation reached his head, everything appeared different. Or perhaps it really was different – he could not tell. But soon after, perhaps just seconds later, perhaps minutes, like a receding wave on the beach, his mental faculties returned. All the while that infernal burning in his limbs remained. The wave was receding as Will processed Arthur's question. 'Your eyes have gone yellow and your head is too big and ... and ... *it's you*, all along – it was you, and now you've poisoned me!'

'Not poison, lad – it's St Anthony's fire. Will help you make the journey.'

'Surely you don't believe that stupid prophecy!'

'I'm staking everything on it, lad, and when you get to my age, you'll take any hope life's brought you. As I said before, there's nowt worse than a fella with no hope.'

'But I don't want to die,' Will cried out, twisting his head as he felt another wave come in and his head start to swim again.

'Hey now, don't distress yourself,' Arthur said, gently resting his hand on Will's forehead. 'You'll get too hot, and it won't help the visions. Anyway, we all got to go sometime. I thought at least you'd understand, bein' a believer and all.' But Will could not answer, for his mind drifted into cavernous regions of lava and jagged rock. Winged creatures skulked on cave ceilings and harpy-like demons rifled through his pockets as his weightless body lay helpless and contorted in despair. After an eternity, his eyes opened, and he saw one of the demons holding his mobile phone. The creature had long grey hair and an evil, twisted face, angular and full of purpose. The creature thumbed a text message using his phone keypad. As Will looked and stared, the wave of ergot-induced hallucination receded and the harpy slowly changed into his matron. The clock showed 1.25 a.m. Arthur was nowhere in sight, and Will supposed that she had come to save him. *I've been found, thank God. She's calling an ambulance.*

'H … h … help me!' He tried to say the words but they came out as a dribbling croak. 'Please, help me.'

She looked up and smiled. 'Good, he's coming round.'

Arthur appeared from the hallway with his coat on. 'Ah, good lad. You all done, love?'

'Nearly; hate these things. Why anyone would want to use them …' She finished punching in the text message on the phone. 'Right, how does this sound? "Darling Hannah, please forgive me. I just couldn't go on any more. Too much pressure and bullying. I'm going to end it all tonight. Forgive me, my love. Forever yours, W." Don't think it's a bit soppy?'

'No, I think it's sweet,' Arthur said.

Matron pressed "send" and then dropped the phone back in Will's pocket. She threw the thin rubber gloves that she had been wearing onto the fire and said, 'Right, I'd better get going to the wood or the others will miss me. You got everything you need?'

'Aye, right enough.'

'Good, well, get going. You haven't got long.' She gave him a long, sensuous kiss and, grabbing his wrists, said, 'Tonight! It'll happen tonight.' She looked at him hard and added, 'Don't forget what I've told you.' She kissed him again and left.

Will tried to move his limbs but there was still no response beyond the spasms. As he slouched, helpless, he began to work through what her parting comments meant. When Arthur came back from washing his hands yet again, Will said, 'The others don't know, do they?'

'Them lot in the woods!' he said with disgust. 'They're just playing at it, saying the prophecy is allegoricalistic or some such. No, chickens and goats is all them lot are good for. Matron knew that back in '96. It's why she got me. Like I always say, If aught wants doing round here, they get old Arthur to do it.'

'So you're not a Druid?'

'No, takes years, it does, but Sarah's training us up for an Augur. It's what's needed for this job; they read the signs and that.'

Will started to feel sick at the thought, and his stomach knotted with dread as the autopsy photos came back to his mind. 'Please don't do this Arthur, it's all rubbish, this Celtic stuff. There's no evidence – but Jesus –'

'Gave his life for a better world, and that's what you and Percival are doing. I thought you'd understand that at least, you having faith and all?'

'You murdered Percival and it didn't work. Can't you see that?' Will's voice was faint.

'We had to be sure with the other date. I'm sorry for young Percival, but it was an honourable death.' Arthur's hands began to tremble slightly and he went back into the kitchen to wash them again.

He came back a minute later. 'Come on, we'd best be off.' He picked Will up in a fireman's lift with surprising ease and carried him out to his wheelbarrow. 'I've put some sacking in so it'll be comfy for you.'

'Please, Arthur, don't do this. I mean, why me?'

'Come on! You came to me, remember? Can't you see the spirits have singled you out, like they did young Percival? This is your destiny, lad.'

'But the card – the card was in Rawkins' jacket.'

'Got the wrong coat, but it still brought you all the same – like I say, it's fate.'

Will was laid carefully in the barrow, his feet facing forward and head tilted back, looking up at the old man and the bobbly fleece he was wearing. *How ridiculous, after all this time imagining men in dark robes, that this was probably the last thing that poor Percival saw – a gardener in a bobbly, old fleece.*

They passed the shed and Arthur stopped to tap on the window. The collared dove cooed and flapped inside. 'Aye, think he'll be all right, and so will you, lad, in about ten minutes.'

Will tried to cry out but there was little more than a whisper in his voice. 'Help … Help … Please don't do this – you don't have to go through with it.'

Arthur passed the school gates. 'Oh, I do, lad. Like I always says, nowt worse than a job half-done. Now, you just rest easy there; it'll not be long now. Listen to the sound of those waves.' Arthur spoke gently as he trudged up the coastal path to the Druids' circle. 'It's like they're calling us. There's magic about tonight and no mistake.'

Will had ceased to talk, and in his more lucid moments, he tried to formulate prayers, but it was as hard to prepare his soul for death as it was to actually accept that it was going to happen to him. *Please forgive me, forgive me for meddling, for not listening to Hannah. Oh, if I'd only listened.* He tried to think of them all at his funeral: his mum crying, his dad wondering what he'd done wrong. Will began to hate, more than anything else, the lie that they'd be made to believe: that he'd killed himself. He tried to move his arm, but he could not feel it, nor would his legs as a fresh rush of heat swept through him. *So tired, so very tired.*

He opened his eyes and saw the stones looming above him and Arthur wheeling him to the centre of the circle. 'Now, tell me about the visions. Have you seen aught I need to know about?'

'This is madness, Arthur. Please don't do this.'

'Come on, now, best avoid any unpleasantness. Besides you'll soon be in a better place.' He unbuttoned Will's clothing and took off his duffle coat. Will's arms jerked in spasms, as Arthur bent them to get his rugby top off too, 'That's it lad, easy now, don't want any bruising, do it just like matron says.'

The cold bit into Will's skin like a thousand ice daggers.

'The police will know – you know that, don't you? They'll suss it this time when they autopsy me.'

'I'll take my chances. Anyway, why would they suspect me? You didn't.'

'But when the heat's on, they'll sell you out.'

'Nah, they've all got alibis. There's village folk up at the wicker-man. Anyway, it's only Sarah what knows about this, and she won't blab. Now come on, let's have you. Get the job finished.'

Will tried in vain to get his limbs to react as Arthur picked him up out of the barrow, but it was no use; they tremored and contorted as if he had cerebral palsy. Arthur's rough fingers grasped his ribs and hauled him onto the central stone. Grit scraped his skin. He shook more than ever – not so much with the ergotism but as a reaction to the cold. 'Please, God, don't let this happen,' he sobbed. *Please God, please, please, no, not this way.*

Arthur put his hand on Will's forehead.

'Come now, lad. Have courage. It'll be over soon. It's 1.47, with 20 seconds to go.' Arthur's eyes were moist with sympathy but his hand now turned to hold Will's forehead. 'It's a whole new dawn. Now, don't wriggle if you can help it; I don't want to get this wrong, me being all fingers and thumbs and all.'

Will looked down his nose to see the knife in Arthur's right hand. It hovered over his upper belly. Arthur drew it across a few times. Oh God, its actually happening and I can't feel it. His head swam and his eyes rose above the stone and floated above the circle. A foul demon held the knife over his blood-soaked body. *I'm dying, oh God, I'm dying. It's actually happening. Why does it feel so confused, so dark?* His thoughts seemed very lucid and clear to him. He tried to raise his arms to ascend upwards to heaven, but they juddered and chaffed on the gritty stone. *No, I'm still here; this is not real.*

He then heard Arthur's voice: 'O great spirits of the earth and the seas, we bring this offering to you for the renewal of this precious land, to save us from the violence we have done to you by greed and pollution. Accept, we pray you, this blood, and bring to pass what was said of old by our ancestors.'

Will blinked, looked again and saw the knife still above his belly, though now he felt the cold steel on his skin. Arthur cleared his throat. 'Goodbye, lad, greet my loved ones for me.' His lips tightened and his brows furrowed as the muscles in his arm, neck and forehead tightened for the final thrust.

Will closed his eyes and gritted his teeth. He heard a hideous growl. A thud. His head fall back on the stone. Arthur cries out. *What is going on? What noise is this?* Will opened his eyes. Two figures scuffled to his left. One snarled like a dog – no, it was a dog. Grendel! *Dear God, it is Grendel. Good dog! Must have slipped her kennel.*

Arthur shook his arm from her teeth and rose to his feet. He put a hand to his cheek. It gushed blood. Arthur staggered and held the knife forward. 'Bitch,' he spat out. His hand cupped his wounded cheek, and he began to circle with the snarling dog in order to get back to Will. But Grendel stood her ground between the knife and Will, her lips hideously peeled back, her jaws wide as death. She must have known what a knife was but she did not back down.

'Now, easy, girl. Let me past,' Arthur said slowly, glancing for a moment at his watch, but she only snarled more. 'Come on. Let me past. Can't you see – there must be blood tonight.'

'Will!'

Will tried to twist his head, as he heard Ben's voice screaming his name.

He saw jostling torches, then Ben and his brother running in. Will turned back to see Arthur's expression of defeat, then a steely resignation. 'Very well, but there will be blood. Old Arthur will see the job through.' Arthur dropped to his knees and plunged the knife into his own side, drawing it across his middle with an almighty scream.

The head boy grabbed his brother. 'Don't look – please don't look.' After a moment he said, 'Go to Houston, but don't look at the old man, promise me.'

Will felt Ben's hand on his shoulder, but when he looked around, Ben's head was turned at the ghastly spectre of the old man slumped in his own gore. The head boy approached slowly as Arthur called out, 'Oh, Master Pitt, forgive me for Percival. I know it hurt you, lad, forgive me.' He coughed blood and groaned. Pitt shook his head slightly and walked away in Will's direction. 'Come on Ben, let's get his clothes back on. You all right Houston?' His face was hard, his voice unfeeling.

Will looked in Pitt's cold eyes. 'You must tell him. You must.'

Pitt paused, frowned, then said, 'Come on, quickly, Ben. Will's going delirious again.'

'No, I'm not. You must tell him that Jesus is the only way.' Will looked at the older brother. 'Man can't die without hope. Please, Pitt; tell him.'

Willie Pitt's head dropped for a moment and then he turned to his brother. 'All right. Ben, get Houston back to the house. I'll see to Arthur.'

Epilogue

Will remembered little of the remainder of that night, other than that he had insisted that someone other than Matron treat him. As it was, he was treated at the police emergency unit where Hannah was waiting. It was she who had called the school and roused the prefects. Dundas had gone to Necropolis, but the older Pitt, acting on a hunch, had gone to the circle instead. Peel arrested Matron that very night upon the strength of Will's garbled testimony, though she had left not a single trace connecting her to either crime. Will recovered from the ergot poisoning within forty-eight hours, but it was some weeks before he was fully back to his usual self, some scars taking longer to heal. He had come very close to death and said often afterwards how surprised he'd been at how unready he had felt for it. It had shaken him greatly.

This one thought alone took any edge off his pride when he was later hailed as the great school hero, and the first time he mentioned it was at a reunion of the Invisible College on the last day of that term. The usual suspects were invited, but also some of the original members. Will arrived early with Hannah – they brought along some salads – and they saw Mr John and the elder Pitt saying goodbye to a visitor. They both hugged the man, and Will saw a few tears on each side as he approached. Will peered curiously at Mr John, this man who had given him so much, and whom he'd betrayed in some way by his doubt. They had talked before today soon after Mr John's release, but he would hear no apology from Will. 'Don't talk rot, lad,' he'd said. 'The whole thing was beyond your control. Main thing is that it's all over. Truth always wins in the end, you know.' And so it had. As the car drove slowly away Will said, 'Who was that?'

Mr John shook his head slightly. 'Someone I never thought I'd see again.'

He did not look round for some time, but when he saw Will's stare, he placed a hand on his shoulder. 'That was Mr Percival; he drove all the way from London, would you believe that. One brave man.'

'Would he not stay for dinner?'

'No, he has to get back. But I'm a happy man, I tell you that. Now, what about these salads?'

He went to greet Hannah and helped her unload the car, leaving Will to chat with Pitt.

'Hey, how you doing?' asked Will.

'So-so.'

'What happened to Arthur?'

'He went peacefully enough – it didn't take long.' Pitt looked out across the bay.

'Did you talk to him?'

'I made my peace with him if that's what you mean.'

'And about Jesus?'

Pitt shook his head. 'He wouldn't hear it. Said he'd made his bed. You know what old people are like.'

Will breathed out long and hard. 'Oh yes – just like us.'

They stood there for another minute, gazing out to sea. The cove was still, with not a breath of wind in it as the sun started its tilt towards the western shores of Scotland, not twenty miles across the Solway Firth.

Hannah organized a long table on the patio outside the cottage, and Father George brought buckets of ice, champagne and tall glasses. He had plenty of reason to celebrate, for, as he said, at his age, every opportunity should be taken for giving thanks. The other boys came trooping over the hill at 6.30 p.m., headed by Dundas. Hannah organized the seating arrangements, and Will noticed there was one spare place. 'Come on Hannah, thought I was the one bad at maths.'

'Whisht, Master Houston!' Father George smiled. 'There is yet one more.'

Will followed his gaze and saw Mr John glancing up the drive. A figure approached. 'It's Mr George. Well, who'd have thought?'

'Who indeed,' the old man muttered under his breath.

Everyone stood as he entered the patio area, and Mr John showed him to his seat, pouring him a long drink. Very little was said – and perhaps very little needed to be said – for just then the magic was to be found simply in sharing the table again together and enjoying the evening.

Of course, many other things were said and speeches demanded, particularly from Will, who stood awkwardly looking into his glass for a moment, then said, 'Been quite a year. Didn't know public school was like this. At least I hope they're not all like this. You people have dangerous lives. Quite glad to have survived in one piece.' He cleared his throat, and looked at Mr John and Father George, 'I want to thank you – both of you – for what you did for us – me and my friends, everything you taught us. You gave us new eyes to see the world, a new awe of the Creator, a new passion to see Him glorified.' Will went on to thank the others, speaking for some minutes and with great emotion after which there was a long silence, with people nodding. This was broken by Father George, who rose from his chair.

'Now then,' he said, 'most of you know that I usually leave the talking to my sons, both of whom fancy themselves jolly good at it.'

Pitt and Dundas thumped the table, saying, 'Hear, hear.'

'But as I have both of them here at my table tonight, and for once they both have their mouths too full of fresh salmon to speak, I will speak in their place. I am brought to mind, by Master Houston's speech, of the things which I used to tell them when they were boys themselves, not so very long ago.' Mr John and Mr George laughed and their eyes met.

Father George banged his glass with a fork to get order back. 'I have heard – thank you – I have heard that the classics have been in decline at St Columba's since the retirement of a certain nameless venerable headmaster some years ago, but if I may be permitted a little Greek at the table, I would remind you of John's name for Jesus in the first chapter of his Gospel: "In the beginning was the word" – or *logos* in the Greek – "and the *logos* was with God, and the *logos* was God. The same was with God in the beginning, and nothing was made except it was made by him; and though he made it, he came to the world and they did not recognize Him", etc.'

Will watched Mr George staring into his wine glass, biting his lip while his father spoke. Will followed the headmaster's eyes as he looked around the table at the expressions on the boys' faces. Their eyes were wide with longing, their mouths half open in anticipation and wonder. *Hmmm, bet he's remembering what he'd been like once; what he'd wanted for his students and what he'd seen less and less.*

Father George continued, 'Of course, my sons remember who coined the word *logos* years before John used it.'

As if the thought had never left his mind, Mr George said, 'Heraclites, one of the founders of ancient science.'

'Yes, my boy – but can you remember the rest?'

'Something to do with reason?' Mr George replied.

'Yes, the purpose, or the *reason why*, to be precise; he looked for the "reason why" behind whatever he observed. He, like you George, looked for the *logos* behind the *bios*, and now we have *biologos* – biology. He looked for the *logos* behind the cosmos and now we have cosmology. My younger son has looked for the "reason why" behind ancient cultures, bones and pots and so on; some call it archaeology, others call it *not settling down!*'

Both brothers laughed again, and Father George continued, 'But my boys remember; Jesus is not only the creator of the universe, He is also the "reason why" it exists. So love one another. Here endeth the first lesson. Shall we have a toast?'

Mr George raised his glass. 'To the Logos.'

Mr John joined his glass to his brother's. 'Yes, the Logos.'

After the others had left and the washing-up was done, Will, Hannah and Adam sat on the beach with mugs of cocoa, talking about all that they intended to do that summer, which wasn't much. Adam told Hannah about his disease and about the progress of his medication. Following Will's advice, he had broken the news to his family after the headmaster's lecture and, though they had taken it well, he still didn't fancy an entire summer in London. It wasn't just the risk of infection; he had resigned himself to the fact that, in his current state, he might not live long in any event. It was more that he had a craving to be away from England, from the stench of the city and the boredom.

Soon after Adam had finished speaking, they realized that they had not been alone. Mr John stepped forward and sat down beside them. 'So, you're all looking forward to the summer, then?'

'Yes,' Hannah said, adding with unusual sarcasm, 'Adam can't wait to get back to the city, and I can't wait to lose Will to his father's building site.'

'Hey, come on,' Will said. 'I need the money.'

'Pity,' Mr John said.

'Why?'

'The *Argonaut* will be looking for a crew this summer; bound for Alexandria, on the Nile delta.'

'Wow – the site of the ancient world's great library and first university!' Adam said.

'The city of Cleopatra and Mark Anthony,' Hannah added, squeezing Will's hand.

'And what's there for you?' Will asked.

'Well, the boys might remember me talking about the scientific work of King Solomon, David's son. The Bible says that God gifted him with incredible insight, which he used to study many different branches of science.'

'Of course,' said Hannah. 'But what happened to his work?'

'That's just it. Probably the most profound scientific treatises, maybe surpassing those of Newton and Einstein, were lost when Israel went into captivity in Babylon.'

'So what's Alexandria got to do with it?'

'Well, after Alexander the Great died in Babylon, one of his generals, called Ptolemy, who had a passion for science, took as many manuscripts as he could back to Alexandria and started the great library.'

'And you think Solomon's work is there somewhere?' Adam said.

'Perhaps. The library was destroyed in various fires, but last summer we were working in the catacombs and we found inscriptions on a first-century tomb that read, "Apollos, keeper of the great works of Solomon, king of Judea", and –'

Hannah interrupted, 'Apollos – you don't mean the one in the Acts of the Apostles? He was from Alexandria?'

'There is that possibility – we'll know more next summer; but, of course, that's not really the big thing. If we found even a fragment of Solomon's work – just imagine it: the greatest human mind, except the Lord Jesus, writing on flora, fauna and cosmology, and that five hundred years before Aristotle – well?'

'Yeah,' Will said. 'That would be a revolution!'

'Think of it,' Adam said, 'The Lost Treasures of King Solomon's Mind! Reckon we could make a film about it!'

Lightning Source UK Ltd.
Milton Keynes UK
UKOW04f2006041017
310419UK00001B/1/P